THE RELUCTANT QUEEN
THE BONE THRONE

TERINA ADAMS

AUTHOR'S NOTE

Hi Dear Reader,

Welcome to book 2 of The Bone Throne series, The Reluctant Queen. I'm thrilled you've continued the journey with Tressya and Tamas.

In case you missed it in book 1 I have a bonus for my VIP readers. I have a letter Tamas wrote to Tressya when he was back in the north after the final battle. If you're interested in reading this and staying ahead of everyone else and keep up-to-date with my new releases, as well as receive bonus goodies, you can sign up for my newsletter via the QR code or VIP readers

AUTHOR'S NOTE

CHAPTER ONE

TRESSYA

Would I ever enter Emberforge without remembering the man who first enticed me inside?

Standing in the massive entrance hall, encircled by towering pillars supporting a floating roof overhead, I struggled to recall Tamas leading me this way on the day we stealthily entered the temple.

Back then, I had overlooked the warnings. Newly arrived in Tolum, I had already begun showing disloyalty to the Sistern, allowing my enemy to cloud my mind with his presence. That day was etched into my memory, not because I risked being caught by the king and Salmun, or having my true identity exposed, but because of Tamas.

Ensnared in his charm, I had convinced myself that keeping him a secret from the king and the Salmun was wise; after all, knowledge is power. I believed the Sistern's six pillars: loyalty, discipline, precision, courage, secrecy, and discretion, would shield me from any challenge. Too late, I realized I was defenseless against Tamas, both physically and emotionally. Despite the Mother Divine's rigorous training, my heart was not made of stone.

"Your Majesty," Orphus's voice and the soft *swish* of his cloak across the stone floor sent a prickly sensation across the back of my neck. His face remained concealed beneath his hood, for which I was thankful. I preferred not to glimpse the eerie markings the Salmun adorned on their faces, nor endure his deep-set eyes, which seemed to rake over me, heavy with dark secrets.

One week since the fight in the Ashenlands wasn't sufficient to adjust to my new title.

"I'd like a moment." *Or ten.*

I kept my back to him, preferring to gaze at the gap between the stone walls and the roof, out into the gray sky—a fitting backdrop for a funeral.

"Of course, Your Majesty. I shall return when it's time." Before facing what lay inside, I sought solitude to organize my thoughts. I felt unprepared to confront the spirit of King Ricaud without mental preparation.

"You shall wait until I'm ready." Commanding the Creed of Salmun was new to me, but I was quickly learning to enjoy it.

The silence lasted scarcely two breaths. "It is understandable—"

"Thank you, Orphus, that will be all." Silence enveloped me again, this time creeping in like a beast from the Ashenlands. The intensity of his gaze burned through the back of my head, but I refused to turn and face him.

"You've grown claws, my dear, and I love it," Andriet said.

Despite my resolve to ignore Orphus, I spun around, forcing myself to maintain eye contact with the prelate instead of glancing at Andriet.

"The service is timed to conclude at the top of the hour, preceding the vigil of devotion. I'm afraid too long a delay will shorten our time," Orphus said.

"Top of the hour preceding the vigil of devotion is an auspicious time—" Andriet said.

"It is the reason I suggested I return in good—" the prelate interrupted Andriet.

"Fine. Let me know when the service is about to commence."

I turned my back on Orphus again, rewarded by the sound of his cloak sweeping the ground as he moved deeper into the temple.

"I asked you not to come." My voice was low, knowing now I would get no peace.

Andriet appeared beside me, his clothes still stained with blood, the deepest crimson centered around his chest, just below his heart. It was a constant reminder of the horrific night in the Ashenlands.

"And miss my funeral."

"To avoid raising suspicion. We know little about the true extent of the Salmun's abilities. I need to keep my secrets, Andriet."

It was hard to say I'd lost my closest friend when he stood beside me. His death was a violent affront to his soul, preventing eternal peace and leaving him in limbo behind the veil. The night had seen too much death for me to let him go.

Spirits are tethered to their death site, but while he still existed behind the veil, separating the living from the dead, I had freed him from this constraint. Perhaps wrongly—I lacked sufficient knowledge of spiritweaving lore to foresee the potential consequences of my meddling. The veil remained his cage, but he would not spend his eternity in the Ashenlands; rather, he could choose wherever he wanted to be.

"You have no bloody secrets, my dear, considering you brought the entire spirit realm of the Ashenlands across the veil to fight for us. I'm sure the Salmun suspects I'm still here."

I rubbed my brow, turning away from Andriet. Summoning the spirits was a desperate act, disrupting the delicate balance between life and death. As a novice spiritweaver, courtesy of the Mother Divine, uncertainty about whether I had set a dire future in motion plagued me. I'd returned the spirits to their rightful place as soon as possible, but the damage may have already been done.

And now, Andriet. I dared not consider the consequences of my actions that night.

"Of course they know about my abilities." Frustration seeped into my voice, though not directed at Andriet. The last few weeks had been tumultuous. "They can't guess the full extent." I faced him. "You're supposed to be haunting the Ashenlands with your men, not the halls of Emberforge and

Emberfell. I want your presence here to remain a secret from them."

What concerned me was the Salmun's disinterest in my ability to free the dead. I'd expected Orphus to exhaust me with questions regarding that night, but he'd said nothing these last weeks.

"I promise not to tell a living soul." Andriet moved to touch me. Instinctively, I jerked my hand away, then regretted my action the moment I saw the distress on his face.

"There's much I have to get used to," he said.

"I'm sorry, Andriet. It's just—"

"Please, don't apologize. I may no longer touch, feel, or taste, but I am eternally grateful to be freed from that dreadful place, thanks to you." He raised a hand to silence me. "I don't want to hear it, you silly thing. None of this is your fault. If anyone's to blame, it's the Salmun. Their sole duty was to protect the House of Tannard. Instead, they let us all die."

I closed my eyes briefly and sighed. We had argued about this too. The only reason the Salmun abandoned Andriet and his father was because of me and my link to the Etherweave, a power I barely understood until that fateful night when the Salmun declared me the new House of Tannard.

"I'm not ready to face my fate." In my weaker moments, I'd let that slip on more than one occasion in the last few weeks.

"Nonsense. That's not the girl I know talking." Andriet moved to stand in front of me, reciting the same argument he'd used. "Not the princess I rescued from the sea after she'd faced a ship of Huungardred and won."

"They weren't Huungardred."

It crippled me knowing Andriet still had faith in me when everything was my fault. The old House of Tannard was dead because of me. I'd held all my secrets close when I should've let them be known. Andriet knew nothing of my dalliances with Tamas, nor was he aware of how much I knew about the Northerners' planned attack. If the king had known of Tamas's plans to strike while they were on the edge of the Ashenlands, maybe Andriet would still be alive.

"Same nasty beasts," Andriet said.

I gazed up at the fragments of sky visible through the floating roof, harboring yet another secret deep in my heart: I was struggling. Andriet was right. I wasn't the same princess who had faced the Razohan on the ship. The war against our enemy in the Ashenlands, the deaths I was responsible for— I had killed one of my sisters, for mercy's sake; a betrayal so grievous against the Sistern—had sapped my strength.

If I confessed the truth, would Andriet think less of me? I was a coward, afraid he would abandon me when I needed him most, because I didn't know how to be a queen. I needed him by my side, guiding me through difficulties, supporting me when I faltered, correcting my mistakes. But more than that, I needed a friend.

I turned from him, feeling the shame every time I saw his ethereal form floating beside me, knowing I had forever deprived him of the warmth of the sun on his skin, the pleasure of good food, and the tenderness of a lover's touch.

"That's all behind us now. You defeated them spectacularly. And now you're queen. The House of Tannard lives on."

I lowered my head, yearning to hide from his ceaseless praise.

"It's...Andriet, I—"

"Hush. That's enough of that."

In response to Andriet's questioning about my connection to the House of Tannard, I simply shrugged. He was adamant I was a displaced great granddaughter, or rather, and joked about us being nearly siblings.

The Mother, true to her nature, seldom disclosed her knowledge or intentions to her disciples. Our role was to obey, not to question. However, I was aware of the Sistern's purpose: to strengthen their influence in the world through strategic births. I had initially believed the Mother's scheme in arranging my marriage to the crown prince was to secure a link to the throne of the most powerful kingdom in the neighboring realms; an heir born of a disciple on the Tarragona throne. But I was mistaken. The Sistern's manipulation of my lineage had consequences far beyond what I had imagined. It wasn't an heir she desired on the throne. It was me.

The Mother had guided me, trained me in the six pillars, gave me the strength to survive my cruel life. My thanks to her for elevating me above my sisters within the Sistern and placing me upon the Tarragona throne as queen was betrayal. Yet, by leaving me under-prepared for my role as queen and transforming me into a spiritweaver without my consent, I would say she'd also betrayed me. Even so, I'd sent word to the Mother, needing her counsel.

I stared up at Andriet, unable to mirror his wicked smile. You shouldn't have so much faith in me.

Beside me, Andriet straightened. I looked over my shoulder at hearing footsteps moving toward us on the stone floor. Gusselan approached, flanked by Merrilda, her lady's maid, confident and fellow Levenian.

I'd had little time to speak with Andriet's mother since his death. Gazing at her sallow complexion and gaunt frame, I yearned to reveal the truth to her: that her son was always by her side, invisible yet ever-present.

Freeing Gusselan from the Salmun's cruel, deathly enchantment had been my first purpose on returning from the Ashenlands. She'd survived their poisonous magic, but I now questioned if she would survive the pain of losing both her sons—the loss of Henricus, her husband, I was sure she celebrated in solitude.

Andriet glided forward as if to ease Merrilda's burden and support his mother's weight, which he couldn't, of course. Watching his helplessness as he moved beside her was difficult, hands splayed outward, ready to catch her if she stumbled, yet knowing he would never succeed. Nor would he ever be able to hold her or comfort her again.

"You look stronger," I said when she reached me.

She locked her eyes with mine. "I doubt that."

Judging by the harsh tone in her voice, it was clear Gusselan still didn't trust me. "The Salmun won't harm you anymore." Andriet's presence made me cautious in selecting my words. "It's up to you to decide if you want to survive."

"You think you have that much sway over them?" There

was no accusation in her reply. She was, perhaps, too sickly and tired for such emotions.

"Please wait for me. I have something I wish to attend to first. I won't be long," I said, ignoring her question, because she was right. I doubted I had little sway over the Salmun, whose sole duty was to protect the House of Tannard.

I caught her frown as I retraced her steps, giving a subtle jerk of my head to Andriet, hoping he wouldn't decide to be stubborn and ignore me.

To my relief, he followed. I led him out of the main courtyard, away from Gusselan and Merrilda.

"Please, Andriet. I need time alone with your mother."

"There's no point in secrets, Tressya."

"Your mother has many. In respect for her, please let her keep them. She may never have wanted you to know."

"What are you talking about? You're an enigma, little queen. How could you know anything about my mother? The short time you've been in Tarragona, she's kept to her bed? I have spent the last twenty-six years by her side. Are you suggesting you know more about her than I do?"

I reached for him before I remembered I could never touch him again. A sudden sharp pain stabbed at my heart. "Nobody is without secrets, Andriet. Some they might not even be aware of themselves." The last I added under my breath, for the mystery of how I became linked to the House of Tannard, and heir to the Bone Throne.

Dammit. I had no power to stop myself from thinking of Tamas and all the secrets he'd kept.

"Please." Once again, I reached for his hands before stopping myself, my hands helplessly hovering over his, unwilling to feel the chilling sensation of touching a spirit. "Give your mother the privacy she deserves. It's the day of your funeral. Daelon will be..." Was it cruel of me to mention Andriet's former lover?

Andriet ducked his head. Curses. It was insensitive of me to use Daelon to distract Andriet.

I swallowed the hardness thinning my throat. "I'm sorry. I shouldn't have—"

"No. It's all right. But it hurts too much to see his pain."

"Then I'm truly sorry—"

"But you're right. I'll go to him. It's wrong the Salmun refused him entry to attend my funeral."

"That was something I had no power over."

"Only heirs to the Bone Throne may enter Emberforge. I know that. That they accepted Mother is a blessing, at least."

There was a sudden wildness in his eyes. "I want Daelon to know about me, Tressya. I want him to understand that I am with him."

"But you can't. You're a spirit. Besides, I'm not sure if that's a good idea."

"I have not abandoned him. And I never will. He needs to know that. We promised each other no matter our futures we would always find a way to see each other. He'll know I'm there."

"Andriet, that's not a good idea. Daelon needs to learn to live his life without you. If you—"

"I know what I'm doing." And he was gone.

Curses, I was a fool. I shouldn't have brought Daelon up, but I needed a way of distracting Andriet from his own funeral, giving me time with his mother.

There was nothing I could do about his decision now, nor was I prepared to command him to my will, a capability he didn't even know I had as a spiritweaver. Exerting such power would be the ultimate betrayal of our friendship.

If only I had that level of control over Tamas.

Whenever I thought of Tamas, the skin around the bite mark tingled—the mark he'd given me the first time we met on the ship, during the Razohan attack intent on killing me. Instead of killing me, he had spared me, marking me by biting my wrist and forging an intimate connection between us he had no right to impose.

His audacity to do such a thing infuriated me. However, with each emotion I felt towards Tamas, there was a contradictory twist of elation; it was twisted because, as my greatest adversary, I should abhor being bound to him, but there was also a sense of elation: our connection allowed me to feel that he had survived his grievous wounds.

I was as sure of his survival as I was of the inevitable doom of anything that might exist between us. I was now the new House of Tannard, with my duty to ascend to the Tarragona throne, and eventually, according to the Salmun, the Bone Throne. But that was Tamas's ambition, the reason his people risked crossing the deadly Ashenlands. I could be nothing but his greatest enemy now.

Then there were the unexpected emotions that overwhelmed me when he stood against his friend, the Nazeen, to protect me during the fight in the Ashenlands. At that moment, I was convinced the emotions I felt were not my own, but his, which seemed impossible. A week later, as the clarity of that night faded in my memory, my certainty waned. I longed to confront him about the consequences of his bite, yet I was equally apprehensive about the prospect of ever seeing him again; finding common ground seemed unlikely now I'd usurped his position on the throne.

I pushed my problems aside and headed back to Gusselan, conscious I'd left a sick woman waiting too long for my return. The guilt increased upon seeing her leaning heavily on Merrilda, so I took the other side of her.

At first, she was reluctant to accept the silent offer, but she was still too weak to protest. Perhaps the Salmun had ignored my demand to release her from their death spell.

"I'll take care of her from here," I told Merrilda, who glanced at Gusselan, unsure if she should comply, yet unable to refuse the command of the queen.

Gusselan acknowledged her loyal friend with a nod. Following this, Merrilda excused herself, leaving me to support more of Gusselan's weight, which felt akin to holding up a skeleton. Tall in stature, Gusselan's illness had caused her to stoop, reducing her to my height. "You want secrecy?" she asked, her voice as frail as her form.

"I speak better when alone, and there is much we can learn from each other."

In the corner of my eye, I spied a spirit keeping pace with us two pillars across from us. He wore the uniform of a soldier, dirty and bloody as the day he died in battle. I scrunched my eyes, forcing my attention back to our conversation.

"You mean there is much you can learn."

"There is that. I know nothing about being a queen."

"You think I can help you?"

"Some advice—"

"A queen beside her king is nothing more than an ornament." I allowed her a few moments to catch her breath. "I can't help with what you want."

"I think you can. You're a disciple of your order. You weren't sent here to birth the next heir to the Tarragonan throne because you're weak. I know much feels beyond you at the moment, but that will change. You'll get stronger," I said.

The sudden rigidity in her body showed she had more to say, but needed a moment to muster the strength to speak. I slowed our pace, recognizing that there were many things I wanted to express before we encountered the Salmun.

"I know nothing of the Salmun, but you have spent all these years living beside them. And I know little of Tarragona's court."

"The Salmun hold their secrets, and you destroyed much of Tarragona's court." She glanced around her. I did the same, noticing the spirit soldier continued to keep pace with us. "This is my first time inside Emberforge. That's how much they allowed me to see."

"I don't believe you learned nothing."

"And you're not my friend, so stop pretending to be."

My steps faltered, a sudden surge of shame hollowing my chest. I bore responsibility for her profound losses—her children, her husband, her queenly title, her duty as a disciple to her order. It was no wonder she harbored loathing toward me, despite all my efforts to save her life.

"I'm sorry for everything you've suffered. Losing your

sons was never my intention. I tried everything I could to save Andriet."

Liar. I kept Tamas a secret.

"What is it you really want from me?" Gusselan said.

I hesitated before answering, uncertain myself. I'd freed Andriet from the Ashenlands because I needed a friend to stand by me as I faced my uncertain future, and there was more at stake. The prospect of bowing to a queen enraged the nobles. It was an unprecedented event in Tarragona's history. Many expressed dissent, accusing me of having no true links to the Tannard line, claiming me as bloodborn—which I was yet to fully understand—or a ruse, a sleight of magic beyond their comprehension. Even the assurances from the Salmun couldn't pacify some of the influential voices that survived that dreadful night.

This fate I didn't even want. The Mother had thrust it upon me. "You and I are alike."

"We're nothing alike."

I glanced at her profile, noting a slight mottling of her skin, ever so faint I at first missed it. I shifted my vision, searching for her death echo and was pleased to see the fringes of her aura, the areas that had once darkened like a coming storm, were slowly turning into the vibrancy of life.

"What's your order called?" I asked.

"Why should I tell you?"

"There's no longer any reason for us to be hostile toward each other. You succeeded in your duty to your order, birthing two heirs to the throne—"

"Succeeded, you think. Where are my sons now?"

"Your order left you to die."

"Duty is sacrifice."

I inhaled, then steadily released my breath. Was being queen my sacrifice to the Sistern? After everything that had happened, it certainly felt as though it was.

"In all honesty, I don't wish to be queen."

Gusselan sagged on my arm but kept her eyes forward.

"It's the truth. I was naïve to the Mother's real plans. I never suspected she wanted this of me. You must realize I have no idea of my heritage. Someone claimed I was bloodborn. What does that mean, exactly?"

Tamas had called me a bloodborn, which was then echoed by a nobleman's declaration when Orphus named me heir to the Bone Throne, though Orphus himself denied it. Andriet had scorned the term bloodborn when I brought it up, proceeding to denounce it as an abomination—a lineage tainted by heathens, liars, and murderers. When I asked Orphus to explain the term, he confessed he didn't understand what it meant. *Liar.*

"It means you're cursed." This time, she faced me with accusatory turquoise eyes.

"I don't understand."

A wicked smile brought creases to the corners of her mouth. "It means the Salmun have lost. After a millennium of protecting the Levenian line of Tannard rulers, they have finally lost the throne to a northerner."

"No. Orphus said that night in the cave I wasn't bloodborn."

"That's because he doesn't want anyone knowing the truth of who you really are." She glanced around as if checking for unwelcomed listeners.

I now spied two spirit soldiers hovering some distance away.

"Who am I?"

"No illegitimates of the Levenian line of the House of Tannard are born. A strict rule enforced by the Salmun for a millennium. It's impossible. Their magic makes it so."

It seemed she'd dismissed my question. "That seems improbable."

"A binding of their fertility until their marriage. It's an easy enough task when you wield magic."

"But why bother?"

"The Salmun aimed to control anyone with a claim to the Bone Throne—a task that would become impossible if history were teeming with illegitimate children fathered by successive kings over a millennium."

She glared at me, reminding me of the Mother's stern gaze when I displeased her.

"Heirs born of the Levenian line within the House of Tannard inherit the ability to master the Etherweave." She leaned into me, needing my strength for support.

This was the reason her order and mine had sought to influence the Tarragona throne.

"They are not the only ones capable of wielding the Etherweave. A link to the House of Tannard, placing them beyond the Levenian line and outside the Salmun's control, persists in the north among the Razohan, thanks to witches loyal to the last king of the Bone Throne. That is the essence of being bloodborn: a child born with the power to wield the Etherweave, untainted by the Levenians and free from the Salmun's control," she continued.

Now I understood why Orphus openly refused to acknowledge my heritage as anything other than of the Levenian line. The council already balked at the idea of a queen's rule; what would happen if they discovered I was bloodborn?

"However, it is said that only one bloodborn exists," she said.

"Only one?"

She huffed, then coughed. I took her frail weight and waited for her to gain her strength again. "It would seem it's a falsehood."

"I'm not from the north."

She narrowed her eyes at me. "You know nothing of your heritage."

"I'm not beast-born. I can't shapeshift like they do."

"Yet."

"That's impossible," I whispered, pulling away from her, but she sagged, losing her balance, forcing me to come in close and take her weight again.

Tamas knew. From the beginning, he'd known who I was. That was the real reason he'd attacked our ship—not to assassinate the betrothed of the crown prince, but to eliminate another rival for the Etherweave and the Bone Throne. Yet he'd chosen to mark me rather than kill me. If any of this was true, it meant the extent of the rivalry between Tamas and me was bigger than I thought. And yet, even knowing the truth about me, he'd saved me. Repeatedly.

Tamas, where are you? I yearned to see him, hold him, tell him... I didn't even know what I would say. These revelations were too fresh; I barely believed everything I'd heard. And now, I'd lost Tamas to the northern realm. Was his witch turning him against me? Did he regret keeping me alive? I ached inside at the thought.

"According to the prophecy, one of the beast-born in the north, a bloodborn, would challenge the right to the Bone Throne."

"That's Tamas, not me."

"Who is Tamas?"

I shook my head, thinking fast. "A rival I faced in the Ashenlands during the fight. He's long gone."

Gusselan's lips thinned as she continued to stare at me. Under her gaze, my thoughts felt too raw and open for her to dissect.

"Your Majesty." Orphus appeared at the entrance to the temple sanctuary.

I gritted my teeth in frustration at his appearance and was about to snap at him to leave us alone, but Gusselan moved on, forcing me to walk beside her.

I fisted my free hand as I forced some calming breaths.

Mother, I need you.

CHAPTER
TWO

TAMAS

Slumped in the oversized chair, I buried myself in my tankard of ale and stared into the fire pit. Leaving Osmud and Garrat behind, I'd ridden hard, punishing my horse through the driving snow only to find myself at Thaindrus's court. I had wanted solitude to think over everything I'd done and beg his forgiveness.

I wasn't a fool. I recognized my hard ride for what it was, an escape from myself more than anything else. But as was my habit throughout my years, I sought Thaindrus's company and wisdom when my heart was deeply troubled.

I savored my solitude and the warmth of his court, which gave me time to brood on my thoughts. Given where I was, the most forceful was my betrayal to Thaindrus. I sat here abusing his hospitality and withholding my honesty. He deserved to know I could never accept Bryra because I'd bitten Tressya, forming an intimate bond that could only be broken through death. I was no longer free to be with another. In truth, I didn't want to be.

I'd also omitted revealing the truth to Bryra, coward that I was.

The fire spat sparks. One landed on the shin of my pants. I smacked it out, then set down my tankard and launched to my feet and paced. Too much raged through my head to keep me settled.

Thoughts of Tressya were in my mind the moment I woke and were there to lull me to sleep. Then came the other concerns, seeping in throughout the day, draped in shame.

It had taken weeks of negotiations to gain the allegiance of the stronger clans—thank the stars for Garrat and his hard work and diplomatic prowess—and it took one woman and my foolish, weak heart to destroy all our plans. Because of me, we'd failed; because of me, the northern clans suffered terrible losses; because of me, the northerners had lost faith when I had promised them hope.

I didn't need to look to know it was Thaindrus, my dearest friend, who approached me from across the great hall. I could hear his ailing in his footsteps, which only doubled the guilt already clouding my head.

He'd offered me his daughter's hand to ensure the survival of his people, the Huungardred, mighty beast-men and women of the north, whose lands were slowly encroached upon by an ever burgeoning population of people growing more hostile toward them with each generation. And as a friend, I'd betrayed him.

"Tamas," Thaindrus bellowed as he eased down into his

seat. The fluid grace of his young years was long gone. I swear I found more grays on the beast-side of his face since I last saw him a month or more ago.

He eased himself back into his seat, fixing his dark eyes on me. Old as he may be, his gaze still held the wisdom and intellectual acuity of a shrewd diplomat. I tried to avoid his look as long as I could, knowing he absorbed my emotions through my expression and movements. Feeling uncomfortable with how much I revealed in my silent pacing, I slumped down in my seat again.

I could attempt to hide what dwelled inside of me, but that was not what drove me into the deep north. It was only here, in Thaindrus's court, I truly felt free to unburden myself, and Thaindrus knew that.

The heavy sigh that slipped from my lips said it all, as did my slouch. The two of us stared into the fire pit for a long silence, me thinking of a dozen ways I could say all I needed to say.

"I failed." What came out of my mouth surprised me. The painful honesty was more than I anticipated saying so soon. I'd agonized over several ways of explaining myself. All of them were nothing but concealed excuses. I ditched them all in the end.

"A difficult task you'd set before yourself," Thaindrus replied, keeping his gaze on the fire.

"Difficult but achievable."

"One man cannot hold the burden of defeat for an entire army."

"In this instance, this man can."

"It's not your fault the woman commanded the dead?"

"The princess was meant to die on the ship and not reach Tarragona's shore. That she survived to win the war for the Tannard line and Salmun is because of me."

Thaindrus eased himself back in his seat, splaying his arms on the armrests. "You spared a life, Tamas."

"So that many more would die."

"That is the outcome of war."

I arched my head back, stretching my neck.

"More often than not, it's easier to strike than to hold your blade. There was a reason you spared the princess's life. At some point, you'll understand why."

I was watching him closely now, noting the fatigue around his eyes, even if they remained sharp and fixed on me.

"I believe I already know."

Thaindrus nodded. I wasn't sure what rumors had reached him and how much resembled the truth.

"Yes, I think you do."

So he'd heard something, if not all of my escapades.

"It was hard for me to come here, even if I couldn't stay away."

"If it makes this conversation any easier, I know, Tamas."

A great wash of relief rushed through me, followed swiftly by shame.

"It was wrong of me to ask what I did of you."

I sat forward, resting my elbow on my knees. "No, dear friend. It's not wrong for a great leader to wish the survival of his people."

"And now you wish to ease my guilt." He chuckled.

I slumped back in my seat, feeling as though someone

had removed a great weight from on top of me. We both stared into the fire, perhaps sharing the kindred feeling of eased burdens.

"Bryra told me." He waved a hand when I snapped my eyes to him. "She's disappointed for sure, but she long suspected your heart was not set on her. She's lived with that knowledge for some time and foolishly hoped my request would soften your feelings toward her, maybe reveal something deep down you didn't realize was there."

"I wish—"

"Not with me, Tamas."

We'd shared a deep bond of understanding and respect for so long. Apologies, defenses, evasions or rationalizations did neither of us justice.

"She's a bloodborn, Thaindrus."

Surprising me, Thaindrus snorted a short, hard laugh. "I can well imagine Romelda's response."

The Huungardred paid little attention to the concerns that dogged the Nazeen. They cared little for augurs and their ramblings. The threat of the Etherweave meant little compared to the threat of their own demise.

"I haven't seen Romelda since that night. Her own have taken care of her. But I'm curious what you may know about her response."

Thaindrus quirked a bushy brow. "You question my loyalty, young Razohan?"

"Stars, no. Not at all. Thaindrus, you know I would never do that." *Damn. You fool.* There were a myriad of better ways I could've posed the question.

He chuckled again and smiled to himself as he looked at

the fire. Huungardred weren't known for their humor. Thaindrus's appeared rarely and was equally less understood.

I took a swig from my tankard before resting it on my belly. "'Twain is the bloodborn'. Those were the augur's words. Romelda was there. She heard them too. I can't believe she didn't suspect Tressya."

There was only supposed to be one bloodborn. Me, or so Romelda's lectures schooled me to believe. No augurs had pronounced a twin fate until the ramblings of Sirillious, the last augur she'd dragged me to see before sending me on my task to kill the princess.

"Do you think perhaps that's the reason she was determined the princess should die before she reached Tarragona?" Thaindrus said.

"I hadn't thought of—No, she was surprised when I told her what I suspected."

"But she's a disciple?"

"You've been well informed." Thaindrus's knowledge shouldn't surprise me. It was as though the Huungardred listened to the wind and the whispers of the trees, for their knowledge of the greater world, despite their isolation and habit of keeping to themselves, never ceased to amaze me.

Thaindrus sighed, as if receiving such information was a burden, which it probably was. The outside world was forever encroaching on the old Huungardred's peace.

"As to the fact she's a bloodborn. It could've happened easily enough. It would take nothing for a disciple to seduce a lonely Razohan roaming the depths of the north."

"Not just any Razohan. That's too random if the Sistern were chasing a bloodborn."

"You speak wisely. And I have long held my tongue on my suspicions."

I sat straight. "Suspicions?"

"Fewer and fewer of the Nazeen accept the path of the blooded. A millennium is a long time to hold many's devotion."

I discovered on the eve of our assault that few of the blooded remained to join our war against the Salmun. A millennium had passed since the death of the last king of the Bone Throne, and it was a long time to maintain loyalty to the old king and uphold their oath to prevent the Levenian and their pets, the Salmun, from ever possessing the Etherweave. With one thousand years gone by, many could be forgiven for doubting that the bloodborn would ever return. And while I couldn't blame them for losing their faith, had we crossed the Ashenlands with a good contingent of blooded the outcome would've been different. Or maybe not. Thanks to Tressya surprising us all with her ability to bring the dead across the veil.

I huffed a sigh as I gently shook my head with a wry smile. She really was something: brave, resourceful, cunning... *Enough*. Now was not the time to give free rein to my thoughts regarding her.

"Does our conversation amuse you?" Thaindrus's interruption helped restore my thoughts.

"Only my stupidity. Though it angers me more than amuses me." I sat straighter. "So you think some of the Nazeen have betrayed the blooded and shared secrets and knowledge with the Sistern?"

Romelda was one of the rare Nazeen who held true to her

promise as a blooded, and remained loyal to the Bone Throne and the heir destined to sit upon it as any Nazeen who lived during the reign of King Ricaud, the last ruler to sit upon the Bone Throne and command the Etherweave.

"Aye."

Thaindrus kept such things to himself because the Huungardred preferred to keep themselves apart from the problems outside their borders. This was one reason the Huungardred as a people were threatened. Strangeness threatened many. Despite their ancient ancestral links, few northerners knew a lot about them, giving them a feeling of otherness that frightened and angered the clans. Thaindrus already knew my thoughts on their habit of keeping themselves to themselves and fostering feelings of *otherness*, so I moved the conversation on.

"To what end?"

"Betrayal is always for the same reason," he said.

"Do you think Romelda suspects?"

"If she does, she's never confided in me. But you can be assured the princess is not one of my offspring. Every woman I've bedded, I'm still in contact with. And I can vouch for my father. He was devoted to Mother until he died."

Huungardred had very long lives. Generations of men would pass before one Huungardred died.

"She knew nothing about shapeshifting."

"Hmm. So she can't shapeshift." Thaindrus murmured into his beard. "Then it happened so long ago that it's almost bred out of her. Perhaps it will return to her in time."

"The most important link to her heritage is still very much alive within her," I said.

"So you're sure she's a bloodborn?"

"She found a splinter of rock containing a fragment of the Etherweave. I'm not sure if it led her to it, like it did for me, but it reacted to her touch."

"There's no refuting that."

"But even before that, I knew. I knew the moment I first saw her. It's the reason I bit her."

"You're a bloodborn, she's a bloodborn. It's not surprising you recognized your own abilities in her. Perhaps you need to speak with Romelda."

I snorted. "I'm not sure she'll be too willing to speak with me. And neither am I in any hurry to do the same."

"Many regrettable words are spoken and regrettable actions taken during times of war. Do not let such things make enemies out of your allies."

I heaved a sigh, feeling his wisdom entangle my emotions, making it hard for me to separate my anger from my shame, which remained embedded deep in my heart.

"She thinks me a weak-hearted fool for biting Tressya. I wonder if she even sees me as worthy anymore."

Thaindrus eyed me for a long while before he spoke. "She would change her mind if she understood."

"She knows what I did, and so far, a weak-hearted imbecile is the friendliest of the names she's called me."

"Not even the Nazeen grasp the true depth of a Huungardred union. For us, it is a sacred bond, one that is never shared with those who cannot comprehend the profound depths of such a connection." He sat forward. "There's a reason I have never given my mark to another or agreed to take one in return; it's the same reason few Huungardred do.

The young are advised against such commitments until they are much older because, at their age, they cannot fully comprehend the true nature of what they are committing to. At that age, love is often more about lust, and such feelings can be fleeting. Even my darling Bryra is too young to fully understand what it truly means. She knows it's a deep bond, unseverable by years, but she cannot yet grasp the full extent of the union at her tender age. She'll learn in good time. It's a connection unrivaled by any. To agree to exist as bonded partners is to make yourself raw to another."

As the years deepened my friendship with Thaindrus, he took it upon himself to explain the intricacies of the partner bond. Romelda had already declared me a bloodborn, and Thaindrus aimed to safeguard me by advising extreme caution in choosing who I would bond with if I ever chose that path.

I drew my fingers through my hair, feeling unjustifiably frustrated with his lecture. "I understood the depth of the bond the first time you told me."

"I believe you, young Tamas." He nodded. "I do." Leaving me feeling guilty for my sudden show of anger.

"A bond is never made until one fully understands what it truly means to be bonded. It's why I wanted you to know. And a bond is never made without both partners' full understanding and agreement." He held up a hand to silence me before I spoke in defense of my actions. "No one would understand your reasons like I do, so rid yourself of your shame for having forced the bond upon the young princess. These days are dark, my friend. No one would judge you if they knew the truth."

"I want to be honest with you. I have my doubts about what you said. I feel nothing, Thaindrus. I've not broken the soul vow." I grimaced. "Maybe I slipped up a little, but only for a moment. I withdrew from the connection the moment I first felt her emotions. But I've felt nothing else."

"You're too impatient, young Razohan. Time and the heart deepen all connections. Willing or not, soon she will share everything with you. *Everything*, Tamas."

The possibility seemed too implausible to fathom.

"Her ability to command the Etherweave was she ever to reach it before you. There's nothing she can keep from you. Any of her powers are now yours."

I sat forward, rubbing my forehead.

From our first encounter, Tressya had captivated me. She possessed unique qualities seldom found in this world, meriting her survival. Faced with moments to decide, I acted with the knowledge I possessed. While others deemed me reckless, I knew I was prudent in forcing the bond. Aware she was the second bloodborn the augur had foretold, I had the power to spare her life, protect my people, and potentially alter the fate of the seven realms by bonding with her.

"With this knowledge, young Razohan, it's now time to use much wisdom. Always remember, a Huungardred bond is made from the heart with pure intentions. Not made for gain. It's made for a love that lasts eternity."

It was desperation, not love, that drove me to make the bond. Though my feelings had changed, deepened, since then, the sort of love Thaindrus spoke of felt unobtainable.

Upon seeing Tressya at Romelda's mercy, I was prepared to cut out my heart and offer it as a sacrifice to spare her life.

That was my first response. Someone as selfish as me, who'd killed his own father to take his seat, I didn't know if that was pure enough? Was such a sacrifice worthy of a love meant to last an eternity?

I couldn't know. But the only reparation worthy of what I'd done was to offer my blood in exchange, so that she may take all that I had, making us equals, giving her the advantage if I were to win the Etherweave.

Right now, I couldn't make that decision.

"Much afflicts you, young Razohan. And I must torture you further by bearing you more grave news."

It was doubtful anything he said would conflict me more than what he'd already shared. I took a swig of my ale.

"Romelda's here."

I choked on my mouthful.

"She's been here for days."

"Why didn't you tell me first?" Dammit, I didn't want to see the woman.

"So you would ride home again when you'd just arrived?"

"I feel you've set me up, old friend." And that was unfair. Thaindrus was not to blame for Romelda's actions.

I sighed. Would this week ever end?

"She's been waiting for you to arrive."

"She knows where I live."

"Did it occur to you that Romelda is also ashamed?"

I snorted. "I doubt it. The blooded care for little else than their sworn task. I can't forgive her. Not yet."

"Blooded they are, but blooded still have hearts."

I scratched my head. "This is you saying I'm being irresponsible, callous, and obtuse."

"This is me saying that every choice you make going forward must be made with wisdom."

"I can't sulk, then?"

"You may sulk all you like, young Razohan, after you've done right by those who give you their allegiance, and one who has no choice."

I scrunched my eyes closed at the reminder of what I'd done to Tressya, then glanced at Thaindrus before sighing one more time as I went to rise.

"No need. Sitting close to this fire for so long and I long to feel the snow on my pelt."

My old friend rose, taking his time to ease out his joints. I stared at the fire as he strode from the hall, brooding over everything we'd spoken about.

It took little time for another set of footsteps to grace Thaindrus's great hall, and I wondered if Romelda had been waiting close by for this moment. I kept my gaze on the fire, knowing it was cowardly to shun this meeting.

Romelda took Thaindrus's seat without a word. Her appearance shocked me. I'd never been able to guess at her age, but with the knowledge she carried, I'd guessed she was moving into middle age or beyond. Seeing her now, I could be forgiven for thinking she'd once lived alongside the long-dead King Ricaud.

Instead of black streaked with white, her hair was now the color of dirty snow. Her pale skin was ashen, her cheeks and chin slashed with silvery scars. But it was her eyes that shocked me the most. Once the color of blood that signified her loyalty to the Bone Throne, they were now black.

It seemed there would be no end to the shame I would

suffer for my decisions. For two days, I'd raged on my sickbed, cursing Romelda. She'd promised to protect Tressya, not kill her. My anger still throbbed from the betrayal, but facing her, I was forced to acknowledge that she'd suffered because of me.

I could not blame her for her loyalty to the Bone Throne. The blooded held the memories of their ancestors, those who'd sworn allegiance before them. If there was anyone who understood what was at stake, it was the blooded. Their fight to prevent the Levenian line from taking the Etherweave had cost many their lives and haunted those to follow.

Her choices came from her memories and knowledge, just as my choices came from my heart—a pitiable place to make choices from, according to Romelda; especially for a would-be king.

"I'm trying to feel forgiving." It came out weaker than I had intended when I'd felt ready to face her and have this conversation.

"I've not come here seeking your forgiveness. It is you who should ask the same of me."

"Tressya was on our side," I snapped.

"You're a blind fool," she hissed. "The mark you gave her has twisted your head. A disciple is loyal to only one."

"She holds no more love for the Salmun than we do."

"Did you not just hear what I said? It makes no difference what she feels for the Salmun. The Mother wanted a child of the Sistern on the throne. But now she's got one better. She has a loyal disciple on the throne. And not just a loyal disciple. A bloodborn. One who can take the Etherweave and claim the Bone Throne. We couldn't be in a worse position."

I fisted a hand, gently banging it against my temple to keep my anger in its cage.

From outside eyes it looked bad, but Tressya's and my last moments in the Ashenlands together fed my dreams and waking life. She may not have taken my blood, our bond may not be as secure as a true bonded partnership, but there was something special between us.

"She's like no other disciple."

Romelda slapped a hand to her thigh and huffed a frustrated breath.

"She killed one of her own…" I was going to give a list of all the ways Tressya had betrayed her order. Only in my ears, I heard a child's excuses for bad behavior. "That's certainly not the actions of a loyal disciple."

"You're not the man I sent to fulfill his destiny. The mark has blinded you. It's enslaving you." She shook her head, closing her eyes as if she couldn't bear to look at me.

I stared at the heavy lines on her face, the deep inset of her eyes, as if her face was caving inward. Then there were the scars, wounds made by Salmun magic, and no doubt terribly painful to heal.

"She's a bloodborn. She's one of us."

"Once I was well enough, I searched for evidence of such a link and found none. Since the Huungardred's lives are very long, it appears her ancestral link is distant. She's barely Razohan, Tamas."

"But she is Razohan."

If I told her my mark on Tressya's skin gave me the ability to wield the Etherweave through her, the revelation would end this argument. I wouldn't. Romelda was not a Huungardred or Razohan, she wouldn't understand the intimacy between bonded. According to Thaindrus, it was sacred, not to be shared with anyone outside of the Huungardred. I wouldn't even offer the truth, knowing it would ease her fury.

Tressya and I needed time to feel our way through this relationship... No, wait. What was I saying? I'd forced the mark on her. It was one-sided. But it didn't have to be. She was Razohan, meaning there was a chance... I blew a strong breath through my nose. I was grasping.

I snorted a mirthless laugh, then raised my tankard in a toast. "Cheers to our failure." And I took a large swig.

"The clans demand a meeting. Has Thaindrus told you that? And when you face them, will you continue to be so irreverent toward their losses?"

I stared into my tankard, deserving every lash she made. I'd promised hope and delivered tragedy. And here I was, the defeated, with too many miles between the woman I'd bonded.

"You should know that she's sent word to the Mother."

"What?" Could it be true, or was this Romelda's cruel way of punishing me further?

"Another blooded has kept a close eye on her while I've been recuperating. She sent word not long after her return from the Ashenlands. It seems the Mother was the first person she thought of once she was named queen."

I launched from my seat and turned my back on Romelda as though she were to blame for everything.

"Things have turned out for the better and now she's seeking guidance from the Mother."

"No. That's not what she's doing."

"Oh, Tamas."

I wanted to lash out at her for the pity I heard in her voice. Not for the first time, she made me feel like a child.

"A disciple is always a disciple."

Romelda was not there in our final moments together. She didn't hear the words we exchanged, and our silent promises. For all her wisdom, there were many things Romelda didn't understand, particularly anything that involved the heart.

"I fear the Mother will be on her way."

I turned back and stared into the fire. "She wouldn't dare step foot on Tarragonan soil while the Salmun protects the throne."

"You underestimate the Sistern. To your peril."

You underestimate Tressya. "Besides, these last few months have revealed the Salmun's complacency after a millennium with little disruption to their rule."

I threw the rest of my ale into the fire, having no stomach for it anymore. The fire hissed and subsided, releasing a haze of smoke before reclaiming its strength.

"The war for the south was lost, but we still have time. Every day we move closer to the Etherweave rising. You must find the Senjel Oracles."

This felt like déjà vu, like we were arguing in circles. It would take more than a few timed disclosures to pacify my anger at her betrayal, but to ignore what she asked was to turn my back on the north after failing them; the people who'd earned my fealty.

Even so, I couldn't decide without considering Tressya.

Finding the Senjel Oracles meant entering Tolum again, seeing her again.

I closed my eyes as I rubbed at my brow. *She'd sent word for the Mother.* Was that a sign of her true devotion? Regardless of the way I felt, the bond was one-sided, meaning separation and time may have weakened her feelings toward me, reigniting her loyalty to the Sistern. She would see my hunt for the Senjel Oracles a threat. It would divide us further. Maybe this time Tressya wouldn't be so willing to keep my presence her secret.

Being the coward that I was, I couldn't bear the thought of uncovering her true feelings if they were less than favorable toward me, especially since I had relinquished my only chance at true love.

I fixed my gaze on the contents of my tankard, unwilling to meet Romelda's haunting black eyes. "Tamas," Romelda barked.

"Yes," I replied, my tone dry and strained.

"You must be the only one present when the Etherweave rises from its entombment."

It wouldn't matter, but again, I held my tongue. Romelda had not earned back the right to know all my secrets.

"I need not speak aloud the outcome were you to fail once again."

I lifted my gaze and locked eyes with her. "It's impossible for me to lose control of the Etherweave now."

I smirked at her confusion, but soon my mind was no longer on our conversation, but in the south with a certain headstrong and courageous queen.

CHAPTER
THREE

BRYRA

I stretched my legs, increasing my pace, thrilling at the speed in which the ground disappeared underneath me, the feel of the wind caressing through my pelt. It felt too long since I could take my beast form, racing on four legs instead of two and roaming unhindered through my father's lands.

In beast form, our minds and bodies melded with the untamed wilderness of our home, untethering us from the inflictions which bound the two-legged kind and setting us free. It was why Huungardred favored their beast form, why many buried themselves within the wilderness for months at a time. Most would choose that way of life for longer, forever perhaps, if it weren't for my father's rule, forcing them back into their two-legged, half-beast half-man form occasionally so that none would forget they still had to live in the world of humans.

Weeks from the fight in the Ashenlands, and I'd yet to release my Huungardred form. I needed the beast to heal my terrible wounds, but that was not the only reason; I needed to forget.

Sadly, it seemed the memories wouldn't leave me so easily in beast form. For once, the freedom of burying myself within the wilderness would not cure all my ills.

Finally, I slowed and as I did so, I returned to my two-legged form. Weeks spent as a beast and there was a strangeness to walking on two legs such that I tripped over my own feet and nearly fell into the snow. I growled at my clumsiness, then, for some strange reason, chuckled, which then gave way to laughter.

I paused, resting a hand on rough bark and laughed some more. It felt silly and good, but in many respects hollow. The true merriment of my laugh was absent, the laugh echoing around as though there was nothing inside of me to mute the noise. I sobered on the thought and straightened.

Light flakes of snow fell, tickling the end of my nose. I raised my head, eyes closed, angling my face so the tiny flecks of the snow chilled the human side of my face. The skin prickled with the feeling.

It was good to be home. If only I could bury the memories and return to my father's court. But I'd had a taste of the malignant hatred and wickedness of the two-legged kind of which my father warned me about.

We lived our lives in the north, shielded far from the reach of humans. Our power and might as Huungardred kept our neighbors from our borders, but father had argued that it would not always be the case, and we needed to prepare for the day when they would become bold.

Garrat and Osmud were good to their word, protecting me from the worst of the clans' prejudices against the Huungardred, forcing them to accept me as a warrior fighting alongside them. But what I'd not revealed to either Razohan—to save them pain—was the terrible things they sought to inflict upon me once the fight began. Not even as allies were they prepared to shed their hatred for my kind.

And then there was the fight. Despite having traits that made us the perfect warriors, Huungardred were loathed to fight. Father took his place on the Huungardred throne by force, any other way and a leader would not be respected, but that didn't mean we spent our lives intent on tearing each other apart; I couldn't say the same for the two-legged kind.

Terrible things were done that night, as was with war. But I'd not been prepared for the attacks on me by my allies, or the rising of the dead. The world was changing. It seemed the tales of long ago would surface again as cyclic as the seasons.

My father cared little for the babbling of augurs or anything the Nazeen proclaimed. As his daughter, I'd believed in him and stopped listening to myself. But the dead had risen, and now I struggled to turn aside all Romelda had said. Perhaps the life we knew really was about to be destroyed.

I shook my head, sending the little streams of water created from the melting snow on my hot skin in a tiny spray around me. The world of humans was not mine to worry about. I was my father's daughter, the plight of the Huungardred should be my sole concern. I'd given myself to Tamas's course because I believed in him, but I couldn't do that anymore. Now I was fully healed, it was time to return to my father's side, give myself to the plight of my people.

About to take the beast form again, I stopped when the sound of horse's hooves reached my ears. I sniffed the air, smelling horse sweat and burned wolfrow.

Nazeen. And I knew which Nazeen I would find were I to continue along the path behind me. Curiosity made me turn around and head back the way I'd come.

It didn't take long before I saw Romelda's horse's gray head shifting through the snow-covered trees. Next came the Nazeen. Her appearance shocked her.

She'd fared little better than most of us during the fight. I'd not seen her once the fighting began, but word from Garrat informed me she'd survived a Salmun attack. It seemed such an attack was dangerous indeed, for the Nazeen looked aged beyond her time. Healed lacerations slashed across her face like silvery rivers and the skin on the back of her hands looked as frail as dead leaves.

"It's a long way for you to travel," I said in way of welcome as I walked toward her approaching horse.

"And now my travels are at an end." She reined her horse in and slid from the saddle, retaining the agility I remembered.

"You've ridden through the snow to see me?"

"I have."

Her blood-red eyes were now black. Perhaps the most shocking difference in her appearance.

"My father's hall would've made a more comfortable place for a chat."

She glanced around her. "This is the perfect place for the chat I wish to have with you."

I nodded, unhappy to hear this. Though father concerned himself rarely with what the Nazeen said, his hospitality was as boundless as his courtesy. The Nazeen were our allies, and the Huungardred had so few. Because of this, I strode toward a fallen log and brushed it clean of snow, then motioned for her to join me.

Anything Romelda had to say would relate to the greater realm, the south, Tamas and the Etherweave. Except for Tamas—a man I could never push aside, even if I wanted to—the rest was no longer my concern. But out of deference for the Nazeen, I would at least listen.

She sat with ease, no sign of lingering aches or wounds from the battle.

"You must have some idea why I've sought you out in private?"

Straight to the point. The Nazeen always presented themselves honestly, never hiding their true intentions behind deceptive words—a trait my father and I deeply respected.

"You wish to draw me back into the troubles of humans."

For three breaths, she replied with a stare. "The war has only begun."

"A war that has nothing to do with the Huungardred."

She straightened in her seat, as though she were drawing in strength to forge ahead with her goal.

"There was great loss. An unavoidable toll in war."

"I learned that the fight of the two-legged is not a fight for the four."

"You're wrong." She leaned forward, as if to emphasize the sharpness of her retort.

After a moment, she eased back. "This is everyone's war." She placed her hand on mine, resting in my lap. The skin on her palm was rough, as though she'd labored long and hard.

"The war for the Etherweave will consume everyone in the near realms. And then it will stretch to the far realms until it consumes everything.

"As a Huungardred, I know you're reluctant to get involved. You have many significant concerns of your own. But Bryra, you were once willing to get involved. You rode south with the rest of the clans to fight alongside the Razohan."

I turned away, avoiding her now black eyes. Romelda would not know at what cost I did so, and there was no point in telling her.

"I did," I intoned. "And now I have returned to my father's side. He needs me. The clans weren't happy to have me there. I now understand my father's concerns. This land is my future, as are my people, not the poisonous greed that festers in the heart of the two-legged."

A light dusting of snow coated her hair. She didn't bother to hide her impatience with my speech. Yet again, I couldn't help but respect her. Many would simper and nod, pretending to understand my meaning, all the while planning their tactic to undermine my reasoning.

"The greed of the south is your greater danger. Forget—"

"And what can I do? I followed the Razohan in to battle

because I believed in Tamas, but it made no difference to the outcome. What difference can I make now?"

"Tamas betrayed us," she snapped.

I gasped. Shaking my head, I said. "No. You're wrong."

"Don't let your feelings for him muddy your intellect, Bryra. From the start, Tamas went against my command."

I wouldn't have guessed a Nazeen would show such a pitiable emotion as bitterness.

"His choice led to our failure. And now he'll bring devastation upon the seven realms if he continues to turn from what needs to be done. I fear, though, his mind is lost. He can no longer see clearly."

"What're you saying?"

Romelda leveled her black eyes on me. "The princess must die."

I leapt from the log. "You can't ask that of me."

Romelda joined me standing. She was a tall woman, but was forced to look up at me.

"You love Tamas."

It wasn't a question.

"He doesn't love me. I know that. I've always known, even if I choose to dream."

"He's blinded by this woman."

"You think love is blind?"

"This time it is," she continued, not thinking of what she'd said.

"He bit her." There was no greater intimacy than that. No greater demonstration of love than that.

"Tamas is not a full-blooded Huungardred. He doesn't

understand the depth of his actions. The bite was not made out of love, but fragility." She spat the last word.

"Maybe not in the beginning. He did so because he's an honorable man. And honorable men don't kill innocent women. But I think much has happened while he was in the south. There's no denying where his heart now lies."

"It's not his duty to think with his heart."

"Honorable men will always think with their heart, so they don't act in tyranny."

Romelda's face flushed, even though her lips were now a deep bluish red from the cold. "You're ignorant of what she's capable of."

"I know she raised the dead."

"She's a bloodborn."

That stole my words. At reading my shock, Romelda's glare held a tinge of triumph.

"You made us think Tamas was the only bloodborn."

"For centuries it is all the augurs proclaimed." She turned from me and paced a short distance, as if to hide her shame for her false guidance. "Sirillious said differently the last time I saw him. 'Twain is the bloodborn'. Those were his words. The first time I'd heard them uttered. Curses it would be this woman. Anyone else and they would already be dead."

"How can you be so sure?"

"Tamas is sure."

That Romelda was confident in Tamas's belief made me believe it, too. "My feelings are unchanged, regardless of how he feels about me. You're willing to place this burden upon me, knowing Tamas will hate me for eternity if I kill her."

She at least had the decency to look abashed at what she was asking. "Believe me Bryra, no one understands better than I the burden I'm placing on you. The blooded gave their life to the servitude of the Etherweave. I have sacrificed everything in my life to ensure the rightful heir will one day sit upon the Bone Throne. And that rightful heir is not Tressya.

"I ask you to make this sacrifice to save someone you love from their folly. Tamas is blind to what fate he'll create with the choices he's making."

"What if you're wrong? I trust Tamas to do what's right."

Romelda inhaled, arching her neck and turning her face to the feathering of snow. "And what if I'm right? Are you willing to take that chance?"

"I've already said my place is by my father's side. My concerns are for my people."

Romelda looked as though I'd slapped her. Then, regaining her composure, she glanced around us to the snow covered forest. "It is very peaceful here. I can see how you would easily believe everything beyond these forests can't affect you." She shifted her gaze to me. "I wish it were so. You think the clans are your enemy, but they are nothing compared to who will come for your lands and come for your people if we fail, and Tamas fails to ascend to the Bone Throne. As a bloodborn, controlled by the Salmun, the princess Tressya is now our greatest enemy."

She held up a hand to stem any argument I may have.

"She was an innocent before she arrived in Tarragona. She would've stayed that way had Tamas completed his task. Evil is not born, but it is easily made, and Tressya is now in the grip of the Salmun, under their influence, learning their lies."

She took my hand in hers. "As a Huungardred, I know romantic notions of love didn't blind you. Their bond is one-sided. And it's all from Tamas's side. She'll remain untouched by the bond while he falls hopelessly and deeply under her spell. In the end, she'll become his master. There'll be no hope for him, and no hope for us. His pain will be great when he discovers the mistaken choice he made."

I pulled my hands from hers. "But what if you're wrong?"

Romelda was right in saying it could only ever be one-sided. It was impossible for anyone without Huungardred ancestry to ever form such a bond. But if the princess was bloodborn, didn't that make her Razohan with a bloodlink to the Huungardred? Didn't that mean at some point she could choose to accept Tamas's bond?

"With all my heart, I wish I was. I know I'm not."

I turned my face, giving Romelda my less expressive beast side because my human side was vulnerable to revealing my confused thoughts. I didn't want Romelda to see how much I was breaking inside; all over again.

Tamas had always been my dearest friend. And for the last five years, my feelings toward him had changed, grown deeper, more enduring, more precious. I'd dreamed he and I would form such a bond, longed for it to be so. My heart was ripped apart to know it would never happen, to know he'd chosen another, yet I would never blame Tamas for my feelings. He'd never promised me more; it was my own fanciful desires.

I found escape from that pain in knowing their bond

would never be complete because Tressya was not blood linked to the Huungardred. It was petty and cruel of me to have such feelings, so I intended to keep them a twisted secret I would hopefully shed once I grew through the pain in my heart.

Romelda's words ripped my bleeding heart anew. And what if Tressya chose not to reciprocate and strengthen their bond? It would be as Romelda said, with Tamas a slave to his love while the princess remained unaffected.

I couldn't bear the thought of him enslaved because of his love, his heart torn like mine because he'd made the wrong choice.

"Look at me. I can't move amongst humans."

It was my excuse; an excuse, which meant I'd not entirely dismissed all she said. I was curious whether she could provide a solution to my appearance.

"With my help, you can. I'll disguise your true-self, give you the form of a woman. It will not last, but you'll have enough time in disguise to finish what Tamas should've done at the start. I'll spell a letter of recommendation, which you shall give to the seneschal once you reach Emberfell. That will ensure you're given the position as lady to the queen."

I didn't want to agree to such a thing. I wasn't a murderer of innocents. But I couldn't dismiss the fact Tressya was living within Emberfell, guarded and influenced by the Salmun.

Tamas couldn't have foreseen this when he saved her life by marking her on the ship. He didn't love her then. The bond would enhance his feelings, blinding him to the truth.

He really was falling into a trap of his making, all because he acted honorably and saved an innocent woman.

"All right. I'll do it." I couldn't believe the words I was saying. It was as though someone else was speaking from my mouth.

"I'll make this burden easier for you to bear. Poisons are a tidier way to kill. And you can be long gone before it takes effect."

I shook my head. "This is wrong. My heart tells me so. How can you ask me to betray my dearest friend in such a way?"

"Listen to me," Romelda hissed, her patience fraying with my refusal. The blooded were bound by their oath, their resolve hardened by a millennium of shared memories. It made sense that she was solely focused on what she believed must be done.

"There must be another way," I interrupted before she could continue.

"There is no other way." Then she gently touched my arm. "I understand your hesitation because I know your heart. You're a true and loyal friend, like your father. But Bryra, the fate of the seven realms surpasses your personal feelings. If the Salmun seizes the Etherweave, then all the seven realms are doomed, including everyone you love. Whatever hatred you fear Tamas will harbor towards you will matter little if we cannot ensure he alone wields the Etherweave. Remember, Tamas will be the first to die if the Salmun succeeds. Are you willing to let that happen, knowing you could have prevented it?"

Turning my head from her, I closed my eyes. "When?"

The words were like flames pouring from my mouth, burning my throat and tongue.

"It's best it's done as soon as possible while Tamas is still in the north. And Bryra. This is our secret."

I turned to her. "I won't be able to keep it a secret from Tamas always."

"I respect that. It's a secret until it's complete." She squeezed my hand. "There'll come a day when he'll see the truth and understand why it had to be done. He won't hate us forever."

Maybe so, but Romelda didn't understand the depth of a bond. Neither did I, for that matter, but I understood it more than she. Regardless, to save him from his terrible mistake, I had to accept he may never forgive me. But I would rather he hate me than see him enslaved by a false love.

What if she falls in love with him and surrenders herself to the mate bond in return?

That was a wound too great for me to bear, and a possibility if she really was a Razohan.

CHAPTER FOUR

TRESSYA

Daelon still struggled with his loss. His cheekbones were now jutting ledges, pronouncing the hollow groove of his cheek, and his clothes fit loose. In profile, he remained a striking figure, but when he turned his face to me, I couldn't miss the wretched abuse that ravaged his heart. His once expressive eyes appeared flat and hollow.

Three weeks was not enough time to push aside the pain of losing someone you loved. Surprisingly, Andriet listened to what I'd said and kept his distance. As a spirit, his influence was limited, but I was sure he'd find a way to make his presence felt. The separation pained them both, but I felt sure Daelon would learn to live without Andriet before Andriet had time to get over his ex-lover.

I couldn't help feeling guilty at the thought. Maybe I'd been selfish in bringing Andriet home, but forcing him to spend eternity in the Ashenlands was a cruelty I couldn't bear.

"It's best to stay invisible," I warned Daelon as we sat upon our horses at the dock awaiting the Mother's ship.

"I'll do my best. But I'm yours, Tressya. If she threatens—"

"Daelon. She's not like any other you've met before. Trust me. Men are useful instruments to her, nothing more. I know how to deal with her."

I lied, but I wasn't about to admit to Daelon that my stomach twisted in knots, and I'd woken with an erratic heartbeat. Of course I knew the Mother would come, even before I wrote. Her audacious plan had worked. Now all that was left was to shuffle the pieces around until everything suited her fine.

"I'm not afraid of this Mother Divine of yours."

I stared ahead, watching the small rowboat bring her closer to the dock. My wounded heart had betrayed so many, including me, making me believe I was strong enough to standalone outside the Sistern, but I wasn't sure if I could fit this role as queen without the Mother's guidance. I'd appealed to Gusselan, but she was yet to see my overtures as anything but manipulative. The Sistern had always been my foundation, my walls. I felt stripped of strength without its instruction.

I felt alone.

Not for the first time I thought of Tamas, thought of our time together in his bed before the war began, when I allowed myself to believe one dream of mine would come true. Yet one more ache, raw and brutal, stabbed at my heart, as my yearning for his touch throbbed like relentless drum beats through my body.

You naïve fool.

I bit my bottom lip on feeling the thickening in my throat. How many times have I dreamed only to find I live with nightmares? I was fine with nightmares if it meant Tamas and I would fight them together. But that was not to be.

"I can't wait to meet the craggy beast," Andriet said from beside me.

I was being miserable again. It took me a moment to shake myself out of my melancholic thoughts. Thinking such things would not help me survive my new life.

I straightened on my horse. As a disciple, discipline was my life. Embodying the six pillars was my only hope of surviving.

I turned to Andriet, hovering beside my horse, and gave him an impatient look—I'd warned him to stay away, given I would ride with Daelon—but he ignored me and now he gazed longingly across to Daelon. Seeing the turn in his expression, his yearning, the open wounds of his heart, I stare back out to sea.

What wrong have I done in releasing him?

This was one more demonstration of how far I'd strayed from the six pillars. Discipline. Courage. Loyalty. The three pillars I'd lived by. Discipline to fortify myself against the weakness of a fragile heart. Courage to face what must be done regardless of the sacrifice. Loyalty. I'd betrayed the Sistern too many times to call myself a disciple.

I deserved no forgiveness, but I would ask for it all the same. I needed the Mother now more than ever.

Who am I to sit upon a throne?

Now I was the heir, Andriet lectured me senseless on all the legends relating to the Etherweave, but I was cautious with what I believed, aware the Salmun's teachings influenced Andriet's version. The one thing I couldn't dismiss was his belief in the Etherweave's return. And soon.

"Listen." I turned to Daelon. "This is your greatest secret."

With the rowboat almost at the dock, I could feel the tremor in my hands.

He nodded. "I know. I understood after the tenth reiteration."

"The Salmun—"

"Can't know who she is."

"She's come as my spiritual advisor."

"I can't wait to play." Andriet attempted to clap his hands together, but they passed through each other instead.

"No. You can't," I snapped.

"Can't what?" Daelon said.

I shook my head. "Never mind. Just...please." I wasn't sure who I was speaking to.

Daelon reached across from his horse and took my hand. "It's all right. I know how to play the game. I've done it all my life."

I regretted glancing at Andriet, seeing the pain cripple his smile as he glanced at our joined hands, likely wishing he could do the same. Hopefully, it wouldn't take eternity for him to get used to all the losses he faced.

Mother, what have I done? With my insides in tight little knots over the arrival of the Mother, I couldn't cope with the emotional fog swirling around me, so I nudged my horse forward.

"Wait here." I meant both the living and the dead, but Andriet was unruly in spirit form and wafted along beside me.

Though out of earshot of Daelon, I still mumbled. "If I'd known you'd be so stupid, I would've left you in the Ashenlands."

"Liar. You love my interference. Who else is going to whisper sense into your ear?"

"Please, Andriet. You don't know the Mother Divine. You don't know—"

"My sweet. I have spent my entire life within the Tarragonan court, and watched a silent war waged with truculent egos seeking to ingratiate themselves close to the seat of power."

"This is different."

"Your judgement is clouded because her arrival has made you anxious. You're a queen. And this Mother Divine of yours is sneaking ashore in disguise. That's how much power she wields in Tarragona. I ask why has she come?"

He didn't ask for me to answer.

"For the same reason, everyone else lies, tricks or kills to get close to the king, or in this case, queen," he answered for me.

Andriet was right in saying I couldn't see through my anxiousness. But there were too many twisting tales and heart pain I'd have to recount for him to truly understand what the Mother meant to me, what strength and power she'd given me to survive a life within the vicious court as a loathed illegitimate princess. I owed her my loyalty. I needed her strength while mine failed me.

A simple carriage pulled up at the dock to greet the Mother's arrival. Everyone at court would know her as my spiritual advisor and substitute mother, an acceptable disguise given my illegitimacy was well known.

"I should warn you, the Mother knows about my spiritweaving ability."

"Oh good. If I feel she's getting too high on herself, you can play intermediary between us."

"Never," I snapped, wishing I could punch him. "I don't want her to know you're here. You were meant to be a secret, Andriet. Our bargain, remember?"

"Tressya, my dear, you really need to release your secrets. It's time us spirits got to influence the living. Stars knows there's a lot who need a good kicking."

I tightened my hold on my horse's reins as I fought against using my ability to command him to disappear. "Honestly, Andriet, if she knew you were hanging around, she'd find a way to use soul voice to command you."

"I know the rules. I'm safe. You said soul voice is only for the living. And this Mother of yours has not a drop of Whelin blood, so she's not about to command the dead."

The traitorous disciple I was, I'd confessed my secrets to Andriet, knowing across the veil is where they would stay. It felt great to offload the burden of secrecy. Only now I wished I hadn't been so forthright about everything—everything except my dealings with Tamas, coward that I was.

"I wouldn't put it past her to find a way."

The small rowboat had disappeared behind the dock. I dismounted and handed my reins to a footman who was waiting to help the Mother into the carriage.

Andriet sucked in a breath. "Here comes the crone now."

Black was her usual attire, so the Mother's simple gown of deep blue, suitable for a woman of good breeding, surprised me. She wore a plain white headdress, covering her hair, but leaving her craggy face exposed to the sun's weak rays. Despite looking too advanced in years to walk unaided, the Mother shunned any offer of assistance and strode toward me, her bearing straight and strong just like her mind.

Though she'd yet to leave the dock, I could already feel the heavy weight of her stare, those dark eyes whipping me with judgement.

As she drew near, my knees bent, my first instinct to fold to the ground and kiss the emerald ring on her finger.

"Steady now, Tressya," Andriet warned me, understanding what I was about to do. "The queen gets on her knees for no one."

I straightened, but dipped my eyes to the ground in respect.

"There's a lot of eyeballs on you right now. Including the Salmun." Andriet continued to instruct me.

I sucked in a breath, forgetting about the Salmun. I'd argued with Orphus about my guard, not wanting the shadow of the Salmun everywhere I went. He'd relented with his snake smile, sending them in secret. The secret lasted no time once we arrived at the dock, the two Salmun positioning themselves where all could see when they knew it was too late for me to argue or send them back.

"A lot of tongues to recount tales of this exchange. If you want your Mother's true identity a secret, don't give anyone reason to question it."

I nodded, acknowledging his wisdom.

My eyes were still on the cobbles when her black boots came into view.

"Child." Her voice was as I remembered: a precipice over which the weak fell.

For a moment our eyes met, then to my surprise, she dipped into a curtsey, but only so far, feigning stiff joints and bad back.

I stayed like stone, feeling too awkward to move. Never had our interactions ever been like this. The Mother demanded subservience and obedience, a necessary discipline, only now our roles were reversed, and the Mother was expected to be subservient to me.

"Mother." It was all I could say, taking her hands in mine as a show of affection. "Your journey went well?"

Her thin smile was my signal to shut up.

"She's as warm as ice, I see," Andriet said from beside me.

"Come." I swept my arm wide, motioning toward the carriage, and, in my awkwardness, accidentally passing my forearm through Andriet's body.

As the stabs of ice speared through my skin, I recoiled with a gasp.

"Ooh, that did feel good," Andriet purred.

"Your Majesty," came the slippery voice of a Salmun. "Are

you all right?" His hands were the only part of his body I could see. The skin discolored and wrinkled like old parchment.

Damn, when had he gotten close?

"I'm fine," I snapped, casting a side-eye to the Mother.

She remained still, eyeing me with one thin black-marked eyebrow arched high on her forehead. She knew. Damn her. The Mother was far too cunning to miss what a reaction like that meant.

"Go away," I mumbled to Andriet, with a lame attempt at not moving my lips.

"No way. Things are just getting good." He continued to pester me while I walked across to the carriage. "You never told me you could touch me."

"I can't," I hissed under my breath.

"Then what was that? Not a full sensation granted. But I felt something. Death will not be so gloomy."

"Andriet," I growl-whispered in warning.

"Don't worry, Tressya dear. I shall be wise with my newfound knowledge." He went to rub his hands together and failed, but he didn't notice. "We're going to have some fun."

It was like being squeezed between two rivals with Andriet taking the seat beside me and the Mother the one opposite.

"This is cozy," Andriet crooned. He'd sunk below the seat to his torso, but rested his hand on the seat, his arm threateningly close to my thigh.

I shifted my leg, trying to make it appear as though I was resettling myself after the jolting of the carriage as the horses moved off. Catching on to what I was doing, Andriet sidled up a little closer, while I side-eyed him.

Forcing Andriet's games from my thoughts, I looked across to the Mother and found her watching me intently, her thin lips almost disappearing into her mouth.

"Trouble?" she said.

"Mother?"

"The six pillars are your shield."

"Of course, Mother. Something I'll never forget."

She snorted. "All six? It seems you have decided to pick and choose those you wish to hold on to."

"I..." This was a test. "The one is useless without the others."

"Yet you deem to condescend to me," she bit in before I could say any more.

"Oh, she's good. A right little viper. She makes Radnisa look like a harmless lizard in comparison."

I couldn't stop the fluttering of my eyelids in frustration. "No, Mother."

Shut up. Shut up. Shut up.

"Tell me. How far have you progressed with the death arts?"

She knew. *Dammit, Andriet.* She knew a spirit was here. I dared not lie. "I have much to learn of spiritweaving."

"You're the queen, Tressya. Act like one," Andriet admonished me.

I relaxed my clenched fists on seeing the Mother's gaze settle on them. She was too sharp to miss my frustration, too smart to wonder why I couldn't sit still.

"It seems you have progressed farther and quicker than I

envisioned." She glanced to the right of me, looking to where Andriet would be if he'd not sunk halfway through the seat.

"That snake. Do you think she suspects I'm here?" Andriet cried. "Oh, she's very good. This will be quite the challenge."

"I was surprised that you chose me," I choked out.

"Pathetic as you were, it was necessary."

"The wicked little fiend. I want to officially announce I don't like her. You're the queen. Tell her to mind her tongue."

I tried to shut my ears to the pest beside me. "What did you do?"

"What needed to be done?" As I expected, the Mother wasn't about to tell me anything beyond which she deemed necessary knowledge for her cause.

A good disciple never questioned, but after everything I'd done, I wasn't a good disciple, and I was sick of mysteries. "How did you..." I flicked a look at Andriet, then remembering the Mother's shrewd gaze remained on me, looked beyond him to the streets of Tolum, finding it easier to ask when not looking at the Mother.

"How did you do it?" The Sistern's power was soul voice, not wielding magic, which meant whatever the Mother had put inside of me was the help of a magic wielder.

There was a dearth of magic in Merania. An ancient yet dying skill in the death arts and an order controlling soul voice, but little else. There were the occasional traveling seers, peddling their fortunes for money, but none proved reliable, and few paid them any attention.

Magic was the only explanation for what the Mother had done to me. Secrecy and discretion, two of the pillars we lived by, was the reason for the Sistern's success, which meant the Sistern always acted alone, yet this time, I was sure the Mother had used an accomplice.

The Mother gave me another arched eyebrow, her lips thinning in displeasure, and I dropped my gaze to the floor of the carriage.

"Go on, Tressya. It's impertinent of her to dismiss your question like that. And what's with the death stare? Honestly, the woman needs a good shakeup."

I needed my calming breaths to get through this ride. Andriet bleating in my ear on one side of me and the Mother staring me into the seat in front of me, I wasn't going to make it to Emberfell sane in the head.

"The Salmun are expecting my spiritual advisor and..."

Dare I say the word? When I was young, my heart yearned for the mother I lost at birth, slotting the Mother in her place. Stone, ice and an implacable heart. That's what the Mother became to me, but also my protector, my liberator, the one to show me I could be more than the accident I was at birth. Those were her gifts to me in the form of the six pillars and relentless training.

I'd left the sentence hanging, and by her expression, the Mother was waiting for me to finish it.

"I said you were like a Mother figure to me. I thought it would explain your arrival."

She tilted her chin up. "Very well." And glanced away.

"I'd blunt an axe on this one, I'm sure." Andriet was not going to be quiet.

Since the Mother had finally stopped glaring at me and was now looking at the scenery, I darted Andriet a sour look, to be given a smile and a wink. Then he sat forward, reaching out a hand as if to touch her knee.

"No," I snapped.

With the Mother's attention diverted to me, I waved to the opposite side of the carriage. "This side is of more interest. That's Emberforge. The Salmun's temple."

"I know." There was a weight to her tone, a condescension burying me in my place.

I thought of another perplexing question about myself I wished to ask the Mother but feared doing so with Andriet beside me. He knew many of my secrets now, I shouldn't care, but anything linked to the Razohan felt sacred, and a secret I wished to keep as my own.

Besides, Andriet was adamant my connection to the Tarragonan throne and the Etherweave came through the Levenian line, his own bloodline. This belief stemmed from the prophecy he had always believed in, which stated an heir from the House of Tannard would rule the Bone Throne. However, he never once doubted or questioned which specific ancestral branch of the House of Tannard the prophecy referred to.

If what his mother had told me was true, that I was of the North, I wasn't ready for Andriet to learn of my true heritage, forcing me to keep one more secret from my dearest friend, adding to my guilt and shame.

I remained silent, making the rest of the ride uncomfortably tense. If it weren't for Andriet, who constantly teased me by shifting in his seat and repositioning himself—his arms or legs always threatening to brush against the Mother—I might have found some peace. Had I known how provocatively he would behave as a spirit, I would have left him confined to the castle.

"You have been inside Emberforge?" Rather than a question, it sounded like an accusation.

"Yes, Mother."

"And the Bone Throne?"

"I've seen it."

And, of course, any talk of the Bone Throne reminded me of the man I was with when I entered Emberforge. What had he felt when the last ruler to sit on the Bone Throne had passed through him?

"Aha, the serpent shows the true colors of her scales," Andriet shouted.

The Mother's stare was like nails. I pressed myself back into my seat with a gasp as Andriet leaned over me, waving a hand in front of my face, as if trying to distract the Mother's glare.

"Omissions are lies," she hissed. "You have secrets."

I shook my head.

"Go on, tell her, the old crone. Tell her if she doesn't show respect for your title, I'll tickle her insides until she pukes."

"Never, Mother." I shook myself, gritting my teeth, a warning to Andriet.

"Don't make me, child." Her voice slithered like a snake.

She was threatening me with soul voice.

"Oh how I long to see her eyes pop when my hand slips—"

"I've summoned spirits." The words tumbled out. It was the only way I could think to prevent Andriet from touching the Mother. It was a confession I was reluctant to make, but I knew the Mother would expect me to eventually master spiritweaving, especially since she was the reason my skills in the death arts had advanced.

I knew my defense against soul voice, but that was my secret from the Mother; an irreparable disloyalty in my heart because I wanted to keep it a secret, just as I'd wanted Tamas to remain my secret—everything we'd shared remained cradled in a special place in my memory and heart.

"As was my intention. But that's not all you want to tell me."

"Tell her, Tressya. Tell the bitch that if she doesn't mind her tongue, I'll stuff my fist so far up her—"

"There is nothing else, Mother."

"Don't let her win."

"The position you find yourself in is because of me, but it seems you have willingly forgotten that." Her voice was a blade, my soul word hanging on the tip of her tongue.

"Your charm, skill and courage placed you on the throne, and she's arrived to claim the glory. I'm sorry, Tressya, but I've had enough."

"No," I cried, then corrected myself. "...Mother." I lurched forward, following Andriet as he slid from beside me to hover in front of the Mother, blocking me unless I wanted to go through him.

The Mother's eyes flared at my sudden movement.

The small carriage gave me no room to maneuver with Andriet separating the two of us.

"You're right, Mother. So much has gone on since I arrived in Tarragona. It's distracting and confusing, and with

Radnisa..." I sucked in a breath, unable to mention my greatest disgrace: that I had killed Radnisa, a fellow disciple.

My babbling and shouting were my feeble ways of stopping Andriet.

"Please, just...stop," I pleaded. I stared at the back of Andriet's head, and my eyes landed on the Mother.

She mustn't know about him. I wanted to keep everyone I cared about as far from the Mother as I could. There was no telling what cunning she would devise to take what was mine from me.

Her eyes narrowed on me before they flittered around the carriage. "You'll tell me now whose presence is here with us." Her voice was like a chilling wind blowing through a dusty hall.

"And you'll prostrate yourself before Her Majesty and beg forgiveness for your insolent tone." Andriet gave a breath. "You refuse to do so? I thought as much." And plunged his hand through her chest.

The Mother sucked in a breath, her mouth gaping wide, eyes bulging in surprise.

I smothered my cry, about to command Andriet to stop, but a traitorous corner deep in my heart thrilled at seeing her like this. And I would never slip up and command my good friend to my will.

"Where's that cursed tone now, old crone?" Andriet cried in triumph, twisting his hand around inside her chest.

"*Aether*—," the Mother cried, at the same moment I cried. "Stop," keeping the command from my voice.

"You're no fun, Tressya dear." Andriet sighed, pulling his fist from the Mother's chest. "She needed a good lesson.

Look at her." He chuckled as he wafted back into the seat beside me. "She needed to know her place. And if you're not going to do it, my dear, then I'll make it my extreme pleasure to teach her."

The Mother sagged forward, gasping breaths. Because I was a fallen disciple, I took delight in seeing her like this, but it was wicked to do so. I had no integrity if I held no loyalty to the Mother.

The Mother lifted her head, her eyes sparking like fire. "It's a good thing I've arrived. I know how to restore your faith in the six pillars." She kept her voice low.

"That stunk of a threat. Perhaps a little more..." Andriet waved his hand.

"Of course, Mother." I intervened. "I'll devote myself to my training."

She straightened, checking her headdress remained in place. "You'll leash your pet. Or I'll do something about it."

"Pet!" spat Andriet.

"Yes, Mother."

I gave up hiding his presence and glared at him. As a spirit, he thought he was beyond the living world. But I was sure the Mother would find a way to manipulate him from across the veil.

"Never forget who you are, Tressya," Andriet continued. "But I understand the hold the old bat has over you. You've spent your life in devotion to the Sistern. Such loyalty is not easily dismissed. If it were, then there's little honor in your heart."

Shut up, Andriet. He wasn't making me feel any better after everything I'd done.

"But you needn't worry, my dear. The Salmun is on your side. Use them as your shield if the serpent continues with such impertinence. Threatening the queen." He huffed. "That's treason."

The Mother had made an enemy of a spirit free to roam where he pleased. There would be no stopping him from haunting her every move.

A wicked part of me delighted at the idea.

CHAPTER
FIVE

TAMAS

THE GREAT HALL at Ironhelm filled fast with the raucous chatter of the clan leaders. I spied Kaldor, Macmillan and Giraldus amongst them, heads of the three strongest clans, each having fought bravely during the Ashenlands war. Now they were without their strongest warriors.

I'd put on an excellent feast, filling the great hall with mouth-watering aromas of succulent roast meats, scores of deer, boar and pheasant and ensured braziers burned in each corner of the hall. Then I instructed the most troublesome and the powerful clans to be separated at the tables. All for nought, as I was sure they'd aired their fury to each other behind my back already.

There was a restless prowling energy taking hold within the hall, not least of which came from my heart. I wasn't ready to face them, but not doing so was the greatest cowardly act of all.

This is what it meant to be a strong leader: solidarity during hardship and failure. Truth was, I didn't want to be anyone's leader, not even the Razohan. It was Romelda's influence that won me my place. Her persistent demands, sharpening the haunting voice of my shame, refused to let me free. And this is where I found myself, promising success, then condemning them all to failure.

Had I not spent the night with Tressya, I would have killed King Henricus in plenty of time to take his soul, then his place as king, which would have changed the outcome, making us the victors. Perhaps the war need not have happened. However, that's not how it went. And I was forced to face the consequences of my actions and the fury of the clan heads.

Garrat, ever the diplomat, tried his best to pacify their anger, but somehow the rumors grew wings, and everyone was talking about the queen of the south, listening to whispers of our secret liaison. Garrat and Osmud argued that resentment fed the rumors, but with so many grievances, the rumors stuck. And why shouldn't they? After all, they were true.

I sprawled in my seat overlooking the hall and the vast stretch of filled tables before me, and wished, for one spineless moment, I was far from here, far in the north, running with the Huungardred, leaving the woes of men behind. But I was a Razohan, living firmly in the world with them.

This was all my doing. It was time I faced my responsibility.

Garrat left Kaldor's side and approached my seat, raised on a wood dais, so that I may see every corner of the room and everyone in it.

I studied his face as he approached, reading the mood of the conversation he had with the Wildelm clan leader by his expression. Gratitude for the blessed arrival of the two orphaned boys, Garrat and Osmud, into the Razohan clan never once failed to humble me. I owed my sanity, perhaps even my life, to my two best friends. And I was doing a poor ass job of repaying them for the unrelenting loyalty they gave me.

Garrat climbed the steps and slid into the seat I ensured remained beside mine for moments like this, when either of the two needed a private word, usually to talk sense into my stubborn head.

"Kaldor's eating his weight in deer," I said.

"You've provided it."

I gave a subtle nod. "He's furious then?"

"It doesn't help when he believed my words of glory and is now forced to provide for the widows who've lost husbands, sons or daughters, most both."

I sunk my head to my chest, staring at my belt buckle, unable to look Garrat's way. I couldn't even say I had tried my best because I hadn't, far from it. My best would have seen the line of the House of Tannard destroyed before any of the north stepped foot inside the Ashenlands. With the line destroyed, the Salmun would have no choice but to accept me. I, who knew Tressya was the second bloodborn the moment I met her, did nothing to eliminate the threat she posed to our success. While I was finding love, the northerners were suffering defeat. Was that the true way of a king?

"The clan heads have not come to hear your feeble excuses or listen to your sorrows." Garrat read my mood, like he always did.

"I can't give them back their sons or daughters."

"But you can give them assurance you'll right the wrongs."

Not *my* wrongs. Such was his loyalty, Garrat would never blame me.

"I'm ready to atone for what I've done."

Garrat surged forward in his seat. "But you won't, at least not verbally." He nodded his head toward the clans filling my tables. "They haven't come to hear you moan and weep. What's done is done. You'll stand up there and tell them how you plan to fix everything. Because I know you have a plan."

I met his unflinching gaze, then couldn't stop the smallest twitch of my lips. "Perhaps we need to trade seats."

"Not on your life."

"You're a better man than I."

"We're better men for having each other." He clapped me on the shoulder. "Each of us have our skills. Mine is for diplomacy—"

"A skill for true leaders, or kings."

"But it's a most effective skill for the king's advisor. Talking rather than fighting—"

"Again, it's a trait all good leaders or kings should possess."

"There comes a time when talk no longer works and action is best," growled Garrat, sounding exasperated with my interjections. "That's when a true leader is needed. One that won't hesitate regardless of the cost to themselves and... the cost to others if it ultimately achieves the right end."

I stared at my boots stretched out before me. I knew Garrat too well, knew this for what it was, approval, cloaked as a lecture.

It all came down to that one moment when I stabbed my blade through my father's heart, the moment I believed I'd truly cursed my soul. I'd shut out the songs of praise surrounding me when he lay at my feet. During endless, sleepless nights, I had to learn to shut out the vision of Father's cheeks puffed and flaming with rage, eyes dark and wild with savage hunger, lips pulled back in fierce fury.

In the north, there was no hesitation in killing the deranged. They were a lethal blight within the clans. A sword through their heart was the only cure for their insanity.

Some told me I was strong in making the choice, taking it upon myself, when many would've accepted the offer from another to spare any pain. But no one understood. It wasn't a weak will that allowed the evil spirits in to twist his mind, neither was it a sickness developed from something he ate or for exposing himself to the rare blood colored moon for too long, or a curse buried within the Razohan bloodline for Sophila's crime of mating with a Huungardred. It was grief, so deep and profound it ate him up inside. He simply couldn't live without my mother.

I liked to think my sword through his heart ended his

suffering, but I knew deep down that was my attempt at easing my own. But his torment would've only intensified when he discovered he'd killed his only son because of a lie; he was not the bloodborn, and would never inherit the Etherweave or sit upon the Bone Throne.

"You know I don't like to rant," Garrat said.

"When you do it frequently with gusto."

"I do it when it needs doing. And if you think it's frequent, then it's because you're a stubborn fool who won't listen."

I raised my hands in surrender. "Okay. I'm listening."

Garrat snorted, then repositioned himself in his seat. "Then let me lend some friendly advice."

"Is that what you call it?"

He huffed a sigh. "Fine. This is what you'll do. You're going to stand up and tell these people exactly what they want to hear. You're going to praise all for their fealty and courage, pay homage to those who fell, then tell them the Ashenlands fight was a setback, but not the end of the war."

At my grunt, he said. "Stop wallowing in your self-pity and think of all those before you. They didn't send their sons and daughters to die so that you could hang your head and brood on all your mistakes.

"Yes, you fucked up, Tamas. For your own good, I won't hide that fact. But they don't want to hear that. They want you to tell them how you're going to win because winning is the only way to replace their losses."

Their willingness to knock sense into me was one in a very long list of things I cherished about Osmud and Garrat.

I glanced across at him. "Succinct as always. No wonder you're the diplomat." Osmud would've punched me in the face, which was usually just as effective.

I covered his hand with mine, giving a firm squeeze of thanks, before I rose from my seat and faced the crowd. The raucous din, echoing through the great hall, quietened in moments as heads turned to face me.

I surveyed each of their faces before I spoke, gauging my audience. There was not a friendly expression amongst them, and I didn't blame their hostility.

Glancing once at Garrat, who gave me a subtle wink, I sauntered down the steps and paced closer to the tables. I stopped beside a young man and placed my hands on my hips, sliding my gaze across the crowd once more, ensuring to meet all eyes.

"Words are inadequate to express my gratitude for the courage you all displayed during the Ashenlands war. It was a brutal conflict against a deadly foe. I can only imagine what it must've felt like for you all when you first faced the Ashenlands' beasts and the Creed's magic. Yet." My voice rose as I continued to trawl my gaze across all the turned faces. "Not one of you baulked. Not one of you deserted. You fought brutal, and you fought hard because you fought for the north: your loved ones, your homes, your future."

I allowed the silence to cloak the room and pull us all in tighter.

"For that, I'm grateful beyond measure. And for all the vacant seats at your tables, I bestow the great honor a brave warrior deserves."

I reached across the young man and swiped up the closest tankard, then raised it into the air. "To the fallen."

The room erupted in chorus as everyone chanted my words as I gulped down the warm ale. Once the tankard was finished, I slammed it down on the table, silencing the room once more.

"But you didn't make the long journey from your homes to hear me praise your worthiness as fierce warriors of the north. You came here with questions."

"Too right we did," someone yelled to a jeer of agreement.

I waved my hand to settle the crowd as I nodded. "And you all deserve answers."

"Is it true you fucked that bitch?"

Hands on hips, my head sunk, eyes softly closing as I inhaled. I owed them the truth for their fealty and for their losses. But would the truth ease their suffering or their fury? Or was I thinking only of myself in hiding the shame of my choices? "I had not expected Tarragona's new queen. Her presence was unforeseen. She is..." I paused, searching for the right words to use in front of these men that would neither be a lie nor the whole truth.

"But you spared her life when you were meant to kill her," shouted another voice from far across the room.

Only those who had sailed with me knew of my plans to kill Tressya that fateful night, which meant one of my own had confided in others outside the Razohan. Stars, this was bad if even my own people were speaking against me.

"I won't deny it. I made a fateful decision to spare her. The consequences are heavy upon my conscience."

A tall, aged man, thin and stooped, struggled to his feet. "What about our slain? I doubt they would accept your heavy conscience as punishment enough for their deaths."

A round of agreement rippled through the hall.

"You're right. But not even the Nazeen can unravel time and undo the wrongs."

"You may not be able to undo them, but we still demand reparation for our losses." Kaldor rose to his feet, amongst claps and cheers.

He was a short man, with a graying beard that reached his middle and thick club like arms covered in tattoos. His gray eyes were like wolves, his sneer as savage because Kaldor had come here to cause trouble. He wasn't looking for apologies, but a way to gain advantage.

Historically, the Razohan were the strongest clan in the north because of our shapeshifter abilities and powerful ties with the Huungardred. That didn't mean we were favored, just feared. If he could muster enough hatred toward the Razohan, gather all the clans behind him, it would strengthen his position and perhaps his courage to rise against us. Already it seemed at least one within my clan had betrayed me.

I ran my tongue on the inside of my cheek and slowly nodded. He'd sensed an opportunity, felt it ripple as agitation through the crowd. This was his moment, what he'd been waiting for. And now he was sinking his teeth deep like a predator with its prey. I was powerless to do anything but listen to his demands lest I lose the faith of everyone present.

"You will take my daughter, Luecia, as your bride."

The sudden uproar spun my tumbling mind. I placed my

hands on my hips, head bowed as I tried to think of something plausible that would not turn all in this room against me. Unfortunately, I could think of nothing they would want to hear.

"That's not possible," I managed over the fracas.

"Not possible!" bellowed Kaldor, determined to be heard as much as he was determined to see me chained to his demand.

"It's the only way to demonstrate your loyalty to the northern clans." He glanced around him, agitating agreement. "Take a bride from amongst us and prove the rumors are false."

It was in Kaldor's nature to manipulate each opportunity to align with his interests and exploit the defeat of others to further his advantage. I rubbed my forehead, furious with myself for not seeing this coming.

"It's not possible..." Garrat said as he strode up behind me. "Because Tamas has already received such a proposal."

He stood beside me, casting me a sad smile before facing Kaldor.

"What is this?" Kaldor said.

"This is a private matter. One Tamas is considering very carefully for the good of all northerners."

Kaldor's face reddened.

"It can't be an offer from anyone here," shouted a voice from my right.

Looks and shrugs were exchanged. People shook their heads, but it was only a matter of time before someone worked it out.

"Thaindrus," roared Kaldor. "Is it not enough you bed

that witch in the south, but now you plan to bed a beast?" He made no attempt to disguise his disgust.

Claws punched through the tips of my fingers before I could douse the flames of my fury. Unable to control my actions, I demolished the distance between us, hand gripped tight around Kaldor's throat and dragged him backward onto the table, slamming him down on top of a plate of meat, sending a tankard of ale sloshing to its side "Utter one more word against my good friend," I growled, leaning over to goad him, my claws indenting into the skin at his throat. "One word." Then I bared very sharp and long teeth. A drop of blood-stained saliva dripped to his chin.

A hand rested on my back.

"Ease up, Tamas." It was Garrat.

Only his soothing voice of reason could break through the black vision of my fury.

I squeezed Kaldor's neck a little tighter, allowing one sharp claw to pierce his skin just below his chin, then released him and stood away. The hall remained draped in a silence so heavy it felt like it would burst through the stone floor.

Claws retracted, I forked my hands through my hair, turned my back on Kaldor and paced away. I couldn't look at him again lest I unleash more than fangs and claws.

"Do you see that?" Kaldor bellowed. "The Razohan has shown us where his allegiance lies. He chooses beasts and evil whores over his own people."

I closed my eyes, arching my head back, feeling the strain of the last few weeks turn me to stone. It seemed I was destined to follow one mistake with another until I met my demise.

Like one gigantic slow moving beast, everyone in the hall came to life. The harsh cries of outrage rang through my ears until they dulled to a constant wail. I shut out the noise, fearing if I heard anymore remarks like Kaldor's, it wouldn't be claws I sprouted. I wasn't in the mood, and I feared not even Garret's sane words would pull me back before I did something unthinkable.

"I withdraw my allegiance, Razohan. You'll get no support from the Wildelm clan." He raised his voice. "The rest of you would do well to follow my lead. We find ourselves standing amongst traitors."

I kept my eyes closed to the chorus of agreement as the sound of chairs scraping across the stone floor ran a vibration down my spine. The hard smack of boots followed, like a great army on the move, as clans stomped out of the hall.

Above the clamorous departure of the crowd, Kaldor's voice bellowed, ensuring all would hear, perpetually seeking an audience and a throne to deliver his declarations.

"It's not wise to make enemies of your neighbors, leader of the Razohan."

Those exiting the hall stopped as he spoke, while I slowly turned to face him.

Locking eyes with me, he said. "Your love of those beasts shall be your ruin, as much as theirs."

Threat delivered, he turned to go.

"You have no idea what I'm capable of." My voice was like the sharp edge of a blade, but I didn't bother to raise it.

"Is that a threat?"

"Was yours?" I slowly prowled toward him.

I gained no satisfaction in seeing the glint of fear in his eyes because I was deadly serious. Kaldor, being Kaldor, stayed his ground as I came close, towering over him.

"Be careful, young Razohan. A threat against me is a threat against the northern clans."

"No threats, loyal friend. But I will say this." I leaned down to speak in his ear. "I can become your worst... nightmare."

Kaldor jerked his head away, then did the one thing I didn't expect him to do. He spat at me. Given his size against me, it landed on the top stone button of my shirt.

Without waiting to see my reaction, he spun on his heel and marched away. Like a wave clawing sand from the shore, his departure drew the rest of the clans after him, none looking back as they left the hall.

"That didn't go exactly as I planned," Garrat said, coming up beside me.

I grunted, suddenly feeling as tired as I did when I arrived back in the north, bleeding half my blood from the sword wound.

Garrat slapped me on the shoulder. "He's a conceited, arrogant fool."

"With a big mouth, a lot of coin and a gift for stirring trouble. And I have done a sufficient job of turning the clans against us."

"That may be, but men like him will cause no more trouble once you take the Etherweave."

It all came down to the bloody Etherweave.

"You've been spending too much time with Romelda."

"Curse that witch. You know me, Tamas. I respect the woman, but I am not about to spend any of my valuable time listening to her pronouncements."

"But you believe in the prophecy. You believe I'm the rightful bloodborn."

He leveled his gaze at me. "No. Tamas. I just believe in you."

CHAPTER
SIX

TRESSYA

THE COLOR WAS BACK in Gusselan's complexion. She was no longer a threat to the Salmun or their cause now her sons were dead, which had to be the reason the Salmun obeyed my command to halt whatever vile magic they were using to slowly kill her. They had me to achieve their goal, or so they thought.

"Perhaps this isn't wise," Gusselan said.

"You have to be in the Mother's presence at some point. Let's just get it over with."

I stepped aside and allowed Gusselan to enter the combat room first. The ex-queen was under my protection, and I was determined the Mother knew as much, so I encouraged her to join me during my training. I'd spent the morning reading through petitions presented by various noblemen, all expecting me to appoint the queen's council without delay. According to them, important decisions regarding the realm could not be made until I'd completed my council. The Salmun showed no interest in the daily administrations of the kingdom, which left the queen's council as my only *living* advisors. Having suffered through their boring lectures, I was eager to stretch myself with some hard physical training. For now, Gusselan could watch from the edge of the room, but at some point, once the Mother became accustomed to her presence, I hoped she would participate.

"My ability's still weak," she whispered, hesitant to step inside.

I'd never seen her nervous, though I could understand why. After a lifetime, I still had flash daydreams of becoming invisible when forced to face the Mother. Perhaps her claim of immunity to soul voice didn't extend to someone as fiercely adept as the Mother Divine.

This was the first time Gusselan hinted at any skill she may possess. I longed to know her secret and had thought time and subtle encouragement would win her over.

"Oh, and what may that be?" I prodded gently.

Gusselan's eyes darted from mine, her lips pressed thin. Conflicting emotions flashed unrestrained across her face before she gathered her reserve. I didn't blame her for her resistance to sharing her secrets. As part of our training, the Sistern schooled us in discretion and secrecy as assiduously as our ability to kill. I'm sure her training was no different.

"I know what you hope to achieve by asking me here. But I think it's a terrible idea."

Her loyalty to her order was an impenetrable barrier. If

she knew the long list of my indiscretions toward the Sistern, she'd never trust me: a woman with such a fickle heart.

"Please, Gusselan. Emberfell is your home. You're not leaving. I promise you that. It's best to face the Mother as soon as possible."

"I was queen for twenty-five years, and never once did I forget my duties to my order. My devotion remains steadfast."

A lecture. Great, she believed I thought myself better than the Mother now I was queen.

"I understand why you were chosen."

"And I know why you were chosen." Her expression remained solemn.

The Mother chose me not because of my dedication to the Sistern or my cunning skills, but because I had the right heritage and gifts.

"Perhaps I would have made different decisions had I known the Mother's real intentions." Or maybe not. Tamas was my defense for every action I made; the enigmatic asshole obliterated any hope I had of acting sane. I had to resist rubbing the mark and soothing the tingles that flared on thinking of his name.

Would I ever see him again? Right now, I would surrender my place on the throne to see him one more time. Was that a display of my weakness?

"Perhaps," she replied.

I itched to take her hand. "We're not enemies."

"My High Priestess would say otherwise."

"No one will tell me how I shall rule." The words were heavy in my mouth, but the conviction emboldened my heart. I would speak the truth even if I lost Gusselan's support. "Especially when it comes to the Etherweave." I knew so little about it. There was so much I had to learn; in secret, so the Salmun couldn't influence what I discovered.

"You have no trust in your Mother?"

I glanced inside the combat room, where the Mother waited.

"You may judge me negatively for this, but since arriving in Tarragona, I've learned sometimes it's best to follow your own instincts."

The words strengthened me as I matched her gaze.

"My ability is not too dissimilar to your own." Her first offer of trust.

"You use your own soul voice?"

"No. It's not verbal. It's to do with the mind."

"You use your mind to compel others to your will?"

"It takes singular focus and immense discipline to master. For most, myself included, the practice is limited."

"How limited?"

She eyed me for three heartbeats; her gaze like an iron trap. Either she was trying to penetrate my mind, or she was deciding how much of the truth she would surrender, and I'd wasted little time dismissing my loyalty to the Sistern upon arriving in Tarragona.

"My control is of short duration. Those with a strong will are difficult to bind. Some minds, like the Salmun's, remain impenetrable."

"If you're no threat to them, why did they want to kill you?"

"King Ushpia is King Bezhani's greatest rival. The

animosity between the two has held for centuries and deteriorates with each passing decade."

"Your order is loyal to King Ushpia?"

"King Bezhani's a tyrant. There's little he wouldn't do to further his ambitions. He would crush Avaloria given the chance, but he's failed his many attempts so far as Avaloria is not without support."

"Your order, for one."

She nodded. "Some of the Salmun have broken from the Creed and given their fealty to King Ushpia."

"That seems strange. Unless they see a way it would benefit them."

"King Ushpia can be most persuasive."

"How were you chosen as King Henricus's bride if the Salmun in Tarragona are loyal to King Bezhani?"

Her sly smile was my answer. Mind control was a potent skill and a terrible ploy for seeking revenge and power. "The High Priestess's ability in mind binding has long-lasting effects. Unfortunately, we were betrayed by one of our own. Word was sent to Tarragona of my true identity, and the Salmun began their persecution of me in secret ever since."

"Then I'm glad I came when I did."

Her lips tremored as she fought against her smile, then she nodded. I'd thought it would take longer for us to reach this far in our relationship.

I motioned her inside the combat room, which was not the real name for the room, but one the Mother was swift to label.

The mother waited at the far end, seated upon a wide wooden chair with ribbed high backing to make it look like a throne. She'd insisted I return to a rigorous training schedule, something I'd thrived on in Merania. I'd always thrown my anger into perfecting the six pillars, especially discipline, the pillar I held closest to my heart, which ensured I accomplished precision, my second favorite pillar.

In Tarragona, I'd grown lazy. Training and mediating on the six pillars was my only defense against the cruelty of the life I'd led in Merania, which was far from my experience now. Complacency replaced my training. I'd likely be sluggish in a fight; something I should be ashamed to admit.

I was sure the Mother resumed my training with a vengeance because she wanted to remind me of my place. She was right in doing so. I thought of what Andriet had said in the carriage days ago; it wasn't so easy to turn my back on the Sistern. Because of the Mother, I was queen; yet another reminder of who deserved my allegiance.

I groaned inwardly when I spied Albert, Turret, and Borat hovering on the far side of the room. At least the three spirits had bothered me little since the Mother arrived, so I was surprised to see them here now.

Gusselan dropped behind me as I made my way across the room to where the Mother sat. A Salmun stood at the other side of the room, his face shrouded by his hood. It wasn't Orphus. Even under their shapeless cloaks, hiding their tattooed faces with their hoods pulled low, I could pick the prelate from amongst his men.

The Salmun remained my constant shadow. The knowledge prickled along my skin, but it was something I would have to get used to. There was no way any of the Creed members would let their last surviving link to the Etherweave out of their sight. I would have to become cunning to slip their noose, as I doubted they would encourage my self-learning on all things to do with the Etherweave.

At first I was surprised when the Mother rose gracefully to her feet, then I remembered her supposed position in relation to me. A fine tickle of pleasure coursed through my body on seeing her ever so slight curtsey, though her face remained like chiseled rock. She wasn't pleased with her rank, or me, not after Andriet's attack in the carriage.

Luckily, Andriet left me in peace and spent the day following Daelon. I had no faith in his promise to keep his distance from his ex-lover, and I was fast learning he was deaf to my pleas. At some point, I feared I would be forced to command him to obey, or he was going to cause havoc.

The Mother's eyes passed over my shoulder to Gusselan, and the creases in her brow deepened. Her lips thinned so much they disappeared into her mouth.

"She's not welcome." The Mother kept her voice loud enough to reach Gusselan, contained enough no one else in the room would have heard. "I summoned you."

I swallowed. "She's in no one's way."

The Mother's eyes flared briefly before her gaze turned lethal. "Is that so?"

The air thinned, and I couldn't get enough breaths. I didn't want to be antagonistic, but neither would I be compliant. Not now. Not with who I'd become. I'd lied, kept secrets, fell for my enemy, killed a sister; there was no end to my disloyalty.

However, I wasn't yet ready to turn my back on the Sistern. I still needed the Mother's brutal training to nurture the strength and will I would need if I was to be queen of the Bone Throne. But it was time I forged myself a path. One that allowed me to stand for myself while harnessing the strength of the six pillars through the Mother's unforgiving training.

"The woman from Merania is long gone, I see." It wasn't praise.

"Yes, Mother."

"A warning. Those who grow too quickly make the biggest mistakes."

I lowered my gaze to her feet, my heart devoid of subservience the gesture might imply. "As always, I'm at your command."

The Salmun was at one end of the room, leaving Gusselan's only escape from the Mother in the adjacent corner, which is where she headed before I could say anything else.

As was their habit, the Salmun's hood stayed low, concealing his face, making him appear as though asleep while standing. I knew differently, knew that everything that transpired here today would pass back to Orphus, and not my training, because that meant nothing. Their interest lay in any power play between the Mother and I. While seemingly a harmless old woman, she was an unknown entity they would watch closely, especially if Orphus found her mind an iron trap. Then there was Gusselan, the woman with talent they'd failed to kill.

I turned at the sound of the soft padding of bare feet to see two thick-set men entering the room. Dressed in linen loincloths tied at the front, their chest and legs remained bare to display their defined musculature. A sheathed sword was on one's hip, the other carried a quarterstaff in his hand, the end studded with a metal spiked star. The way they moved around the room, alert to everyone present, I would say they were from amongst Tarragona's top fighters.

"This will not end well," Turret said. "Why the Salmun allow it, I cannot guess."

Great. I was too out of practice to be sparring with the best. This was the Mother's punishment for what had happened in the carriage. I'd already confessed my infrequent training, yet she'd chosen two men guaranteed to set me on my ass. She also knew with the Salmun present I wouldn't dare use soul voice on either of the fighters, if that was possible, which it wasn't because I'd grown lax on perfecting the skill.

Tamas, you're an ass. He'd sucked up all my attention, leaving me no time to focus on anything important. I clenched my teeth, ignoring the fine tinkles on my wrist over Tamas' mark. What I couldn't ignore was the aching emptiness spreading within me like a growing chasm. Why did it feel like I was now cleaved in two, a part of me lost in the north?

"Fear not. I will intervene if things look terrible for the queen," Borat said.

"You will do no such thing," interrupted Albert. "You are an imbecile at the best of times. What can you hope to do?"

"The queen—" Borat continued.

"Stop calling her that," Albert demanded.

I dragged in a long breath as I paced across to the wall of weapons the Mother had the weapons master erect, ignoring the spirits argument and the tingles running along the skin of my inner wrist all because I thought of Tamas.

It would show timidity and weakness to argue against her choice in my combatants. I would have to suffer her lesson. Pain and sacrifice honed my mind and were my vessels to greater strength. This is what I needed.

I chose a sword, my primary weapon, but I would also use it as a distraction. The dagger was my follow up surprise at close range.

"This is unheard of," came Albert's cry of indignation. "A woman with a sword. It is bad enough she is queen."

Fluttering my eyes closed, I took a deep breath, searching for my calming breaths. *Discipline.* I'd need exact breaths to shut out those three spirits if they continued to comment from the sides.

Sword heavy in one hand, dagger clasped firm in the next, I drew in another long breath and slowly filtered it through my noise, washing my body free of agitation while I gathered my wayward concentration.

This felt good; it felt right, familiar. Control of the mind and belief in my ability to win were the two safeguards I needed. Before Tamas, my only cherished moments were with a weapon in my hand, exertion and pain coursing through my limbs. Pain was transitory, defeat was not.

Feeling like myself again, I sheathed the sword and dagger, then turned to see the warriors had positioned themselves on either side of the room, both eyeing me like predators. I strove to reveal nothing of my skill as I paced toward the center of the room.

The tall warrior with the sword cracked his neck. He

wore tattoos on the knuckles of each hand, spreading as dashes on the backs of his hands as far up as his wrist bone. Perhaps a tally of his kills. His face was stone. Eyes of deep blue stared out like a flat sea, empty of his schemes for the fight.

Snarling like a feral animal, the second warrior shifted his weight from foot to foot, barely restraining his instincts to fight. Smaller by half than the sword wielding warrior, his muscles quivered with anticipation. Veins protruded on the back of his hand, knuckles whitened from his fierce grip on the quarterstaff.

Neither I could dismiss, but the prowling, snarling warrior on my right concerned me the least. He'd burn half his energy in the first few strikes, hoping to use his hulking strength to do the damage with a few powerful blows. Dancing just out of reach would entice his fury, break his focus, force him into foolish decisions. The taller warrior was the lethal predator staying hidden, ready to strike.

The shorter warrior spun his quarterstaff over his head in a show of deft skill, then brought it down and slammed the end into the stone floor. Reenforced with a head of iron fashioned into a ball, the sound cracked through the spacious room like a clank of bells. The other end was also encased in iron, sharpened to the lethal spike of a starred arrow.

I spared him a look, but always my thoughts were on the taller man, who'd taken the stance of a fighter, legs apart to center his balance, soft in the knees to enable swift movement, sword relaxed by his side, eyes firm on me.

Unable to restrain his savage desire to crush me any

longer, the warrior on my left stomped forward, baring his teeth while he raised his staff to mid chest. I tensed. *Fool.* After one forced breath, I eased the tension from my limbs. Agility was the secret of winning against the shorter foe.

"I cannot look," Borat groaned.

In three breaths, he'd covered the distance. At the last he shifted his hands to the bulbous end of his staff, telling me his intention. I waited until the last, watching the staff crash down. He'd come in with such speed, swiped down with stunning force, catching his balance in the strike's momentum.

I dived before the iron end broke my skull and tucked into a roll while pulling my sword from its sheath. The reverberating crack of iron on stone sheared up my spine as I came out of my roll onto my feet, only to face the rapid slash of a blade flashing in front of my eyes.

Instincts saved me. I jerked left, into the path of the shorter warrior, tucking myself into another roll rather than stagger out of balance. This time, as I came out of my tight tuck, I swiped my sword low, slicing the side of the staff wielding warrior's thigh.

A fierce roar raged through the room, but I was already dodging away, and none too soon, when the sharp end of the staff stabbed through the vacant air where I'd been. I would use the staff wielding warrior as a shield to the taller foe, burn him down, then slice him through, before I concentrated on the greater challenge.

"You can look. The queen is unharmed," Truett said. "I cannot say the same for her opponent."

Keeping the shorter warrior between me and the taller

foe, I danced and dodged the swings, stabs, and blows of his staff. The warrior threw fire and muscle behind each swing, chewing up valuable energy, fueled by fury, while seeping blood across the floor, turning it into a slippery mess. If I could keep him fighting in his tight circle, he would slip on the crimson pool he'd created.

A quick glance at the larger warrior, I noticed he kept his distance, his eyes tracking my every move. He'd seemed content to allow my plan to play out. Perhaps he, too, was eager to tussle with me one-on-one.

After years under the tuition of the Mother, our bodies moved without thought, relying on instinct and years of relentless training. After months of doing nothing, being suddenly propelled into action, I felt my body slip the shackles of lethargy, growing limber.

I continued my dance, striking and stabbing when I spied openings. Unfortunately, he was agile enough to swerve just out of reach of my sword, so I reserved most of my strength and taunt him instead. I smirked at every missed swing and followed it with a wink, then ensured he caught my eye roll when his staff split the stone pavers once more. The bellow of his fury sent relief seeping deep into my limbs. He grew impatient, raging at every failed strike.

My next smile wasn't a taunt. I read each move he made, predicted his next as my eye for the game grew more acute the longer we fought. All I need do is keep my strength and focus for the next bout while I waited for the stout warrior to become sloppy.

When he did, I wasted no time, diving low, keeping from his wildly swinging staff, and slid close on my knees to spear him in the thigh. My slice cut from his inner thigh all the way back, opening his flesh to the bone, then quirked a brow at him when he cursed me with names I didn't hear because my concentration shut out the sound.

His blood soaked my pants legs, and the stone floor turned a deep black red. His leg gave out, but he gritted his teeth and stormed forward, the spear end of his staff barreling toward me along with spittle soaked rage.

I doubled back, braced as he came, but at the last heard the swift pad of slight feet, felt the eddy of wind from the fast moving blade.

I dove right, moving too fast to tuck into a roll and instead staggered, tripped and went down heavy, my grip fierce on my sword. Pain lanced through my knee, but my mind screamed for me to keep moving.

The chink of the blade on stone split the air beside me, but I was already climbing to my feet. Still crouched, I lurched further right, catching the raised staff in my periphery. Behind the stout fighter leered the face of the taller warrior who'd made his surprise attack.

I spun, dove under his staff onto my back, sliding across the blood-soaked stones, and speared upward with my sword to catch him low in his belly.

Wasting no time, I sprung to my feet and faced the taller warrior while behind me, the bellows of agony rose like a thick fog.

"Bravo," Borat shouted.

"It is not over yet. The next looks meaner," Truett said.

Half an ear to the stout warrior behind, I crouched, balanced and waited for the sword wielding warrior to make his move. He'd benefited from watching me fight, assessing my moves and learning my skill.

Damn that I'd given little time in Tarragona to develop soul voice, not that I could use it here.

His hesitation gave me time to calm my pounding heart and harness my focus. I had to fight to keep my eyes on him and not look to the distant figure of Gusselan behind him.

I gauged the distance between us gave me enough space to breathe a little. It would take him at least three strides for the tip of his blade to reach me. But his stillness distracted my mind. The Mother was there, the Salmun too.

Don't.

Now was not the time to lose concentration. I clenched my teeth as a subtle punishment to force my attention to the fight.

In my periphery, two men scuttled forward and dragged the stout warrior away by his arms, leaving a trail of his blood across the stone floor as the silence descended, thickening the air with anticipation. A tick started in my cheek as the remaining warrior stood like stone. I knew his game. He wanted me agitated, thinking he could draw me into an offensive position; not my preferred way of fighting. The delay gave me a chance to catch my breath and allowed me to center myself into discipline.

The tension eased from my muscles the longer I waited. Calm attuned my focus, cleared everyone from the room.

When he moved, less patient than me, I was ready for his first strike. Knowing his strength, I opted to glide my blade the length of his; the tip aimed for his chest, rather than exert force to try and push it away. But he yanked his sword downward, bowing his body as he jumped backward to avoid my tip.

I grunted, danced left to avoid the strike I knew was coming only for him to read my direction before I moved. In a breath, I twisted my body, feeling another eddy of air across my stomach from the near miss. Then a hard thump hit my shoulder and forced me from my feet.

"She has lost. This is madness," Borat shrieked.

I bit my tongue as I hit the stone on my side, then rolled and gathered my feet, springing away seconds before his sword sliced close to my face.

"You must stay on your feet, Tressya," Borat shouted.

Panting, I spun to face him, steadying my sword in both hands.

I swung with my sword. He caught the strike on his blade, sliced his down the length of mine, and shunted me with all his strength.

My feet left the ground as I flailed, falling backward. My spine cracked, then my head smacked the cold stone floor and agony split through my skull at the same time something inside me burst.

"Get up," Borat yelled in my ear.

A cage flew open and cold rage clawed its way out, ripping a snarl from my lips.

"Mercy on our souls," Borat cried, disappearing from beside me.

"Come back, you coward," Albert shouted, as Borat faded from the room.

The warrior jerked to a stop and frowned down at me. Taking the advantage, I sprung to my feet, swimming in a haze before blinking my vision clear. I puzzled at his surprised expression until I realized I was still snarling.

Still entombed in his confusion, this was my chance to slip under his indomitable attack. I jumped forward, sword poised to stab while my mind prepped my body to dodge right, away from his retaliatory strike, but the same strange feeling that had pummeled through my chest like a battering ram and sparked my body like lightning, drove power through my arms, feeding a ferocious determination.

I would win this. It was a knowing, foreign, and yet familiar at the same time.

Such was the strength of my downward strike, sparks flittered at the clash of our blades. With teeth clenched, muscles flexing under the strength at which I drove my sword, he grunted as he tried to deflect my blow.

Tried. *Tried.* A wicked glee thrilled through my chest, and if I wasn't emitting lusty snarls, I would cackle with excitement.

Never had my attention remained singularly focused on one goal, neither had I felt so supple, agile and strong. My body and sword were melded as one. I fought with a relentless savagery, surpassing his masterful strikes, his unbeatable strength and aggression. It was as though he were a child, learning sword play for the first time. What were once bold moves, I now thought were clumsy. I was gone before each lunge, blocking before he struck, enticing him, infuriating him, toying with him.

I could smell the iron tang of his blood, the sour sweat slick on his skin, hear the sawing heaves of his breath through his lungs as though I'd pressed my ear to his chest.

I felt magnificent, powerful, reborn.

And watched. Whatever strange yet wonderfulness growing within me needed to be quelled in front of those I'd yet to decide were my allies.

I quickened the warrior's end with a few perfectly sequenced, brutal attacks, crippling his defense, sending his sword across the room to *clatter* against the stone floor and forcing him to his knees.

Panting through my exhilaration, the tingles pulsing around my body would have driven a wild cry from my mouth if I'd not swallowed it back down.

The warrior bowed his head, hands limp by his sides. His chest was a bloody mess. The lacerations oozing a deep black, red, which pooled around his knees and into the cracks in the stone paving.

I blew out a deep held breath to steady this fierce otherness, still wanting more of the fight, like a feral dog, snapping and snarling on the end of its chains. A crack off my neck, and I clawed my sanity back and slowly turned to face the Mother, noticing the pesky spirits had disappeared.

What I saw on her face made me struggle, yet again, to maintain my calm and not whoop with joy. She was shocked, perhaps even appalled, to find her plans had not worked. Or was she, perhaps, shocked to find her manipulations had worked too well?

CHAPTER SEVEN

TAMAS

There were four, two men and two women, richly adorned in warm colored clothes of luxurious fabrics of silk and velvet, intricately embellished, elegantly designed and tailored to perfection.

The men's long cloaks were trimmed with ermine, their belts studded with gemstones, and their fingers covered with thick gold bans. The women sumptuously attired with brocade bodices threaded with gold and the hems of their skirts covered in elaborate embroidery, intricate lacework, and embellishments. Their hair, woven into braids, were pinned using jeweled clips and ribbons of silk.

I rose, thinking I was on my bed only to find I was lying on a stone floor underneath the starry sky, which couldn't be right. Osmud and Garrat had thrown me into my bed after the fateful clans' meeting, and I continued to sleep fitfully.

Not even enough ale to drown a bullock would rid my mind of the dozen or more problems I faced. I shook the heavy feeling from my mind, then rubbed my eyes, feeling like I'd run all night with nothing to eat or drink.

'Welcome, young Razohan,' said one man. His thick gray beard and mustache concealed the movement of his lips. 'I am Carthius.' He extended his hand.

I simply stared, my brain refusing to wake up.

'Time, Carthius. He is understandably confused.' The woman's face was narrow, her nose long, but her deep green eyes were striking.

'Wisdom is yours, Fivia. Impatience is mine. Forgive me, young soul.' Carthius withdrew his hand and backed away, allowing Fivia and the other woman to come forth.

The second woman smiled down at me, her small, wide-set eye seeming to grow wider with excitement the longer she stared at me. 'My name is Ovia.'

'O-k-a-y,' I replied, drawing the word out as I tried to clear my head. I glanced around me, noticing the large flaming torches set to the wall by great iron brackets, casting a flickering yellow glow around the room.

I swiveled on my ass to see behind me the great expanse of the room, then curled my fingers in, drawing my nails along the stone floor. The white flecks in the floor mimicked the starry sky above, but it was not the sky I was looking at. With the realization, I lurched to my feet, then staggered sideways, clutching my head, feeling like hammers pounded my skull from all sides.

'We were too eager,' came the other male voice.

Looking out from under my palms, I watched as the last

man came toward me. Tall and willowy in his long robe of rich purple. I could see patches of scalp through his thinned hair.

'Humble apologies.' And he bowed before me. 'My name is Ineth.' One eye focused on me, the second appeared to be looking to the side of the room.

I ignored the four people and turned slowly in a circle. 'If this was at all possible, I would say I'm standing in Emberforge. In the room of the Bone Throne. Only I don't see the throne anywhere.'

'Yes, my friend. And no,' said Ineth.

'That makes no sense.' I pinched my brow in a lame attempt to rid the pounding in my head while I tried to tease apart what he said.

'We stand within Emberforge, but what you see is not where you are? It is an image found inside your mind. The details are poorly sketched, I am afraid.'

I buried my head in my hands, pressing my fingers into my temple. 'Romelda,' I growled. 'What're you doing to me?'

'There is much anger in you for this woman,' Fivia said.

'I get it. This is a dream, right? Either that or I'm going mad.'

'Not mad like your father,' Ovia said.

I jerked at the mention of my father. 'What's going on here?' I backed away from the two women who'd moved suffocatingly close.

'Perhaps we should be clear,' Carthius said, moving in front of the two women. 'We found a memory comfortable for all of us.'

'Wait.' I jab a hand to my hips, pointing a finger at Carthius. 'Is this real?'

'Very,' replied Fivia and Ovia in unison.

'Who are you?'

'It is my turn,' Ineth said, moving Carthius out of the way. 'We are the Eone.'

'Am I supposed to know that name?'

Fivia gasped, placing her hand on her heart. 'Forgotten. After all we did.'

Ovia fingered one of Fivia's braids. 'Not by all, and not for long.'

Fivia rested her head on Ovia's shoulder. 'We must speak plainly. I am feeling weak.'

'Yes,' Ineth announced. 'We are not yet strong.'

My throat felt grazed with sand. My pounding head was making it hard for me to concentrate. If this was a dream, it was the most real dream I'd ever had. I dragged one of my extended nails down my palm and stared at the split skin; the blood beading out, and felt the sting.

'Dream, huh?' But why was I dreaming about strange people I'd never seen or heard of before? 'This is my repayment for the things I said to Kaldor.' I turned slowly in a circle as I eyed the room.

It seemed I was destined to continue my mistakes, this time plunging the Razohan into a possible war with the northern clans. If Kaldor could gather enough support, he would choose to take my threat as an incitement to war. And judging by how quick he emptied the hall, I'd say gathering clans to his side would not be difficult. Fear could be manipulated or redirected as easily as loyalty. And Kaldor had evoked fear for the Razohan.

'We are the Eone,' Ineth reiterated, interrupting my thoughts.

'Tell me what that means, before I throw up at your feet.'

Carthius came alongside Ineth. 'We are the makers of the Etherweave.'

'That's impossible.' They would have all my attention if the pounding in my head had not intensified.

Fivia joined the two men. 'We were once the greatest power, ruling over all the land and seas. Unfortunately, great power does not grant immortality, no matter how hard we tried.'

'We struggled to beat our end,' Ovia continued.

'So you forged the Etherweave,' I finished for them.

'And failed,' Ineth said.

I shook my head. 'The Etherweave is the greatest power to have ever existed.' As far as I knew, but all I had to go on were ancient tales, given the Etherweave's entombment for a millennium.

'We still died,' Carthius said, his expression as sombre as his voice.

'But there is hope,' Fivia interjected. 'An ember of our combined life-force lives on in the Etherweave. We ensured it would be the case. Weak as it is, it is enough to give us the power to enter your dreams when your mind is not full of other thoughts.'

'What? Twenty-seven years and you turn up now.'

'Young Razohan, you have touched the Etherweave. It has entered you, become you for a brief time.' Carthius said.

'And that's given you a way in?'

'To your mind, yes,' Fivia said.

'You have no right to invade my mind, and I'm pretty sure I won't like it.'

'Trust, my friend,' Carthius said. 'Soon, the Etherweave's tomb will no longer hold it. But the power of the Etherweave is great.'

'It needs a great mind to wield it,' Ineth added. 'The four of us barely managed. Yet there is only one of you.'

My first instinct was to protect any memories of Tressya from their prying.

Given the Etherweave was forged so long ago, there were no lingering tales. We called the people responsible the ancients because we had no better name for them and had always supposed they were allies.

But were they? Memories, thoughts, emotions were private affairs. Anyone who violated the inner privacy of another like this was a foe in my eyes. Bonded to Tressya through my mark, I could destroy Tressya's emotional privacy, but I never would cross that boundary without consent. The Eone had done worse. They'd entered my memories without welcome, rummaging through them to find a place they felt comfortable within.

'What about those that came before? King Ricaud for one. Were you also interfering with his dreams?'

'Interfering is an adversarial word, young Razohan.' Carthius's cautionary tone flared hackles along my back, invisible in my human form, but felt nonetheless when my emotions were strung. It seemed, as always, my instincts didn't deceive me. 'I take that as a yes.'

'Without us King Ricaud—' Fivia said.

'Any of those who came before,' Ovia interrupted her.

'Thank you, sister. Any who wielded the Etherweave's power without our help would not survive.'

Carthius moved alongside the two women. 'It was forged by four, to be wielded by four. You do not stand a chance on your own. The Etherweave will burn through you, consume you if you do not let us help.'

I retreated a step, partially turning away as I pondered their words and reflected on the moment in the cave. There, I had miraculously liberated a fragment of the Etherweave from its entrapment, using it to save Tressya. This feat had nearly cost me my life, as I had wielded it without the aid of the Bone Throne to harness and amplify its power. Instead, the Etherweave had come perilously close to depleting my life's energy. At least, that was my understanding of the harrowing experience.

'Wasn't the Bone Throne created for that very purpose?'

'The Bone Throne was not our doing,' Ovia said.

Carthius gently placed his hand on Ovia's arm, subtly raising his eyebrows as she turned to look at him. The silent exchange between them was inscrutable to me. Whatever understanding they reached, Ovia dipped her head in agreement with Carthius. She then directed her serene gaze back toward me, offering nothing but a simple, enigmatic smile.

'Who created the Bone Throne, if not you?'

'One who became corrupted by the Etherweave's power,' Carthius said. 'For some, no amount of power is ever sufficient. The one who carved the Bone Throne was a king whose ambition exceeded even what the Etherweave could offer. He grew restless with our warnings and the threats of withdrawing our assistance if he failed to curb his insatiable desire for something greater.

'Using the Etherweave's power, he carved himself a throne to amplify his already formidable abilities. The Bone Throne achieved what he desired, intensifying the power of the Etherweave, but in doing so, it made the power uncontrollable and volatile. Sadly, without our help, he greed consumed him.'

This was not what our legends told us. 'You're saying the Bone Throne makes the Etherweave dangerous?'

'Yes, without our assistance. The successors of the Bone Throne learned from King Agropea's errors. They embraced our wisdom and guidance.'

'And how did you deliver your wisdom and guidance?'

The four glanced at each other, each sharing a thought neither seemed willing to speak. I assumed the truth was not something they felt I should hear.

Possession was merely a superstition, a perspective that placed me in the minority. For the northern clans, however, superstitions were the bedrock of their existence. Their laws, religious beliefs, and daily life practices were all deeply entrenched in fanciful tales.

Finally, Fivia spoke. 'Through cooperation and trust, young soul.'

I eyed each of them thoughtfully as I mulled over their words. I'd never heard of this king before; our legends only extended as far back as King Ricaud, the last monarch known to wield the Etherweave. We knew nothing beyond his time.

If King Ricaud had been guided, influenced, or even

possessed by the Eone, then they must allies, their motives righteous, for our legends spoke of his courage, bravery, and benevolence, suggesting any force aligned with him would have virtuous intentions. The blooded Nazeen, whose linked memories transcended time, would not have dedicated their life and loyalty to a throne corrupted by power.

'What do you want from me?'

'Countless lifetimes have elapsed since the Etherweave fell into slumber, and there are no longer any who recall the lessons of King Agropea. These realms are as much our home as yours, and though we may no longer walk with the living, the reawakening of the Etherweave summons us as much as it does you. We hope to prevent the same devastation wrought by King Agropea's greed from befalling these realms once again.' Ineth said.

Thoughts of Tressya fought to surface, but I forced them away, filling my mind with Kaldor and the clan problems I faced.

I didn't believe unequivocally, and although much of what they said seemed plausible, I couldn't ignore my instincts. The tightness in my gut urged me to proceed with caution.

Ovia came toward me. 'For now, young Razohan, we only ask for you to consider what we've said.'

'And do you plan on invading my dreams often? I warn you, I won't be happy if the answer's yes.'

'Your privacy is of the greatest concern to us. However, we strive to be honest with you in all endeavors,' Ineth said. 'For your own good—'

'For the sake of your life.'

'Thank you, Fivia,' Ineth replied. 'To prevent you from succumbing to the same folly as King Agropea, we urge you to open yourself to us and welcome our guidance. It is the only path to your survival.'

Each stared at me with candor, their expressions imploring me to believe in their sincerity. Unfortunately for them, it wasn't my way, and with this niggle, irritating my instincts, I wasn't about to make promises. Rather, I took what they said as a warning for what lay ahead.

Power could become an addictive curse, tainting the souls of the honest as easily as the wicked.

Again, thoughts of Tressya flittered around in my head. I couldn't let the Eone know about her being a bloodborn. Given she'd also carried a fragment of Etherweave within her for a short time, did that make her mind susceptible to their invasion? At the moment, they seemed ignorant of her, and I needed to keep it that way.

Before committing to any promises with the Eone, I needed a deeper understanding of the four and King Agropea. Was he even real, or a fabricated tale used as leverage to secure my cooperation? I was sure within the sanctum of solmira, I would find the knowledge I needed. And this meant returning to Emberforge in the disguise of one of the key masters: Tortilus, Plesy or Selisimus. Tortilus, as lore keeper, was my first choice, but I'd take the souls of the three to gain what I needed.

'You've said your piece. And now I demand you let me rest my pounding head.'

'Of course, young Razohan,' Carthius said.

'I want a warning next time you plan on dropping by.' I

pressed a finger to my temple. 'Or I swear I'll find a way to shut you out. I'm sure the Nazeen should be able to help me with that.'

The four exchanged another look. This time, I scrutinized their faces, hoping to detect any subtle sign my threat had garnered their attention. However, they were adept at communicating with few facial expressions, revealing little.

I felt the slightest tickle in my head, like small spider feet creeping across my mind, as Ovia turned her narrow-eyed gaze on me, my first hint at her thoughts. But then she smiled, and the warmth carried up into her eyes. There were definitely conflicting emotions warring within her, and she'd adeptly covered one for the other in the eye's blink.

'Yes... The Nazeen,' Fivia drawled, but I didn't for one beat accept her nonchalant tone, not after Ovia's slip.

'I thought you said my inner privacy was your concern?'

'As it is, young Razohan,' Ineth counted.

'Then perhaps Ovia needs to stop rummaging around in my head.'

Ovia's eyes flashed, the change almost imperceptibly.

I prowled around the four. 'Yes, I felt it.'

Each turned to follow my pacing. 'This will only work between us if you follow my rules.'

Fivia inhaled, opening her mouth as if to speak, but Carthius placed a silencing hand on hers.

'Of course, young soul. We aim for cooperation.'

'A fragment of your life-force lives within the Etherweave, you said, which means your ability to influence me is weak.'

Fivia straightened her shoulders and tilted her head

upward, seeming to look down her nose at me while Ovia's eyebrows arched.

'This is how it will go. You'll give me a warning first before you invade my head, or drag me from my sleep for your entertainment.'

'This has nothing to do with—'

I held up my hand. 'I'm not done yet.'

A faint ripple of unease wafted through the air, causing the hairs on my arms to bristle. The four exchanged sidelong glances, seemingly making a silent decision to avoid direct eye contact with each other, suggesting they were communicating with their minds—an ability I'd never encountered before. But, considering I'd never heard of the Eone before, this shouldn't come as a surprise.

'I'm also yet to decide if any of what you've said is true. Give me time to think on all you've said.'

'The time draws near when the Etherweave will be free,' Ineth said.

'Then you all better hope I've decided before then. Now, I'm going to lie down right here.' I lowered myself to the starry floor. 'And close my eyes. I expect when I open them again to find myself in my bed.'

'You have—' Fivia began.

'We have said what we came to say,' Ineth intercepted her. 'Now it is up to the young Razohan to decide.' Ineth turned back to me. 'We hope your decision is wise, Tamas, for the sake of the seven realms.'

Closing my eyes, his solemn warning echoed in my mind, stirring up dormant fears. Was I truly worthy of ascending the Bone Throne? Would the will of Tressya and myself combined be enough to control the Etherweave and prevent it from consuming us? What if the power corrupted one of us, or both of us?

With the weight of such a thought, I lurched up to sitting and found the dawn sunlight filtering through my window. The sudden movement roused the pounding in my head. I bent forward, cradling my head in my hands until the pounding eased, then dragged my fingers down my face and sat straight.

At least I was in my bed. I slid to the edge and stood, stretching through my headache and stiff limbs, then paced to the window and stared out onto the gentle falling of snow.

Resting a hand on the windowpane, my breath hitched with the sudden cold. I left it there until my fingers felt numb, while I pondered on my dream, then turned my right hand over to see a red tear now healed, running down the length of my palm. The scar didn't prove the reality of the Eone's fragmentary existence, just that the dream was real.

CHAPTER
EIGHT

TRESSYA

Walking beside me, the Mother gave me little room, as if she expected me to disappear if she didn't keep close. The rustle of her skirts sent prickles along my arms like tiny creatures crawling across my skin. It was either her proximity that plucked and pulled at the fine hairs on my neck or a sense that someone lurked behind us. But when I glanced around, there was no one there.

Orphus had refused the Mother entry into Emberforge, claiming only royalty and its immediate bloodline were allowed. We'd argued for hours, Andriet adding his voice to the debate, which muddled my head until I surprised everyone by shouting. In the end, I got my way.

Entering Emberforge was the Mother's idea, keen as she was to see the Bone Throne for herself. I was also eager to see it again, minus the entourage, but the Salmun acted predatory toward the temple. No one entered, not even the queen, unless escorted by one of the Salmun. Hopefully, I could escape them all for some solitude with the spirits. King Ricaud was the real reason I was eager to come. I needed answers to my many questions, and he was the one person who could reveal all about the Etherweave.

The Mother held her normally lithe and agile body erect and taut. The tension emanating from her seized my throat in a stranglehold. Her smoldering fury at the silence and subservience she was forced to keep felt like a furnace, and I continued to relish her predicament.

Once we were alone, she compensated for her public composure by adopting Radnisa's cruel taunts. She had never been one for kindness or compliments; now, she became openly spiteful and antagonistic. I excused Radnisa's acidic words, believing she was born spiteful, but the Mother's venom I questioned as fear.

Our relationship had definitely taken a downward turn after I'd snarled like a feral beast through half of the combat training yesterday while defeating two of Tarragona's best warriors. Anticipating the delightful spectacle of my defeat, she was instead made to witness my unexpected ascent. The hard set of her features, like storm clouds threatening rain, told me she was less than pleased I had won.

In private, she demanded I complete the most menial tasks for her, including soaping her back in the evenings and spreading out her night attire while she soaked in her bath. But while I gathered her discarded clothes from the floor and arranged her nightgown out on the bed, I smiled to myself, knowing the Mother was now forced to confront the outcome of her scheming—the woman I had become. I could only imagine the taste it left in her mouth.

The little peace she could claim was in believing she had mastery over my soul word. That I knew my shield against soul voice was my greatest secret; along with this other mysterious existence growing inside of me. The Mother had no idea Tamas had bitten me, had claimed me as his bonded partner. It was a secret I would keep from her at all costs: my very special secret.

Once again, thoughts of him flared sudden tingles around the bite mark, pleasurable tingles. I closed my eyes, arched my head back, feeling his presence, his hands on my body, his lips on my skin. I was back in his tent, on the cusp of war, taking what I needed, delighting in what he gave, savoring that one moment when I spread my wings.

My body ached with grief for what it had to endure; a coldness where there had been warmth, an emptiness where there had been loving hands and a loving mouth, teasing and caressing me until I couldn't breathe and only saw stars, until the ecstasy stripped my strength, leaving me vulnerable, raw and needing, needing Tamas like I needed air.

I smothered the mournful moan that escaped my lips, unconscious I'd stopped.

"Your Majesty?" Orphus's voice slithered over my shoulders like a snake.

"I'm fine." I walked on, keeping my gaze fixed on the pylons ahead, avoiding the Mother's glare, which felt like snakes piercing fangs into the side of my head.

Again, that irritating niggle ran across the back of my neck. I gave in and glanced one more time, then cursed myself for feeling so jumpy. It had to be because of the Mother. My nerves were suffering from spending this much time in her presence.

Our footsteps echoed across the vast opening of the Arunian Hall as we passed through the pylons and into the temple sanctuary. Moving further inside, again my steps faltered, plagued as I was with indelible memories of Tamas coaxing me further into the temple sanctuary.

Tamas, where are you?

Instinctively, I reached for Carlin's necklace, only to remember I'd lost it in the cave with Tamas. This realization added another memory to the collection associated with him. Struggling for a deep breath, the feeling of entrapment engulfed me. I'd spent scant moments with Tamas, yet it appeared he had been the pivotal figure in my existence, given how memories of him filled my mind.

I jerked my arm away at the feeling of the Mother's gentle touch. "I'm sorry," I uttered. My head was a muddle.

"We should keep walking." And I strode on, unable to look at the Mother.

Two apostles stood beside the pylon and bowed as I passed into the inner temple sanctuary, a realm of deepening gloom with its labyrinth of smaller temples dedicated to long-forgotten deities. I slowed as I passed them, scrutinizing each, but neither was Selisimus.

The key to the dungeon library that Tamas had stolen belonged to Selisimus, and there was at least one other, Tortilus, who also possessed a key to the library. If both owned keys, then perhaps they knew about the contents inside the library. Maybe they could assist me in discovering what it was Tamas was searching for. To find out, I'd have to rid myself of my escort, then hunt Selisimus down. But perhaps that would have to wait for another time.

Orphus picked up his pace to move alongside me. "Pardon, Your Majesty, shall I lead the way?"

I slipped aside, creating as much distance as I could between us. Orphus showed no sign of noticing. He simply waited in silence, his face perpetually covered by his gray hood—thank the stars. The thought of seeing his eyes made my stomach curl in on itself.

"Yes, of course." No one knew I'd entered Emberforge with Tamas, that I'd already seen the Bone Throne, so I gestured for him to keep walking.

This time I wasn't quick enough to turn my head from the Mother's glare. She arched a smooth brow when she caught my eyes. Damn her shrewd perceptiveness. She knew something was off with me.

Orphus guided us through a maze of narrow corridors, past empty temples and shadowed alcoves, trailing a chilled silence behind us. The Mother's footsteps gradually quickened, outpacing mine. Her eagerness to see the Bone Throne was palpable, even though it wasn't her right to sit upon it. I attempted to remain inconspicuous as I stole furtive glances at her profile, noticing her eyes intently fixed on the dimly lit corridor ahead. Normally alert to her surroundings, I was sure she was blind to my presence beside her with the Bone Throne so near.

The straight, sharp line of her nose was like a blade, cutting a harshness to her features. A sudden, intense hatred flared in my heart for the woman who had taught me how to survive. She'd risen me above my sisters for her own gain. In her eyes, I was merely a valuable possession, the sole person capable of aiding her in attaining her true ambition.

The hatred only intensified, burning within me like a glowing poker as I reflected on the intricate manipulations of the previous leaders of the Sistern, whose role the Mother had assumed, just so I could be here today. For generations, women in my lineage were strategically matched with suitable men, all to ensure I would eventually take my place on the Bone Throne. How many generations ago had it been since a disciple ventured into the northern lands and seduced a Razohan? If, as many had always believed, there was only one bloodborn, how did the Sistern determine which Razohan would father the child that would start the long line of generations leading to me, the second bloodborn? Was augury involved in their choice of the right Razohan partner, or did they use other means I couldn't fathom? The depth of the Sistern's scheming was beyond my comprehension.

"Perhaps it is time for some answers." With Orphus present, now was a terrible time for this conversation, and the words escaped me in a harsher tone than intended, and it was too late to take them back.

I wasn't expecting her to stop. I glanced ahead to see Orphus turn.

"Is something the matter, Your Majesty?"

"No. You may go ahead. I wish to speak with my spiritual advisor before we enter the throne room." I tried to keep the command in my tone, though I was sure he heard the faint quiver in my voice.

I'd never meant for this conversation to be antagonistic. I blamed the anger, like fire in my veins, which had vanished the moment the Mother faced me. Eager as I was to hear the truth about my heritage, I'd yet to find the courage to confront the Mother. Now I had no choice.

She fixed her venomous gaze on me, and it shocked me to see the extent of her fury laid so openly bare. We had ventured deep into the inner sanctum, where the only light came from flickering torches, casting shadows that masked our features. Yet, no amount of darkness could conceal the Mother's intense glower.

"Your Majesty—"

"Orphus, please. Just give me a minute." My nerves were jangling.

Although my mind screamed for me to instruct Orphus to lead us to the throne room, to escape the Mother's wrath, I couldn't yield to cowardice. To repeat Andriet's mantra, it was time I acted as queen. I should demand more of myself, and I was certain Andriet would agree any moment was an excellent chance to assert my authority over the Mother.

I was determined to extract what I needed from her: the discipline and strength honed through her rigorous training, the insights on how to rule. But as queen, it was imperative I surpassed my creator. I had to prevent her from using me to seize control of the Bone Throne's power for herself.

Orphus's gaze flittered between us both.

"Leave," I shouted at him, unable to keep my calm.

"Very well." He inclined his head, bending ever so slightly into a stiff bow, but the way his head shifted to the Mother, I knew he blamed her for my sudden dark mood. I couldn't see his eyes, but I was sure they were sharp as daggers.

I turned my back on him, staring at the stone floor, listening to his footsteps move further into the sanctuary. Once I could no longer hear him, I lifted my eyes to the Mother.

"I want to know my heritage. That's all."

The Mother knew of my bloodlink to the Razohan. She knew every disciple's heritage, something of prime importance to every Divine Mother. Apparently, within the library at the temple of the Divine Order, you could find scroll after scroll containing every lineage of every disciple since the order began, almost a millennium ago. But if my heritage was from the Razohan line, why could I not shapeshift like Tamas?

She pressed her lips together, deepening the lines above her upper lip.

Breaths passed. I felt sure she wouldn't answer me, but then she spoke. "You dare give me an order."

"No. I'm asking, not ordering. I think it's only fair." I cupped my hands to steady the tremor and rested them in front of my skirts.

The Mother lifted her chin. "You know more than you need to know."

I wouldn't let the conversation end there. "That I'm... is my bloodline from the beast-born of the north?"

"What would make you suspect that?" Her words were ice shards falling from a storm ladened sky.

"An augur spoke of it."

The poor light couldn't conceal the sudden flare of her

eyes.

"I deserve the truth of my heritage."

The Mother moved so suddenly, I couldn't catch my breath. There was a sudden jolt in the back of my legs, and I went down, spearing a sharp pain in my knees as they hit the stone floor. The Mother's arm was around my throat in a tight hold that prevented me from taking a breath as she wielded a blade in front of my face. "As a bastard child, you deserve nothing," she hissed in my ear.

Slowly she feathered the blade across my cheek, holding back from cutting my skin. "How eager you are to forget the pillars and leave the Sistern behind you."

"No—" I could hardly get the word out before she tightened her hold.

"You're queen because of me." Her warm breath blew strands across my cheek and tickled my ear. "I gave you everything," she spat. "Yet at the first glimpse of power, you turned your back on your sisters."

I shook my head, then stilled the moment I felt the sharp edge of the blade dig into my chin. I couldn't take a breath around the Mother's choke hold, and she didn't appear willing to relent her hold.

"Your disdain for me will be your end."

She pushed the tip of the blade into the soft skin behind my ear. I felt it like a nail being slowly worked through the side of my neck. "How many lies have you told me? How many secrets do you keep, you filthy bastard child?" The blade drove deeper, lengthening the cut. "Which part about your mother do you want to hear? That she gladly surrendered you to me, eager for her arms to be rid of you. You were weak and sickly at birth, a disgrace to the Sistern. She was ashamed at birthing such a thing."

Jealousy and fury fashioned her words. She could say anything, and I had no way of knowing the truth.

"Your soul word is on the tip of my tongue."

Discipline.

I could summon King Ricaud and his deceased soldiers, commanding them to wrench her away from me. Alternatively, I could tap into the raw, captivating savagery I experienced in battle against the warriors, harnessing that agility, strength, and cunning to make her rue her actions. But as queen, I had to be smart. There were too many I couldn't trust, more I would likely have to fight. Now was not the time to start with the one woman who could further my training, hone me into the weapon I needed to be. Besides, she was unaware of my true strength; she underestimated my power. The Mother had yet to comprehend the full magnitude of what she'd created. And I wished to keep it that way for now.

Instead, I did what I always did. I stayed silent, let her venomous words wash over me while I fought to find my calming breaths, knowing the Mother wouldn't keep me like this for much longer. Orphus would return soon, and she wouldn't dare risk exposing her true identity.

I waited, trying to gasp in what breaths I could while focusing on the piercing pain of the blade and my wild heartbeat. The Mother would say every moment was the perfect occasion for practice, so I opened myself to the pain, allowed it to infect my mind, and absorbed the lesson she taught: mastery over fear and pain.

THE RELUCTANT QUEEN

Careful, Mother, for you're only strengthening me.

I caught a flicker of movement in my periphery but was unable to turn my head to see who it was. Perhaps it was one of King Ricaud's soldier spirits, or maybe the king himself, though I doubted the king would remain in the shadows.

As I expected, she kept her suffocating hold for one beat longer before releasing me on the smack of Orphus's boots coming toward us.

Once she stepped away, I rose, ungainly, fumbling to find my feet amongst the layers of my skirts. On my feet, I glanced toward the movement, but only saw dancing shadows cast by the gentle flickering torches.

The Mother shoved a kerchief in my hand and gripped tight, jerking me close. "You're a fool to think your soul word is my only weapon."

She shoved my hand away and turned toward Orphus's approach.

I wiped the trickling blood from my neck, then pressed the cloth to the wound as Orphus came into view, my mind a dizzy mess pondering on what she said. Of course, the Mother would be smarter than to leave my soul word as her only means of controlling me. My hand jerked up, following the urge to touch my old wound, the entry point for the black oily mist she'd placed inside of me, but I stopped myself before my hand made it halfway.

I'd never questioned how the Mother could do what she did to me when such a thing required magic. I simply accepted what she'd done, like any good disciple would, believing it was for the good of the Sistern, my sisters. Radnisa would argue, what benefited the Mother benefited the Sistern. Months ago, and I would have agreed. But too much had changed; I had changed.

Damn her conniving ways. I was her instrument, with no way free.

At first, Orphus was nothing more than a dark shape skulking in the shadows. By the time I could see him clearly, I'd stuffed the kerchief into my pocket and walked to meet him.

I waited until he stood in front of me. "You may take the Mo—take her to the throne room. I want a minute alone."

"Your Majesty, this cannot be done. I acquiesced to your demand she attend Emberforge with you, but she shall not enter the throne room alone."

I glared at Orphus. "Then take her to the door and wait for me."

"This is a most unusual request."

"It's not a request. I wish for a few moments alone… In here," I indicated the small sanctum behind us, shrouded in darkness, except for a weak candle flame resting on the altar at the front of the room.

"For what, may I ask?" There was a deeper question Orphus didn't voice.

"I shall wait with you," interrupted the Mother.

I kept my gaze on Orphus, ignoring the Mother. "The both of you will do as I say."

I looked to the Mother. "You'll wait for me in the corridor, outside the throne room."

She jerked her chin up with as much defiance as she dared, then strode past me.

"Thank you for this." I'd taken the kerchief from my

pocket and offered it to her as she passed. "It's no longer needed." I'd scrunched it in my hand, so Orphus wouldn't see the smears of blood.

A muscle twitched in her jaw, but I held her stoney gaze. "And thanks for answering my question. I take your answer as a yes." My heritage was with the beast-born of the north.

Her eyes narrowed, but I turned away, giving her my back.

"This way," Orphus intoned from behind me.

The temple was tiny, with a small altar of stone at the front and two rows of pews either side, enough for a handful of worshipers. I waited, staring at the candle flame as Orphus led the Mother away.

It surprised me Orphus had yielded to my command. Commands were what a queen gave, and I'd not overstepped my bounds, at least not yet.

"You can come out now." I wasn't sure who I would encounter, but ever since entering Emberforge, the subtle movements I'd caught in my periphery assured me that someone was here—not a spirit, as they invoked a distinct sensation.

I waited, attuned to the soft shuffle of slippered feet, reminiscent of a doe's cautious steps. Gradually, I turned to see a tall, lean apostle with a gaunt face and a shaved head enter the temple. The candle's flame flickered in his eyes. Then, he leaned forward into a deep bow, remaining in that position for three breaths before rising before me.

"Your Majesty, forgive me. I didn't mean to intrude on your solitude. If you wish to be alone…" He half turned, jerking his thumb in the direction he'd come.

"Why would I want you to leave when I've been waiting for you?"

"Yo...you were? Forgive me." He bowed again. "It's just that...Your Majesty. I wasn't following. I was—"

I sighed, not yet used to the way some people fell to pieces when in the presence of royalty. "Relax. I'm not going to cut off your head." I headed to the left row of pews and eased down on the hard stone bench.

"I'm glad you've found me." Once I'd fidgeted and made myself comfortable, I patted a place beside me.

He watched me pat the stone, his mouth agape, but made no move to come closer, as if his legs were carved from stone.

"I want to have a little chat, and I'd feel more comfortable if I didn't have to look up at you all the time."

"Of course, Your Majesty."

I smelt the oily blend of pressed herbs mingled with the scent of burned candle wax as he slid down onto the very edge of the pew, maintaining a distance of at least three bodies' length between us. He reminded me of a mouse caught in the open with a predator lurking nearby.

"What's your name?" I said.

"Plesy, Your Majesty."

"You can drop the title."

"Yes, Your—If you wish... I didn't intend to take offense."

I arched my head back and stared up at the wood beams crisscrossing the roof of the temple. "Relax, Plesy. It's just you and me. We'll get nowhere if you keep stumbling over your words. The Salmun won't stay away forever, and I've a lot of questions for you. For starters, why were you following us?"

His eyes flared wide. "I wasn't, Your—I'm sorry. It's hard to—But I wasn't."

The poor agitated man seemed about to leap from the pew and scuttle away.

"I've disturbed you, and I'm sorry. But I was curious. That's all. There's been rumors about you, and I was curious. They didn't say you were so young." His mouth sagged in astonishment. "I'm sorry, Your Ma—" He clawed his hands down his scalp, perhaps forgetting he no longer had hair. "I should go." He leapt up.

"No, don't," I shouted, then sucked in my voice. Curses that was loud and would likely draw Orphus back.

Plesy remained hunched, as though expecting a blow.

"Just sit down," I sighed. "Please. I won't hurt you."

"But the Salmun," he squeaked.

"Yes," I drawled. "They are a problem. But if you stop apologizing all the time and answer my questions, you can disappear back from where you came before Orphus returns. Now sit."

Plesy eased himself back down on the edge of the pew, keeping his shoulders hunched, looking as though he would peel forward and hit the floor at any moment.

"I'm sure many have spoken about me. How I survived the Ashenlands, defeated the northerners and returned as queen."

"There was never anything said about you defeating the northerners."

"Oh. That's all right. I was going to warn you not to

believe all the rumors you hear. Are you curious how I became queen?"

I arched a brow, and he nodded. "Only one who can take the ancient power of the Etherweave can ascend to the Tarragonan throne. The Salmun would not accept them otherwise, which would make you a descendant of the House of Tannard." There was a hint of awe in his voice.

"True." But not in the way he thought my heritage was linked.

"And you're a woman." He ducked his head. "I'm sorry, Your—I'm sorry. I didn't mean to be rude, it's just."

"There has never been a queen on the Tarragonan throne before."

"Yes. Which means the Salmun were desperate." His eyes widened in horror. "That was also not said to be rude."

"Relax, Plesy. I understand. And yes, I am the only heir left capable of wielding the Etherweave. Let's move on with my questions. I want you to tell me everything you know about the Etherweave."

"Now?" Panicked raised his voice.

"You have a point. Maybe not now. But soon."

"Forgive me, Your Majesty..." He winced at his slip of the tongue before continuing. "This conversation won't be easy. The Salmun..."

"You can speak plainly."

His gaze flicked to mine. "You're a foreigner."

"Who knows little about the Salmun and the workings of Emberforge. Is that what you were about to say?"

He nodded slightly.

"Where does your true loyalty lie?" Was he merely a

curious apostle, or was there a deeper reason he followed me through Emberforge?

"I'm sorry, Your—?" He paused, shaking his head in frustration.

How much should I reveal to him? "I need answers to questions that I cannot ask the Salmun. Do you understand?" My instincts assured me he was someone I could safely ask the questions I needed answered, beyond what the Salmun would tell me.

For the first time, he met my gaze and nodded, then leaned in closer. "There is a group of us within the apostles. Our loyalty... Let's just say it diverges from the Salmun's thoughts on the rule of Tarragona. On a lot of things."

"Then it's a good thing we've met." I frowned. "It's difficult for me to get inside Emberforge without the Salmun. And I'm sure they'll grow suspicious if I'm constantly asking to come back."

I launched to my feet and paced. "It's frustrating. Everyone expects me to be queen without telling me how to be one."

"Forgive me, Your Majesty—Sorry." Plesy hammered a fisted hand against his temple as he rose to join me. "It's a habit I can't stop. I don't suppose the Salmun expects you to know how to be a queen. It makes you reliant on them."

"That would be their plan. They can't have a queen with claws, now can they?" I didn't bother to keep the sarcasm from my voice. "Unfortunately, they don't realize I've already grown mine," I mumbled as I paced, speaking more to myself. "Then there's the Bone Throne. I'm sure they want me naïve to the extent of the Etherweave's power. But I must know. And you must tell me about the Etherweave and how it's connected to the Bone Throne."

"Your Maj—Sorry. But you're wounded." For the first time, Plesy noticed the wound on my neck.

My hand came away smeared in blood, but I'd not felt the trickle running down the side of my neck because our conversation was more interesting.

"It's nothing," I bit out, not wanting any distractions, fighting against thoughts of Tamas and the bite mark he gave me on the ship. Then I groaned with annoyance when the tingles flared around the mark. This was not the right time to daydream about him.

Plesy was already bent over, tearing at the hem of his smock, renting the silence with a violent ripping noise that seemed to hang in the air long after he'd finished.

"What're you doing?"

"It's fresh on this morning. I washed it last night." He offered me a strip of material.

"Oh. Umm...thank you." I pressed the material to my neck, smelling the rich herb oils tinged with a stringent citrus odor. I huffed a breath to clear my thoughts and turned back to Plesy. "What's your place within the temple?" I eased myself back down onto the stone seat, Plesy joining me, though keeping a polite distance.

"I'm scribe master."

"What does that entail?"

"I translate the old teachings."

I suddenly sat straight, finding more interest in him. "That would mean you have access to the dungeon library and would know all the volumes within it."

"Dungeon library? You mean the sanctum of solmira."

Such a fancy name for a dungeon.

"I can't claim to know all the works contained within. There is too much, and I have not been long in my position."

"What about Selisimus? Does he have anything to do with the sanctum of solmira?"

Plesy stared at me with an expression I could only read as admiration. "He's the scroll guardian."

It didn't sound like he would know a lot about the contents in the library. "But you both have keys?"

"And Tortilus, the lore keeper."

"Lore keeper. That sounds like he knows a lot about the teachings within the solmira."

"We all do..." He was likely about to use my title, but finished with a humble smile. "But there is much within we have yet to learn. Some works are so ancient, I've yet to devise a translation."

"What about anything around the time of the great war and King Ricaud?"

"Hmm... I can't say for sure. I've yet to come across any works regarding him. But Tortilus would know more." He leaned forward, casting a look over his shoulder as he did, hinting at a secret he wished to share. I, too, leaned close, hoping to encourage him.

"The Salmun have their own private library, filled with teachings they deem too sensitive for our eyes."

"Do you know where this library is?"

"Beneath the Bone Throne."

I sat back. "That makes access very difficult." Perhaps what Tamas sought was hidden within the Salmun's library, something he'd not realized when he took Petrulus's form to enter Emberforge. Whatever teachings he'd sought would be connected to the Etherweave and the Bone Throne, which meant it was something I needed to find.

"You won't get in. Only the Salmun are allowed. They have their means of keeping everyone else out."

"And you have no idea what they keep in there?"

Again Plesy glanced over his shoulder, as if expecting to see the Salmun looming upon us. "Dark teachings."

I frowned, unsure if that was true or if Plesy believed it so because it added an enticing air of mystery and danger.

"The Salmun's links to the Throne of Tarragona stretch back as far as the great war. That's a millennium of time to search the realm, gathering all the ancient teachings and translating them for themselves. We have no idea what they have hidden to keep from our eyes. We've spent a great deal of time in the sanctum of solmira, but there's little we've learned from what they've left us about the Etherweave, or anything to do with the ancients responsible for its creation or that of the Bone Throne. We believe the Salmun kept all that knowledge for themselves."

"It keeps them relevant and ensures their presence as advisor to the ruler a necessity. But for how long? Surely once the ruler of the Bone Throne consumes the Etherweave, the Salmun will lose their authority or ability to control them?"

"Remember, they've had a millennium to work out a plan to ensure they never lose control."

I arched my head back, thinking on what he said. "You're

right. That leaves me little time to work out a plan to ensure they never control me. I must get into their private library."

I also needed a plan to free myself from whatever schemes the Mother devised to keep me chained to her command.

"We'll help you. We may not have access to the Salmun's library, yet, but we are forever trying to find a way past their magic. And we're getting close. Besides, there is much we do know. And there is much the Salmun don't know about us. We've crafted our own lore, our own magic—"

"Wait? Magic?!"

Plesy hushed me with a finger to his lips while he glanced around. "We aren't the first of our order to try. We're simply building on those apostles who've come before us. A millennium is a long time. Our secret order has roots spanning at least five hundred years, working in the shadows of the Salmun."

I studied him. I'd lived a court life long enough to detect liars and deceivers, and Plesy was not one of those. "Then it's very fortunate for me we've met."

He bowed. "No, Your Majesty, it's very fortunate for me. My brethren will be very keen to hear of our conversation."

He rose from his seat. "The Salmun must not catch me here with you. I fear they'll ask too many questions about our conversation."

"I'll find a way for us to meet again. Perhaps outside of Emberforge. It will be less suspicious."

"The apostles rarely leave Emberforge. This is our home, but it's not unheard of. We need fresh air and sun occasionally. But I'm curious how the queen will walk the streets of Tarragona without the Salmun's protection."

"Damn, you're right. Then I'll find a way to sneak into Emberforge."

Hearing the distant sound of heavy footsteps, Plesy bowed once more and was on the verge of slipping out of the temple when I posed another question.

"Are you aware of any spirits inhabiting Emberforge?"

From his position by the archway at the entrance to the small temple, his expression was indiscernible. "We have no magic to communicate with spirits."

I nodded, and he vanished into the darkened corridor. I may not get a chance to speak with King Ricaud's spirit, but I'd discovered equally valuable secrets today.

CHAPTER NINE

BRYRA

The clothes were a good fit, but they felt foreign on me, coarse and scratchy, giving little chance for my skin to breathe. The maid's long skirt caught between my legs as I walked, and I found myself stomping around in irritation and yanking at my skirt for most of the day. The buttons on my blouse tightened all the way up my neck to below my chin, feeling like fingers gripped tight around my throat. I pulled at the collar constantly and was tempted to open all the buttons just so I could breathe. I wasn't sure how long I could remain in this outfit before I snarled and ripped it from my body.

Romelda gave me the perfect two-legged form, yet she couldn't do a lot about my size. While I wasn't my usual Huungardred height, I was taller than all the women I worked alongside and a lot of the men, which inadvertently made me the focus of their attention. Countless times, I touched the side of my face where my beastly features would be, anxious Romelda's spell had faded and exposed my true identity. Feeling only smooth skin where my beast form should've been was disconcerting, leaving me feeling estranged from my body.

For days, whenever I glimpsed my reflection, I paused and stared, disturbed by the woman looking back at me. Although the face was mine, the missing beastly aspect left me profoundly unsettled, and I couldn't help but loathe the change. In my reflection, I saw little of the woman I truly was, a woman with pride, resourcefulness, and strength. Instead, I saw a tall, ungainly woman, little different from those around me who were fragile of mind and preoccupied with nonsensical ideals like physical flawlessness.

The seneschal struggled to find me clothes that fit. She'd tutted and frowned, rummaging through the men's supplies to find boots large enough. My hands were too big for the delicate jobs expected of me, making my work clumsy. I soon discovered it took one stern look for any who dared find complaint in my work to send them scurrying away. After that happy discovery, I frowned at everyone, even the friendly servants, such was my mood at being forced to endure this two-legged form.

I would endure for Tamas, but it needn't be for too long. Romelda was true to her word, providing a letter of employment, which somehow captivated the seneschal. Whatever magical craft Romelda wove into her letter, the seneschal sent for the queen's lady's maid and dismissed her in front of me. She was young and her tears stirred my pity. I knew little of life in Tolum, or the castle, but enough to know employment was a necessity to survive and scarce. But she was young and would surely find another position soon enough.

I couldn't afford to be distracted with the fates of any two-legged, whose lives were insignificant to my murderous task. To succeed, my sole focus had to be on my goal, especially given Romelda's warning that her spell wouldn't last indefinitely.

The one obstacle to my employment I'd not expected was the Salmun, who'd read Romelda's letter with interest, then inspected me with equal interest. I had no knowledge of magic, yet I had always held the Nazeen in high regard as a powerful and ancient order of witches. I trusted in Romelda's abilities and felt a smug satisfaction in seeing them outwit the Salmun.

When I first arrived, I felt the fine hairs on my neck prickle at the proximity of all the people. Walking the roads to Emberfell, the two-legged jostled beside me. I swerved around bullocks pulling carts, dodge running children, and bat away persistent hawkers trying to sell me useless trinkets. Many times I wanted to bare fanged teeth and snarl. Even now, days later, the temptation to flee north to the solitude of the forest sometimes overwhelmed me, and I would have to find a solitary corner to close my eyes and calm my breathing, while suffering the sensations overriding my body for control. I'd clutch at my stomach to survive the waves of nausea while jittering nerves rode along the race of my heart.

A Huungardred from the north, I was stronger than this; my experiences would put the night terrors into many a feeble mind.

But the Salmun, who shadowed Tressya closely, made my task difficult. And if it wasn't the Salmun observing everything she did, countless others surrounded her, ladies in expensive clothes and jewelry so fine it shone around their necks like the sun. But the one to really make my skin shiver was the Mother of the Sistern. I wasn't scared of her, only what I would lose if she were ever to discover my true identity; of all the people within Emberfell, I felt the Mother would be the one to uncover my deception. Romelda had cautioned me to maintain my distance from the Sistern's Mother to ensure that she would not become suspicious of my true identity for even a moment.

Though aged, she stood tall and moved with catlike grace and ceaseless energy, as though her muscles were constantly coiled to spring. Too many times, I'd felt her shrewd gaze peeling the clothes from my back. A Huungardred didn't scurry like a mouse, and neither could I hide easily amongst the crowds. Instead, whenever she was around, I endured her eagle like stare, kept my back to her as best I could and avoided catching her eye while I completed my chores.

I'd visited Tressya's room this evening, supposedly to prepare her bath, but she wasn't in. I'd left in a tangle of nerves because I'd spent most of the last hour preparing myself for what I had to do. In my mind's eye, I'd watched myself walk through my plan, moving around the room as

I'd done for the last few nights, completing my tasks, secretly carrying the vial of poison in my skirts.

Romelda had warned me of Tressya's skill with a dagger. Her ability as a disciple was of no concern, as our beast form was impenetrable to their talent. She controlled spirits too, but if I acted swiftly, a claw laced with poison lancing her skin would end her before she could breathe a word.

I returned to the servants' passages, a cloistered warren of dimly lit corridors within the thick stone walls of the castle, filled with cobwebs and smelling like dead vermin. It allowed the servants to move about Emberfell without being seen. I'd not gone far when I ran into a short redhead, carrying an armful of linen. She pressed herself against the wall as she neared me, seeming intent on passing without touching me.

I filled the narrow passage, blocking her way, ignoring the way she shrunk against the wall. Cobwebs caught in her thick curls, which she didn't seem to notice.

"Where's the queen?"

I rarely spoke to anyone, so it was no surprise she shrank back further. The whimper caught me off guard. In my agitation over losing my quarry in the hunt and my eagerness to complete what I'd steeled myself for, I might have let a snarl creep into my voice, plus my frown was a permanent facial feature, and I suppose my question sounded accusatory, but I didn't think I was that scary.

I had strong features on the human side of my face as a Huungardred. Romelda's spell enhanced those features, giving me a broader forehead, sharper cheekbones and thicker lips and nose. It was as powerful a face as I could hope for while taking this two-legged form. Combined with my height, her reaction as she approached me shouldn't surprise me.

"She's...she's," she shook her head, "in the king's garden."

"Where's that?"

Her voice tempered as she rattled off instructions on how to reach the garden, which required me to remain inside this terrible dust filled corridor, with the stench of death, mildew and ages of neglect for longer than I wanted to.

At times, I was forced to stoop, and when I finally faced the wall at the end of the corridor, I knew I was in the right place. I pushed through into a room of wonder. Greenery filled every crevice, stretching to the glass ceiling and climbing along the windows as if seeking escape to the world beyond.

Tolum was a dead place, without a blade of grass or a tree. The two-legged had built over the natural wonders, replacing green with gray, the fresh, living smells of the wilderness for the odor of rot and decay. Only days I'd been in Emberfell, but already I grieved the vibrancy of the wilds. And here it was, tucked away in a secret captive garden.

I rushed forward, running my hands along the thin boughs of the trees as I passed, grasping the fat leaves, weeping downward as if in greeting, burying my face amongst the splendor and inhaling deep to smell the sweet oily fragrance. A tingle feathered through my blood, exciting my senses, as the first twinge of my fangs pierced my gum.

I reared back, running my tongue over my upper gum, at

the same time feeling the side of my face where my beastly form would normally be. I was still human looking. Even so, my fangs itched to extend. And I longed to release them as much as I longed to rip these clothes from my body and run.

I stepped back into the garden, immersing myself amongst the foliage, wrapped broadleaves across my body and closed my eyes while focusing on my raging heartbeat; let the captured forest nurture me and restore me. Here I would find my peace, for however short a time. Now that I knew this captive garden existed, I would seek its comfort whenever I felt the immensity of my task, drawing the walls of this castle in on me.

Stepping out from the shelter of the foliage, I noticed an iron table positioned at the heart of the garden. From this central point, two paved paths branched out, weaving into the thick greenery until they vanished from sight. A third path stretched towards an open glass doorway.

The table was set for tea, the cups still warm. Unfinished sandwiches remained of their feast. Who was Tressya entertaining?

I headed out the open doorway and onto a gravel path that followed along the side of the castle. Despite the majesty of the captive garden, little life was to be found out here. The tree's limbs hung heavy, their leaves dried on the ground. Someone had tamed the hedges into square shapes and left the flower beds to wilt and brown.

With the sun low on the horizon, Emberfell's black stone cast an eerie gloom on its surroundings. The aged, drab colors of my maid's clothes concealed me against the stone as I moved further along the path.

I encountered no one by the time I reached the back of the castle. Ahead, sprawled a field dotted with shabby circular garden beds. I was still a distance back, but with my keen Huungardred sight, I spied the ladies in their expensive dresses of velvet and fur, their hems trailing in the dirt, milling around a small fountain. Further along, I saw Tressya and Gusselan, the dead king's queen, sitting on a large swing seat, supported by thick chains slung from a large boughed tree. They appeared to be having an amicable conversation.

Though I knew little about the minds of the two-legged, this much I understood: those with power were often adversaries, so I hadn't expected a friendship between rivals. Reluctantly, I admired Tressya for befriending the ex-queen. I shouldn't. It didn't help to feel any goodwill toward the person I was here to kill.

Maybe Tressya was being strategic rather than generous. Gusselan wasn't much of a threat anymore. Stripped of her title and no sons to claim the throne, Tressya could afford to align herself with someone who knew a great deal about the court Henricus built. It was better I believed in her cunning than her charity.

To accomplish my mission, I simply had to familiarize myself with Tressya's routine and strategize accordingly. Nevertheless, I wasn't opposed to eavesdropping, considering it advantageous for everyone in the north to gather as much intelligence as possible on the new queen and her potential schemes while I was here. However, my towering size, coupled with this damn skirt that seemed intent on twisting around my legs and tripping me up, and the boots making an awkward noise against the gravel, stealth was near impossible. Although I didn't need to be close, given my hearing was as superior as my eyesight.

I diverted from the path across the barren field, gritting my teeth with every crunch of the dead grass under my boots. If luck was on my side, I'd reach the small thicket of dead trees close to the swing seat without being spotted.

I kept half an on eye on the courtiers huddled around the fountain and loped along, doubling over in an effort to reduce my size. With the darkening sky, I couldn't have chosen a better time to spy.

Two Salmun were present, their backs to me, keeping their distance from the courtiers while giving Tressya and Gusselan room to talk in private. I wasn't close, but even a distant proximity to them ran spikes across my neck. So far, I'd kept out of their way, not wanting any reason for them to scrutinize me further than they'd done on the first day of my employment. I feared they would see through my disguise once Romelda's magic waned. And that was one more reason to accomplish what I was here to do as quickly as possible.

Once I reached the thicket, I buried myself deep amongst the scrappy branches of the dead trees, swatting twigs threatening to catch in my plait. The loamy soil swallowed my noise, enabling me to move as close as I dared. Once their voices were clear, I sunk to the soft bed of decayed weeds and rested my head against the tree to listen, while burying my fingers in the damp soil, savoring the feel of the soft crumbling texture digging into the beds under my nails.

"I guarantee your safety," Tressya said.

There was a slight pause before Gusselan spoke. "I want to believe you."

I watched Tressya shift on the seat, turning her body toward Gusselan. "The Mother grows frustrated with her place in Emberfell."

"And with you, I would say."

"I'm no longer the disciple she sent away."

In their shared glance, I read a shared sentiment. Gusselan, too, felt changed.

"She has no allies in Tolum, which makes her situation precarious. Powerful people don't like feeling caged. I would be careful, Tressya."

The ex-queen spoke wisdom. I would guess Tressya had thought the same for she appeared pensive, her brows closing together as she sat in thought.

Gusselan stared ahead to the drab garden. "I've sent word to my superior, requesting a safe passage home. I feel there is nothing keeping me here."

"I understand, but I don't want you to go. You agreed to help me navigate the court, teach me my friends from my foe."

Gusselan let out a short laugh. "You killed most of your foe during the Ashenlands war."

"Yes, but you must have heard the talk, how the peerage are loathed to acknowledge me as queen. I feel I'm making new enemies every time I breathe."

Tressya leaned her body ever so slightly toward Gusselan, perhaps unconsciously, in a desperate bid to convince the older woman to stay.

"The crown will always have enemies. The Salmun will ensure none can touch you."

"Like they did your sons," Tressya snapped, then her face

fell the moment the words were out. She expression appeared repentant by what she'd said.

Gusselan turned her face away.

"I'm so sorry. That was spiteful and cruel of me to say."

"And true." Gusselan's voice was strained.

Tressya closed her eyes, as if searching for something to bridge the silence.

"You're right, Tressya. You're no longer the same woman. Your Mother Divine knows that. I see the way she looks at you when she thinks she's not been watched. I know loathing when I see it, but I also know the look of fear. You've grown into a woman she no longer knows how to control."

I didn't know the young queen well enough—it was in my best interests to keep it that way—to feel confident I could interpret her thoughts through her expressive face. But I was sure she was keeping a secret. Her eyes shifted beyond Gusselan, unfocused as though she'd fallen inside of her head, thinking on dark thoughts.

"Then I'm going to have to be smart. And I need allies around me. Perceptive and cunning allies like you."

"Tressya—"

"Listen. Your goal was to keep anyone connected to King Bezhani from taking his place on the Bone Throne." She seized Gusselan's hands. "Maybe this is not the way you expected to succeed, but you've succeeded, nonetheless. I'm not of the Levenian line. You, yourself told me so. I have no links to King Bezhani or the Salmun.

"What do you think this wicked king of yours will do if he ever discovers a queen with a bloodlink to the north sits on the Bone Throne?" Tressya continued.

It made sense the young queen would know of her heritage.

"I don't wish to think about that possibility. But you realize once the Etherweave rises, once the new ruler sits upon the Bone Throne, Bezhani will set sail for Tarragona, bringing with him the might of Yaslana and the Salmun with him."

Tressya laughed. "If this Etherweave is so powerful, I don't know what he thinks he can achieve going up against me."

The arrogance of the young queen. Already she believed herself the ruler of the Bone Throne.

"I ask you never to underestimate a man such as King Bezhani. His cruelty is limitless, and his desire for power is insatiable."

"But he is just a man. Is he not?"

"He's lived longer than any normal man." Gusselan fidgeted. "I can't say. There are rumors. He's immersed himself in the Salmun's teachings and practices. It's possible he's found some way with the aid of the Salmun to transcend his human limitations, but we've lost too many of our order in trying to infiltrate Yaslana to learn if the rumors are true.

"Whatever monster he may be, the king is not my greatest fear. The Salmun possesses unparalleled knowledge of the Etherweave. They harbor a library beneath the Bone Throne, dedicated, I believe, to all ancient lore regarding the Etherweave. Andriet once shared that all except the Salmun are barred from the place—the king himself wasn't an exception."

"Yes, I've heard of this library."

"Given their millennium of research and study, it's logical to say they've devised means to either harness the Etherweave for their own ends or to bind its wielder under their control."

Tressya sat back, puffing her cheeks before noisily exhaling the air. Then she ducked her head, pressing her thumbs into the corners of her eyes. "It's such a headache." Lifting her head, she said. "And all the more reason for you to stay here with me. Together we are stronger."

I rolled my head along the trunk of the tree, turning my head away from their conversation. I felt as though I wasn't ready to hear anymore, for everything I'd heard was deeply disturbing.

If all Gusselan had said was true, by removing Tressya, I placed Tamas in grave danger of being controlled by the north's greatest enemy.

I came to the south for Tamas, agreeing to Romelda's scheme because I wanted him free, only to cast him into a fate far worse, if I was to believe what was said.

I was not pure of heart. Tressya was a Razohan. Distance as her bloodlink may be, she was capable of forming a full partner bond with Tamas. I couldn't bear the idea. Yet, listening to her now, she didn't sound evil at heart, nor the manipulative shrew Romelda had me believe. No one conniving and greedy for power would care for the fate of another.

I slipped from my hiding spot at the base of the tree and hurried back toward the castle. Compelled by conflicting emotions, I yearned to run, strip myself free of my confines and run until I was choking for air and my legs quivered and spasmed with exhaustion. I wanted to escape the evil thriving in the hearts of our enemy, those who walked on two-legs. I didn't, because there was far more at stake than the ache in my heart. The problem was, I simply didn't know what to do next. It seemed Tressya was no longer under the sway of her order.

CHAPTER
TEN

TAMAS

A SAVAGE GALE whipped through the blackened trees, howling like a hungry pack of wolves on the heels of their prey. It was an ice wind with a fierce bite, mean enough to reach my heart. I clapped my hands across my arms hoping to find some comfort, even if for a few seconds, but it felt as though the unceasing wind had almost turned my body to stone.

Thick, rich, loamy soil weighed my boots, turning each step into additional labor. Thick knotted branches broke the sun's weak rays. They shone like shattered glass across the forest floor.

A curious feeling drove my quest, despite not understanding where I was or where I was going. There were no such places as this in the north, no forest so cursed that nothing thrived, not even the creeper underfoot. This had to be another dream. And not my dream, unless my mind was not yet free of the Ashenlands.

Damn those Eone. There was nothing else to explain why I was wondering through these dead lands. I would find great pleasure in demanding they show themselves so I could roar with fury at their faces for dismissing my demand, but I had to keep going. Why? I had no idea. But this ever present, mysterious feeling was like rope lassoed around my legs, pulling me forward. Even my heart agreed, pulsing signals of encouragement with every step I took.

Was chaining my body to a silent command also the Eone's doing?

If I ever saw them again, I'd introduce them to one of the many twisted aberrations of my soul. That's once I freed myself from the binds of this feeling. And something told me I would fail at that unless I reached my destination wherever that may be. Upward. That's the only way my legs seemed willing to go.

Rather than stay furious at the Eone for how easily they had manipulated my dreams, I was best turning that fury into strength and getting me out of this cursed forest. Stomping up this mountain would warm me up, so would becoming a Huungardred beast, but I thought best in human form.

Fisting my hands, I increased my pace, and found the faster I moved, the more urgent my need became. I had to reach it. The idea was so profound my cry almost sounded like a howl.

Soon I was pounding up the slope, using the boughs of trees to hurl myself onward, sinking newly emerged claws into the bark, shredding strips in my wake. I kept my human form, but called on the strength of the Huungardred so I could move silent and swift.

I punched out of the blackened trees as the sun dipped low on the horizon with the flare of an ember glow. Sucking in deep breaths, I stared at the ruined castle before me, splashed with evening colors. Thick twining branches of dead creeper and mold tarnished the stone. A millennium had destroyed its walls, but enough of it remained standing for me to recognize its resemblance to Emberfell, if not for the color of its stone: bone-white stone contrasting against Emberfell's black.

The broken battlements and crenellations resembled broken teeth and the remaining towers, that once pierced the sky, now stood fractured, their tops jagged against the backdrop of the early evening stars. Archways and windows stared beyond into the distance like eye sockets in a skull. Time had stripped its glory leaving it looking forlorn and fierce upon the mountain top.

Stumbling on the castle was surprise aplenty, but the biggest shock, if not my biggest hurdle, was the creatures soaring overhead. A menagerie of everything winged and foul, second only to the nightmare.

And there was the answer to my riddle. I had to be in the Ashenlands, for surely there was no other place in the realms where such evil spawn existed.

Turning into the nightmare was out. While my pet spanned the width and length of these creatures, it was more convenient for me to either take to the air as an eagle or merge fully with my Huungardred beast and race the creatures to the entrance.

I spread my wings within seconds of releasing my human form and rose onto the wind. The gust caught my tail, lifting my feathers and pushed me forward like a slingshot. I tried to keep low to the ground, but the wind danced over the city of rubble and bobbed me about like a small boat in a ferocious sea.

I wasn't even halfway there when one beast dipped its barb tipped wing and plummeted, and I was at the mercy of the wind, which refused to blow in a straight path. Instead, I surrendered to another form, hitting the ground at a gallop, once my four pawed feet emerged.

I sought the cover of the rubble on hearing the great downward beats of leathered wings, sending a sweep of wind barreling over the top of me.

With an ear shattering shriek of fury to hackle the fur across my shoulder blades, the beast gave one sweeping downward beat and rose above the rubble, gouging shards of stone as it scraped its barbs on the tips of its wings across the columns.

I kept my head low, ducking and weaving my way through the boulders of stone, and edged my way forward with a ferocious song of furious shrieks echoing overhead. When the song became a chorus, I glanced up to see more of the creatures brethren had joined the hunt.

The entrance was nearby, but reaching it meant leaving the shelter of the rubble, where a swarm of winged beasts had already landed.

The next shriek overhead spurred them forward. They

spiked the barbs on their leathery wings into the dark soil, darting their beaks outward, hoping to spear me. I craned my head back, looking up to the underbelly of the creature above.

Fine.

I soared skyward, clearing the tallest column in one leap. Then unfurled my wings, arched my head back, opened my mouth wide to swallow the creature in one gulp. A panicked frenzy broke out as the rest rushed to escape.

In this form, my mind became a tangled maze. The other creatures retreated in a chaotic flurry of torn wings while I was locked in a fierce battle against the nightmare's overwhelming instincts to hunt and fight and instead tried to focus on reaching the castle.

The urgency to rescue Tressya had cut through the internal jumble in my mind during my first transformation into the nightmare's form. However, the second time, amidst the tumult of the Ashenlands war, there was a disturbing allure in succumbing to the nightmare's dominant desires.

The temptation to surrender to the nightmare's urges was strong, yet the curious feeling that had set me on this path to climb the mountain proved the greater force. I turned from my prey and soared above the castle, tilting my head to look inside, then I folded my wings and plummeted, landing on the rubble strewn stone floor as a man.

Gnarled creepers clung to the walls like black veins, so dense in places that they likely were the only thing keeping the walls standing. Above me, the first stars peeked through the dusky blue-gray sky, and occasionally, winged beasts soared overhead, too high to pose any concern.

Inside the castle, the corridors and halls were a maze of shadows and whispers. No furnishings or tapestries remained to soften the brutality of time, or deaden the sound of crunching grit under my boots.

Now I was inside the castle, the curious feeling became a pulse in my chest, soon spreading as far as the tips of my fingers and toes. I followed the pulse as though it was a path laid out before me, weaving around the castle's decay and through empty cavernous rooms open to the dusky sky.

Before long, the pulse merged with my heartbeat, vibrating through my body and infusing my legs with a tingling energy. A surge of excitement propelled me into a run, as if an invisible map unveiled in my mind. I raced through the labyrinth of hallways and crumbling rooms, never questioning my destination.

I was close. The hum vibrated through me like fierce winds, relentlessly driving me deeper into the castle's heart, until I reached a gaping cavity in the center of a vast room. Stairs, now devoid of their banisters, spiraled down into the shadows. Peering into the depths, I tasted the stench of stagnant water and stale air on my tongue.

I was meant to descend into the darkness, where shadows danced and whispers echoed. Feeling a disaster was imminent, I leaped from where I stood, reaching the first landing, then sprinted the rest of the way down, following the spiral staircase to the cavern below.

Light came from the open cavity and a soft infusion of white flecks, like tiny stars, embedded in the rock walls. I slowly turned in a circle, seeing no other passages for me to follow. The impulse to keep moving had vanished, which had to mean I'd reached my destination, but all I saw was a desolate room.

Then, a bluish glow emanating from behind me illuminated the cavern walls, coinciding with the threading vibration in my body reaching its crescendo.

I turned to see a rock pulsing with blue light. The Etherweave. It had to be. I closed my eyes, resisting the urge to move closer, to touch it, knowing it's what the Eone wanted me to do.

Curse them. This was a test or a lesson, and I was sure it was the latter. They wanted me to touch the rock, suffer the potency of the Etherweave's magic, and understand the impossibility of wielding it alone.

I was sure the Eone rendered an existing scene within my dream rather than fabricate a fantasy, so instead of staring at the pulsing blue rock, allowing myself to fall under its mesmeric spell, I closed my eyes and tried to map out the trail I'd taken to get here. It took all my resolve to do. The ache to move closer grew more painful with each second I resisted, but I had to teach them my own lesson. My mental restraint was greater than they believed.

The prickling sensation warning me I was not alone overrode the pain in resisting the Etherweave's call. I dove left as I opened my eyes, crouched, battle ready in time to catch the dagger as it flew past. On instincts, I went for my weapons as I spun, to find none. I was still cursing the bloody Eone when I instinctively raised my arm to deflect a strike, knowing it was coming even without seeing my opponent.

Coming in low, I blocked the blow. The impact of my

forearm against theirs forced them to lose their grip on their weapon. About to swipe the lost dagger mid air to claim as mine, I faltered on hearing a female voice gasp.

I jumped away in case she planned a retaliatory attack while I shook my head, then rubbed my eyes. She was invisible to me. Somehow the Eone was blinding me to a part of my dream.

Sensing the change in the air, I danced away, then turned toward the sound of the gentle tread of a soft soled boot. The longer she delayed her strike, the better she could prepare her attack, so I leaped forward, cutting into the distance between us, shortening her ability to strike with my senses alive for any sound, the eddies of air across my skin, and the innate prickling that came with proximity to another.

I sensed her next attack and threw my arms outward, catching her forearm once again, pushing her strike wide. I shot my other arm forward and ceased her throat, having judged the distance and my aim, on hearing her frustrated grunt.

'Okay, wildling, time you stopped trying to stake me,' I snarled.

As though pulling a veil from my eyes, Tressya stood before me.

'Tressya,' I gasped, and released my grip on her throat. Her eyes narrowed, lancing me with a glare sharper than any blade. Her lips pressed thin, cheeks flushed pink with building savagery. But as quick as I'd freed her, she found her next dagger, and launched forward, stabbing straight for my heart.

I seized her wrist, a manacle grip, forcing her to drop the

dagger. She growled and hissed, thrashing like a true wildling, her eyes wide with fury.

'Release me, beast, before I gut you.'

I did, shoving her out of reach. 'I thought when we first met again, we'd at least talk first before we fought.'

Mercy, where did she keep all those daggers? Already she ran the hilt of another along her palm.

She snorted in derision. 'How can I talk to a beast? You have no wits about you, no sanity in your head. You wouldn't understand a word I said.'

'You're angry. I get it. You have every right to be. But at least let—'

I caught her next throw. 'That was careless. You should know better than to use me for target practice.'

Then finally I understood. This wasn't my Tressya. The Eone hadn't bothered to match their fabrication to my memories.

'You'll pay for this,' I yelled, glancing around the room as if expecting to see the four of them observing from the shadows.

'You've got that wrong,' Tressya intoned. 'It's you who'll pay.'

And she charged toward me. From her clumsy attack, I would say the Eone had little understanding of how to fight. I slipped left, ducked low and snagged her around the waist, lifting her off her feet. She kicked and yelled in a language I was sure no longer existed.

'How dare you corrupt my memories,' I shouted, trying to save my shins from her vicious kicks. 'I won't do as you want, so you might as well give up this fantasy.'

'You already question if you're the rightful heir to the Bone Throne,' Tressya gasped through awkward breaths.

I dumped her on the ground. Her legs weren't under her, so she landed on her ass. I paced around to stand in front of her. 'I'll give you to the count of ten to get out of my head before I cause some harm.'

'You are strong to resist the lure of the Etherweave, for sure. But you are not strong enough—'

Tressya spoke with Fivia's voice. I snapped my arm forward, seizing her neck again, no longer merciful in my grip. She grabbed my wrist with both hands, but her feeble hold was pathetic.

I pulled her close. 'Get rid of her.' I couldn't bring myself to voice Tressya's name in front of them.

'You will fail.'

I would have shaken her a lot worse if I wasn't staring into Tressya's eyes. As it was, I was suffering from maintaining my fierce hold, especially when her eyes bulged and her face flushed red.

'Give her up,' I yelled into Tressya's face, balancing the edge between revulsion for doing this to Tressya and fury in knowing it was Fivia, not Tressya before me—or at least her spiritual representation in the mask of Tressya's body.

Finally, her disguise faltered. The blue in her eyes blended into green. The face I'd adoringly mapped and fallen in love with became narrower and more angular. Fivia's sharp, straight nose emerged, replacing Tressya's small, snub nose.

'We do this for you, Tamas.'

I released her, pushing her by her throat and sending her onto her back. She rose to her elbows.

'I warned you the first time not to meddle in my mind. This was the last time you'll get that chance.'

She shook her head. 'You are but an infant in our eyes.'

'An infant heir to the Etherweave. Remember that. It's what you want after all, isn't it? A way to reclaim the Etherweave.'

Slowly Fivia pushed herself up to sitting. 'Do not praise yourself so highly, young Razohan, for you are not the only one.'

I jerked at the truth of what she'd said.

I launched on top of her, forcing her to the stone floor, a clawed hand at her neck, another clawed hand posed over her chest to rip out her heart. I didn't realize I was snarling until a drip of my saliva hit her upper lip.

'Underestimating us is your biggest mistake.'

'Likewise, bitch.'

'The door has begun to open. What is set in motion shall never be undone. We are growing stronger.'

She disappeared from under me. My hand, only moments ago holding Fivia in a choke hold, collapsed to the bed as I fell forward to my knees.

I was back in my room, and rather than waking up from a dream, I'd been an active participant. I slammed a fist into the mattress as I shouted in frustration, then leaped off the bed, spearing my hands through my hair. I now had one more pressing concern. Tressya.

They knew she was a bloodborn. I'd exposed her to the

fragment of Etherweave. Did that mean they now had an entrance into her dreams?

Osmud burst into my bedroom, not bothering to knock, while I was pacing back and forth and sunk down onto my bed.

"What do you want?" I had little patience at the moment for his smart tongue.

"Good afternoon to you, too."

"What?" I stomped to the window to see the sun high in the sky. I never slept late. Never.

"Your presence is required in the main hall."

I rested my hands behind my head and arched my head back, straightening out the kinks in my back. "Who is it?"

"And have you slip out the back door? You best come look for yourself."

"I'm not in the mood for an audience. I've got some things to think about."

"You can think about those when you're lying in your bed tonight. Day time is not for dreaming."

Too right it wasn't. It was unsettling to think the Eone could keep me trapped in my dreams.

"Where's Romelda?"

"Now you want to get friendly with the Nazeen?"

"I need her counsel."

"She's unlikely willing to give you any since you've proved fatheaded so far."

I spun to face him. "Is there anyone in the hall, or are you here to irritate me?"

"Both. More so to irritate you, but you have an audience."

Edging through the knot of tension holding my muscles

taunt, I felt the first stirrings of a smile. Thanks to him and Garrat, I stayed sane. Most of the time.

"I need to head south." Tressya was my first thought. She was astute enough to not fall for the Eone's lies, but... after the dream, I felt desperate to see her again. I needed to ask her forgiveness and tell her the truth of everything.

"Figured you'd say that sooner rather than later." He rose from the bed. "I'll just go pack a few things."

"You're not coming."

Osmud clamped a hand on my shoulder. "Sure I am." And headed for my door.

"It's personal this time."

He continued striding for the door, speaking over his shoulder. "You're the Razohan leader, heir to the Bone Throne. Nothing's personal."

I heaved a sigh. "Am I going to have to stab you in the shoulder so you can't fly?"

"Just get your ass to the main hall." Before he disappeared out the door, he stopped, glancing over his shoulder at my naked cock. "Since you're sorely lacking, you might want to put clothes on. There's ladies present, and I wouldn't want rumors to spread." Then he added. "Just thinking of your reputation. Though, I don't know why, since you pissed it away on the disciple when you bit her."

The Etherweave was in the Ashenlands, something I'd assumed long before the dream. But the Ashenlands were a produce of the Salmun's twisted magic, meaning the ruined castle could be anywhere within a place that no longer followed the boundaries of reality.

It was time I focused on the Senjel Oracles.

CHAPTER ELEVEN

TRESSYA

I was eating breakfast in the king's garden when they announced Daelon's arrival.

"Oh goodie," Andriet said, clapping his hands together.

"That's the only reason you bothered me at breakfast, isn't it?" I accused.

"Dearest queen, I'm heartbroken you would think I care so little for our friendship. I am and always will be your devoted..." His voice trailed away as Daelon entered the room. Andriet made a small squeak, his eyes set longingly and greedily upon Daelon as he strode toward me.

I couldn't blame Andriet. Daelon was impressive in his form fitting, deep leaf green pants and jacket, tailored to outline his broad, muscular physique. Andriet had hovered by the seamstress, barking orders on the measurements and fit even though she couldn't hear him. And now he was left to drool and pine for his ex-lover.

"I compiled the list of names you requested," Daelon said, placing the paper beside my plate. He no longer bowed to me in private, under my repeated instructions.

Andriet, appearing over his shoulder, leaned in close and sniffed the back of Daelon's neck. I frowned at him while Daelon focused on the list. He couldn't smell, so why risk accidentally touching Daelon or prolonging his ache?

"Everyone should take a seat," I announced, to which Daelon arched a brow and glanced around him, giving me another chance to frown at Andriet. I jerked my head toward the farthest seat from me.

"Yes, you, Daelon." I motioned to the seat closest to me.

Andriet glided into the seat first and mimed patting his lap.

"No," I barked, making Daelon freeze on the cusp of sitting on Andriet. Andriet winked at me, then slipped from the seat before giving an exaggerated bow and waving Daelon to take the seat.

"I'm sorry, Daelon. I'm out of sorts at the moment. Please," and I motioned once again for him to sit. "What have you got for me?" Determined to ignore Andriet's antics, I picked up the list and skimmed it through, recognizing a few names as I pushed the plate filled with pastries toward Daelon. "We can cross off the Earl's second son straight away," I said.

"Hold your girdle, sweet, that won't be easy," Andriet said.

"I'm afraid it won't be that easy," Daelon replied, helping himself to a pastry.

I rolled my eyes at Andriet for interfering. "Why not? The crown gets final say on who will serve her on the council, does she not? Besides, his father was involved in the plot to have me kidnapped. I refuse to reward his father's behavior by rising his son to my council."

"His father was very influential and while the new Earl of Vaelorin is young and a complete ass to hold such a title, many will back him," Andriet intervened.

"The young and incompetent are easily manipulated," I added.

"The Earl may be young and perhaps incompetent, but he's shrewd," Daelon said.

"Which is why many of the lords and barons will want him on the council, whispering in the queen's ear," Andriet continued.

"Most care little for my ear. They would rather see me dead."

Daelon frowned. "Are we still talking about the young Earl?"

"And the closer they are beside you, the easier they are to observe," Andriet finished.

I slammed my hand down on the list. "I can handle only one conversation."

"Right. The young Earl is off the list," Daelon agreed. "Anyone else you wish to strike off?"

"That slut Baroness Deflume will push for Stokrest to take a place," Andriet continued.

I scrutinized the list, running a finger down the names, looking for his. "What about Stokrest?"

"His titles are barely worth mentioning. I wouldn't put him on the list," Daelon said.

"Of course, Daelon wouldn't put him on the list, but the Baroness will push for it all the same. She has a sharp tongue and wields gossip like a blade. Never underestimate what passes through the courtiers and makes its way into their husbands' ears."

"She's influential, right? You need to keep an eye on her, make sure she doesn't spread malicious gossip," I continued.

"Who're we talking about?" Daelon said.

"Baron Deflume. She's Stokrest's lover. She'll push to have him elevated."

"Oh," Daelon responded. "You know a thing or two about the royal court."

"That little turd, Thurrebe. He'll be looking to make a name for himself." I jumped, spilling my tea, as Andriet suddenly spoke in my ear.

"Are you all right?"

I sighed. "I'm fine, Daelon. Right now, I seem to have too many voices in my head regarding all these matters."

"He's Lord Dowel's son. You remember that oaf? Take it from me, my sweet, his impotent son will already have some sordid plan to remove your royal behind from the throne and replace it with—"

"Perhaps we should leave this discussion until later," Daelon began before I slapped my hand down on the list, slamming it against the table. "You're forgetting the Salmun.

They're hardly going to allow an impotent dolt to win the throne."

"Very true," Daelon said, his voice sounding strained. "Who's the impotent dolt?"

"Besides, you said it was best to keep my enemies close," I continued.

"I don't recall mentioning that, but it's wise." Daelon was trying his best to keep up with my seemingly one-sided conversation.

I seized Daelon's hand. "I'm so sorry. This must be very confusing for you because it's doing my head in."

"You've been weeks on the throne. No one's expecting you to act competently in all matters so early in your rule." He looked at my hand cupping his. "Besides." His voice had softened. "You lost those close to you, as did I, and that's going to take time." He sighed, closing his eyes. "Sometimes time isn't even enough."

"Shit. I'm going to cry," Andriet wailed. "Sorry, Tressya, I won't be able to help you with your list for now." And he vanished.

I gave Daelon my warmest smile, feeling my shoulders ease with Andriet's disappearance. I loved him dearly, but he'd become a handful as a spirit, and I was doing my best to fulfill the promise I made to myself never to exert my control as a spiritweaver over him. "You're right. Grief makes a poor leader out of anyone."

"If you allow it, it will strengthen you."

I patted his hand again, then reached for the teapot. "Have you thought any more about my request?" I poured Daelon a cup of tea while I spoke.

"He'll refuse." I jerked, spilling Daelon's tea over the tablecloth at Andriet's sudden reappearance.

"Tressya?"

I gave Daelon an embarrassed smile. "Sorry. I seem to have the jitters suddenly. I'm fine. Go on."

"I'm honored you wish to bestow me with title and rank, but you can't be seen to show favoritism."

"See, I told you."

Gritting my teeth against Andriet's intrusion, I said. "That's ridiculous. Royalty always shows favoritism. Everyone expects it."

"Don't give up on him," Andriet moved across to stand behind Daelon.

"Please, Daelon, don't dismiss my request outright. Think on it."

"Most will turn against me."

"No, Daelon. Don't let that keep you from accepting Tressya's offer."

"You're stronger than that, Daelon. Don't let those concerns sway your decision."

"Listen to her, my dearest. We want the best for you."

"In all honesty, I feel happier where I am."

"Nonsense. Tressya will give you rooms in the palace. You'll have every luxury, servants at your call."

"You mean a great deal to me, Daelon. You're the only one I trust in this lair of liars and murderers."

"She needs you close, Daelon. I need you close."

"You can be with him anywhere you please," I grouched, then gently shook my head at my stupidity for speaking that aloud—for the confusing conversation I'd conducted with Daelon so far.

"Are...are you referring to Andriet?" Daelon said.

I pressed my fingers to my temple as I spoke. "I want the best for you, and if you feel happier where you are, then I—"

"Shut up, Tressya," Andriet interrupted.

"—respect your wishes."

"No, you don't." Andriet paced behind Daelon. "You want him to have titles, land, a place on the council. His—"

"Thank you," Daelon said.

"—advise will be invaluable."

"After all you've lost. I want you to be happy."

Andriet leaned down beside me. "He'll be much happier once you've elevated his rank and given him a place within Emberfell. He just doesn't know it yet."

"That's a tough ask," Daelon said.

"See, I told you he wasn't happy."

"We'll share our tattered hearts." It was near impossible to have this conversation with Andriet hovering between us. "And we'll also share them when they're mended."

"That's a promise," Daelon said.

"Shit. I'm going to cry again," Andriet announced.

Just then the door burst open, a guard rushing forth, the Mother close on his heels.

"Your Majesty, your spiritual advisor."

"She can see who I am," the Mother growled at him as she strode past.

"Oh goody. Just the sport I need," Andriet crooned.

Daelon rushed to his feet, knocking over his chair in his

haste. Face flushed red, he fumbled to right it, apologizing all the while.

I rose from my seat. It wasn't the done thing for the queen to show such curtesy to anyone, but I feared Andriet was about to do something calamitous, like rush straight through the Mother yanking on her heart along the way.

"I wasn't expecting you," I stammered.

Thankfully, Andriet chose instead to stand beside Daelon, like a protective pet.

I fought against my smirk at seeing her stiff attempt at a bow. Then turned to Daelon. "That'll be all." Sparing him the Mother's scrutiny.

"Your Majesty." He exaggerated his bow, as if to make a mockery of the Mother's own.

"I'll be with you shortly," Andriet yelled to Daelon, as he hurriedly retreated from the king's garden.

"I'm very glad we can talk in private," I said pointedly, staring at Andriet because the Mother was already making herself comfortable at the table, despite my not having welcomed her to sit.

She simply huffed at what I said, paying me little attention, her gaze focused on the food in front of her.

"Your position is most favorable." The tone in her voice was like being forced to juggle hot coals—it burned the more you listened to it.

I settled myself into my seat, feeling ill at ease with Andriet hovering behind the Mother. He was both my reward and punishment for all I'd done in the Ashenlands. I'd refused to mourn him, so brought him home as reward, only now he was punishing me by driving me insane.

Deep in my heart, I knew I was still to suffer the consequences of disturbing the balance and dragging the dead from their home across the veil. The suffering, however, had yet to come, and right now I had to concentrate on the position I was in.

"A position foisted upon me. But, yes, you're right. It has its favorable moments." I slid back down into my seat, placing both my palms on the table as grounding for the conversation to come.

Her gaze sliced across to me, and I warred with my choices: hold her gaze, a direct challenge, or dip my eyes and submit to her authority as the Divine Mother. With each passing day, I felt less a disciple. Traitorous of all, I struggled to see the Mother as my savior.

Finally, I lowered my gaze and focused on the half-eaten pastry on my plate. I had yet to feel secure in my position, and with so much still unclear and numerous enemies seeking my downfall, it wasn't wise to confront the one person I still feared. Now was not the time to provoke a conflict with the Mother.

The silence between us was like hands around my throat. I could feel her gaze upon me, but I resisted lifting my eyes, knowing what I'd read in her expression if I did—loathing. Only now, after all these years, have I come to realize my foolishness in holding her in such high esteem, in letting her into my heart as the mother I never had.

"I know a malicious schemer when I see one. Loyal words they may say, it's in their eyes. The greed, the hunger for wealth and power they don't deserve. This one has a black core, the blackest I've ever seen." Andriet said.

I couldn't challenge him on that assessment. Nor could I tell him to back away as he hovered dangerously close to her face, I discovered as I finally lifted my gaze. If he were alive, the Mother would be breathing in his breath.

"Her heart's a shriveled husk from lack of use." He held up his hand, curling his fingers inward and hovered it over her heart, a threat to repeat what he'd done in the carriage on her arrival.

Maybe I'd grown weary of fighting Andriet's antics, but I felt no inclination to stop him.

"Perhaps I'm wrong. She probably doesn't possess a heart."

The Mother's brows lifted as she glanced to the list of potential council candidates beside my plate.

"That's right, you old witch. As queen, Tressya gets to choose the trustworthy to counsel her. She'll surround herself with people of worth who'll give genuine support."

"You wanted privacy?" the Mother asked. "Tell your friend to leave us alone." And she stared ahead out the windows into the garden, as if waiting for me to do as she asked.

"Oh, she's good. And I hate I think so, but it's true."

"Please," I whispered to Andriet, even though the Mother would hear.

"You need my support, my sweet. You're not yet strong enough to stand against her. You're learning, though. Each day I see the fire in your burn brighter, but she still gets the better of you."

I slowly shook my head.

"Come on, Tressya. A spirit's life lacks many things, most of all fun. Let me have some with her."

"Perhaps you're not as adept in your ability as a spiritweaver as I believed." The Mother returned her gaze to me.

This time I wouldn't look away. I watched her brow arch, mockingly questioning my stare. Then her lips thin and pinched in displeasure.

"I don't understand the significance of what she just said, but it's finally pulled out the queen. Bravo, my sweet. Now show some teeth."

"*Aetherius*," the Mother suddenly hissed.

My soul word surged through me like a tempest unleashed from the depths of a raging sea, surging within to flood my mind and drown my heart. My muscles turned to stone as my breath seized, the power in her voice, swiftly crippling my control over my body.

"Tressya?" Andriet queried, abandoning the Mother and sliding close beside me. "So this is soul voice?"

In my feeble resistance, my fingers curled, clawing my nails down the stone table. I couldn't even make my mouth move. The six pillars deserted me. Discipline I needed most to calm my mind, allow me a chance for my own retaliatory attack, but my soul word drenched in the power of the Mother's voice captured me in a suffocating and cruel embrace.

"She even made me jump."

"Fall to your knees," the Mother barked.

Gasping for shallow breaths, I slid from my seat, unable to disobey, unable to even fight.

"Don't worry, my sweet. I'm your protector. Whatever the crone gives, I'll make her receive."

My eyes were the only thing free of her command. I cast a side-ways glance to find Andriet standing behind her, a wicked, gleeful smile on his face, and my heart surged in joy at the thought of what he'd do.

"I've nurtured your naivety for all these years. It was important, you see, ensuring your lack of progress in the Sistern's divine arts of soul voice, and in your understanding of your heritage."

I was sure I didn't want her to continue, but I was as hungry for my past as a drowning man for air.

Andriet's glare stayed on the back of her head, hand raised as though readying himself to chop it off. He wouldn't, because he understood the value of information.

"You'll slowly choke if you speak. Do you understand me?" She quirked a brow.

I nodded, a chill of ice creeping into my heart. I was desperate to hear this, yet I feared it was not something I wanted Andriet to know. But it was too late. By sealing my lips, the Mother had ensured Andriet's presence.

"Many, many centuries ago, there were only a handful of us who had discovered our voice. Even fewer understood the potential of what we could achieve by nurturing this unique ability. Selective breeding became essential, as did the establishment of the pillars, the foundation upon which our order would be built.

"Our order gradually grew, but as women, our influence was restricted in a world dominated by men, regardless of how strategically we positioned ourselves among those in power."

Andriet shifted to the side, for a clearer view of the

Mother. He appeared as captivated as I was by this revelation into the Sistern's history.

"If not for the Razohan and their crucial connection with the deceased king of the south, the Sistern would have remained concealed, merely a hidden force behind true power. Finally, we found a way to be more than just the puppeteer behind the throne. We could become the throne itself. And rulers of the Bone Throne."

"This is nonsense," Andriet interjected, while the Mother slowly rose from the table. He held his arm out to her, pulling up his sleeve to expose his wrist. "In my blood runs the true heirs to the Bone Throne." He jabbed a finger at me. "She carries that blood, from the Levenian line."

I closed my eyes in shame. Though I had no power over my ancestry, only my destiny—even that looked shaky—I'd not been truthful to my dearest friend. But I was shocked and saddened to realize how vehemently he believed what the Salmun had told him: that his line, the Levenian line, were the only true heirs destined to rule the Bone Throne.

"The presence of the Nazeen in the north posed a challenge to our objectives. However, our persistence and patience eventually paid off. Discontent simmered among some of the blooded, weary of their sacrifices. When Sophia, Ammelle's granddaughter, bonded with a Huungardred to create abominations, doubts arose about the legitimacy of her line to the Bone Throne. Thus, the restless amongst the blooded warmed to our overtures."

There was no stopping what she would say. Andriet would finally hear the truth.

"With the Nazeen's help, the Sistern sent one of our loyal sisters north to unite with a Razohan many generations past, long before my tenure as head of the divine order. Your connection to the Razohan began over four hundred years ago. It was a courageous and ambitious scheme, showing great foresight." She took a breath. If only I could shut her up.

"You see, she couldn't just mate with any Razohan. He had to be exceptional. With the Nazeen's help, we selected a Razohan from the men of the north, one whose lineage would produce a very special child."

"This is all lies." Andriet's face contorted in anger. "You don't need to listen to this, Tressya. You're one of us. You're not a disgusting beast from the north."

He raised his hand, ready to punch it through her chest from behind.

I was a coward, because for a breath, I wanted him to do it. I'd dreaded this moment, the moment of witnessing the look of horror on Andriet's face as he learned the truth, and the inevitable rejection I was certain would follow. I wanted him to silence her, so I could maintain the veil over my dirty secrets, keeping them confined between the Mother and myself. But it was too late now. The truth had been revealed and could never be withdrawn back into the shadows.

She strolled the length of the table, running a finger across its surface as she went. "Your mother loathed the blight running through her veins, but as a loyal disciple, she understood her duty and committed herself to the Sistern's goal."

Andriet glanced down at his wrist, the sleeve still pulled up, leaving it exposed to a woman who couldn't even see him. He looked like a man grappling for sanity, looking utterly defeated.

"It was a mercy she died so early." She halted at the end of the table and turned to face me. "She didn't want you, a reminder of what she abhorred. Your mother wanted to see an end to her cursed blood, but you were important to the Sistern, and she knew her duty, so she obeyed."

"This is her twisted way of hurting you?"

The only thing left to burn me in my shame was to reveal my part in his family's demise. In many ways, the Mother's hold on me was a mercy. It was the punishment I sorely needed. I closed my eyes, unable to bear Andriet's expression after the Mother exposed me for what I truly was: his enemy.

"It's all lies, you whore," Andriet shouted.

I opened my eyes to see the Mother fall forward, slamming her hands on the table with a loud gasp, Andriet behind her, his features distorted with malice and a twisted euphoria.

The moment Andriet punched his fist through the Mother's back, her hold on me vanished. I fell forward, crying out as I cracked my head on the edge of the stone table. Dizzy with pain, I tried to right myself as blood trickled into my eyes.

"Tell your pet to release me," the Mother shouted, then, through gritted teeth, she straightened, forcing Andriet's fist to protrude through her chest.

I understood the sensation of being invaded by death, of feeling overwhelmed by their emotions. I had believed it was my spiritweaver ability that made me susceptible to such feelings. However, as with our time in the carriage, the Mother appeared to experience the same as me.

"Arrh," she growled, hands fisted so her knuckles turned white, her lips pulled back, revealing yellowed teeth and gums. Then, after a moment, she tilted her head back and laughed, filling the room with a maniacal sound.

"That's all you have? You pathetic fool. The dead can't hurt the living."

She said as much because she had no idea of what I'd done in the Ashenlands, which meant she didn't realize the extent of my ability as a spiritweaver. One word from me would bring Andriet across the veil and into the world of the living.

"You better listen carefully," the Mother said, though her voice sounded strained. For all her strength and power, she still struggled under Andriet's touch.

"Andriet." My voice croaked as I spoke.

"It's time to silence those lies," Andriet growled, deafened to my plea.

"Our lives are now connected," the Mother gasped, her eyes seeking mine across the table.

Andriet's face turned bone white.

"You know I'm telling the truth," she continued.

Mercy upon me. It was the black mist she'd placed inside of me before I'd set sail for Tarragona.

"That's right, child. I see you remember."

Andriet was staring at me, his eyes imploring it not to be true. I could only shake my head, feeling yet more shame for something beyond my control.

He backed away from the Mother, mimicking spearing his hands through his hair. Shaking his head, he turned his back and paced away, and kept pacing until he left the room.

Why had he not done that in the beginning? *Because he needed to hear the truth. And you would never find the courage to tell him.*

The Mother eased herself down in the closest seat, inhaling deep as she arched her head back.

"The mist was to enhance my spiritweaver ability."

"Yes. And more. As if I'd leave something as important as assuming power of the Bone Throne and the Etherweave up to someone as pitiful as you."

I pulled myself from the floor, sliding into my seat. "What have you done?"

"I've elevated the Sistern to its rightful place."

"What have you done?" I repeated, my voice sounding dry and rough.

Her dark eyes resembled deep wells leading into a perilous lair. I wanted to leap across the table and smack the smirk from her face, but her answer was more valuable to me. Thanks to Andriet, her dark secret was out, and once I knew exactly what she'd done to me, I would reverse it. There had to be a way. I'd stop at nothing to find a way. Then I would teach her the mistake she made in thinking me pitiful.

"Had you followed your duty and remained loyal to the Sistern, you wouldn't have to suffer." She rose. "You have only yourself to blame."

Discipline. I swallowed, easily shedding the sludge of her gloat. There were far more significant matters for me to consider than allowing myself to become angered by her smugness.

"How are our lives connected?"

She strode toward me. "You have forgotten so much of how the Sistern works since arriving in Tarragona. I suppose I'll have to excuse you, given the company you've kept for all this time."

I'd anticipated her silence, but it was worth attempting to see what I could get out of her. I'd hoped her conceit would make her believe she'd already triumphed, loosening her tongue. The Mother was too shrewd for that. Which meant I'd have to work this out for myself.

I rose, so we were facing each other. "Thank you, Mother, once again for your valuable lesson."

Magic was how this started, so it would be the cure.

I left her smirk faltering and marched from the king's garden.

The Salmun were the last on my list to consult. I needed to sneak back into Emberforge and meet with Plesy and his brethren. There was also the Nazeen who'd betrayed their sisters to side with the Sistern. I was damn sure they would not sit idle and let the Sistern win prime place in this race for the Bone Throne.

Did Tamas know of the Nazeens' betrayal?

I tried to ignore the tingles flaring on my wrist where his bite mark remained.

Tamas, the bloodborn. The only other bloodborn; the man who had bonded himself with me. The man who should be my greatest rival for the Bone Throne. Yet, he was the only rival I felt certain wouldn't want to see me fail.

You need to come back to me.

I felt sure if I was ever to wield the Etherweave,` I needed Tamas by my side. It was time I shed my foreigner's naivety and understood my inheritance.

It was time I learned how to be a queen; ruler of the Bone Throne.

CHAPTER
TWELVE

BRYRA

Her blade skills were exceptional, a fact I couldn't help admire, as to her fortitude in the face of potential and gruesome defeat. Her cursed Mother must surely have faith in Tressya's abilities to have thrown her into such an unfair fight.

I shifted uncomfortably on the small log I'd selected, close to the weapons cart. As a lady's maid, my duties were confined to the castle, and while the queen was preoccupied, I was supposed to attend to other household tasks. Yet, no one could compel me to do anything.

Dressed in my maid's attire, standing as tall as a lot of the men present, I felt conspicuously out of place. Therefore, after observing Tressya's initial battle with a tall, sturdy man, I positioned myself at the fringe of the crowd of men, hoping to draw minimal attention to myself now that the fight had intensified.

I'd risked a lot leaving the castle and joining the growing crowd gathered to watch the queen fight, but I'd become increasingly restless locked behind walls. While Romelda's spell concealed my beast side, it didn't prevent me from turning into a full Huungardred if the need arose, and I was sure remaining cooped inside would weaken my restraint until I grew fangs and claws and sprouted hairs across my back.

From where I sat, I heard the whispers of astonishment from many of the young men to see their queen wielding a sword. It was uncommon because the men of the south cruelly cloistered their women and expected them to stay meek and idle, which made them frivolous and pathetic.

But not the young queen. Her fighting style was efficient and clever. It was obvious the Sistern were masters of the sword.

For a breath, I turned away with an unfamiliar feeling infecting my heart. It was the disease of jealousy. Here was the reason Tamas favored Tressya, likely the reason he'd surrendered his chance at bonding with another.

At a glance she looked feeble, reaching below my shoulders, with little muscle to keep her clothes fitting snug. But she was bold, and that alone was enough to catch a Razohan like Tamas's eye. Yet there was plenty more about her to make him fall. Her moves were perfectly executed, her cunning and agility unmatched by any man who stepped into the arena. Her tireless energy contested each strike and blow, sending many men bleeding to their knees. There was also the Razohan blood in her veins, which would give her the advantage over any two-legged male.

How could I not admire such a worthy fighter?

Compelled by the rising tension, the clash of swords, and the cries of shocked anguish from the male fighters, along with the onlookers' sympathetic and pained responses, I left my seat. I stretched to see over the men who had pushed their way in front of me, obstructing my view, to see Tressya's swift and decisive blow that ended the fight by sending her opponent to his knees, bleeding from too many places.

Tressya called an end to the match and offered her hand to the loser, which he initially hesitated to accept. Then, remembering himself, and who he was refusing, he slapped his hand in hers, but tried his hardest to scramble to his feet unaided. His exertion flushed his cheeks, but I was sure his embarrassment deepened the rosy hue.

I pushed a man in front of me aside, keen to hear what Tressya said to the inept man who'd misjudged the fight, underestimated Tressya as a worthy opponent, and squandered valuable strikes. He deserved to be expelled from the king's army, assuming that was his rank.

"Heya," grunted the burly man in front when I pushed him away.

I curled my lip as I stared at him. His eyes dropped to my booted feet then all the way up, then he smiled. "Well, little lady. Looks like you'd be a handful of fun."

Before he breathed another word, I twisted his arm behind his back and kicked his knees from under him. "Not the sort of fun you're looking for, I assure you," I spoke into his ear, then released him, pushing him forward to his knees and smirked when the men surrounding us mocked him.

Perhaps it wasn't the wisest decision, but I found it difficult to ignore brash insults from contemptible men who were beneath my notice. Unwilling to draw any more attention, I slipped from the crowd and headed back to my seat by the weapons wagon.

Now the fighting was finished, the crowd scattered, causing a ruckus as they departed, which meant I had to concentrate to discern Tressya from amongst the crowd. By familiarizing myself with the sound of her footsteps, I could distinguish her approach from others around me and knew she was heading in my direction. Anticipating she would return her own weapons, as the queen appeared to prefer handling most tasks herself, I'd strategically positioned myself near the weapons wagon.

Huungardred were supreme hunters, never making foolish mistakes, like revealing themselves to their prey. Yet, here I was, daring to leave the castle confines, watching her fight when I should be dusting the bannisters, or worse, sluicing her chamber pot.

The allure of the young queen made me forget I was the predator. This same queen who'd attempted to befriend her tall, clumsy lady's maid as she quietly went about her tasks, rebuffing the queen's overtures of friendship with mere mumbles of yes or no to any inquiries, even those that warranted a more elaborate response.

The truth of my coming to the arena was as complicated as my burgeoning complex and torturous emotions toward her. As a maid, I was privy to most of the gossip, so I knew the difficult task she faced convincing the noblemen to accept her as queen. And I shouldn't care that she had few to confide in, as far as I could see; the Salmun made my hairs prickle; the Mother made me want to grow claws.

While Huungardred craved their solitude, they were fiercely loyal to their kind. We considered all Huungardred our family and that meant we were never truly alone, and so I felt the queen's isolation acutely, which infuriated me.

The more I was in her presence, the more I witnessed her fortitude and her guile, but it wasn't the side of her I wanted to know. I should despise her, see her merely as a manipulative schemer, as shallow and greedy as the rest of her court. Instead, I saw her as an intelligent and brave woman battling for her rightful place in a realm that privileges men.

"Ryia!" she exclaimed.

Perhaps it hadn't been wise choosing a name so close to my own, but I feared forgetting anything else.

Looming behind her was the ever-present Salmun. Instinctively, I half-turned, shielding what would be the beast side of my face from their potential scrutiny. With their hoods drawn low over their faces, it was hard to know if they were watching us. However, it seemed likely, considering their sole reason for being there, Tressya, was standing right in front of me.

I curtseyed awkwardly, dipping my head and holding my tongue.

The queen's cursed Mother had yet to raise from her seat, and I spied Gusselan also present, seated with ample distance between her and the Mother.

"You escaped?" Tressya said, unbuckling her weapons

belt. Her voice was good-humored, easing my discomfort. It was difficult standing so close to my target while grappling with admiration and guilt. Praise our ancestors, *guilt*. I should have no room for guilt in my heart—guilt for what I intended to do—but also a persistent and growing niggle of doubt. Why did I feel she wasn't meant to die?

I wasn't an augur, nor did I possess the inexplicable intuition that some Nazeen seemed to have, but I sensed that Tressya's role in all of this was more significant than Romelda had assumed. Was this how Tamas felt on meeting her? The reason he saved her? Bit her?

"I don't blame you," she continued, drawing her dagger from a separate belt. "I'd go crazy forced to stay indoors all day."

She seemed genuinely interested in making conversation with me; her supposed maid.

"I heard rumors you were battling with the army's best."

In mock horror, she said. "Spare us all, a woman with a blade."

Despite myself, I smiled.

"And you had to see for yourself if the rumor was true." She turned to me, holding out her arms. "Well, here I am." She spun in a circle, parading herself in front of me, opening herself up to my scrutiny without a care. Her pants and shirt were stained with smears of blood and dirt, evidence of a tumble or two, yet no more so than her opponents. The underarms of her shirt were drenched, as was her hair, with strands adhering to the beads of sweat on her forehead. The most striking feature, however, was the exhilaration in her eyes. That, coupled with her raw energy, gave me the impression she could spring for freedom into the trees at any moment.

I understood that feeling. Just looking at her roused the same desire in me, joining us in a wordless bond of kindred need.

"I hope you were impressed."

"You outranked every opponent. Though, to be fair, I believe all were frightened of hurting you."

"True. And that's the most frustrating thing about it."

"But only in the beginning. As the fight went on, they became distressed by your obvious skill, then humiliated once they realized no amount of effort would help them win. Then some became angry and others became vengeful, as is common when conceited men are humbled."

She quirked a smile. "You're very observant."

It seemed I'd lost control of my tongue. "Some were inept. I wonder why they've been given their place in the army. Some were sluggish, as though they'd woken late from their sleep." I should shut up before I accidentally revealed myself, but I couldn't seem to stop. A week of near silence, and my mouth was now loose, mostly because I was now on my favorite topic. "Most read your strategy wrong and were too quick to anger. They were arrogant and impatient and foolishly believed brute strength would win them a bout. I would rank two of those you fought mildly worthy of another fight."

She was staring at me, her mouth slightly ajar. I should've stopped at the start, but there was a twinkling mischief growing in her eyes.

Her laugh was like a cool wind fingering its way through

your pelt during a hard run. She had a plain face, but I believed it would grow enduring the longer time spent with her.

"The outdoors has made you very chatty. I believe that's the most you've said to me since you arrived."

"You're queen." To explain my near mute responses.

She rolled her eyes. "I'm far more comfortable when I forget about that. You know, before they dressed me in this title, I was the king's blade."

"Oh." My surprise wasn't convincing because Tamas had shared that piece of knowledge.

The title King's Blade suited her better. I sensed she would slowly suffocate on the throne. I have the same intuition about Tamas, but sitting upon the throne in the north carries a different meaning than it does in the south. He would fare better in the north, where freedom to run through the wilds was still valued, even for those who ruled. However, Tamas would ascend to the Tarragonan throne. I felt sure he would lose a part of himself when he did.

She sighed, as if burdened by the memory that she was now queen. "You seem to know a great deal about sword play."

I wasn't ready for the change of direction in our conversation. A faint tingle of unease snaked inside my belly, signaling how perilously close the question came to triggering my admission. "I grew up surrounded by a lot of men. Though, they mostly liked to use their fists. Close blood ties to my...family would often visit and with them came their love of sword fighting. That's how I learned most of what I know."

She was looking at me with fresh eyes, as if looking beyond the tall maid with clumsy hands and seeing me for the first time.

You're such a fool. I should leave before I exposed myself, but hers was the first sincere smile I'd seen and genuine interest I'd felt since arriving at the castle.

"You sound fortunate in your family."

"Very."

"Do they live close?"

"No." This was dangerous. I shouldn't have seated myself where we'd run into each other, nor should I have stayed.

"Your current employment must be stifling after your adventurous childhood?"

"I'm deeply appreciative of what I've been given."

She glanced across at the Salmun, waiting a distance off to the side, then turned to the wagon, rummaging around inside. With her back to me, I couldn't see what she was doing.

Suddenly she spun, releasing a dagger that seemed to fly from no-where. In the second I caught the tip with my Huungardred reflexes, I realized my mistake.

"That's impressive," she said, easing out of her thrower's stance.

My heart spiked into a jagged beat. I glanced beyond her to the Salmun, relieved to see they were positioned in such a way, the wagon plus Tressya would have blocked their view. Tressya looked over her shoulder, following my gaze.

Seeing the Salmun remained like stone, she turned back to me. "I'd ask you to join my next fight, but I'm sure that will raise some eyebrows."

My mind was in such a panic, all I could think to do was escape. Rather than reply, I curtseyed, mumbled an apology, then tried to hurry away.

"It's customary to wait until you're dismissed."

I froze, taking in subtle breaths to calm myself. No one here was a match for a Huungardred, except the Salmun. I couldn't reveal myself.

"The dagger."

I glanced down, noticing it in my hand without having felt its weight.

Tressya held out her hand.

I returned it, averting my eyes as I assumed was expected of me, then waited in torturous silence. Finally, Tressya spoke. "I enjoyed our chat, Ryia. I look forward to a time when we can continue. You may go."

I felt her shrew gaze on me as I dashed away. And then I felt something else, a funny sensation, like small vibrations, sending ripples across my chest. I staggered, clutching a hand to my heart.

This was the disciple's curse. Tressya was suspicious. I found my feet, then doubled my pace, resisting the urge to bolt for the trees and instead headed back to the castle.

Romelda was a skilled witch. I could only hope her magic was powerful enough to bury my true nature beneath my disguise, sealing it from intruders.

CHAPTER
THIRTEEN

TAMAS

Razohan would never demean themselves by taking the form of a rodent, yet I had to be cunning. Taking another apostle's life would rouse too many suspicions, especially considering the inexplicable events Tressya and I had undoubtedly caused the last time we were here, so I spared an apostle's life and took a rodent's instead. I soon discovered rats were quite intelligent, though their minds were easily manipulated. And while I loathed placing myself in such a vulnerable position, the rat proved my best disguise when it came to entering fortresses fortified by the Salmun's presence.

I'd arrived in Tolum not long prior to entering Emberforge, taking longer to reach the south because of unfavorable winds. Perched atop the grand entrance gates of Emberfell, I observed Tressya boarding a carriage alongside an older woman, garbed in what appeared to be mourning attire, yet clearly not the former queen. A single glance at her taut body, confident gait, and stern expression told me it was the Mother. She moved with swift, deliberate steps, vigilantly surveying her surroundings. It was a good thing I remained in eagle form, for staying hidden from someone as perceptive and skilled as the Mother would be a challenge.

I'd followed the carriage from up high, until I was confident of where they were heading, then took the direct route, beating them to Emberforge.

From my vantage point on a spire, in a quandary as to the quickest way enter Emberforge, my eagle eyes had spied a rat. Rather than making it a meal, the urge governed chiefly by the eagle, I decided it was the perfect disguise—once I swallowed my prejudice.

Entering the throne room, I discovered my feelings had changed. I couldn't explain how or why, but I no longer felt the incessant craving to sit upon the Bone Throne once again.

During the weeks I was kept in the north, I longed to return to the Bone Throne and feel what I could only describe as the late King Ricaud's spirit pass through me. This desire filled my head as much as my need to return to Tressya. Yet, here I stood with mere feet to reach the dais upon which the throne sat and I balked.

I had come here to find one of the three apostles, holding the keys to the sanctum of solmira, determine to finally find the Senjel Oracles, but once I'd stepped foot in Emberforge, my feet brought me to the throne room.

Coming upon the hour, Emberforge would fall silent during the vigil of devotion. Apostles without duties would spend their quiet contemplation in one of their favorite temples, emptying the corridors. There was no better time for me to sit upon the throne, given it was right in front of me.

Instead, I listened to the quiet shuffle of slippered feet as a handful of apostles moved along the corridor outside the throne room. No one was to enter the throne room without the presence of one of the Salmun, so I felt sure I wouldn't be discovered, and it was a simple matter of assuming my new form if I heard someone approaching.

Just get up there.

I was running out of time to hunt down one of the three holders of the keys. Fists palmed, I strode the remaining distance across the dark stone floor and up onto the black stone dais. I slumped heavy onto the throne, then inhaled long and deep before easing against the backrest, feeling the carved faces of the long-lost deities jutting into my spine—presumedly, King Ricaud didn't make a habit of sitting on the Bone Throne for long.

I eased out a few more breaths as I gripped the skeletal armrests, fighting against a sudden surge of revulsion that felt like claws scraped across my stomach. I could feel the corners of my lips pull back, feel the slight sting in my gums as my fangs descended and a soft snarl escaped, vibrating across my lips.

The Eone had warned me of the Bone Throne's corruptive power. Perhaps this was the reason it was so difficult for me to remain seated? But the Eone's words were likely lies. I would be naïve to believe any of what they said after they'd invaded my dreams and memories, looking to manipulate me for their gain. More likely, my reluctance to remain on the Bone Throne was born of the Eone's dishonest influence.

I didn't want to believe that our legends of the benevolent King Ricaud were lies. The blooded carried the memories of their ancestors, according to Romelda, which meant they would know the truth. The Nazeen wouldn't stand beside a tyrant. Unless their memories were corrupted.

I launched up from the throne, unable to remain seated any longer. Too many conflicting thoughts muddled my mind. This was the curse of the Eone. Their poisonous whispers were infecting me, causing me to doubt everything I'd known to be true, to doubt the blooded Nazeen, unmatched in their loyalty to the Bone Throne

Movement cleared my mind, enabled me to think, and there was little room for me to pace on the dais, so I leaped down onto the stone floor to stand amongst the flecks of white embedded in the black floor marble.

I gazed at the starry floor beneath my feet, realizing it resembled a scene from my dreams; a single dream, crafted by the Eone. They either drew upon my memories of this throne room to recreate that scene, or the ruined castle atop the mountain and its surroundings were the source of the stone used to build Emberforge's throne room, indicating that the ruined castle indeed existed.

Two apostles in conversation approached. I recognized them by their shuffling feet and the respectfully subdued tone of their voices. Did this mean the vigil of devotion had ended, showing I'd lost track of time? I ignored them, trusting they wouldn't wish to face the Salmun's sanctions for entering the throne room alone.

My heart skipped a beat when the slippered feet paused outside the door, their conversation turning to a whisper. I glanced over my shoulder, checking the door was firmly closed.

At the sound of the door handles turning, I transformed back into a rat and scurried toward the shadows cast by the stone dais, thanking my luck the room was dim.

"I fear this isn't wise."

Thanks to Petrulus, I recognized Wellard's voice.

"The time for keeping secrets has ended. We have to be bold."

And that was Plesy, the scribe master and member of a small band of apostles disloyal to the Salmun. Encroaching where he shouldn't, alongside a member of the rebel apostles, meant Wellard was one of them.

"This is too great a risk. The whereabouts of all the Salmun are not accounted for. And we don't even know if this will work. We've failed so many times, I'm afraid we'll never succeed."

Though he knew of their presence, and was slowly surmounting his fear, flirting with the idea of joining them, Petrulus was not a part of this rebel group. The day I took his soul, I'd learned from Petrulus all I would learn about them. But I wanted to learn more.

"Courage, Wellard. We can't afford to be cowards. The queen needs us. She needs all the information we can gather for her."

My nose twitched at hearing her name.

"We don't even know if we can trust her. She's one of them, and this is her herit—"

"She's not one of them, you fool. How can she be? You know that. The Salmun's curse has remained for a millennium. There are no Tannard bastards within Tolum."

There was nothing within the throne room except the throne to interest them, so why were they here?

"The prophecy said the bloodborn would come from the north."

"It seems likely now the prophecy actually meant a bloodborn with links to the north. Someone must have transcribed it wrong. An easy mistaken given the complexities of the ancient tongue and augurs' penchant for speaking in riddles. I said nothing about this when I spoke to the queen."

Tressya spoke to him?

"That you spoke to the queen is something I'm still recovering from."

That cunning little minx. She'd already learned of the apostles' betrayal of the Salmun. And now she had them on her side.

"It's as I said, Wellard. It's time to be brave. We must trust the great Goddess Ovia is protecting us and steering us on the right path. She sent us Tressya."

I almost released a squeak on hearing the Eone's name.

"If you think so." Wellard sounded far from convinced.

Goddess Ovia. If I was a man, I'd spit. This proved the apostles had found some reference to the Eone in their extensive library. However, not understanding their true nature, they assumed the Eone was part of the old religion. Though, it was possible the Eone falsified the historical accounts by ensuring they were recorded favorably, or perhaps they really claimed divinity.

"I know so, brother. And that's why we must at least try our best to help the queen."

"We'll be no use to her if the Salmun catches us in here."

"Courage, brother."

I remained in the dais's shadow, watching the two of them pass close by, heading to the back of the throne. For what reason could they head back there? Once they'd passed, I followed, scuttling beside the rock, using its shadow for shelter.

The last glimpse I got before Wellard blocked my view was Plesy placing his hand on the rock underneath the throne. It grew even more bizarre when Plesy fell to his knees. Was he going to pray to Ovia for divine help?

The two chanted in whispers, using a foreign or ancient tongue, perhaps passed down by the Eone, through whatever teachings the apostles had found. My ears twitched as I tried to catch most of the words. I had a good ear for foreign languages, but whispered and then filtered through the rat's brain, meant what they chanted was too difficult to decipher.

Wellard dropped to his knees beside Plesy, joining his hands with Plesy's on the rock under the throne.

"It's taking too long," Wellard said, interrupting the chant.

"Trust, Wellard. Just a little longer." Plesy continued his chanting. Wellard soon rejoined him.

The dim golden light from the flaming torches bracketed to the walls, failed to reach behind the throne, making it safe for me to creep closer, though I suspected neither would bother about a rat.

Staying close to the rock, I halted upon feeling a burgeoning warmth at my side. Turning my head towards the rock, I noticed the warmth drying my nose. Could it be the rock was slowly heating?

With my curiosity ignited, I dared crawl forward until I was next to Wellard's slippered feet. At the corner of my sensitive eyes, I spied a flicker of dim light and not the sunset glow of the flaming torches. This light was a true milky white. I was too small to see what was happening upon the rock, where the two apostles laid their hands, but whatever was happening involved magic.

The apostles wielded magic—perhaps only rudimentary at best, but magic nonetheless; the air was imbued with its distinctive aroma. Although the Razohan did not wield magic, my time spent with Romelda allowed me to witness her craft and recognize the smell. I doubted the apostles were natural-born magic wielders, suspecting instead that their abilities might have been gained through centuries of managing and studying the vast collections in their library. However, I had never heard of such a phenomenon occurring before.

I was profoundly curious about their intent. Did they hope to tap into some residual dormant magic within the Bone Throne, if such a thing even existed? The apostles were a great puzzle, far more interesting than I had initially surmised when I assumed the form of Petrulus on my first visit to Emberforge. As a peripheral member of the rebellion within the apostles, he had given me little valuable information about them. I now regretted not taking the soul of someone more deeply embedded in this rebel faction.

For a moment, I pondered their reaction if I revealed myself to them, then pushed the thought aside. They would see me as a direct rival, Tressya's nemesis. But if I could convince them that Tressya and I were united in our fight against the Salmun—which we might not be—would they help guide me to the Senjel Oracles? Time was my true enemy, and a simple path to the Oracles would be invaluable.

The sound of running feet, heading toward the throne room, silenced their chants.

"We're caught," Wellard shrieked.

I had to be quick to dodge Wellard's feet as Plesy dragged him up. "Don't be a fool. It's not the Salmun. Though they're likely the reason for the haste."

The heavy doors creaked open.

"Plesy, the Salmun have arrived," someone yelled from across the room—another member of the rebel group.

Plesy grabbed Wellard's cloak and pulled him around. "We were so close," he grumbled.

"No time now," Wellard said. "We have to get out of here."

Curses they were disturbed. I was curious to discover what it was they almost achieved. While they hurried from the throne room, I scaled to the top of the rock and sniffed my way to the spot where both had held their hands.

The rock still held the warmth of more than their hands. The tiny pads on my feet grew almost too hot, but I resisted scuttling away. Instead, I tuned into the faint pulse of energy now tickling up my legs. Magic.

Either the apostles' magic was weak or far greater magic

protected the rock: Salmun magic. What would the Salmun want to conceal? I had no time to contemplate this before others entered the room.

The throne room door burst open. From between the throne's legs, I saw Tressya. The first time in too long, and it left me reeling. Could it be possible she'd grown more beautiful during our separation?

Whether by her choice, she'd shed her dowdy fashion and was dressed in the splendor of Tarragona's finest fashionable gowns. The deep green of the fabric contrasted against her brilliant blue eyes. The gown of silk and lace, cinched at the waist, disguised nothing of her lithe frame. She was small and lacking the muscle I usually found so attractive, but she made up for that in the agile way she moved her body and the cunning of her mind.

It was totally inappropriate for me to think on all the other ways she knew how to move her body when the Salmun had entered the room with her, but damn if my eyes wouldn't leave her, and I couldn't stop my thoughts straying to our night spent together.

You're still poison for me. The perfect poison for me.

I shuffled back into the shadow cast by the legs of the throne. The faint pulse of the residual energy still tickled and warmed the hairs on my belly; irritating, but I couldn't afford to move about else I might draw the Salmun's attention. It wasn't in my nature to hide, but the Salmun would have means of ridding pests with a wave of one finger.

Tressya's stride faltered as her left arm twitched. Her eyes briefly flared, and she glanced around the room.

She knew I was here. My mark would give me away. But I

was safe as long as I stayed still and no one went poking underneath the throne, and I wasn't sure how she'd react to our first meeting. Regardless of my craving to speak with her, I had to remember Romelda's warning. Tressya had called for the Mother. I was uncertain of her allegiance—had she returned to the Sistern? Yet, there was a method to uncover the truth.

Curses. I would never breach the soul vow merely for clarity. Having bonded my soul to hers, there was a deep yearning within me for our souls to merge, our bodies likewise—in a more primal way. However, I couldn't act on these desires until she made the choice to reciprocate, to accept my blood and unite us in an unbreakable bond.

"This way, Your Majesty." The Salmun nodded his head, showing as much respect to the queen as he thought she deserved, but Tressya appeared not to hear him.

And where was the Mother? I'd seen her enter the carriage with Tressya. At some point, between Emberfell and Emberforge, they seemed to have lost her.

"I wish to be alone." There was no authority in her voice.

"Your Majesty, I don't understand."

"It's quite simple. I wish to be left alone."

"In the throne room, Your Majesty?"

"Give me time."

"May I ask why?"

"Why am I forced to explain myself?" There was sudden grit to her tone. "I want solitude to contemplate my fate. And the Bone Throne is very much a part of my fate, or so you've led me to believe. And since you've avoided my questions regarding anything to do with the throne, particularly the

Etherweave, I believe it's fair you at least grant me this one wish."

"It's understandable Your Majesty would find my silence in such matters frustrating."

"I've presented the list of those I've selected to sit upon the queen's council. They'll arrive in Emberfell by the end of the week in time for the convening of the first council. What else are you waiting for?"

"Your grief, Your Majesty. You lost those precious to you. We're simply giving Your Majesty time to adjust."

"Cut the shit, Orphus. Your silence suits your purposes only. If you were so worried about my grief, you wouldn't hesitate to grant me this one wish."

Was it possible I would find new uncovered parts of her to love? The queen was finding her voice, and I loved it.

"Of course, Your Majesty. There is no question of granting you time in the presence of the Bone Throne. If you promise me not to sit upon it."

Tressya fixed Orphus with a quizzical look for several moments, her expression one of puzzlement. "That's an odd request."

"Not odd, Your Majesty. I'm only thinking of your protection."

She glanced at the throne. "Are you superstitious, Orphus? Do you think the bones will come to life and strangle me?"

"No, my queen. But the Bone Throne is a relic of a turbulent past when dangerous powers were alive in the world. It's a caution, Your Majesty."

Her refusal to yield to the Salmun was admirable, but his

concern about the Bone Throne was confusing, unless it was as the Eone had forewarned and the Salmun knew. The ache in my head was bound to worsen as I tried to discern the truth from the lies given many intended to control whoever sat on the Bone Throne.

I couldn't read the snake's eyes with his hood drawn low on his forehead, concealing his face. If I could, I'd know where his true intentions lay, though I would guess they weren't respectful, honorable or loyal to the crown.

"Very well. I give you my word. And now I want my solitude."

Orphus inclined his head. "We can spare some time before the ritual begins. I shall wait by the door."

"There is but one definition of solitude." Tressya didn't even bother to glance in his direction.

If I was a man, I'd reveal my presence by chuckling.

"Your Majesty is wise," was all Orphus said.

"Make sure my spiritual advisor also respects my privacy."

"She shall not pass." And with that, Orphus departed.

Spiritual advisor. For someone of the Mother's power, it was a belittling position, and I couldn't help but smile at the irony. She had to be somewhere within Emberforge, yet her absence from Tressya's side was peculiar, unless the Salmun had barred her from entering the throne room.

When the door to the throne room closed, Tressya released a sigh, then turned toward the throne. Eager as I was to speak with her, it took effort to stay where I was, and not transform back into a man. But I needed to satisfy my curiosity.

Why did Tressya want to be alone? Did it have something to do with the two apostles, and what they were doing behind the throne?

Tressya strode toward the dais. She hitched her skirts and leaped upon the rock, as agile as a predator. Yards and yards of fabric to tumble on and slow her down, I couldn't imagine it was easy. The way she moved momentarily distracted me from my curiosity about why she sought solitude, leading me to ponder something else entirely. Could it be possible Tressya was gaining the traits of a Razohan?

No sooner had I thought the question than I was seized by my tail and dangled in front of Tressya's eyes.

"I never dreamed our first meeting would be like this. And if you dare think to bite me, I'll put you under my heel."

She was, as ever, breathtaking in her guile. I released my hold on my rodent form, maneuvering myself as I transformed into a man so that I landed in her lap. "I knew you'd be pleased."

Tressya shoved me off her lap. I relented, catching my balance and landing feet first on the stone floor.

It seemed neither of us had words for this moment, and I was content to stare at her face through my eyes, and not that of the rodent, for as long as she would let me. I wasn't sure if she consciously sucked on her lower lip, but doing so distracted me by kindling a desire that never grew dormant.

"You've just arrived, and you came straight to Emberforge." She relaxed back into the throne, crossing her legs with the air of someone in repose, but her accusatory tone revealed her emotions. Dare I believe she would have preferred me to visit her first.

"What makes you think I've just arrived?"

"Are the Razohan known for their rotten memories?"

"The bite mark." I nodded in understanding.

Bonded partners, through their shared blood links, could effortlessly track each other, yet Tressya had not accepted my blood. Had she sensed my return to Tolum the instant it happened? For anyone else, I would deem it impossible. Even if my mark on her revealed my presence in the throne room, it wasn't potent enough to disclose my exact location within Tolum. Only fully bonded partners attained such a profound connection. But Tressya was extraordinary in the most charming ways, and it wouldn't surprise me if she had developed some Razohan ability surpassing our own.

"You promised me I wouldn't turn into a beast."

I folded my arms across my chest. "If you are, it has nothing to do with me."

"I snarl, for mercy's sake."

"You realize that's a love poem to a Razohan."

She sucked in a breath. "I have no intention of wooing you. And if I sprout fur, I'll gut you."

"Surely your Mother shared your heritage with you."

"Under duress and with limited details. Needless to say, I was horrified."

"There's nothing to be horrified about, Tress—"

"Your Majesty."

"Thanks, but I don't deserve the title just yet."

She rolled her eyes.

"I'll teach you all there is to know about becoming a Razohan. The Salmun and your Mother won't understand what it means to become a shapeshifter, they won't understand the changes—"

"And you understand what it is like for someone like me?"

"Considering that's my nature."

"You were born a Razohan, of course you do. But I grew up believing I was human. How can you understand what it means for a human to turn into a beast?"

"You must feel stronger and faster than you ever have. Isn't that worth something?"

She tilted her head up, seeming to ponder my question. "There's that." And her lips twitched, before she glanced off to the side with a frown.

I followed her gaze and saw nothing that would make her frown. She straightened in her seat as if trying to shrug what had bothered her, then she rose from the throne and jumped lightly down off the dais as if she wasn't lumbered with reams of clothing. That was something she wouldn't have been able to do without tripping over her hem if not for the Razohan's blood in her veins.

"We're out of time, Razohan. Orphus will be back soon, and we're gathering a crowd."

My brows rose. "We're what?"

"It's a quirk of mine you'll never have."

"I'm confused."

"Yes, you were never bright."

I lurched forward, seized her arm and pulled her close—at least my speed still surprised her, giving her no time to dodge or squirm away. Unless I'd misread her soft gasp and the slight part of her lips, I'd subdued her outrage at being manhandled.

"We need to talk." *And I need to kiss you.* "But not yet." *On both accounts.*

She still smelt so good, fresh, sweet and with a hint of the fire that I knew ran through her veins.

"I agree," Tressya said.

I required time to discern her allegiance before disclosing too much. With that consideration, my yearning for an intimate connection with her intensified, yet I restrained myself, pulling back from inquisitively probing her emotions before delving too deeply. "Is there a time when you're alone?"

"Unless you're planning on entering my bedchamber. No."

"Your bedchamber it is then."

She leveled her stern gaze at me. "Don't even think about entering as a rodent."

"I'm glad that's the only thing in this conversation that concerns you."

Weeks apart, yet we effortlessly slipped back into our familiar conversational rhythm; I hadn't realized how much I missed it.

"I have means of dealing with any surprises."

"I would have been disappointed if you didn't." My traitorous eyes wandered to her lips.

Strangely, Tressya's attention seemed to be drawn off to the side of the room once again, though I knew there was no one there. She remained the enigma. That thought circled my mind to the dangerous mysteries of the Eone. "Have you had any bizarre dreams of late?"

"I haven't dreamed of you once."

"I'm sure that's a lie. What about anyone else? A group of four, perhaps?"

"You're weird."

"Is that a no?"

"I'll likely suffer nightmares tonight now I know you're back. Is that good enough?"

Why should I expect a straightforward answer to my questions when she had never provided one before? She would remain frustratingly obstinate as much as she was addictively alluring.

I smirked. "I see the Mother hasn't softened your demeanor."

She struggled out of my embrace, but I tightened my hold. She swallowed, her eyes blazing blue like the sky on fire.

"I'd argue against that. I can't think of any important reason for you to know my fantasies."

I flicked the tip of her nose. "I only asked for dreams. It's you who thought of fantasies. Perhaps when I come to your—"

She shoved me in the chest, pressing her lips to hide her smile. I resisted her escape.

"You're wrong about me." I lowered my head, coming in close. "I reached Emberfell first, in time to see you enter the carriage beside a crow of an old woman who turned out to be the Mother Divine. I followed for a while, but once I knew for certain where you were heading, I came direct. This meeting was not entirely by chance. Where's your Mother Divine, by the way?"

"You do nothing by chance. And the Mother is none of your concern."

"Neither do I ask questions without a good reason. And she's a blade that needs blunting."

"Your reasons are your own and have no influence on my decisions or actions. And the Mother is currently entertained by the Salmun elsewhere in Emberforge."

"Wise of the Salmun not to trust her. She must prickle with such a demeaning rank."

"Such trivial matters do not distract the Mother."

"I know you're no longer loyal to the Sistern, so stop defending her." A sting laced my voice, my annoyance sharpened at her continued pretense of caring about the Sistern. But maybe Romelda was right, and Tressya had returned to the stronghold of her former order.

She leaned in closer, tilting her chin up, locking her eyes on mine. I swear I couldn't look away if I tried.

"I won the war. How's that for loyalty?"

I flinched at the reminder. "You fought for Andriet alone." Please let me be right.

She swallowed, blinked, then turned away.

"I'm sorry. In the end, I didn't intend for him to die."

I resisted hauling her close when she backed away. This was the wrong place and the wrong time to have the difficult conversation we needed to share—no breaking the soul vow. Tressya and I were equals, both destined to sit upon the Bone Throne and wield the Etherweave. I yearned for a deeper connection, but for now, we needed to compromise, and that could only be achieved with honesty, which required trust, and I doubted she was ready for the vulnerability trust required. Neither was I.

There was a curious glint in her eye when she returned her attention to me. "Do you believe Orphus's excuse to keep me from sitting on the throne?"

The change in conversation jarred me. I thought I'd wounded her by mentioning Andriet, yet I'd done the opposite, enlivening her astute mind. Unfortunately, it wasn't a question I could answer right now.

"In all honesty, I don't know."

"You're not normal by any means, but you sat upon it once."

"Is that your best compliment?"

Ignoring my attempt to ease the conversation in a different direction, she continued. "Why would he say such a thing? It's a pile of bones."

"Magic is never just a pile of bones. If you haven't come to sit on the throne, why has Orphus brought you here?"

"You've only just arrived on my soil, and you're already demanding answers," she snapped. "Since when have I had to answer to Tarragona's foe?"

I tried to keep my expression neutral, even though her words felt like a slap to my face. "Foe, is it now?"

Dare I believe she looked abashed? She was definitely at a loss for words. Perhaps the first time I'd ever seen her fall silent. She turned away from me, taking a deep breath. I watched the small crease in her brow deepen and could almost hear the thoughts whirring in her mind. Finally, she returned her gaze to me. "I don't know. Are you?"

I stared deeply into her eyes, unable to voice the words I

dearly wanted to say. *I'll never be your foe.* That was the truth in my heart, but did she carry the same conviction? Was the Mother her anchor, the Salmun her guiding force?

Our eyes became our tethers, binding us together as we searched deep within, hoping to discover the truth we both hesitated to voice. I was acutely aware I hadn't answered her question. She once knew my answer; I wanted her to remember, to see it in my eyes.

The longer we held each other's gaze, the softer her expression became. In that moment, I realized I hadn't lost her completely. My fingers twitched with the urge to smooth her brow. I'd come for the Senjel Oracles, to save my people and the realm, but mostly, I'd come for her. I'd always believed this was *our* journey, that my foes were her foes, and that unity was our only path to success. I sincerely hoped she believed that, too.

It was Tressya who broke our gaze first. She clenched her fists beside her. "I'm sick of the Salmun keeping their secrets."

I understood why she broke the spell between us. The moment had become too intimate for two people on opposing sides, whom everyone said were adversaries. The last we saw each other, I was waging war on her people, and she was defeating me.

"They've told you nothing about the Bone Throne or the Etherweave? What about your Mother? She must know a thing or twenty, since she went to all this bother to place you on the throne."

"Talking to the Mother is like talking to stone."

I loved that she so easily confided in me, something

usually reserved for friends, family and lovers. I cherished this glimpse of vulnerability, a conspiratorial moment that could only bring us closer.

"Sounds like there's a disgruntled chick within the nest."

Tressya reared on me. "And you're no better. You felt something when you sat on that throne. I know you did. But you keep quiet."

"Do you trust me?" Perhaps it was too early in my return to ask this question. I couldn't hardly expect a truthful answer. But this was pivotal.

She blinked, then snapped. "What?"

"It's a simple question."

She folded her arms across her chest in a defensive pose. "You never give me straight answers."

"Touché. But I'm asking in all sincerity. Do. You. Trust. Me."

She blinked again, then sucked in a long breath. "I ask the same of you."

I was surprised by how much it hurt that she refused to answer. "Then we have a problem." Maybe I was being childish, playing her game and hiding my true feelings. A lot was at stake. All it would take was… I stepped back, half turning away from her, exhaling deeply. No, I couldn't break the soul vow and force my way inside to learn her true feelings toward me.

She dipped her head, avoiding my gaze, but relaxed her arms to her sides. "I'm a queen in a foreign realm with no idea how to survive the challenges of my throne." She spoke in a low and measured tone. "Then there is this." She waved her hand toward the Bone Throne. "I'm expected to rule from the Bone Throne when I don't understand what that means, and no one can or will inform me."

That was why she called for her Mother. It had to be. She was drowning in a realm where she had no allies, and the only person she could trust was the woman who'd taught her from birth to be strong. My heart lightened with the thought.

Instinct drove me forward, a yearning to hold her close, reassure her she was not alone. The Salmun, the Mother, the Eone all hoped to control the ruler of the Bone Throne using whatever magical and vile means possible. But Tressya was not alone. Hers and my fates were linked. I wanted her to know that. That together we would survive a destiny neither of us chose.

But I was too late. With the sound of the door handle turning, I transformed back into a rodent and scuttled behind Tressya's ample skirts.

"Orphus," Tressya almost shouted. "As you can see, I've barely moved. And you'll be interested to know I don't dream. At least nothing I remember."

I disappeared into the shadows of the dais, sneezing chuckles as I went. I'd missed my opportunity to gather the keys from one of the three who guarded the sanctum of solmira, but something told me learning the reason the Salmun brought Tressya into the throne room would be of greater value.

CHAPTER
FOURTEEN

TRESSYA

He remained as prideful as I remembered, unfortunately he also remained as gorgeous and masterfully adept at infiltrating places he wasn't welcomed. I'd struggled to gather my thoughts, warring with the desire to throw myself into his arms and kiss him like he was my last breath. At the same time, I wanted to punch him in the face. To deepen my confusion, the skin around the bite mark felt as though a thousand butterflies were fluttering across the surface like a caress, reminding me of our special night.

The room had grown crowded since Tamas transformed into a man. The spirits of King Ricaud's army gathered to the left of the throne, while Tamas had likely disappeared back into the shadows at the base of the dais.

"I'm ready to go on," I announced to fill the sudden awkward silence.

Half of me dreaded what this ritual would entail, the other half was curious. The prelate had approached me late yesterday afternoon, informing me we had to return to Emberforge tomorrow. I didn't believe his reason but was eager to return, thinking perhaps I could talk with Plesy again. It had been over a week since we last spoke, and I'd struggled to find time to escape my constant entourage. I wanted to meet more of his friends, those secretly practicing their magic in the shadow of the Salmun. Then there was the Salmun's secret library. I was certain whatever they kept down there was exactly what I needed to read—what Tamas had hoped to find.

Apparently, the Salmun intended to perform a ritual to solidify my position on the Bone Throne, enhancing my connection and ability to wield the Etherweave. The Salmun claimed the ritual was as ancient as the throne itself and asserted that without it, my mastery over the Etherweave was doomed to failure. I was sure most, if not all, of what he said was a lie, but I was powerless to refuse. Besides, my curiosity and desire to know more wouldn't let me.

If only I'd asked Tamas if he knew of any such ritual. He'd likely omit the truth in his reply or weave a tale to his liking that had nothing to do with my question, but for a moment there, before Orphus entered, I'd grown apprehensive about going through with the ritual.

I was already tied to the Mother in ways I couldn't imagine, and believed Gusselan's warning regarding the Levenians. The Salmun had a millennium of time to share their knowledge of the Etherweave with their master, King Bezhani. I doubted such a ruthless king would arrive on

Tarragona's shore expecting to bow before a woman, even if she sat on the Bone Throne with the Etherweave in her veins. Like all ruthless men, the king would have a plan enabling him to seize the power for himself, and that plan likely began with this ritual Orphus hoped to perform.

Unless I could come up with my own plan in time, I was stuck. Perhaps I should've insisted the Mother's presence. She was familiar; the Salmun were an unknown. As much as I now loathed her presence, she was better than the Salmun with magic I had yet to understand. At least I felt I had a chance of outmaneuvering her and overcoming whatever she'd done to me to force our link.

However, for the first time since I had assumed the throne, Orphus was adamant; the Mother was explicitly forbidden from attending. While Orphus relented, allowing her to travel with us to Emberforge, a wall of Salmun guard barred her from entering the inner sanctum.

As Orphus lead me toward the back of the Bone Throne, I wondered where Tamas had disappeared to. The shadows cast by the rock and throne were the only decent hiding places, unless he scurried into the dark at the edges of the room, away from the flaming torches, but I couldn't see Tamas as a man willing to bury himself far inside the shadows.

I forgot about Tamas once I realized exactly where Orphus was leading me—the Salmun's library beneath the Bone Throne. How could I be so fortunate to have the prelate lead me to the one place I most wanted to discover? Unfortunately, it would be impossible for me to search the library with Orphus so close beside me, but at least I would get a look inside and perhaps learn something I could share with Plesy and his group of rebel apostles.

In silence, Orphus placed a hand upon the rock underneath the throne, closed his eyes, then mumbled a chant too low for me to discern.

I shielded my eyes when the rock beneath his palm glowed a brilliant white. I tried to peek through my fingers, but the light became so bright it obscured Orphus. The tinge of magic tickled my nose, and an audible vibration rung in my ears.

No wonder Plesy and his friends were having a hard time finding a way in. I had very limited experience with magic, and what Orphus did now seemed to take a lot of skill and power to achieve.

"Your Majesty," Orphus said.

The light was gone. Orphus stood in front of a hole in the rock, disappearing down into the darkness. Coming closer, I saw steep, stone steps leading into a rock carved tunnel heading deep beneath the throne.

A heavy sensation swelled my stomach, spreading tingles to my feet as I stared into the opening. It reminded me of a dungeon.

"Down there?" My voice sounded small.

"There is nothing to fear, Your Majesty. This is a sacred place created by those loyal to the Bone Throne and devoted to the ruler of the Etherweave."

"By those loyal, you mean the Salmun?"

"We have given our lives to serving the Tarragona rulers. The heirs to the Bone Throne."

"Did Andriet and Juel know of this place?"

"Of course, Your Majesty." Orphus inclined his head. His usual way of bowing without bowing.

I knew he was lying. I was sure Andriet would've told me about the secret library had he known.

It was on my insistence Andriet remained at Emberfell, haunting Daelon's every move. I was desperate to protect his presence and feared his constant interruptions and outburst would muddle me so much I would accidentally reveal him to the shrewd Salmun.

The prickling hairs on the back of my neck told me King Ricaud's men were drawing near. They were an unsettling sight. Their hatred and disgust for the Salmun was unmistakable in their expression, impossible to disguise beneath the fatal wounds they bore. If Orphus wasn't present, I would question them about the hidden library, but the extent of my spiritweaving was one secret I would keep from the Salmun.

"You may enter." Orphus moved aside, welcoming me to descend.

Anxiety made my heart beat stronger, sharpening my focus. *Think quick.* The understanding I was about to get caught in a ritual tempered my desire to know more about their secret library. I was sure this ritual would bind me in ways dangerous to my free will.

I caught movement in the corner of my eyes, but resisted the urge to glance towards it for a better look.

"I would feel more comfortable if you went first. Dark places make me anxious."

"It won't be dark for long." And Orphus turned toward the entrance. A resonant noise echoed deep in his throat and a small glow of light emanated from the center of his palm. He flicked his wrist, tossing the ball of light into the opening, where it hovered just below the first few steps.

This was the second time since the Ashenlands war I'd seen the Salmun's magic. There was already a heaviness in my stomach, but the sight of Orphus's magic dragged that heaviness lower still. I was no match for magic. But if any mention of the Etherweave was to be believed, I would experience the touch of magic firsthand. I felt the welling darkness of dread as much as I felt the blooming lightness of excitement at the thought.

"I'd feel more comfortable if you go first."

"As you wish, Your Majesty."

Orphus disappeared through the cavity in the rock under the throne. I stepped closer, watching his descent, then placed my palm flat on the rock. Within a heartbeat, Tamas scurried out from his hiding place and up my arm. I plucked him off my arm, and shoved him inside my pocket bag, hidden under my layers of skirts, then dared to tickle him under the chin. He didn't bite me, which had to mean the gesture wasn't demeaning to him. If I wasn't descending into danger—my instincts told me this was so—I'd smile.

I kept a hand on the tunnel wall for balance as I descended. The rock was cool on my skin. The residue of age and magic tinged the air and tickled the inside of my nose, made my tongue feel furry and spiked the fine hairs across my neck.

There was something else about the tunnel that made me shiver. Instinctively, I reached for my throat as though expecting to feel hands inching their way around my neck.

I slowed and leaned close to the wall, inspecting the cracks and juts of rock, thinking I would find creatures making homes in the wall, like the Ashenlands pit. I got the same nervous feeling.

Our footsteps echoed off the tunnel walls and tumbled into the darkness beneath us. Orphus's light stayed close overhead, guiding us down the treacherous descent.

I stumbled on my next step as a chill creeped along behind me. I jerked, hitting my shoulder on the stone wall to avoid one of King Ricaud's men, who'd glided down to join me. And he was not alone. Taking advantage of Orphus's ignorance, as he continued to descend into the darkness below, I slowed as I glanced over my shoulder to see a group of King Ricaud's men following along behind us.

As one, they stopped and watched me with somber expressions. Devoted to King Ricaud, they endured the existence of their mortal enemy for a thousand years, observing as the Salmun debased their sacred spaces and denounced their faith. Yet, these violations diminished in significance when faced with the possibility of the Salmun seizing command of the Etherweave.

The soldier beside me overtook me to block my way. He was gruesomely attired in his death clothes and missing his right arm. His clothes he would wear with pride for the significance they held, only now they were ruined with slash marks and blood.

"You are not to descend."

I couldn't speak to him with Orphus this close.

"You will not deliver the heir to the Bone Throne into their hands."

It was a weird way to speak about me in my presence. Unless they meant someone else.

Tamas wriggled in my pocket. Perhaps curious why I'd stopped. I could feel him climbing his way through the pocket fabric, looking for the opening seam. I placed my hand over the pocket, gently pressing it closed.

"Your Majesty?" Orphus's voice carried up the tunnel steps.

"We will not let you pass."

"Give me a moment," I yelled down. *To clear my headache brought on by these spirits.*

So he wouldn't see me talking, I turned my back on Orphus, facing the way we'd come. The prelate would think I'd lost my brain, or grow suspicious with my bizarre behavior.

The last thing I needed was spirit trouble. Although the Salmun were aware of my talent, their silence since the Ashenlands war led me to believe they underestimated my capabilities, confident in their own supremacy—perhaps rightfully so. This arrogance, I suspected, was why they allowed the Mother into Emberfell. It was likely they knew she was not as she appeared, much like myself, yet they dismissed her as being an insignificant threat, which concerned me more than I wanted to admit; the Salmun were too conceited, or they had a genuine reason to feel superior. And I wasn't ready to find out.

"I'm not what you think," I whispered.

"The man concealed in your clothes—"

"I have the power to command you." I kept my voice barely above a whisper.

"Do you need help, Your Majesty?"

"No," I yelled, giving way to my frustration.

"We will not let you deliver the heir to our enemy."

This was an awkward moment to ask questions, but I would guess the spirits knew what the Salmun planned.

"Fine. Come with me then."

"We refuse to aid our ene—"

"I've got little choice but to continue down these stairs. But I may have use for you if you'll come with me."

Hearing Orphus climbing the steps, I spun.

"I'm ready."

My descent was clear. The soldier who'd blocked my path moved to one side, allowing me to pass unmolested by his touch, even if his gaze remained severe. I wasn't sure what help they could be, but the heaviness in my stomach eased, knowing my spirit army followed behind me.

Orphus waited at the bottom of the steps, standing on the stone floor, smoothed with age. Ahead lay a single passage wide enough for two people walking side-by-side. I leaned around Orphus to peer further down the corridor, spotting a faint light emanating from the right.

I counted fifty steps before we reached the end of the passage and turned right into a vast chamber. A breeze touched my face just before I entered, and I licked my lips, tasting a bitter sweetness.

I felt Tamas wriggle in my pocket once more. Afraid he would reveal himself, I placed a hand over my pocket to settle him, but he resisted. Instead, he made his way up to poke his head out of the seam in my dress.

The walls were illuminated by flaming torches, spaced

well enough apart to cast a warm glow around all the chamber's edges. In the center of the room stood a raised stone altar, dwarfed by the soaring ceiling that vanished into darkness above. Ten Salmun stood in a circle around the altar, partially blocking my view from a pedestal positioned directly under a bracketed torch at the far edge of the room. A tome sat atop the pedestal, its inlay catching the torchlight in such a way that it seemed to swirl. To be placed in such a significant way, this tome had to be special.

Except for the tome, magnificently presented, there were no other books inside this chamber as far as I could see, which made me wonder if there were other secret passages or rooms the Salmun magically concealed. I focused on the tome sitting atop its pedestal. Could it be this was the book Tamas had been searching for? The book he was still searching for, and likely the reason I found him in the throne room.

"Your Majesty." For the first time, Orphus exaggerated his bow, welcoming me into the chamber with a broad sweep of his arm.

"What is this place?"

"It was carved before the great war."

"It's a place belonging to the old king's?"

"Yes, a place where they worshipped their deities."

"Isn't that what the small temples within the inner sanctuary are for?"

"For the people, yes, but the king chose a private place for his worship."

"I thought you no longer believed in the old religion, nor

felt kinship toward any of the bastard kings that ruled before the great war."

"This is the Salmun's sanctuary now. No remnants of the old kings taint these walls."

Only your own foul deeds.

I strode further into the chamber, holding my left arm by my side to hide Tamas from prying eyes. If only he stayed buried in my pocket, but I could understand his desire to see for himself.

Behind me, my army followed through the now closed door and thick stone walls, ignoring the expansive chamber to stare solely at the Salmun. They weren't curious about the room because they'd been here before.

"This is where you practice your craft?"

"Yes."

The Salmun maintained their circle. As their queen, they all should've acknowledged my presence. Instead, they stood like stone statues, their hoods drawn low and their heads bowed. This sanctum was their stronghold, shielding them from the people's scrutiny, where they could act as they pleased. The Salmun weren't loyal to the Tarragonan throne, neither were they loyal to the heir who would one day sit upon the Bone Throne. They gave their allegiance to the Etherweave alone, and King Bezhani—perhaps not even him—a millennium was a long time to stay loyal to a distant king.

I paced around the large chamber, moving in such a way that the shadows cast by my body shielded Tamas, all the while maintaining my distance from the circle of Salmun. I was keen to get as close as I could to the mysterious book.

"What does this ritual entail?"

My hand twitched to push Tamas down into the pocket when I felt him move again.

"Very little from you, my queen. Your presence and a few drops of your blood."

"My blood?" I gasped, stopping in my tracks.

"A prick of your finger is all. You won't even notice it."

"Yet you've barely explained what it all means. If you want my blood, you'll have to give me more than what you have." A tightness welled in my chest, shortening my breath. Tamas had bound me by blood; now the Salmun would do the same. I had to think fast to escape this ritual.

"Of course, it is only fair. Perhaps this will help explain." He motioned for me to follow him as he headed toward the pedestal, and I was keen to follow.

"Before the great war, Tarragona languished under the tyranny of a succession of kings, each as malevolent as their predecessor. It wasn't until Tarragona was purged of its oppressive overlords did the benevolent victors, the Levenians, realize the source of such tyranny stemmed from a single source of power. The Etherweave."

"This is all lies!" shouted one soldier.

Of course, Orphus would give me his version of the tale, but it was handy having confirmation of his lies.

"If the Etherweave is so perverse as to corrupt those who wield it, why are you desperate to have it? Would you not be content to see it remain locked away?"

By now, we stood beside the tome. This close, its age was evident. The swirls of light I'd seen from a distance formed an ancient symbol, its meaning long lost. The book was bigger than any I'd seen before, encased in thick leather and enclosed by iron clasps spiked like the thorns crowning the serpents' heads that adorned the Bone Throne. This was definitely what Tamas had been chasing. It had to be, which meant I needed to steal it. Somehow.

For a moment, I was overcome with nervous excitement, yearning to reach for Tamas and show him exactly what I'd discovered, but what saved from my stupidity by Orphus's reply.

"The Etherweave will free itself from its tomb, whether we like it."

The soldiers who'd followed us across the chamber now circled us.

"Thus, it is our duty to prepare the next heir. For the sake of Tarragona's people and the security of all the realms, we must ensure the heir will not inherit the fates of those who have come before."

"As heir—" I began.

"Heresy," cried a soldier.

"Our king claimed the male was the heir," yelled another.

"He is a descendant of Ammelle," came yet one more cry from the spirits.

I closed my eyes against their voices and spoke. "The Etherweave has yet to rise. How do you know if this ritual will work?"

Tamas's restlessness would betray him soon. We stood under the torch flame, so there were few shadows for him to use as cover. I pressed my hand to my pocket, feeling his whiskers poking out.

"The Salmun have spent a millennium preparing for this

moment." He placed his palm on the book. "The essential knowledge is safeguarded within this sanctuary. Our powers will take care of the rest."

"What essential knowledge? You mean to say everything about the Etherweave is contained within this book?" I wasn't even looking at Orphus. The tome consumed all my attention. All my unanswered questioned, all the knowledge I longed to know about my fate, were held within these pages.

"The Senjel Oracles were written before the Great War, the result of an augur's prophecies that foresaw much of what was to come. It tells us that the true heir to the Etherweave lies within the line of the House of Tannard and foretells the rise of the Etherweave, entombed for a millennium."

"He does not speak of Ammelle's descendants," said a spirit who stood beside me. "She was daughter to our great king. The Nazeen, who entombed the Etherweave, bound its power to King Ricaud's lineage to ensure the Levenian could not use it for themselves. But the Salmun conveniently dismiss Ammelle's descendants in favor of the king's sister, who they forced into bondage by marrying her to one of the Levenian invaders once they learned of what the Nazeen had done. If you have ever heard an augur speak, then you would know this book is a maze of ramblings. The Salmun have twisted its translations to suit their own purposes."

The prelate remained silent, his hooded face turned in my direction. I couldn't see his eyes but felt his scrutiny all the same. It was as though he suspected my silent conversation with the spirits. Normally, I would say that was impossible, but with the Salmun, I couldn't be certain. To ease my discomfort, I said. "What will a drop of my blood do?" hoping to draw his attention from the book and the spirits.

"It serves as a symbol, Your Majesty. For sacrifice, unity, and allegiance."

"All that from one drop of blood."

"One must understand that to gain significant power comes at a cost. We need your oath of allegiance, a drop of blood as testament to your loyalty and dedication to Tarragona's people."

"They are nothing but whores to their foreign king," continued the spirits.

I was inclined to believe him. "Oaths are easily spoken, as easily broken... unless they're binding." That was the reason for the blood, but he hoped to bind me to the Salmun, not the Tarragonan people.

"What you say is true," Orphus murmured as he opened the book.

At once I forgot our conversation, peering down into the open pages of the book. The spirits formed a tighter circle, as though equally drawn to the Senjel Oracles, until I felt the chill of their presence creep across my back. However, it was not enough to distract me from what lay inside.

The penmanship was tiny, cramming all the yellowing pages with a small cursive scrawl. Splotches of ink blotted some of the page, and no doubt sunk through to obscure what was written underneath.

I couldn't read any of it.

"You're showing me this because?"

"Its teachings are power."

"But I can't read any of it."

"We have spent a millennium translating its teachings."

"Are those translations handy?"

"You need not bother yourself with reading them."

"Next you're going to tell me I'm to trust you know best."

"A wise queen is cautious about the nature of all things."

"Yet you expect her to accept what you're saying without question."

Orphus turned more pages with great care. Each page was the same as the last, tiny writing looking like ants running across the page. There were more ink splotches that appeared to move as he flipped gently through each page.

What could Tamas want with the tome? He had the Nazeen to tell him everything he needed to know. I doubted he would understand a word of it, though the Nazeen likely had magical means of translating what they needed.

Orphus stopped flipping on a blank page in the middle of the book, and there he left it, gently smoothing his hand across the yellowed pages.

"While the book holds many secrets. These are the most significant."

I frowned at him, then peered down at the open book, seeing only the flecks of discoloration from fibers and filaments used to make the paper.

"He is not the rightful heir," shouted a spirit.

"The Nazeen witches faithful to our king concealed the truth from their evil eyes to ensure the Salmun never discovered the location of the Etherweave," explained another.

"Because you can't read them?"

"The words rest in slumber, awaiting the heir's touch." Orphus placed his palm in the middle of the page. "The prophecy proclaims the touch of the Bone Throne's heir will bring the words into the light."

"Do you know what they'll say?"

"The Etherweave was lost for a reason," cried one of the soldiers behind me. "The words stay invisible for that same reason."

"No," Orphus admitted.

The Etherweave was lost! So that was the reason Tamas was searching for the book. Not even the Razohan knew its location because the Nazeen witches faithful to King Ricaud lost track of where it ended up. Which would mean it wasn't the Nazeen who concealed the writing from all but the heir, else they would know what was written, they would know the location of the Etherweave. Was it the augur or whoever compiled the augurs ramblings over a millennium ago who concealed the words on these pages?

"Then how do you know these blank pages are the most significant?"

"Because the most important secrets are heavily guarded."

Thank the stars, Tamas had been unusually still. Perhaps preferring to listen. He was smart enough to know it was far too risky for him to stick his little head out now.

"You want me to touch the pages?"

"There is one last essential piece of knowledge for us to glean from the Senjel Oracles. We must learn the resting place of the Etherweave, but we can only do that with your help."

"Then you know what is written?"

"We can only presume. Your Majesty, we have waited a

very long time for this moment. The Etherweave is close to being released from its binds. And when it does, it's imperative the true heir is present."

Tamas, as they believed, was the false heir.

It mattered little to the Salmun that northerner blood ran through my veins—which they knew because they were the ones to place the curse on the Tannard line, ensuring no bastards were born—I was the true heir because I was within Emberfell, under the Salmun's guard. And with this ritual, which had nothing to do with sacrifice and unity, was a magical binding.

"All you need do is place your hand on the pages, Your Majesty."

"I..." *Dammit.*

Tamas wriggled in my pocket, eager to climb out. I pressed him firm to my thigh to hold him still, knowing he was on the verge of doing something idiotic, like exposing his presence to the Salmun because he wanted to be bloody heroic.

My only escape was the spirits. I was loathed to bring them across the veil, as that in itself could cause unforeseen consequences, but it was the only way they could help me.

"I need time to think about this."

Murmurs from the circle of Salmun were like sharp claws grazing along my skin.

"You should've explained it all from the start." I backed away from the book as the murmurs became a discordant melody.

"As queen, your loyalty to Tarragona is unquestioned. And that is why I did not see the need to be explicit."

An irritating vibration began in my ears. Pressing my palms over my ears only made it worse, because it wasn't outside in the room. It was inside my head.

"Tell them to stop."

"Tell who to stop, Your Majesty?" It was the voice of a snake slithering through my mind. Orphus was standing by the pedestal, but I could've sworn he spoke in my ear, hissing his innocence when all he did was lie.

The circle of the Salmun remained shrouded in the dim torchlight, their hoods drawn low, concealing their faces. These were men who'd once knelt before me in the Ashenlands, pledging their loyalty, but only because they foresaw a time when they could compel me with their magic.

"Stop this!" I shouted, unable to shut the chanting out.

I felt Tamas wriggling in my pocket. They mustn't know he was here, and I didn't trust him to be sensible and stay hidden.

I inhaled, sent the breath deep inside as I funneled my attention even further, right down into the core of my beating heart.

Discipline. In my mind, I floated inward along my calming breath, plunging into the protective darkness of my void, my shield, and there I found my soul word. Waiting. The power of my soul word surged through me, coursing with a potent force I wasn't expecting, nor had felt before. It seared through my chest as if intent on shattering my heart and released with as much ferocity as a raging storm, leaving me feeling cleaved in two.

With the intensity at which I wielded my soul word, I swayed unsteadily on my feet as my soul word's force exploded forth. Within breaths, I realized the irritating vibration in my head caused by the Salmun's chanting had ceased. This was coupled with a noise akin to the sound of the roof caving in, and I opened my eyes to witness the devastation I'd caused. The circle of Salmun lay scattered on the ground like fallen branches from a dead tree. Orphus lay on his back amongst the rubble of the stone pedestal, unmoving. A short distance away, the Senjel Oracles lay open, its spine facing the ceiling.

I rushed over and picked the heavy book up. A quick glance over my shoulder reassured me none of the Salmun was moving. In my haste, I juggled the book, almost dropping it, then tried to balance it on my knee so I could flip through the pages. I stopped when I reached the two blank pages in the middle. Carefully, I ripped them out so as not to tear them.

Once done, I shoved them in my pocket, stuffing them on top of Tamas, then turned and ran for the door. I was almost there when the ground beneath my feet rumbled.

CHAPTER
FIFTEEN

TAMAS

The earth shook beneath Tressya's feet with enough violence she stopped mid-flight, and I swayed along with the folds in her skirts.

This had to be the Salmun's doing, and I was damn sick of hiding in this pocket, once again feeling useless to counter the forces against us.

I fought clear of the parchment, determined to escape this damn pocket and transform back into a Razohan. On seeing the seam of yellow candlelight, I leaped upward, already releasing my hold on the rat's form before I'd even cleared the pocket. I heard a rip of fabric at the same time I realized the back end of my boot was caught. I staggered on one leg before I could gain my balance, and fell forward, saving myself at the last before I crashed to the stone floor.

"Tamas," Tressya gasped. "You fool."

I seized her around the waist, flushing her against me, as I dodged toward the wall away from the large metal door.

"No wait," she struggled to get out of my arms, reaching a hand toward the parchment that had fallen free of the ripped pocket.

"Stay there." I gave her no time to argue. Instead, dived forward and scooped the folded parchment up and shoved it into the pocket of my breeches.

"You shouldn't—"

Reaching her again, I held her close, palming her mouth to silence her before she used her whip-sharp tongue.

"You've been busy," I said as I glanced across to the Salmun scattered on the ground like fallen logs. Did Tressya also possess magic now? She really was a tempting bundle of mysteries. The pedestal, home to the Senjel Oracles, lay in ruins, the ancient book itself, carelessly tossed amongst the rubble now Tressya had what she wanted.

"Did you ripped pages from the sacred Senjel Oracles, little queen?" I quirked a brow.

"Was that the book you were looking for?" She was using her customary way of avoiding answering my question.

"I didn't even know of this place." And I did the same, gazing around me, taking in the vast chamber empty of anything but a stone altar in the center and the now crumbled pedestal, home to the Senjel Oracles. "I never would've found the book," I half said to myself.

"You can thank me later. But right now, we need to escape. I don't know how long they'll remain like that."

"Any minute, little queen."

"The door's likely sealed by magic, and I don't even want to think what the cause of that unearthly rumble may be."

"The unearthly rumble was..." Any second now, we'd both find out the answer to that riddle.

My keen senses had smelt and heard the oncoming horde. I couldn't say what they were exactly, but my best guess was some twisted form of Ashenlands evil. It made sense the Salmun would refuse to confine all their pets to that dead place.

"While I'm eager to discover what you did to the Salmun, I fear whatever it was has unleashed their abominations."

"What?" She struggled against me.

"Steady now. We need to be ready. They're going to burst through this door any moment."

"I have nothing to fight with."

"Really? You proved more than adequate unarmed against the Salmun." I regrettably released my hold on her waist—which had been a brief but nice distraction—and withdrew a dagger from its sheath buried underneath my cloak.

"It's not much, but hopefully you won't feel so vulnerable. I'll have to transform into the nightmare."

"You won't fit in here. Leave this up to me."

"Tressya," I growled. Now was not the time to become unwisely heroic.

Our argument was cut short as the massive metal door exploded inward, hurtling like an arrow released from a bow. It sped through the air before slamming against the far wall with a thunderous crash, the impact reverberating with enough force to threaten the chamber's ceiling. Wood pieces from the doorframe splinted away under blade-sharp claws as a swarm of grotesque shaped creatures fought to enter as one.

They emerged from the shadows, moving forward on all fours, yet their body was an unsettling union of strength and deformity with broad and muscular chests, supporting powerful forelimbs, ending in long, razor-sharp claws, gleaming menacingly in the dim light. In stark contrast, their hind legs were diminutive and almost frail, making their movements a disturbing blend of grace and awkwardness.

As they advanced, their claws left a harrowing high-pitched screech across the stone floor, chorused by a low rumble emitted from their throats. Elongated snouts allowed for plenty of formidable teeth, and their leathery hides, interspersed with patches of fine, bristling hair, shimmering in the candle flame, looked like armor. Every inch of their form spoke of a creation forged with dark magic, a living weapon created to inspire terror and awe.

"This is going to be tight," I whispered into Tressya's ear, subtly reaching for my second dagger.

Sensing what I was doing, Tressya slowly shifted her hand, placing it over mine, preventing me from unsheathing my weapon.

By now, a dozen of the creatures had entered the chamber. We were pressed against the wall, so the creatures had yet to see us, their bulbous eyes focused on their masters. If we stayed still, we could last undetected for precious moments longer.

"I hope you have a good plan," I whispered.

But Tressya didn't answer me.

Tressya tried to step forward, but I flexed my muscles, keeping her flush against me. "I don't think that's wise," I whispered.

I struggled to understand what she was doing, what was happening, when she pushed away from me, falling into the wall, and closing her eyes with a deep inhale. Suddenly she yelled. "Come forth."

Dammit, Tressya. Now I understood.

At her shout, the creatures turned to face us. I spun around to confront the horde, ensuring she remained behind me, while pulling my dagger clean from its sheath.

"No, Tamas," Tressya shouted.

She had lost her mind, but then, she had won the Ashenlands war by raising the dead.

Having witnessed the resurrection of the dead during the war, I thought I was prepared. Yet, it was not enough to steady me as I witnessed the miracle once again. Scores of the dead appeared on the far side of the chamber, facing the horde of creatures. It was as though they were being painted to life, limb by limb, piercing the veil with a subtle shimmer of light, hugging each form as it appeared.

Unlike those in the Ashenlands Tressya had brought back to fight the war, these were soldiers—macabre visions of brutality. They existed in death as they were killed in life, emerging not fully human yet with enough of their corporeal bodies to form an impressive army.

"Not what I'd expected," I breathed.

"Save us," Tressya yelled. Her voice was the command. The army attacked, swarming over the beasts like a plague.

With no weapons, their shouts of fury were the only sounds accompanying the fight as they threw themselves upon the hideous horde before them. It was a harrowing sight, but the dead could not be killed; each dismembered limb simply reappeared. By now, the chamber was filled with the savage sounds of wild beasts snarling and the furious cries of the resurrected soldiers.

I seized Tressya's hand. "Let's get out of here." And dragged her toward the exit, leaving the army to their fight.

I swung Tressya left. Ahead, the passage was dark, but my keen eyes allowed me to see enough of the passage to the steps ahead.

Tressya jerked on my hand. "Wait. That wasn't there before."

I looked over my shoulder, noticing another passage behind us.

"This was the way you came, right?" I nodded toward the stone steps in the distance.

"Yes, but this other passage is new. It was a wall when the Salmun led me down here. The Salmun's chamber was at the end of the passage, but it's not now. There's a new tunnel."

"Heading in the opposite direction to the way out. I'd say that's how the Salmun's creatures came through, so we're definitely not going that way."

"What if it's another exit that saves us from moving through Emberforge?"

I pulled her toward the steps. "We're not exploring unknown places, which undoubtedly lead further underneath Emberforge. That's the best way to trap yourself, and I have no intention of discovering why the Salmun hid the tunnel using their magic."

Over the calamitous noise of the fight coming from within the chamber we'd just left behind, I heard the distinct noise of footsteps atop the steep steps in front of us. "Shit, our luck's not holding out."

"I hear it too," she said, gazing toward the steps.

We hadn't ventured far enough from the chamber to escape the reach of the torchlight, which, though dim, suffused the darkness with a soft, yellowish glow. Ahead of the steps lay nothing but darkness.

"More Salmun?" Tressya said over the noise of the fighting raging within the Salmun's chamber.

"We won't find out." I spun, taking Tressya with me away from the steps and the exit. "Looks like we'll have to explore this new passage after all." It was risky to pass the chamber in case we attracted the wrong attention, but the dead were still fighting the creatures.

Before we'd taken a step, I heard voices from those who'd descended the steps.

"Plesy," we both said in unison, as the apostle came into view.

"You know Plesy?" she said. "Of course, Petrulus."

The gentle flicker of a candle flame lit their way as the apostles descended. Changing my mind, I pulled Tressya toward the apostles, and by the time they reached the bottom of the steps, we were there to greet them.

"Your Majesty," Plesy gasped.

"No talking," I barked, and pushed past him and the three other apostles who'd descended with him: Selisimus,

Tortilus and Wellard. Petrulus had been naïve to the exact number of rebel apostles, and I doubted this was all of them.

"Wait, you can't go that way. Salmun is moving throughout Emberforge."

I rounded on Plesy. "We can't go *that* way." My voice was close to a snarl as I jabbed a finger back down the tunnel to where the fighting continued in the chamber.

"We have to," Tressya said, and this time I let a small snarl escape, as she tugged me off the first step. "Hurry."

There was no time to argue with the stubborn little queen, so I did the next best thing, and that was to swipe her up in my arms and retraced our steps back down the passage, passing the chamber as fast as I could go, plunging us into the darkness of the mysterious tunnel.

The apostles struggled to keep pace, and at one point the candle flame went out, but I refused to break my stride.

"No, wait," Tressya hissed. "Tamas, we're losing them."

"I've got no problems leaving them behind."

She struggled in my arms. "You can't."

I growled as I came to a halt, reluctantly releasing Tressya from my arms. "Plesy," she whispered into the darkness.

"Coming, Your—Sorry."

Behind him, a small candle flame struggled to life again.

"Please, Your—Sorry. If we could give Tortilus time. He's performing a spell to seal the passage behind us."

"You have that sort of magic?" Tressya sounded impressed. Stars, I was impressed and hopefully it would work.

"A little. We're no match for the Salmun, for sure. But our

practice dates back centuries to the brave apostles who dared first go against the Salmun. We call ourselves—"

"It's nice you're here to help, but we've no time for this conversation," I countered.

Plesy eyed me cautiously in the flickering candle flame, his gaze traveling the entirety of my body before flicking between Tressya and I.

"He's rude, but we can trust him." She side-eyed me. "I think."

I flashed her a mirthless grin, then turned to Plesy. "Is your friend done yet?"

"Magic takes time and concentra—"

"We'll meet you at the other end, then." I grabbed Tressya's hand, but she shook me off.

"It's safer if we travel together."

"Arh, here he comes now. That was fast, Tortilus. You're improving a lot since your first attempt at that spell."

"Let's skip the praise, shall we?" I grumbled. "Are you ready now, little queen?"

Plesy's eyes rounded in surprise. As he continued to eye me, his lip curled in disgust.

I bared my fangs, making his eyes bulge, and dragged Tressya into the darkness ahead. I felt unnerved because we were entering a tunnel the Salmun had magically concealed, from which I was sure their hideous creations had poured forth.

Tressya stumbled to keep pace with me. "Do you know where this leads?" She said, looking over her shoulder, her question directed at the apostles behind.

"No... We've never succeeded in our endeavor to open the

secret entrance underneath the throne before," Plesy said with an excited edge to his voice.

"Were there any Salmun following you?" I said.

"Perhaps. Most likely. Myself and Tortilus were close to gaining entry to these passages when Wellard arrived in the throne room with the warning that the Salmun was coming. Miraculously, we finally won through and entered the passage under the Bone Throne."

"Did you know I was down here with the Salmun?"

"Yes, Your—" Tortilus spoke up.

"Call me Tressya."

"Yes. We were sure the Salmun brought you down here for something maleficent," Tortilus continued.

"And you came down here, ready to face a dozen Salmun to help me?"

The idiocy of what they'd done, coupled with the courage needed to make such a decision, and I couldn't help but respect the four of them. I would've done the same in similar circumstances, but I was prone to making foolish decisions.

"It may sound stupid, but we're not as useless as we may appear," Plesy said.

"That never crossed my mind," Tressya said.

It had crossed mine, and I remained skeptical about their ability to stand against the Salmun, but given neither Tressya nor I had any ability to wield magic—for now—they were welcome to join our escape.

"We call ourselves the Umbral Luminae, and we've existed for half a millennium," Tortilus said.

"That's a long time to exist under the Salmun's notice," Tressya said.

We had an unknown stretch of dark passage to navigate and stars knows what creatures may come our way, and Tressya seemed willing to encourage the apostles' conversation.

"That's half a millennium to perfect and protect our secrecy. The order started with the three: the Lore Keeper, the Scribe Master, and the Scroll Guardian, entrusted with the preservation and interpretation of the ancient lore. To become one of these esteemed three was to enter a clandestine pact with the Umbral Luminae, committing oneself to our covert manifesto. This solemn vow was a pledge to devote our lives to safe-guarding the order and to guarantee its prosperity," Tortilus replied.

"And what is your manifesto?"

"How about we focus on our escape?" I interrupted.

"To overthrow the Salmun," Plesy quickly added.

"Tortilus," I barked. We were stuck in an underground maze of the Salmun's making, possibly the lair for their disgusting beasts, and they only seemed interested in touting their credentials to Tressya. "How secure is the seal you placed over the passage behind us?"

"It will hold...for now."

"How long is 'for now'?" I snapped, resisting the urge to seize him by the throat while he answered, when I shouldn't blame the apostles for our predicament.

"As long as we find a way out soon, we should be safe."

"So it won't hold a serious attack."

"I don't want to make a prediction," Tortilus mumbled.

"You tried your best," Tressya said.

I was sure she glared daggers into the side of my face for my surly voice and ungrateful attack on the apostle, but that was the least of my concerns at this moment. The trace of something pungent hit the back of my nose, some animalic stench and fetid decay wafting in the stagnant air. There was something ahead we probably didn't want to face, and even though my eyes were keen, they couldn't pierce absolute darkness.

"I smell it too." Tressya spoke beside me, keeping her voice low.

"Give me your candle," I ordered whomever was carrying our single source of light.

Wellard stepped forth, passing me the candle holder.

Tressya turned from the apostles and whispered. "The dead will come to our aid."

"They're best left with the beasts back in the chamber."

"There are more. Many more. So many have died within Emberforge over the millennium." Her voice rose as she spoke.

"Yes, that's true," Plesy said. "Many by the hands of the Salmun."

"That's our army if needed," Tressya whispered again, her expression somber in the candlelight.

"Many were buri—" Plesy continued.

"We need to keep going," I interrupted him, feeling impatient at the thought of a lecture on Emberforge's history.

Knowing Tressya would find a cutting remark for my suggestion, I swallowed anything I would say, as the stench thickened the air, burning the hairs in my nostrils.

"What's that smell?" Tortilus said.

"We're about to find out," I replied.

"It's dead, surely," Selisimus said.

"With that smell, I would say there's more than one dead thing down here," Plesy added.

"Perhaps you'd all like to stop signaling our position," I growled.

The four apostles were as stealthy as bullocks, and we were all guilty of speaking aloud. Besides, whatever was out there probably possessed the keen senses of a predator, but my patience toward the apostles was almost at an end.

Tressya said nothing beside me, which drew my attention. "You've nothing to worry about. I promise we'll get out of this." Having silently blamed the apostles for being too noisy, I kept my voice low.

She huffed. "You think I'm worried?"

"You're quiet. I thought that was your way of worrying."

"I'm preparing myself to call on the dead the moment this beast arrives."

"How about you let me save us for a change?"

"Because this isn't a sport, Tamas. We don't win points for—"

"That's the first time you've said my name since I arrived back in Tolum."

"And it will be the last if you—"

I squeezed her hand as we continued down the passage. "Hush, my fiery queen. I've reserved a few tricks for you."

She arched a brow as she glanced at me. "Fine. But if you continue to interrupt me when I'm talking, I'll tell the dead you're my problem."

The faint rasp of nails on stone silenced my reply. Tressya heard it too, tugging on my arm as she stopped. Mirroring us, the noise ceased, the creature stilled, which implied it had intelligence. I'd also guess superior eyesight, given it lived down here.

"Is there something wrong, Your—Tressya?" Plesy said.

"This way is crowded," was Tressya's reply.

Plesy and Selisimus tried to look beyond us to the passage ahead, needing to confirm what she said for themselves.

"I can give us more light," Tortilus confessed. "Magic, of course." As if neither of us would've guessed what he referred to.

"That's a handy skill," Tressya said.

"All you'll do is scare yourselves," I replied. "Stay behind and you'll all survive. Now shut up." The creature was on the move again, the rasping still faint, but growing nearer.

Now the apostles were quiet, I could discern the differing tones and rhythm of the rasping. "There's more than one."

Beside me, Tressya inhaled. "How many?"

I focused on listening, dissecting each noise, noticing the directional shifts, the change in cadence, and the overlay of tones. "At least a dozen."

"I hope your tricks are impressive," she whispered close.

I turned my head to glance down at her. "And if they are?"

"You'll earn my gratitude."

"Anything else?" I winked.

"I'll stop thinking of you as a pain in my ass."

"That certainly gives a man incentive," I sighed.

The next rasping sounds staunched our conversation.

"What was that?" Selisimus said.

"Any minute now," I breathed.

"I trust you, Tamas," Tressya added at the last, as if she felt I needed bolstering to succeed.

Shadowy figures emerged through the dim light from the insignificant candle flame. It was as I feared. The mysterious tunnel led into the Salmun's lair for all their malformed contortions of nature. What came before us was a freakish sight to send anyone to their knees, paralyzed in fear. Creatures with heads attached in the wrong places, limbs where they shouldn't be, skin the thickness of armor, teeth the length of blades and more weaponry, such as spikes and barbs, than was possible on anything naturally born.

"Sweet Goddess Ovia, save us," Wellard said.

The way forward was through the oncoming horde. Our escape was through whatever barrier Tortilus had created and past the Salmun's chamber, possibly still filled with the Salmun Tressya had disabled and their deformed army of creatures.

'We stand with you,' came the chorus of voices in my mind. I shook my head, pressing my palm to my temple, unsure if for a moment I'd gone crazy, but no it was just the bloody Eone.

"Tamas?"

"I'm fine." I bit out and shook my head again.

The horde approached cautiously, seeming to sense trouble.

"Something or someone is coming along behind us," Tortilus cried. "I swear, I heard something. I'm so sorry, but it seems perhaps my shield no longer holds."

Damn, my focus was divided. I missed those creeping upon us from behind. And Tortilus was right. Now he'd drawn attention to the noise, it wasn't hard to miss.

'Open to us. We will save you.'

'Get out,' I mentally growled.

The creatures continued to draw near.

'You will not survive without our help.' It was Fivia's voice.

'We can save the both of you if you will let us,' Ineth spoke.

'You want Tressya to survive, do you not?' And that was Ovia.

"I don't need your help," I growled. It was only once the words were out did I realize I'd said them aloud.

"Okay, but you better do something fast," Tressya said.

Running footfalls gained ground behind us, guided by a brilliant glow of white: Salmun magic. They were free from whatever Tressya had done to them, and the scraping and screeching of their pets following along behind them meant we were being squeezed in the middle, our enemy coming from both directions of the tunnel, leaving us no way out.

'Only with our help will you live.' The Eone said in unison.

"All of you, get down on the ground," I yelled.

Realizing their masters' approach, the creatures that had

come from deeper within the mysterious tunnel, in the depths under Emberforge, attacked.

In my periphery, I saw Tressya fall to the stone floor beside me. Knowing she was out of the way, I partially released my hold on my human form and transformed my head into the gaping beak of the nightmare.

The passage was too small to take the sheer size of the creature. I couldn't even transform its entire head without feeling as though the mountains of rock on either side would crush my skull. But all I needed was the nightmare's mouth.

I opened my jaws as wide as the passage would allow and inhaled the beasts, feeling their weight swelling in my stomach, until it felt fit to burst. I couldn't hold them all inside, so I took on more of the nightmare's form, being conscious to stay on my feet and not squash Tressya on the ground beside me, until the sides of the passage crushed my body.

Now I was the distorted, maligned form, half human and half nightmare, which was likely horrifying Tressya. But it didn't matter what she thought of me, as long as I kept her safe.

Somewhere underneath me, I heard cries of shock and fear, but none were from Tressya, so I ignored them and continued with my meal.

Once I'd consumed the creatures in front of us. I returned to my human form, then faster than a blink, I spun, taking on my half form again, ready for the Salmun and their creatures coming from the other direction.

Beak agape, I inhaled, sucking in the light and every

other person or thing present in the passage behind, feeling the added weight as boulders resting in my belly.

Once silence settled, I waited, as a lethargy consumed me. Then, slowly, I regained my human form and collapsed against the stone wall, eyes closed, unable to move.

"Tamas," came Tressya's voice in the dark.

I heard her shoes drawn along the stone as she crawled toward me. Behind my eyelids, I caught the sudden flare of light, like a tiny star brought down from the sky and cradled in someone's hands.

On opening my eyes, I first saw Tressya's face close to mine. Behind her, silhouetting her expression, was that tiny ball of light, held in the palms of Tortilus.

"Are you all right?" Tressya placed her hand on mine.

"Indigestion." And I burped.

"What magic was that?" Selisimus said.

"No magic," I murmured, feeling like I needed to sleep off the meal for a century. "That was far too much to consume when I couldn't transform to my full size."

"The passage is clear in both directions," Wellard said. "Everything is gone."

Everything included anyone who'd followed us, namely a Salmun or two, but I wouldn't clarify that to anyone present. The idea only made me want to puke, and no one wanted that happening. I closed my eyes again; it was safer that way.

"I don't understand what happened," Plesy said. "What manner of creature—"

"It's over," Tressya interrupted, then she squeezed my hand. "I'm sorry, but you can't rest for long. I'm sure there'll be more to come if we don't get out of here. And you're not in a fit state to be doing that again."

I cracked an eyelid. "But you were impressed."

Her lips twitched. "You were certainly efficient in clearing our problem."

"Then we agree. I was the hero."

She glanced away for a beat before turning back to me with a wry smile. "If that's what the Razohan needs to hear to make him feel better."

CHAPTER
SIXTEEN

BRYRA

From Tressya's window, I'd watched her depart in the carriage, as a thickness welled in my throat and my heart felt clenched in tight fists. I watched the carriage roll out of sight until the seizure that held me released, and I turned to flee.

Out in the corridor, I swayed, flinging out one hand to clutch the wall while I waited for the churn in my stomach to pass. When I glanced down the passage, the walls of Emberfell seemed to fall inward, threatening to crush me inside this cursed castle forever.

There was only one place I felt safe.

I hurried toward the servants' passage, bursting through the door and inadvertently shoving a manservant to the side. He was a slim, lanky youth, barely older than a child, his thin, wispy hair slicked down wet against his scalp. The smell of fear obscured the crisp freshness of his servant's uniform.

I gave no apology, rather rushed past him and bounded off down the dim passage with the churn of my stomach growing ever more violent. The walls only an arm's span either side, my sense of suffocation grew steadily worse.

Hairs sprouted along my arm, tickling under my maid's sleeve, and I palmed my face, fearful my beast side had revealed itself. The smooth skin worn by the two-legged remained on the left side of my face, but in my anxious state, I struggled to decide if that was a boon or a curse. My disguise made me forget I was Huungardred, made me feel vulnerable, even though without it I would be hunted. I needed to be free, to feel the breeze chill my face and smell the ice and pine on the wind.

I hurried to the only place I knew that would soothe my sudden and inexplicable fear; the king's garden.

Once I reached the only sanctuary I knew in this cursed place, I slipped my uncomfortable shoes and stepped upon the soft, damp soil, burying myself within the broad leaves and closed my eyes to feel my heart beat out of rhythm.

Shame carved a hole in my heart—a shame for the cowardice I had just exhibited; a shame for the fool I had revealed myself to be; a shame for succumbing to Romelda's harsh scheme; a shame for the hurt I was about to inflict on Tamas.

I could only be thankful I was far from my father, so he wouldn't witness my actions.

The last few days, I questioned both Romelda's and my reasoning for committing to this path. I should be angry with her for asking this of me, knowing what I would lose in the end was I to succeed. But I trusted Romelda. The blooded were loyal to one fate, unswayed by glory or greed. However, I feared her loyalty had blinded her.

Jealousy was my reason and knowing this was the biggest source of my shame.

I had dreaded Romelda's prophecy, that Tressya would ensnare Tamas with a false love, only to burn his heart. Yet, my overriding impulse stemmed from the knowledge that she was Razohan—possessing the power to make their bond whole, should she decide to. How could I look upon my father and Tamas, knowing I killed Tressya all for the pain in my heart? And now I was racked with indecision as to the best choice I could make.

Since our disastrous meeting beside the battle arena, demands placed on the queen spared me from speaking with her again, especially in private, given the Mother was present most nights I arrived to tend the queen.

The older woman was a slow, torturous poison, leaving me baffled why any would willingly pledge their loyalty to one so blatantly cruel and hateful. When in her presence, I had hurriedly performed my tasks so that I could escape before my beast burst free.

In three days, my loathing for the older woman raised bile into my throat, forcing me to curl the buds of my claws into the flesh on my palm to stop them from fully forming. Never had I thought someone ever deserving of death until I met this evil woman.

But here in the tranquility of the captured forest, its magic soothed my heavy heart and eased the squeeze on my lungs. I found a place to settle and breathed in the rich earthy smells that reminded me a little of home, and there I stayed for a long time, relishing the restorative power of nature.

Perhaps hours had passed before I felt a persistent and irritating niggle, warning me I should leave the sanctuary before I someone discovered. me

Sadly, I knew the sense of peace I'd found while hiding in the garden was fleeting. Once I left my refuge, the now familiar sensations of anxiety and suffocation would once again slip beneath my skin, but hiding was the coward's way, and Huungardred weren't cowards.

Slipping my feet into my uncomfortable shoes was the first slow demise of my peace. I'm sure my steps would grow heavy the further I moved from this place.

I couldn't bear the thought of entering the servants' passage again, so when I spied the glass doorway leading outside, I couldn't resist the temptation. For a suspended moment, I gazed through the doorway to the grounds beyond, the open air and the cluster of ailing trees in the distance, wondering what awaited me inside the castle. The answer was nothing. The queen had departed, taking her abhorrent Mother and the Salmun with her; her departure had ignited the sudden flare of panic within me, intensifying my feelings of entrapment.

Anything was better than returning to the servants' passage when there was little reason for me to be inside. I relented, heading for the door, relieved to find it easily opened.

Outside, the wind held none of the fresh beauty of the

north, but I continued down the path, this time heading toward the front of the castle. I had a lot on my mind and left my feet to take me where they would while I pondered my choices.

There was only one sensible choice for me to make. I knew it the moment I'd caught the dagger in my hand once I was sure Tressya suspected me. She was familiar with the nature of the Razohan.

She suspected I was one of them, yet she remained silent about my true identity, allowing me to retain my role as her lady's maid. She did this because she would never fathom my true purpose for being here. Her behavior revealed one truth: she bore no malice towards Tamas or the Razohan for inciting the war. Had she harbored any resentment, she wouldn't have hesitated to bind me in chains. Knowing this, I couldn't help contemplating her true feelings toward Tamas. As much as it pained me to think so, I believed they were deeper than Romelda thought. Which would make one of my reasons for coming here a lie.

Now was the perfect time for me to flee. With everyone departed, leaving few eyes upon me, giving me the freedom to escape.

The thought of leaving this place spurred my heart to race. The sun had yet to rise to midday, which meant I should reach the outer limits of Tolum by nightfall. From there, I was free to transform into the beast and disappear through the night to the border in the north.

I halted on realizing my thoughtless meandering had led me to the front of the castle. The churning of carriage wheels on gravel seized me in place. Too late, it appeared Tressya and the Mother were returning, but without the Salmun. Already their carriage had passed through the main entrance gate.

I should take cover around the side of the castle and out of view, since I wasn't where I should be, but I feared I'd already been seen. Sure enough, as the carriage swung around the fountain centering the courtyard, I caught the Mother's eye. It was as though giant arms held me in place, as I watched the carriage come to a halt in front of the entrance doors to Emberfell, and the Mother emerged from inside.

I couldn't explain why I stayed when I realized the Mother had traveled alone. An unfamiliar loathing welled within on the sight of her, churning my stomach until I felt sure this time I really would be sick.

Escape—a word I clung to for solace, letting it linger in the recesses of my mind over the past few days. Now, however, its allure waned, its echo rapidly diminishing. As I stared at the Mother, the churning of my stomach abated, even if my loathing stretched the limits of my heart.

This detestable woman, embodying everything I despised in the two-legged kind, was at fault. She exemplified an order of women whose contemptible greed gave rise to a child whose birth should never have occurred. By her machinations, Tressya was forced into this fate. Because of the Mother, the northerners suffered terrible loss, and the Salmun still controlled the Bone Throne. This was the woman deserved of death.

She treated me as though I were invisible, not even bothering to glance my way as she took the steps to the entrance doors of Emberfell. That was the single boon of this disguise. It rendered me beneath most people's notice.

I observed her, curious whether a woman as astute as the Mother could sense the intensity of my scornful gaze upon her face, wondering if it scorched her skin as fervently as I yearned to set her clothes ablaze. But I had a far greater surprise to gift the Mother than a flame easily doused.

Her outrage was clear in the way she ascended the stairs, each step taken with a force as if she intended to crush them beneath her feet. The downturn of her lips and the tightness around her eyes revealed her fury, and I had a good idea of what might have provoked such ire. She'd arrived alone, which meant Tressya had sent the Mother away, or the Salmun; whomever it had been, the Mother held no power to refuse. For a woman whose words were unquestionably obeyed, she was likely struggling to contain her fury.

As soon as she disappeared into Emberfell, the spellbinding force that had frozen me in place seemed to dissipate. The surge of dark emotions that had overwhelmed me at the sight of her no longer had the power to influence my decisions now that she was out of sight. It was the perfect time to enact my earlier plan. The copse of trees wasn't far for a beast who could move with blinding speed; the thought drew home nearer.

This was not my fight. I was not the person to set right the wrongs committed, nor the one responsible for the fates of so many; that was the arrogance of the two-legged kind. Too long I'd been away from my father's hall.

I retraced my steps around the side of Emberfell until I reached the glass door that led into the king's gardens.

Rather than head inside, I turned and followed the trail I'd taken days ago when I'd hunted down the queen for the first time, which led me to the copse of trees.

A formidable rampart, no doubt constructed during an era when the threat of siege loomed constantly, encircled Emberfell. Now, with the Salmun serving as protection for the House of Tannard, its crenellations remained vacant and unguarded. For a Huungardred, it was barely an obstacle to my freedom.

I itched to leave the cover of the thinned forest but was distracted by the sight of Tressya coming toward me through the small copse of trees from the direction of the rampart.

Her clothes were disheveled, her hair a tangled mess, but her eyes were alive with purpose. She was heading straight toward me. The sickly trees were poor shelter for someone as big as me, so I stood little chance of hiding. Instead, I thought up an excuse and waited to be discovered.

On seeing me standing amongst the trees, Tressya faltered, giving a glance to her shoulder. That's when I spied the rat perched close to her nape.

A rat? What had the queen done to acquire a rat?

Mercy on my soul. The dread was like an anvil.

"Ryia?"

The need to get away twisted my tongue, making me unable to speak.

"What are you doing out here?"

The only sensible thing I could manage was a curtsy.

Tressya glanced to the rampart behind as if she'd already discovered my plan.

"You're coming with me," she announced and stomped off toward Emberfell.

I still had the chance to flee. The queen was no match for my Huungardred speed, yet encountering her this way, as if she'd emerged victorious from a minor battle, compelled me to obey, even with the rat sitting atop her shoulder.

He was the reason I should disappear, but it was too late. There was no escaping a Razohan's perceptivity. Though a rat, I was sure his eyes would penetrate beneath Romelda's disguise.

He'd made it to the south. The two were united. Hiding was no longer necessary for me. As a Huungardred, I was bound to own my actions and confront the consequences.

CHAPTER
SEVENTEEN

TRESSYA

TOO MANY CONCERNS already burdened me, leaving little room to dwell on Ryia. Ever since she caught the dagger I threw, I'd suspected she was Razohan, and I'd spent the days afterward mulling over her reasons for coming here. Part of me hoped Tamas had sent her to watch over me, concerned for my safety while he was recovering. However, I thought it more plausible that the witch, determined to see me killed, had enlisted the help of an accomplice skilled in disguises.

Her motives would remain a mystery until I'd escaped Emberfell and the Mother's grasp. Tamas squeaked when I swept him off my shoulder and attempted to tuck him into my pocket. He resisted, clutching the fabric on either side, thwarting my efforts to push him back inside.

"You insisted on returning to Emberfell with me, so quit it. You'll draw too much attention sitting on my shoulder."

Given Ryia was Razohan, I saw no reason to keep up the subterfuge, so spoke aloud to Tamas.

"Come," I snapped at her as I slipped into the king's garden. After our attack and miraculous escape from the tunnels under Emberforge, Ryia would bear the brunt of my lost patience. Tamas too, if he dared take his human form while I was inside Emberfell.

He was such a stupid ass, who wouldn't listen to reason and insisted we flee Tolum straight away once we escaped Emberforge. I refused, unwilling to vanish without a word to Gusselan. In fact, I hoped to convince her to flee with me, though I omitted that part of my plan when arguing with Tamas.

Once inside Emberfell, I abruptly spun, seizing Ryia by the arm. "Listen carefully, you're to go to the stores where they supply your uniform. Find me two sets of suitable clothing, preferably breeches and boots. The second set make similar to mine in size. Meet me here when you have what I want. I know I don't need to warn you to be silent. And be quick. The Salmun are about to descend on Emberfell, and we can't be present when they do."

She didn't immediately move.

"Hurry," I barked.

"You must take the servants' passages. You'll be able to move about the castle without being seen," she said.

"Oh." So much had taken my attention since the day I'd arrived in Emberfell, and the servants were adept at moving around unseen, so I'd hadn't known such places existed. "Thank you."

I followed her out of the king's garden and shortly thereafter we slipped into a small, dusty passage way with barely any light and drooping cobwebs as chandeliers.

"I'll lead you to your rooms, then head directly to the stores."

If Ryia had come to Emberfell with malevolent intentions, she seemed to have abandoned them, complying with my commands. She might have perceived an ideal chance to execute her scheme, or she might be genuinely cooperating. Either way, I had no time to dwell on the truth. I wasn't fleeing Emberfell dressed in these dirty, voluminous clothes, and neither did I have spare time to find something suitable.

"No. I want to see Gusselan."

Ryia hesitated. "Then I'll take you there."

She moved through the narrow passage with haste, reminding me of her Razohan heritage, making me wonder how much of the Razohans' traits would I inherit. All I hoped.

I noted the minor guides we passed to ensure I would find my way on my return, such as the thick iron nail hammered into the mortar between the bricks that signaled our turn left into another narrow passage.

Soon I felt nervous for how long it seemed to take us to wind through the castle's inner labyrinth, and just as I was about to complain, Ryia stopped at a small door, which required me to hunch to fit through and would have been easy to miss in the poor light. "This leads into the corridor opposite the dead king's rooms."

"Thank you, Ryia. Now be quick. It's imperative no one sees you."

"I know," she said with a solemnity that sent an eerie tingle across my neck.

"And I need weapons." I added, before she hurried away. "I know it's a lot to ask, but you're more than capable." This last week I was getting a sense of how easy it was for a Razohan to perform all manner of tasks.

I left her behind and slipped into the corridor, thankful for the dim lighting in this part of Emberfell. As queen, I was expected to inherit King Henricus's grand chambers, but the mere thought repulsed me. I adamantly stayed in the rooms assigned to me upon my arrival, defying the Mother's insistence I do otherwise, which sent her into a rage, quelled only by her understanding that the queen was rarely left alone, and she was, supposedly, one of my servants.

"She is the most dreadful sight," Albert said.

"Whatever could have befallen the queen?" Borat replied.

Ignoring the three pesky spirits, I gave a small knock, then entered to find Gusselan stretched out on her window seat, peering out the window. Before she could say anything, I ducked inside and shut the spirits out, but unable to restrain their curiosity, they passed through the door.

"That ulcerous hag arrived alone. And her temper was quite the sight," Borat informed me.

"What's happened?" Gusselan rose from her window seat.

"Good luck to you, my queen. This little hoyden has a habit of keeping—" Albert said.

"You look as though someone attacked you," Gusselan interrupted him.

"I have. And we have to leave. Now."

"Wait, what is that hideous thing peeking through the folds of her ruined skirt?" Albert exclaimed.

I ignored both Albert and Tamas.

"What're you talking about?" Gusselan said.

"It's a rat," Truett shrieked.

Borat appeared between us, facing me, with his arms in a mock fold. "We would like to know the same. And why in the seven realms are you carrying a rat in your pocket?"

"There's no time to explain. But you can't stay here. It's not safe," I told Gusselan.

"We cannot go anywhere." Borat said. He glanced at his companions. "Does she intend to quit her quarters, or quit the castle?"

"She cannot mean the latter, you fool. The queen does not simply run away. There is her duty to uphold." Albert said.

Thankfully, Gusselan was too shrewd to ask questions, and took one breath to decide.

I was already heading for the door. "You have no time to pack your belongings, I'm afraid."

"She is serious," Truett exclaimed. "She is stealing off with the queen."

"Both queens," Borat announced. "Something is terribly amiss." Before I reached the door, he slipped in front of me, blocking our escape. "You will go nowhere until you have revealed yourself."

This was an ill-fated time to have an argument with a pompous old spirit. "Get out of my way, or I'll make you. And I know you wouldn't want that."

I didn't bother to look behind to see what Gusselan thought of my conversation with air.

Albert and Truett appeared beside Borat. "You surely do not intend to abandon Emberfell," Albert asserted. "Such an action would bring disgrace to your lineage."

I clenched my fists, preparing myself to pass through all three.

"You can not think to leave us," Truett said, as Tamas climbed from my pocket and clawed his way up the front of my dress. Truett's eyes bulged, then he gave a shriek and vanished.

"Fine. Have it your way." And I plucked him off my bodice and placed him on my shoulder.

"Why do you have a rat?" Gusselan said from behind.

Albert recoiled as Borat's lips curled.

"Look how she touches it like it is a pet," Albert said.

Since I was still holding Tamas, I waved him in front of them, sending both Albert and Borat flinching backward through the door and out into the corridor.

"Sorry," I mumbled to Tamas as I settled him on my shoulder, feeling guilty for doing what I did when he was still struggling to recover from his stomach upset. It had already been a challenge for him to carry me over the rampart without feeling nauseous—a feat he'd have to repeat for both Gusselan and me. Now, having compressed his stomach to such a diminutive size, I was certain he was feeling very ill.

"I'll tell you everything once we're safe," I replied, then peeked out into the corridor. To my relief, Borat and Albert had vanished. But their appearance made me think of another spirit who'd I'd not seen since the Mother revealed my true heritage. I could only guess he sought solace with Daelon, after learning of my betrayal.

I led Gusselan into the cramped confines of the servants' passages, thankful she accepted my secrecy by asking no more questions, and retraced the path I'd taken to reach her.

Hurrying us along the passage, I thanked my sudden change in fortune that persuading Gusselan to come proved quicker than I anticipated. Hopefully, we wouldn't have to wait too long for Ryia to arrive.

The Mother was always a worry, but if my luck persisted, she would remain stranded at Emberforge, unable to return to the castle.

Once back in the king's gardens, I was disappointed to see Ryia had yet to return. "I was hoping she would have come already," I mumbled to myself in frustration.

"Who?"

"Help. She's retrieving suitable clothes and, hopefully, weapons. Though that may be difficult. And with our time constraints. Maybe I shouldn't have asked her for those."

"Do you now have time for my questions?"

"While we wait." But I was already pacing, unable to stay still.

I spoke before she asked; the tale tumbling out along with my nerves and frustration. "We escaped Emberforge." Before I could say anymore, Tamas leapt from my shoulder.

Beside me, Gusselan gasped as Tamas transformed into a man, but his legs buckled beneath him, causing him to stumble. He caught himself before falling, yet his legs bowed, and he wavered before tumbling into a garden bed filled with lush ferns and broad-leaved foliage, his head buried in the loamy soil.

I'd seen Tamas turn once into his beast-like self, shocking me with his swift and graceful transformation. Now he staggered around like a drunk.

I rushed over and crouched beside him. "Tamas." My stomach rose in my throat as I called his name. This was more than a pathetic stomach upset.

He could only muster a groan.

"I assume he's an ally," Gusselan remarked, not at all perturbed by his sudden appearance.

"Help me move him."

"I'm fine." Tamas rolled onto his back.

"You're not, you stupid fool. Grab his arm," I ordered Gusselan.

"Don't treat me like a drunk," Tamas complained.

"I'll treat you like an imbecile if that makes you feel better. You're getting worse, Tamas, don't you see?"

He rolled onto his back with another groan, revealing the damp soil clinging to his cheek. I went to brush it off, but he clumsily grabbed my hand, squeezed it for a moment, then lowered to his side. "It'll pass, so stop fussing."

"Shall I leave your ass in the dirt while I'm at it?" *Come on Tamas. Show me some life.*

"Tressya, Tressya, Tressya," he mumbled as though he really was drunk. "Your temper gets the better of you often."

"When I have to deal with you, it's all the time."

"Are we going to move him or leave him in the dirt?" Gusselan said without a hint of compassion. She was going to make an excellent companion during our escape.

I sighed, wishing I could summon the hardness of heart to leave the fool where he lay, but I couldn't. When it came to Tamas, my heart was like overripe fruit, a soft, mushy mess. He evoked emotions within me I'd believed were beyond my capacity to feel.

"Ignore what he says." I took one arm and waved Gusselan to take the other, but Tamas struggled from our hold. "Take his arm." Why was it so difficult for a man to acknowledge his fragility and accept help?

Tamas relented, allowing us to help him into a seated position, leaning against the leg of the iron table at the garden's center.

I gnawed on my inner cheek, watching him slouch, his head dropping to his chest. His condition had worsened since our escape from the tunnel, and I could only imagine it had something to do with him ingesting our enemy when he took on the nightmare—and I tried not to spend too much time on the idea of what he'd done. It seemed I would forgive any action for us to be free.

The creatures of the Ashenlands might cause plenty of indigestion, but what about those that followed? I was certain some were Salmun. I attributed his condition to their magic. Our greatest enemy, I felt little revulsion at the thought of him swallowing the Salmun whole, but I feared their magic was gradually taking his life.

It must have taken all his strength to scale the rampart with my added weight when he could barely sit straight now? Without his aid, we stood no chance of returning over the wall, which left the front gates, where we would be easily exposed.

"He's one of them, isn't he?"

I jerked at Andriet's sudden appearance and fell back onto my ass. At that, Gusselan frowned.

One of my kind, yes.

"How did he get inside Emberfell? The Salmun should be warned of this immediately."

"The Salmun are the enemy." Gusselan would think me insane for saying such random things, but my emotions were too raw for me to care.

"You say that because..." Andriet shook his head, unable to finish those final words, else they would make the shocking revelation a reality.

"I'm one of them." I finished for him, only for him to throw up his hands and turn away before vanishing from the room.

Andriet hadn't even realized his mother was with me.

"Tressya?" Gusselan prodded, her voice cautiously questioning my sanity.

"One day I hope you don't end up hating me," I said to her.

She gently shook her head, no doubt struggling to fathom why I said the things I did.

Hurrying footfalls headed toward the king's garden. I rose, hoping it was Ryia, but ready for the worst. When Ryia slipped inside, I exhaled.

She arrived with a bundle of clothes in her arms, and to my relief, weapons sheathed in a belt at her hip.

"I knew you would succeed." I waved her closer, but Tamas, slumped against the table leg, caught her eye.

Unexpectedly, she rushed to him and sunk to her knees.

"What has happened?" The sight of Tamas ailing and Ryia dropped her pretense, finding her authoritative Razohan voice.

"Another ally?" Gusselan quirked a brow in question.

I nodded to Gusselan, handing her one set of men's clothes, then sunk beside Ryia. "It's complicated. And I don't have time to explain. He carried me over the rampart, and now he's in no shape to get the two of us back."

"I've never seen this infliction before." Ryia leaned close, placing her hand over his heart. "Tamas." Her voice was like a tender embrace, infused with boundless compassion, and for a moment, my lungs felt scorched by a searing flame. I yearned to swat her hand away, yell that she had no right to touch him.

They knew each other, of course, being Razohan, but her tenderness meant there was more between them. I squeezed my eyes closed, attempting to rid myself of this horrible sensation that made me feel inadequate, made me feel as though I was on the cusp of losing something precious.

Why did she have to be here? The thought was like a snarl in my head. I wanted to cry and scream at the same time, but neither would get us out of here.

"Then it can't be good," I heard myself say, forcing my attention to what was most important, which was not the wound in my heart.

"You say he's gotten worse?" She'd assumed command as effortlessly as the tidal flow, washing over rocks and finding crevices to fill.

"Yes." My voice sounded feeble.

I studied her expression, searching for any sign she

understood the seriousness of his condition, but found nothing in her deep frown to comfort me.

Behind us, Gusselan released a frustrated sigh. We both turned to see her struggling to escape her dress. Without a word, Ryia stood and motioned for Gusselan to turn around. "I'll help you. You next," she nodded to me as she hastily untied the yards of lace strapping Gusselan into her dress.

"There's no point waiting beside Tamas. You should begin with what you can do on your own."

Though not rude, this was no way to speak to a queen, but I respected her sudden command, equally her courage. And I needed strong women by my side. Escaping this merciless place and saving Tamas were my priorities and neither I could accomplish alone, nor with only Gusselan's help. Besides, I was eager to shed this damn crown as soon as I could.

I did as Ryia suggested and thanked her for her help.

"I'll see Tamas safe over the other side," she said. "Both of you head for the Rampart. And I'll meet you there."

I hesitated, again feeling that sudden flush of jealousy. I clenched my fists, desperate to rid myself of the toxic feeling.

The way she'd said his name, with the soft intimacy reserved between lovers, I couldn't imagine it was anything less—perhaps they were still lovers. Maybe all his sweet words to me had been a lie.

Stop this. Rather than aid me in reaching my goal, all such thoughts did was make me feel sick.

"Go," she said, with a gentle strength in her voice.

I hesitated because I didn't want to leave the two of them alone.

Don't be pathetic. What did I think would happen? They were hardly going to canoodle when he was practically unconscious, and Ryia understood our dire predicament and the need for haste.

I glanced at Gusselan, who nodded her agreement.

Before departing, I crouched beside Tamas one more time and retrieved the folded parchment from his pocket, and buried it deep in mine. Then leaving our clothes where they lay, Gusselan and I snuck through the glass door, slowing long enough to ensure there was no one about. I took her hand, giving a squeeze for luck, before I released it and ran. Gusselan remained by my side as we raced toward the copse of trees, while invisible hands seemed to tighten around my throat and ghostly fingers brushed unsettlingly across my shoulders.

It wasn't long before I realized Gusselan had fallen behind, unable to match my pace. Yet, my lungs felt clear, my legs strong, and with each stride, they seemed to grow even stronger—Razohan strength. I felt invincible, overflowing with energy, and I arched my head, inhaling deeply, yearning to shout my exhilaration to the sky.

I wasn't a feeble human. It was no longer just Ryia and Tamas. I was Razohan too.

A blur of movement in my periphery caught my attention, but when I looked, I saw only the disturbance left in its wake. Whatever had passed was long gone.

Once I reached the small copse of trees, I slowed to allow Gusselan to catch up, though the copse of trees provided poor shelter, and I itched to get away. While I waited, I looked back on Emberfell, thinking of the Mother, wondering if she was inside or stuck at Emberforge. I pressed a palm to the scar on my chest; the mark left by the Mother, a symbol of her insatiable thirst to win, a symbol of my enslavement, but right now with the strength of the Razohan pulsing through my veins, I felt more empowered than enslaved. Eventually, I would comprehend the connection her mark forged between us, but for now, my focus was on Tamas and our need to escape.

Gusselan arrived, falling against the sturdy trunk of a tree, heaving in gulps of air. "My years at Emberfell made me lazy."

"Don't worry, we'll get there." I glanced to the top of the rampart. An impenetrable stone wall we had no hope of scaling by ourselves.

"How long have you known?"

"Curses," I yelped, jumping aside as Andriet suddenly appeared again.

"What's wrong?" Gusselan glanced around, as if expecting to see an enemy surrounding us.

"Not long," I replied.

"When I first saw you on the Sapphire Rose, you didn't know then?"

I shook my head. No words were a suitable reply.

"You didn't laugh at the pathetic fool dancing on the end of your puppet strings?"

Wasting moments meant potentially losing our freedom, perhaps even Gusselan's life, yet Andriet deserved more compassion than I could spare. He deserved the truth.

"Tressya, I don't understand what's happening?" Gusselan's voice was calm, but I saw the shadows of concern beneath her reserve.

"Did you kill Cirro?"

"No" I shouted. "Never."

"And my father and brother? What about me?" Andriet recoiled, his face twisted in horror. "Was I to be next?"

I pressed my palms to my forehead, feeling the ground shifting beneath me, as if a fissure might open at any moment, mirroring the chasm that had formed within my heart, ready to send me plummeting through.

"I never—"

"More lies, Tressya. Aren't you sick of those?"

I shook my head, blinking the blur from my vision.

"And the northerner? He's been here all along, hasn't he? An accomplice. Even better, a lover. No wonder you cared so little for my brother's affairs." Andriet's words were like a vise.

"We need to go, Tressya." Gusselan stepped forward and placed her hand on my forearm.

"Stay away from her Mother. She'll get you killed. If she doesn't do it herself."

"You're right, we should go," I said.

Andriet, I'm so sorry. I couldn't give him what he wanted or deserved right now. I needed to think of our lives.

"I won't let you take her." Andriet jumped between the two of us.

"The Salmun will kill her," I shouted at Andriet.

"Tell me what is going on," Gusselan demanded.

"It's futile, Mother. She's adept at keeping secrets and spinning lies, but she's never one to tell the truth."

"Please—" I almost slipped and said his name, and that was one more guilt to throw in my grave. I'd never revealed Andriet's presence to his Mother.

I glanced around to see a sparse collection of scraggly trees standing between us and the base of the rampart, offering scant shelter.

Andriet was safe. While his heart could still be broken, his physical body could no longer be touched. We, on the other hand, were vulnerable. "Have you seen any sign of Ryia?"

Gusselan shook her head. "I caught something in the corner of my eye. The northerners are known for their superhuman abilities. I believe it was her."

She moved faster than the wind. Even the burden of my guilt couldn't stop me from hoping I'd possess her strength and speed one day. Given my tenuous links to the Razohan, that aspiration may remain a mere dream.

"Another northerner inside Emberfell?" Andriet gasped. "Mother, you knew?" The pained expression on his face wounded me as sharply as any spear.

But I was already crippled by what I was about to do: ignore Andriet. "We should continue. Are you ready?"

"I would never admit it if I wasn't," Gusselan said with a wry smile, her first ever directed at me. I reciprocated, and for one dreadful moment, feared it might be the last thing we shared.

"No. Mother, don't leave with her. Don't prove yourself the traitor."

Andriet now blocked her path. "She never told you the truth about me. She never revealed what she did; what she can do, because she knows no other way than to manipulate for her own gain."

I turned away from Andriet. "I don't need to tell you to run as fast as you can."

"You need to know." Andriet passed directly through his mother, enveloping her in the essence of his being.

Gusselan gasped, then staggered backward, pressing a palm to her stomach. There was nothing I could do to change this moment, nothing I could say to right the wrongs I'd made, except save Gusselan's life. I rushed forward and took her hand, intent on pulling her with me. "We have to go."

"Tell her the truth, Tressya. Tell her what you've done."

"Leave now," I shouted, summoning the voice to bend Andriet to my command.

I whimpered in horror at seeing him vanish.

Discipline. Panting my calming breath through budding tears, I pulled Gusselan into a run.

We burst from the copse of trees and into the open air, Gusselan staggering beside me because her mind was no longer on our escape.

"We don't have far. You can do it." I urged her onward.

As I ran, I glanced up, seeing birds of prey high above, circling overhead, invoking my memories of the Ashenlands. Suddenly, I felt vulnerable. The few sickly trees, dotted across the broad expanse of open field, were reminiscent of the barren wasteland. My heart choked my throat, as with each pounding of my feet, I expected the dark gloom of the Ashenlands to swallow me whole.

Without realizing it, I'd left Gusselan far behind, my legs carrying me as if I had wings, so I slowed once more on nearing a tree, and caught hold of its trunk to steady myself while I waited for her to catch up. After my sudden prophetic thought, I wanted her beside me. Finally, I noticed my breathing had hitched up a notch, making me slightly uncomfortable.

Jiggling from foot to foot, I grew impatient waiting for her to arrive. When she reached me, I was eager to be off, but Gusselan was clearly struggling to catch her breath. Hair loosened from her tie, clung to the sweat on her temple and neck, her face a blistering red.

"You're beyond natural," she said between panting breaths, and I couldn't help but detect an accusatory tone in her voice, though that might have been because guilt hung from me like creeper.

"When we make it out of here, I promise you, I'll tell you everything."

Time wouldn't wait for us, yet we needed to pause at this moment; otherwise, I feared I would lose Gusselan's trust. I opened myself to her inscrutable gaze, hoping she would see more than a woman who'd kept too many secrets from the people she loved.

"Do you plan to head north? Across the border?"

I blinked, not ready for such a pragmatic question. "I hadn't thought that far ahead, only to escape Emberfell. I have no idea how to cross the Ashenlands."

"I have a manor north of here. Henricus gifted it to me on our first anniversary. It's been practically empty for the last decade, but I maintained a small household of servants. That's all. We'll find privacy there."

I thought of the parchment tucked into the pocket of my

ill-fitting breeches. To hunt down the Etherweave was my final quest. And once I held that power, I would rid myself of the Mother's dark tendrils, wipe the Salmun from these shores and restore the Razohan's rightful place in the south. I would undo all my wrongs.

I had no interest in the Tarragona throne, and though I was yet to fully understand the intricate link between the Etherweave and the Bone Throne, I had no desire to claim the latter.

"Thank you for your offer. I'm sure Ryia will be keen to take Tamas across the border. As Razohan, they can easily fly."

Taking him from me. My voice choked on the last word, the same horrible sickly sensation inflicting me in the king's garden assaulted me again, only this time, in replace of the scorching burn, I felt a hollowness swallowing me whole. For Tamas's sake, I wouldn't stop her. The witch who desired me dead would do everything she could to save him.

"You'll tell me why both are in Tolum?"

I mentally shook off my maudlin thoughts. The six pillars made me strong, but love, as the Mother always warned, made me weak. But I would rather be weak and in love than strong, yet as brittle as glass.

"I'm done with secrets." I'd turned my back on the Sistern, so it was time to discard the pillars, all except the two that I would always hold close to my heart: discipline, a steadfast mind and fearless heart, and courage, to never waver from what must be done.

I allowed one calming breath, centering my mind to our escape.

"Let's go," my voice was like iron.

"Halt," came the cry behind as I pushed off from the tree, about to leap away.

"Shit," Gusselan hissed from behind me.

I turned to see a row of guard, racing through the copse of trees.

"I thought it was all too easy," I whispered, doubling back and taking Gusselan's hand, yanking her into a run. "Ryia is waiting." She had to be.

"No, Tressya. They have crossbows."

Gusselan struggled alongside me, slowing me down when my feet yearned to run at top speed. "As long as they're not Salmun, I don't care what they carry."

Suddenly, Gusselan fought against my hold, tugging me out of my pace. "I may be able to do something. My ability's grown stronger over these last few days."

"For now, there's only a dozen. There'll be more. We need to keep going." My yearning to escape pulsed through my chest in time with my heartbeat.

"My plan is smarter."

"Against an army," I was yelling at her now.

We both turned back, and the sight that greeted us made my heart clench. Behind the initial guards, dozens more approached, and behind them came the Salmun.

"You can't control them all. Ryia will get us over the rampart. We just have to reach it."

"And what?" She jabbed a hand at the approaching enemy. "Outrun them throughout the streets of Tolum."

"Staying here means giving up," I forced the words through gritted teeth, fully aware that we were trapped. Cold fingers seized my heart, the ice slowly making its way up my throat at the thought of the Salmun's victory.

"You're right. Ryia probably can't carry both of us across at the same time." I turned back to watch the approaching guards, noting their cautious approach. That made me smirk. "We need an army of our own." My conviction was sharp as a blade.

"No." I glanced at Gusselan, puzzled by her harsh tone. "No dead," she insisted, her grip painfully tight on my arm. "We're disciples, are we not?"

I pressed my lips together and nodded.

"Let them come." Her voice remained low and calm. "Let them think they've won."

Side by side, we watched the guards loom closer, their cautious steps crunching amongst the dead leaves, tightening the tension in the already thinning air. Their eyes flitted nervously between us, and I wondered what the Salmun had told them to make them so timid.

As they closed in, they fanned out, forming a circle around us, thinking to ensnare us like animals. I slowly turned, following those on the left, until Gusselan and I stood back to back, keeping our eyes firmly on the approaching Salmun.

I flexed my hands over the hilt of my weapons, knowing there was little point in using blades; the Salmun would ensure none met their mark. They were now well aware of the tricks I could play with my mind, which made me question how effective my soul voice would be this time. If I had magic, we wouldn't be in this predicament; the Salmun wouldn't dare challenge us openly.

When I first learned I was heir to the Etherweave, I felt ambivalent. That ambivalence was far behind me now.

The Salmun's gray cloaks flared outward in the gentle breeze, but they kept their hoods pulled low. For the first time, I noticed the simple gray tunic and pants they wore underneath, a stark contrast to the powerful image they tried to portray.

The guards remained silent, waiting for the eight Salmun to arrive, taking their time and savoring their success like victors after a battle.

"I'll handle the guards," Gusselan whispered.

"I'll deal with the Salmun." Somehow.

"My Queen," Orphus' voice slithered out from under his hood, coiling around my throat. "You've placed yourself in a most unfortunate situation." He stepped into the circle formed by the guards, the other seven following to create an inner circle of their own.

"You have two things of mine. Two...very...precious possessions of mine. You understand I cannot let you flee with them."

I tried not to move, though my hand itched to press firmly against the pocket where I'd hidden the pages of the Senjel Oracles.

"Two?" Of course, he would see me as something he owned if that's what he was referring to.

If only I could see his eyes; perhaps then I could gauge his confidence and discern if he had already found a way to keep me out of his head.

"The pages, My Queen. I'm somewhat irked to find the sacred book defiled, but the pages you carelessly ripped from the center are the most important part of the Senjel Oracles."

"And the second?"

"I would argue, perhaps, the most important part—your soul, My Queen."

I bumped into Gusselan's back before I even realized I'd moved, as a heavy sensation sunk through to my feet, turning me to stone.

"Oh yes, it's quite possible you're not really necessary at all. At least not all of you. As one who commands the dead, do you understand what it is you manipulate when you call the dead?"

I stared at him, my mouth too dry to speak.

"They're souls, young queen. That is all. The body is insignificant, and the mind matters little, especially if you plan to turn them into instruments of your desires. When it comes to magic, the soul is the most powerful tool. As masters of soul manipulation, we would struggle to control a Razohan's soul. But yours…"

"I am Razohan," I spat.

"Not fully, My Queen. Not yet. That's why we must perform the ritual without delay."

Gusselan took my hand and gently squeezed it.

A guard to my left suddenly turned his crossbow and fired a bolt into the back of the Salmun in front of him. The Salmun's cry of shocked agony seemed to signal two more guards on my right, who also aimed their crossbows and fired.

The Salmun spun to face their attackers, raising their arms. A low, reverberating chant hummed through the air, oddly soothing in its melody. Rather than a lullaby, their chant formed a shield, causing the bolts to fall harmlessly away.

My dagger left my hand just as Orphus turned back to face me. In mere seconds, it reached him, embedding in the center of his chest instead of his heart because he'd had enough time to jerk sideways. Curses.

His cry halted the attack, and he staggered sideways, caught by one of his own. His hood fell back, revealing his marked face and the hatred in his eyes. His expression was not of a man in pain, but of one possessed by madness, revenge and a savagery intent on destroying realms. "I'll gladly take your soul," he hissed.

With unwavering conviction, *Aetherius* surged forth, spearing into Orphus' mind without mercy. Orphus was ready, though, with a mental armor I couldn't yet break. But wounded, how long would his barrier hold?

I became dimly aware of the guards trying to break the Salmun's shield, using their bodies and crossbows as weapons in a futile attempt to shatter it.

Thank you, Gusselan. They would fail, of course, but their efforts distracted the rest of the Salmun while I focused on Orphus.

Was the prickling sensation stabbing at my mind him? His eyes were fixed on me, his lips set in a grimace.

"A battle of wills," I muttered. "It worked in my favor last time."

"I'll leave nothing intact this time," Orphus growled.

A pain sliced through the back of my mind, forcing my knees to bend under the torment.

"Tressya," Gusselan gasped, taking my hand.

I shut my eyes, ridding Orphus' evil sneer from my sight, and clenched my teeth. *We're greater than him.* I inhaled, delving deep within, gathering the full might of my soul word, feeling its strength embolden me.

There was a sudden grunt, and I was released from my torment. I opened my eyes to see Andriet flittering around the Salmun, passing in and out of each like a needle and thread.

"I don't know what I'm doing," he shouted at me. "I've totally lost my head." As he continued to pass through the bodies of our enemy.

It appeared even the mighty Salmun was uncomfortable with the touch of spirits. Andriet had caught them by surprise, and all seemed confused and badly prepared to deal with the ill feelings his essence created. However, this, too, was nothing more than a distraction.

I concentrated on wielding *Aetherius* like a giant's fist.

"I should champion the Salmun on. They're on my side," Andriet continued. Then he stopped before punching through the chest of another Salmun and stared at me. "You've hurt me beyond words. My heart's in tatters. It may never recover. But...I don't want you to join me, Tressya. Not yet."

Aetherius slipped from my grasp as Andriet's words echoed in my mind. Tears blurred my vision of him, then an agony like no other shot through my head like a bolt. I screamed, my body seizing, my head arching backward. In the distance, I heard a laugh that could turn embers into a ravenous fire. I heard Andriet cry my name with a fear that could kill the dead as a chilling smugness crept across my mind like molasses.

Just as I realized Orphus had found a path into my mind, ready to rip away my control, destroy my sanity, and take my soul, a black form moved overhead. A massive shadow blotted out the sun, casting everything around us into gray.

The nightmare.

CHAPTER EIGHTEEN

TRESSYA

The looming underbelly of the nightmare descended upon us. Amidst the guards' shouts, my heart surged with joy. Tamas. He must be alright. This had to be a sign he was recovered.

The agony in my head subsided as the nightmare took everyone's attention. Noticing his giant clawed feet flex, I knew what he intended to do. I pulled Gusselan, paralyzed in shock, toward me, hugging her close. "We're saved," I whispered in her ear, my voice trembling with the first hints of joyful tears, as huge scaly claws wrapped around us and scooped us off the ground.

Despite it being only my second time leaving the ground, fear overwhelmed me to where I couldn't even scream. Enfolded in Tamas's giant claws, with no view of the ground below and no way to gauge how high he flew—mercy to our fates for such luck—I squeezed my eyes shut, clung to Gusselan and attempted to find my calming breaths, but they eluded me.

Tamas's swift pace created ferocious winds, the chill slipping beneath my clothes to freeze my skin. The warmth of Gusselan's body kept me from turning to ice, and I was sure my fingers had frozen us in our embrace.

I kept my eyes closed tight and hoped the journey would be short. Such a giant creature would surely cover vast distances with only a few flaps of its wings.

Just when I thought I would survive this flight, I sensed Tamas lose height. Until now, the steady beat of his massive wings was like a gentle, relentless rhythm, assuring our safety, only now the rhythm faltered. I shrieked, my stomach feeling as if it had detached and was floating inside me as we plummeted for a beat, before Tamas found his rhythm again.

I had been mistaken; he wasn't all right, yet he had mustered the strength to save us. Now, however, his affliction resurfaced, placing Gusselan and me in grave danger. I wanted to reassure her, to tell her he was strong, that everything would be fine, and that we would escape, but my jaw felt frozen shut.

Tamas continued his faltering wing beats. All the while, I was sure we were losing height. Any minute we would skim the tops of the trees.

When we finally fell, released from his grasp, my jaw released, and I unleashed my scream. Our fall was brief, yet the landing was harsh, expelling the air from my lungs and sending shards of pain through my left shoulder and hip. I lost my grip on Gusselan and tumbled repeatedly before colliding with a fallen log.

Dazed, in pain, I lay still, feeling as though my head was still rolling.

Tamas. Gusselan. Were they both all right?

"Dammit," I spat when I attempted to sit up. My left side throbbed in agony and a high-pitch tune sounded in my left ear.

Gusselan wasn't far away, struggling to sit herself. I shuffled around further and saw Tamas, face down, laying in a patch of small purple flowers. Deathly still. "Tamas," I shouted, struggling to stand. On my feet, I wavered, my mind spinning in circles. Before I knew it, I hit the log and fell back onto my ass. Clutching my head as if it would help stop the spinning, I took a few breaths before daring to stand again.

I allowed myself two steadying breaths before I staggered toward Tamas. Passing Gusselan, I patted her shoulder. "Are you all right?"

"I'm alive," came her deadpan reply.

Tamas lay on his stomach, his head turned to the side, eyes shut. Resting my hand gently on his shoulder, I leaned down, comforted by his warmth breath on my cheek. "Tamas," I whispered into his ear, my voice barely audible as my heart seemed to cease its beat and an invisible claw constricted my throat.

I squeezed his shoulder when he didn't respond and called his name louder.

Please, wake.

"He's alive." I shouted to Gusselan, not realizing she was

already standing over me. The nervous desperation in my voice did nothing to ease my knotted stomach.

"The flight has taken its toll. He'll improve, I'm sure." She reached down and squeezed my shoulder.

"He will," I nodded, accepting no other explanation.

A small voice in the back of my mind warned we were still in danger, but that voice was too insignificant to gain my attention when a mighty fist clawed at my heart. Tamas was alive, for now, but even Ryia was perplexed by his predicament.

"I rarely left the city limits. Henricus wasn't fond of the country. He was even less fond of the manor he gifted me. I supposed that's why he bothered. I've only been there a handful of times, and that was a long time ago, so I couldn't say where we are."

"Ryia?" I uttered, half listening to Gusselan. She needed to take him north to his witch. "We need to find Ryia."

"An impossible task when we don't even know where we are." Gusselan crouched beside me. "I can see he means a lot to you, but we have to think of ourselves. We have to keep moving. Head north. If we can find a village—"

"No. I'm sorry, Gusselan, but you're asking me to do the impossible. I won't leave him like this. You don't have to stay. You can save yourself, but I can't go on until I know Tamas is safe."

She took my hand in both of hers. "Then I'll stay too. Perhaps we could try to move him further under the trees. I'm sure the Salmun will send out scouts."

I glanced around to see Tamas had crashed us into a

clearing, the only place where he could fit the mountainous size of the nightmare.

"They keep monsters in Emberforge, in tunnels deep underneath the temple. That's what they'll use to hunt us down."

As I spoke, I scrutinized Gusselan's face for any hint of her thoughts, any sign that she regretted her choice to accompany me or her recent decision to stay by my side. But there was no shadow of regret. Instead, I saw the iron will and resilience of a woman who'd weathered hardship and loss, yet remained strong.

"Tamas is heir to the Bone Throne." I'd destroyed my friendship with my dearest friend because of my many omissions. Telling Gusselan the truth was the only way I knew how to make amends.

She glanced from Tamas to me. "Yes, now I remember you mentioned his name once before." She sighed. "You're quite the enigma." It wasn't praise because she didn't smile. "I don't know what to think of you."

"I can't change the past with words. Anything I say would be mere excuses. I'm guilty of so much that apologies alone are insufficient. But I give you my word, I will avenge your sons' deaths."

Gusselan nodded. "Before we escaped..."

I knew what she was going to ask. Perhaps it would make her hate me, if I told her. Regardless, I was committed to telling the truth. "It was Andriet."

"Andriet?" Her voice faltered.

"He wanted to prevent you from following me." *He hurts because of me.*

"You spoke to him."

"I'm a terrible disciple, but an excellent spiritweaver," I said through burgeoning tears.

Gusselan rose, palming her mouth as she turned her back on me, sparing herself the sight of me. Watching her pace through her emotions, I felt guilt spread its tendrils around my throat. I swallowed. I swallowed again, trying to ease the constriction, but there was no ridding the steel clamp of guilt's pernicious grip.

I opened my mouth, felt the banks burst, but said it anyhow. "He's been with you the whole time." The tears were a flood, impossible for me to hold back. "I brought him back with me from the Ashenlands because I couldn't bear—"

She reared on me. "You don't know what you've done." Her voice swept over me like a chilling wind.

"I..." Her ire confused me.

"It's bad enough you disturbed the veil and brought forth an army of the dead, but to free a spirit from its death place..." She no longer paced, she stomped, feeding the earth her exasperation, clearly struggling with knowledge regarding the dead that I, as a spiritweaver, should possess.

"What do you know about spiritweaving?"

"Curse that harridan," she spat, deafened in her anger. "She didn't tell you. She's playing a deadly game that could destroy us all."

I rose to my feet. "I know I've done wrong. I understand there are consequences to disturbing the balance between the living and dead."

I spun, her anger driving her toward me. "And yet, you

continued with your actions." She jabbed a finger at me. "I would prefer to believe you were simply naïve," she scoffed.

"You weren't there. I had no choice." Loathed as I was to turn this into an argument, my voice rose.

"What about your choice when you freed my son from his death place?" Her tone thick with scorn.

"You're telling me you would have done differently?" I shouted.

"When the repercussions of our actions are greater than our shattered hearts," she responded with equal force.

Her pacing, her ire—it wasn't about the pain of her loss, and the terrible secret I'd kept from her, even though that was all that consumed my heart.

"It was the only way to win the war."

"If you wanted to win, why were you consorting with this northerner?" she yelled, jabbing her finger at Tamas.

"Because..." I swallowed, facing her wrathful judgement. "Because I'm a fool who lost her heart." The anger drained from my voice.

Her glare remained like shattered glass, sharp and piercing. In this she resembled the Mother—a heart brittle as glass.

The snap of a twig reverberated through the silent forest. Forgetting our argument, Gusselan and I both turned toward the sound. Through the trees, I caught fleeting glimpses of color and movement.

"Quick," I whispered. "We need to drag Tamas—"

"It's too late," she hissed. "It's probably local folk investigating the noise."

Not local folk, but someone perhaps worse.

A female appeared, unlike any I'd ever seen—half-beast, half-human—flanked by the apostles and another man. Beside her, the apostles looked like children. Even the man, taller and broader than any ordinary male, reached as far as her shoulders. Eye catching was her mixed colored eyes, the left the color of syrup, the right deep bronze, as to the scar, a cruel slash from shoulder to elbow.

She scrutinized us before her gaze fixed on Tamas. Crying his name, she rushed to his side, and in that moment, I realized who she was. Ryia. I also grasped another crucial truth: she wasn't Razohan, but Huungardred. It had to be the witch's magic that granted her the complete form of a woman.

"It's a mercy we found you," Plesy said.

My gaze remained fixed on Ryia's misshapen form. Radnisa had told me about the Huungardred's inability to become fully human, but I'd struggled to envision the image in my mind. She also called it a curse. I saw nothing but strength and power; few would choose to displease someone possessing such formidable form.

"And we would have wandered for days without the aid of our companions," Selisimus added.

The man who'd arrived alongside Ryia drew my attention. He walked with the commanding presence of a Razohan, each powerful stride concealing the agility latent within his muscles. His features were handsome the way rugged cliffs and sharp, jagged mountain rangers were admired for their menacing beauty.

Tamas had mentioned something about leaving the apostles with a friend after we'd escaped the tunnels. In my haste to reach Emberfell and Gusselan, I'd not questioned him how it was a northerner had a *friend* in Tolum.

"Osmud." The man stepped forward, extending his hand while a frown marred his harsh features. This felt like a hostile welcome. "Never thought I'd meet you alive."

One apostle gasped, but I brushed aside his snide comment. Osmud was likely one of the Razohan who'd accompanied Tamas on that fateful night aboard the Sapphire Rose. It seemed he still believed my death was necessary.

I never harbored expectations of making friends, but I always anticipated having enemies. Maybe he would prove otherwise, but for now I would keep my eye on Osmud.

"Osmud," Ryia called.

Osmud dismissed me and went to Tamas's side.

"What happened to him?" Wellard said.

"We don't know—" I replied, joining Ryia and Osmud.

"I must take him to Romelda," Ryia announced.

"How long has he been like this?" Tortilus said, moving to stand over him and rising onto his toes for a better look.

"He's grown steadily worse," I said. "He should never have carried us here."

"There's a lot of things he should never have done," Osmud added, under his breath.

I ignored the veiled reference to Tamas keeping me alive. Tamas's safety and survival were more important than any provocation. Panic had dwelled low in my belly this entire day. Now it was alive, clawing its way up with bladed nails, tearing apart my insides in its wake.

"That's interesting," Tortilus said, overriding my urgency as he crouched beside Tamas and pulled his collar aside.

I strangled the urge to shove him aside.

Tortilus failed to elaborate as Plesy and Selisimus gathered around him. Wellard, standing behind them, peered over their shoulders.

"What's interesting?" Decorum gone, I shunted the three of them aside.

"This discoloration." He exposed more of Tamas's neck. "Look here."

Plesy gently nudged me aside. "Apologies, Tressya." He pointed at where I stood. "But I must see."

"And I," Selisimus remark.

Before I knew it, the three apostles moved me aside to inspect Tortilus's find.

"It is as I suspected?" Tortilus said.

"It's suspicious," Plesy said. "We must roll him over."

"What's suspicious? Tell me," I demanded.

"Well, it's possible," Plesy said, but lost track of his thoughts as Osmud eased Tamas onto his back, allowing Tortilus to lift the front of his shirt to his neck.

My gaze lingered on the face I'd grown to adore, and on lips I hungered to kiss once more. Why hadn't I succumbed to my impulse and leaped into his arms, kissing him with the violence of my joy the moment I saw him in the throne room? I pressed my hand to my lips, my need so intense it was as if I could almost feel his mouth against mine.

Tortilus's triumphant noise drew my gaze to the trail of black marks, like oily snail trails snaking across his chest. A terrible poison raced through his body, leaving a blackish tinge spreading out across his abdomen and chest in the trail of the black veining.

I gasped as I dropped to my knees beside Tamas.

"Malignant magic, Your Majesty," Tortilus said, and my distress was so great, I didn't bother to correct him.

"How did this happen?" Osmud demanded.

"I think he engulfed some of the Salmun in the tunnel," I replied.

Wellard made a strangled cough behind me, and Selisimus audibly inhaled.

"You were there. You knew our predicament. If he'd not done what he did, we'd be caught, dead or worse." *Enslaved to the Salmun.* Their judgement was unfairly given. I glared at each of the apostles, daring them to utter one more noise of disgust.

Satisfied each felt suitably chastised, I turned to Ryia, but caught Osmud's eye. I couldn't decide the true thoughts behind his gaze as he watched me. Neither did he seem bothered that I'd caught him staring at me.

He simply quirked a brow, then turned his attention to Tortilus. "What can we do about it?"

"We're minus our reference materials, but we're not entirely incapacitated without them."

"There are spells," Selisimus added. "Infections such as this, we know a few for those."

"Possession," Tortilus added.

"Yes, possession," Selisimus agreed. "There's a few spells we could perform for those."

"Poisoning," Plesy said. "It's well known the Salmun have black blood."

"Romelda will know what to do," Ryia said.

Tortilus glanced over his shoulder at Ryia. "I'm afraid, my lady, he may not make it."

The beast side of Ryia's face remained an inscrutable riddle, but her lovely, syrupy colored eye flared wide in surprise upon hearing Tortilus use a respectful title.

"I can move faster than the wind," she growled.

"Perhaps we should let the witches of the north deal with this matter," Wellard said, sounding less than sure of their ability.

"It's best we begin work immediately," Selisimus said, frowning at Wellard.

Dammit. I would allow the apostles to work their magic, yet Wellard sounded unconvinced they could save him.

"No. We're vulnerable out in the open," Osmud announced.

"I have a manor in the north. Few know of its existence." Gusselan said. "If I knew where we were—"

"I really think it may be for the best if we allow—" I began.

"He's dying," Tortilus snapped. "We need to begin treatment straight away." He fixed his gaze on me. "Delays give the poison time to spread, reducing our chances of success."

"But you're not sure what is happening to him. How do you know what spells to use?" I counted, though I was sure he was right in saying any delay drew Tamas's death closer.

"Tamas reached as far north as Meltonbea." Osmud rose his voice above us all, directing his attention on Gusselan. It was smart of him to do so. Bickering meant nothing of use was achieved.

"It's not much further. Iredale. The county abutting Meltonbea."

"This is madness. Let me take him across the border," Ryia cut in.

"Through the Ashenlands? How will you manage that?" I didn't mean to sound hostile. Without Ryia's aid, Tamas would still be in the king's garden, face down in the dirt, but this was a truth Ryia needed to consider.

"Romelda gave me a way," she replied, her voice slicing like a knife.

Romelda, the witch who wanted me dead; the witch, I would say, who sent Ryia south to succeed where Tamas had failed. If she cured Tamas, I would hold no ill-feelings toward her.

"The poison has already spread too far, and spreads further by the minute," Tortilus announced. "For his sake, we're best head straight for this manor and begin work on his healing straight away."

If what Tortilus said was true, Tamas didn't have time to cross the Ashenlands.

Wellard cleared his throat. "Perhaps Ryia is right about this Romelda."

"Nonsense, Wellard. The greater risk is the journey, when we're so close to this manor," Tortilus said.

"But, do we have the—?" Wellard said.

Tortilus looked to me. "Our knowledge of the healing arts is vast. We've studied the doctrines extensively—"

"We don't have time for your sermon," I interrupted him. One glance at Tamas, seeing his chest covered in the oily streams of poison, I turned to Ryia. "How fast can you reach the manor?"

I could tell from the expression on the human side of her face, the only side conveying any emotion I could read, Ryia was angry with my decision. After a moment of glaring at me, she surprised me with her reply. "Fast."

"How many can you carry?"

She glanced at the apostles. "Enough."

I respected her for yielding to my decision rather than wasting time fighting me. And for her love of Tamas, I forgave her murderous intentions. "Tortilus, how many of you do you need to perform your spells?"

"Plesy and myself, mostly. Though four is better than two."

"Ryia needs speed." *Please, let this be the right decision.*

I turned to Ryia. "Take the two apostles and Tamas. Osmud take Gusselan. She's show you the way to her manor. I assume she won't be too much for you." I couldn't help the sarcasm. Their priority was speed, so I wouldn't weigh Osmud or Ryia, asking them to carry anyone else.

He sneered at me. "As long as she doesn't pull out any of my fur."

"Then go."

"Your Majesty, what about you?" Selisimus said.

"I'm an added weight to slow Osmud and Ryia down and not important for this to work."

Again, I caught Osmud's impenetrable gaze on me. Then he focused on Gusselan. "I mean it. I don't take kindly to bald patches."

"Then you'd better make sure the journey is smooth, Razohan."

He eyed her, then chuckled. When he turned back to me, his smile slipped. "It's best you keep moving in a northerly direction. We'll find you once we've settled Tamas."

I nodded, and we both held each other's gazes. Rather than disdain, dare I say there was a neutrality in the way he stared at me. For my part, I was grateful for his presence; thankful for the two Northerners amongst us.

The apostles yelped and skittered away when Ryia and Osmud transformed into magnificent beasts, standing as large as a horse, twice as wide, with powerful flanks rippling with coiled muscles ready to be away. Ryia, with the lush red streaks buried within her deep rich pelt, was intimidating in her colossal size.

"Come," I ordered the apostles. "Help me put Tamas on Ryia's back."

As a big man, Tamas was heavy, but with the aid of the four apostles, we positioned him awkwardly across Ryia's broad back. It was an ungainly pose, and he'd be humiliated were he conscious, but he was more secure that way.

"Don't let him fall," I admonished the two apostles before they took their place behind Tamas.

Then the two great beasts were away and my heart went with them, holding tight to the man I couldn't bear to lose.

CHAPTER NINETEEN

TAMAS

'You are dying, young Razohan.'

Ovia was lying. The Eone always lied. I refused to believe her, but if I wasn't, why did it hurt so much?

I tried to recall what had made every part of my body burn like the Ashenlands pits and throb with an agony reserved for the dying, but searching my mind was like peering through an impenetrable fog.

'We never expected nor wanted it to end this way.' Ineth came into view, leaning down over me as though peering down upon my sick bed.

'We are truly sorry to see you fade into the death realm.'

Lying on my back, I was vulnerable. A Razohan never allowed themselves to be in such a position. To prove he was lying, I struggled to sit up, only to discover that my body, bathed in torment, failed me. I couldn't even move a finger.

'You were brave, Tamas. Very brave, for one so young,' Fivia crooned. 'Unfortunately, bravery is not reserved for the victor alone.' Fivia wore a gown of deep green, enhancing her green eyes. In her hair, on the left side, she'd braided green and golden lace.

'If this is my death, then leave me to it. You're not welcome.'

Spasms of agony lanced through my head when I dared turn away from Fivia and Ineth. Even a mere twitch of my muscles ignited a deep burn that kept me prisoner.

'Relax, brave soul,' Carthius said. 'Be at peace in knowing your part in this divine game is over. You have done your best. Know you are not alone. We will stay by your side until the final goodbye.'

Being imprisoned within one's own body was enough to enrage any Razohan, and now the Eone forced me to endure their presence. Their incessant prattle would send me to the death realm quicker than a stake through my heart.

I needed to concentrate, find the memories to explain my predicament, not suffer their insincerities, but the fog wrapped tight around my mind like a blanket.

'You struggle to remember because your mind is slowing as your body begins its final journey,' Ovia said.

'Stop reading my mind. You've disregarded my wishes repeatedly. I refused to listen to you now. You're my enemy.' She was lying. She had to be lying because that's all the Eone did.

Move, damn you. My body remained in its cage.

'We are deeply sorry for the hurt we have caused. It was done with good intentions. So, please, young Razohan, we beg you to cease your fighting. It makes the ending more painful.' Fivia's voice was the softest melody in my ears. 'Peace is yours now, young friend. Embrace it.'

Though she spoke softly, her words had the opposite effect. Instead of comforting me, they ignited a desire to fight, so much so that my heart leaped into a wild beat, willing me to tear from this limbo. Yet, my limbs still refused to awaken, as if my head and body were severed from each other.

'I'm not dying.' Rather than spoken with fury, my voice sounded like a child's feeble refusal.

'Your will is strong, but it brings you nothing but grief. Let go of that which you hold dear and surrender, young friend. It is the only way to cease your suffering,' Carthius said.

If only I could rise high enough to head-butt him in the face. It seemed not even my loathing for him could grant me a snippet of freedom for that small satisfaction.

'As soon as I can move my arm, I'm going to take off your head.' I'd do worse if I could touch any of them because their words drove a fury I'd never endured before. 'I'm not fucking dying.' I infused each word with as much conviction as I could muster.

If I wasn't dying, why was I locked in this torture? Why was every part of my body screaming for a relief that seemed possible only in death? I wouldn't believe it. Not like this, not stuck in my mind with the Eone. If there was to be a deathbed vigil, my closest would be by my side, and the woman I loved: Tressya.

The Eone huddled in a circle, murmuring in a language I

didn't understand. Curious to what they were saying, furious that I should even care, and desperate to climb off my deathbed, I roared, lurching myself forward with every ounce of my strength.

Two hands clamped on my shoulders, pressing me down. Distant voices chimed in my head, voices distinctly not Eone. I wasn't alone, as the Eone would have me believe. This knowledge loosened the fog's tight embrace. I had felt hands on my body, and now I sensed whatever lay beneath me—it was soft, like a bed.

Before I could utter a cry, hoping my shout would reach those beside me, the Eone was at my side, peering over me.

'We have decided to give you one last gift before you fade from the realm of the living,' Ineth said.

I shook my head, squeezing my eyes shut, determined to block them out, determined to break free from the shackles that bound my mind. If I could do that, I was sure I could see, move, and talk. The Eone trapped me with their lies. But with their return, the fog also returned, shrouding my senses once again.

'Tamas,' Fivia said, gently placing her hand on my shoulder. 'These are your last few moments. Our gift is precious. Do not waste it on raging against the inevitable.'

'Your gift is poisonous.'

'Our gift comes from our hearts. A valuable gift for the dying.'

'You're liars,' I shouted, renewing my struggle to break free from the binds on my mind and body. 'You've lost my trust now.'

'That is a pity.'

My gaze shifted to Carthius. My struggle and anger faltered at seeing the sadness in his eyes. It wasn't genuine. It couldn't be. The Eone was manipulative and dishonest. Nothing that came from their mouths could be believed.

"The poisonous infection appears to be spreading," came an unfamiliar male voice that wasn't inside my head. The same man who'd pressed me into the bed?

'Tamas.' Ovia touched my cheek with the back of her hand. 'Your mind is fighting its end, wanting to distract you from its death.'

I tried to roll my head away from her touch, but in this torturous cage there seemed no escape from the Eone.

The voice was real, not a dream I'd woven to fight death.

"We must keep trying. Once Selisimus and Wellard arrive, we shall have more strength."

Who were these people? Not Osmud and Garrat, whom I was sure would be present in my final moments. Perhaps Ovia was right, and my mind was trying to distract me from my impending death.

"Perhaps we're getting the phrasing wrong. It's such a complicated language."

"No. I'm certain of what we're saying."

In my last hours, why would I attempt to find comfort with strangers?

"I fear we made a mistake in insisting they allow us to treat him."

"Have faith, Plesy. These past decades, we've honed our abilities. And now we have a chance to prove ourselves and be of use."

"Something this important, I fear we should've allowed

them to take him to his people. This magic is too great for us."

"Now is not the time to lose faith in your training."

'Tamas,' came a soft, harmonious voice.

I turned my head toward the sound and found Fivia leaning close. 'Come, young Razohan. Let us open your eyes.'

I squeezed them tight. 'To your lies, no thanks.'

'You will soon see for yourself if what we say is lies,' she continued.

I felt a shift in my mind, as if I were leaving it and my body behind, floating. This sensation roiled my stomach and raised a lump in my throat, but rather than being sickness, I gasped in surprise and relief, for the agony in my body had eased. The fight was useless, but I fought death all the same.

'Relax, young friend,' said Ineth. 'You are not yet dead. But close—'

'So close, young Razohan,' continued Carthius. 'We wish to bestow this gift before it is too late.'

When only I saw the Eone, I now saw a stately room, richly adorned with lush rugs, colorful tapestries, dark wood furniture and heavy drapes pulled wide to reveal a shaft of sunlight piercing through a gray cloud. This wasn't Ironhelm.

'Where am I?'

'Look, young Tamas,' Fivia said.

I drew my gaze from the window to look down upon the three people in the room. Suddenly the fog, holding my mind prisoner, parted, and my memories flooded in. Emberforge, the ritual, our flight, the fight.

This was the Eone's gift; sharing my last moments.

The two apostles, Tortilus and Plesy, sat on the bed beside me. Whether it was from moving my body or some other unearthly force, I shifted closer, peering down between the two apostles. Their hands were placed upon my chest and chanting in an ancient tongue unearthed from one of their tomes, attempting to heal me from Salmun magic.

After the apostles insisted we return through Emberforge and not the labyrinth of deep tunnels under the temple, we separated in the streets of Tolum, with Tressya insisting on returning to Emberfell for Gusselan, stubbornly refusing to leave immediately despite my arguments. I made my way to Orbiteen House and Osmud, deciding it was best to leave the apostles with him while I ensured Tressya and Gusselan could escape Emberfell smoothly.

The Salmun's poisonous magic had worked fast, consuming my strength and vitality, ensuring I failed to reach the north with Tressya and Gusselan in my claws. I'd struggled hard to maintain my height, filled with the horror of knowing that if I fell, so too would Tressya.

'Where's Tressya?' I demanded.

She'd be there by my side. In my last hours, she would. I knew she would. That she wasn't... I couldn't bear the thought. And Osmud? If the apostles were here, it had to mean Osmud had caught up with us, as I knew he would. No one was better at tracking than a Razohan, except a Huungardred.

'Young Tamas, we are sorry—' Ovid began.

'We did not agree to this,' Carthius interrupted.

'Shut up and tell me?' I snarled.

Carthius continued as if I hadn't spoken. 'We agreed to ease his suffering. He deserves peace.'

'I want the truth.' My gaze shifted to each of the Eone. 'What're you hiding?'

'Please, Carthius,' Ovid said.

'His final minutes will be filled with suffering. We agreed to interfere to ease that burden, not make it worse.'

'I implore you, Carthius,' Ovia continued. She looked to Ineth and then Fivia. 'Let us grant him his dying wish. To not tell, I believe would be far worse.'

'She's right. If you really want me at peace, then tell me where Tressya is?'

Carthius ducked his head, slowly shaking it as he sighed. 'Very well. We will grant you your wish, but know it burdens our heart to see you suffer when there is nothing you can do to change either your fate or Tressya's.'

'Tell me,' I shouted.

'Tressya is dying, just as you are.' It was Ineth who revealed the shocking truth.

'What?'

'It seems we were wrong, young friend. Yours and Tressya's fates were never to sit upon the Bone Throne.'

'That can't be true. Tressya's not dying.' My mind and heart raged.

'The poison in your veins is no ordinary poison. The Salmun cursed you from within. There is no stopping its spread. You are too weak, my friend. You were too weak to carry your two companions with you.'

I stared down at myself, prone on the bed, seeing the

black striations spreading across my torso, climbing their way up my throat. I shook my head, all the while knowing my refusal was futile. I'd felt the beginnings of the sickness inside the tunnel, only for it to grow worse with each breath I made.

'You tried, Tamas. Your will was strong, but the poison laded your body. Your two companions suffered terribly from the fall.'

I turned, spearing my hands through my hair.

'Osmud rushed you here first, with two apostles intent on curing the poison, which...they unfortunately, cannot. Now your friend has returned to your two companions. But it is unlikely there is much that can be done. The apostles will try, of course, using whatever rudimentary healing arts they have taught themselves. But it is not enough. Not nearly enough. Not for you. And not for Tressya.'

'You're lying,' I growled. 'The prophecy stated an heir to Ricaud will one day claim the throne.'

'Many prophecies are made, my friend. Each countering the last. It seems, perhaps, another was made unbeknownst to the Nazeen.'

I detested how easily the Eone sifted through my mind, yet it seemed in the end, I would endure a fitting punishment, for that was my ability when I took the souls of those I killed.

'This can't be true. It can't be the end. What about the Etherweave?'

'With the deaths of you and Tressya, the last heirs of King Ricaud will have passed. The Etherweave will rise, but with no one capable of possessing and wielding it, it will return to the elements whence it came, and we can rest in eternal peace knowing no one can wield it for evil.'

'I don't believe you. The Etherweave was your creation. You're as greedy for it now as you were when you were alive. If it vanishes, you vanish.'

'We are weary, young Tamas. Too many millennia we've lived. Our final rest beckons us and we long to heed its call.'

'No. You're lying. That's all you're capable of doing.' I spun away from them. "I'm not ready to die." The truth pulsed through my veins, filling me with a defiance that made me feel as if I couldn't die. Yet, I was dying. The evidence was right before my eyes.

'There is only one way to survive this fate, my friend,' Carthius said.

'And to save Tressya,' added Ovia. 'But we do not choose to take such a path. We wish only to take our final sleep.'

'What way is it?' I growled. Two strides and I'd seized Ovia by the throat. 'If there is a way to save Tressya, you'll tell me now.'

'It's risky,' Carthius said.

'Too risky,' Ineth replied.

'Tell me,' I shouted at the two males, releasing Ovia's throat.

She stumbled away into Fivia's arms. Cradled in Fivia's embrace, she said to her two male companions. 'Tell him. We owe him that for our part in all of this.'

Carthius nodded. 'Very well. If you wish to save Tressya's life, you must accept us.' He spoke with such solemnity it was hard for me to dismiss what I'd heard.

'What are you talking about?' This was a ploy.

'Open your mind, Tamas,' Fivia urged. 'Allow us into your mind and soul.'

'We retain remanent power,' Ineth said. 'If you surrender to us and allow us to work through you, together we will save Tressya.'

I backed away from them, huffing my disdainful laugh. 'Of course. I should've known.'

The Eone exchanged glances, revealing nothing of their thoughts.

'Very well. That is your wish. We will understand and respect the choice you have made,' Ineth said.

'We have wronged you. It was kinder to allow you to pass in ignorance,' Ovia said.

'I am sorry for my part. It was I who convinced you all to tell the truth,' Fivia said.

'No, Fivia, do not blame yourself for your kind heart,' Carthius said.

'Shut up. Shut up. Shut up,' I yelled, fisting my hair. 'You always lie. That's all you do. Lie and manipulate. I can't trust you.'

'And we are sorry for your confusion and pain. Please, calm yourself, young Razohan. Allow your final moments to end in peace,' Ovia said.

'Fuck that. And fuck you. Tressya won't die.' *Because of me.* I should never have carried her when I felt so ill.

'There is no holding back death when it arrives for you.'

'You said there was.'

'We have been honest. Yes. That is the only way,' Carthius said.

'But you have made your choice, and we respect that,' Fivia continued.

'If I can save Tressya, then I'll do it. I'll let you in. But you'd better swear on your lives you're telling me the truth.'

'In your final hours, we would never lie. But you must be sure you of your consent.'

'Just fucking do it. We're wasting time and Tressya's life.'

'Very well. If this is your wish.' Carthius held out his hand to Ineth on his left. 'Come.' He motioned for me to take his right hand. Ovia took my other hand and so it went until the five of us were joined in a circle.

'Open your mind, young Razohan. Whatever you do, whatever you feel, don't shut us out.'

I closed my eyes, unable to witness the apostles' pitiful attempt to free me from the Salmun's magic. I refused to dwell on the terrible mistake I might be making in accepting the Eone. All I could concentrate on was my torment in knowing Tressya was suffering because of me. She had to survive. I could accept my own death, but never hers.

Their chanting started as a low hum, growing in strength and intensity on every repeat of their mantra. It wove around my mind and heart like tendrils of smoke, fleeting touches that made me want to recoil. Instincts told me to resist the touch, release both Carthius's and Ovia's hands and back away, but I fought against my instincts.

For Tressya I would surrender.

An awareness nudged at my mind the same moment I felt a stab pierce my heart. I tried to suck in a breath, but instead of air, I sucked in smoke, which coated my tongue in a layer of tar and burned the back of my throat. It felt as though I was breathing through water, each breath gradually drowning me.

I struggled against Carthius's hold, but our hands felt melded together.

Do not fight, young Razohan, came Carthius's voice in my head.

I surrendered for Tressya's sake, to save her as they'd promised. And right now, I was perhaps making the biggest mistake of my life, but I'd rather make this mistake than discover I'd refused my one chance of saving her.

I yielded and let them in, feeling my mind expand as if it were swelling beyond the confines of my skull. My heart raced uncontrollably, and an icy chill seemed to freeze the blood in my veins. I could have sworn my heart ceased beating for a moment, only to restart with such a forceful lurch that it threw me backward, causing me to lose my grip on Carthius and Ovia's hands.

I jerked upright, feeling the bedding beneath me, the gentle breeze caressing my exposed skin and smelling the soft scent of day lilies.

"It worked," shouted a man beside me.

I turned, blinked and stared at Plesy.

"We did it," Tortilus announced.

I clambered across to the other side of the bed and climbed off.

"Wait. What're you doing?" Tortilus said.

"It's best you don't stand. You were badly infected by the Salmun's poison. It's probably—"

"Where's Tressya?" I demanded as I strode for the door.

Halfway across the room, I heard the hurried footsteps

ascending the stairs. I dashed to the door just as it burst open, and Tressya rushed in.

We stared at each other as if no one was there.

"You're alive," we said in unison.

"You survived." We again spoke as one.

"I felt sure—" We both stopped, having said the same words again.

To double my surprise, Bryra walked through the door. "Bryra?"

"Tamas," she replied.

"Bryra?" Tressya said, turning to stare up at the Huungardred.

"It worked," Selisimus announced, squeezing around Bryra who blocked the doorway while her gaze remained steadfast on me.

"I must admit, I had my doubts. I feared we had it wrong," Plesy said.

The apostles' conversation dwindled to a murmur as Osmud entered, trailed by Gusselan. Osmud strode over and enveloped me in a hug, thumping my back as though he intended to punch my lungs through my ribcage. Yet my gaze was fixed on Tressya as I realized how much the Eone had fooled me.

What had I done?

CHAPTER
TWENTY

TRESSYA

From the balcony, I observed Tamas, his solitary shadow, a long tower beside him, as he paced the winding paths through the manicured garden. Already the flowers in their garden beds were closing their petals as the sun slipped lower upon the horizon.

Shunning everyone, he'd disappeared outside and had yet to return, instead choosing the flowers as friends.

I lingered on the balcony for as long as he roamed the grounds below, watching him pace with a heaviness in his stride. His usual agility and grace had vanished, his strides now labored, as though burdened with an invisible weight that trailed behind him.

The pernicious anchor of dread coiled around me like a rope, dragging me into the depths until my breaths turned shallow and my lungs refused to fill.

Watching him was an intoxicating blend of arousal and pain. My desire and distrust for him were enmeshed that I saw no clear path to separate the two. Had I followed my heart, I would never have let him leave. Instead, I would have held him close, compelling him to meet my gaze, searching for the assurance that he was truly free from the Salmun's magic. Yet, I let him go, opting to observe him from a distance, while a shadowy gloom loomed ominously behind me.

Perhaps I would forever remain scarred by the plague of my conflicting emotions.

It appeared the apostles had triumphed. They were, just now, in the kitchen, downing their weight in ale and congratulating themselves on their success, even though I had caught Wellard casting Tamas a sideways glance as if questioning the truth of their assumption.

To me, Tamas remained the untamed beast I yearned to own, as beautiful as he was powerful, as captivating as he was dangerous. On the surface, he appeared unchanged from the day he emerged from the Ashenlands, but what lay beneath what the eyes could see? His aimless pacing spoke of his inner turmoil.

I pressed my hand against the pocket of my breeches, fearing that his troubled mind stemmed from what I had taken from him—the parchment—that his focus, now he was healthy, remained fixed on one outcome, as should be mine.

Earlier, when I had unfolded the blank pages, I discovered they remained blank. Why were they hiding their secrets from me, the heir? I refolded them and slipped them back into my pocket, hoping that with more time and focus, I could unlock their hidden secrets.

The Salmun would hunt us down soon enough, and we were still no closer to discovering the resting place of the Etherweave. Now that Tamas had recovered, deciphering the mysterious pages and finding the great power should be our primary focus. We needed to begin our journey to the Etherweave as soon as possible.

The gentle scent of daisies carried on warm winds reached me before Gusselan came out onto the balcony. She stood beside me, following my line of sight.

"You're worried about him."

"This is unlike him."

"You know him that well?" There was a teasing lilt in her voice.

She was right. All I knew about Tamas was derived from my fictitious dreams. We'd spent little time together and shared only a handful of truths about ourselves. My heart had filled in the gaps in my knowledge, transforming him into a hero. And that could be far from the truth.

Gusselan remained silent, her eyes tracking his movements through the garden. "There's no telling what lingering effects remain. We understand so little about the depths of the Salmun's magic, and the apostles are..." She paused, turning to me as if the significance of her words had just dawned on her. "At least he's walking." Her attempt at consolation did little to ease my nagging worry.

"Perhaps I should've allowed Bryra to take him north to his witch."

"You might never have seen him again."

It was impossible, and not because I believed he was here for me. I had retrieved the parchment from his jacket before Bryra brought him here because I feared losing them, but also because I wasn't entirely sure I could trust Tamas's motives.

"He's still here."

"And you question if that's because he still doesn't have what he wants."

I turned from Tamas and his pacing and rested back against the railing. "Yes."

I pulled the parchment from the oversized breeches Bryra had stolen for me and held them up for Gusselan to see. "He's missing one vital piece of information."

"Stolen from the heart of Emberforge," Gusselan spoke, her voice carrying a whisper of awe.

"The very place."

"You know the Salmun will come for you."

"As will the Mother. I'm not sure who will reach us first, but we have to leave here as soon as possible. If only Tamas would stop his pacing and Bryra would return."

"You wish to continue on with the Huungardred?"

"We need as many powerful friends as we can gather against the Salmun, and Bryra has proved her worth."

"Very well, but don't tell me where you intend to go."

"You're not coming with us?"

"I have no desire to run. I'm too old for such things."

"They won't spare you."

"That's why I prefer not to know your destination. If I'm ignorant of the truth, they can't extract it from me."

"Gusselan. You can't expect me to—"

"You'll respect my wishes." She took my hands. "Without my sons... I've already lived my life, and now I'm free of Emberfell and the Salmun, I no longer care of my fate." Her grip tightened. "But you must promise me this. Return Andriet to his final resting place." She held up a hand to silence any protest I may make. "You must do this, no matter how much it pains you."

"Tell me why."

She released my hands and turned back to the railing, gripping them tight as she spoke. "It's a lengthy story that begins with remnants inscribed on now-broken tablets. The language is ancient and challenging to translate, and since only partial fragments were found, the full narrative remains uncertain."

"It was before the great war?"

"Perhaps millennia before. No one truly knows, but it's incredibly ancient. When I arrived in Tolum, I realized that little of what was uncovered in the fragments had crossed the sea to the near realm. It seems the people of Tarragona are largely unaware of the legend."

"What did you learn?"

"The realms weren't governed as they are today. There were only two distinct powers of influence. One held sway over the distant realms, where my home lies now. The other ruled from what we currently call Tolum.

"Those who painstakingly transcribed the fragments found no mention of the names given to the two distinct powers that ruled millennia ago. However, they were later labeled the Divines for those who ruled the far realms and the Ancients for those in the near realms."

"I've heard of the ancients. It's a name the spirits in the Ashenlands knew."

"Perhaps a millennium ago, the legends were more widespread."

"What does this have to do with Andriet?"

"There is scant information on what transpired between the Divines and the Ancients. The fragments are patchy. But at one point, it seems they were at war. There was brief mention of the Etherweave, and some believe it was created by the Ancients, but the important fragments detailing this part of the narrative were found crushed.

"How and why they created the Etherweave, we'll never know. It's not important."

"But they had something to do with the spirits and the dividing veil?" I said.

Gusselan sighed, arched her head to stretch her neck, then settled her gaze on me. "Through some powerful magic, possibly involving the Etherweave, the Ancients were defeated. However, we will never know for certain. It seems the Ancients—and perhaps the Divines, though we have no fragments to prove it—were trapped behind the veil that separates the living from the dead.

"It is now believed that disturbing the delicate balance separating the living from the dead would weaken the bonds that keep the Ancients—and possibly the Divines—caged. That is why you must return Andriet and promise never to bring the dead across the veil again. For every day Andriet roams free is a tear in the balance and the veil, which may release both powerful factions once again."

I turned to face her. "But you don't know that."

Gusselan rubbed at her temple. "That's what my order believed." As if that was the sole truth.

"You don't even know if they were bad."

"Power is corrupting. That's a truth not even you can argue against."

"You're right, but it doesn't make anything you believe about the two factions true." I shrugged. "You're speculating on a fate that might not even be true."

"And you're arguing against everything I've said because you don't want to do as I ask." Her voice rose.

I pushed off the railing where I'd been leaning. "He tried to help us the day we escaped Emberforge. He tried to distract the Salmun and give us time to reach the rampart." Gusselan's stare remained deadpan. "His final resting place is the Ashenlands. He's your son. Can you bear that thought?"

"What about Juel? He is left to befriend the wild pigs and bees."

I covered my face with my palms as I turned away from her, aware that her piercing, discerning gaze would reveal how little I cared about Juel's suffering.

"Andriet will be welcomed amongst the many hundreds of spirits that lost their lives when the Salmun created the Ashenlands," Gusselan said.

I sagged against the railing, feeling unable to support the weight of this decision. "I'm not sure I'm strong enough to say goodbye."

"You must be ready. You may no longer be a disciple, but you understand what duty means. You have a responsibility to the people of Tarragona, and possibly to all who inhabit the seven realms. Are you prepared to accept the consequences if you release both factions back into the seven realms?"

I pushed off and paced away, needing space from the intensity of her argument. Even Gusselan admitted to only knowing a fragment of the story. It could be there was nothing in this at all, and I would be spared the pain of sending Andriet to his death place. But what if she was right? Was I prepared to ignore that possibility?

"Nothing good can ever come of disturbing the balance of the natural order. If the veil breaks, perhaps it will release more than just power."

I gazed over the balcony, finding no solace in watching Tamas's relentless pacing. He, like me, seemed to wrestle with decisions he found difficult to confront.

Deep in my heart, I knew Gusselan was right. I knew releasing Andriet was a mistake. I was all too aware that life meant enduring suffering and heartache, and that no one was meant to escape that truth. Even if I had experienced my share of suffering, I knew it was wrong to cheat the balance simply because I had the power to do so. Just as I felt guilt gnawing away at my peace with sharp teeth every time I commanded the dead, I suspected the consequences were dire. Though unforeseen, these consequences loomed as a future problem, easier to ignore in favor of dealing with the immediate issue at hand.

She seized my arm. "Promise me, Tressya."

I couldn't avoid her insistent gaze, burrowing into me like termites.

"I know how conflicted you are. But know you're doing the right thing."

Gusselan had the strength to do what was right because she wasn't the one to look in his eyes, to hear his pleas, as she sent him away.

"Promise me."

I swallowed. "I'll try."

She gripped my upper arms, giving me a gentle shake. "That's not good enough."

"I know."

Unable to look at me, she closed her eyes, lowering her chin to her chest. "I've warned you."

"Thank you."

She released me and returned inside the manor. I stared up at the fading sun, seeing the sun's rays tinging the edges of the gray clouds' gentle pinks and oranges.

Tamas, after treading the same path for numerous turns, made his way toward a maze of hedges, meticulously trimmed into neat, boxed rows that meandered out of sight. The hedges began at waist height but grew taller the deeper one ventured into their labyrinth. I strained to catch a final glimpse of him as he turned left and vanished around a corner.

I left the balcony, taking the stairs two at a time, and collided with Osmud at the bottom. He seized my arms, at first to steady me, but then he seemed unwilling to let me go.

"Anxious to be somewhere?" He quirked a brow.

"Have you seen Bryra?" She'd disappeared the moment she'd learned Tamas had survived.

He frowned down at me, as yet to release me from his hold. "She can take care of herself."

"And you question if I can?"

"I question many things about you. Whether you can take care of yourself is not one of them. Why would I care?"

He looked as cuddly as a snake and distrusting as anyone who had faced a cunning and deceitful foe, but I was not his enemy. The color of his eyes was remarkable, but only half as much as their piercing intensity.

"Do you really believe I would save my enemy?"

"If saving him served a purpose, yes."

"You trust Bryra's judgement. She was sent to kill me, but saved me instead."

In response, Osmud let me go, taking a step backward, his shock evident. "That can't be true."

"Can you explain how she passed through the Ashenlands unharmed? And how she reached Emberfell with no one thinking her curious?"

"She was in Emberfell?"

Osmud placed his hands on his hips, half-turning away from me as if what he had heard was too much to bear. "This will gut Tamas," he murmured, speaking more to himself than to me. Then he focused on me again. "How did she enter Emberfell?"

"None of that matters. I don't intend to tell Tamas anything. It's up to Bryra to decide what she wants to reveal. Tamas was already weakened when he arrived at Emberfell. He was in no state to help us escape. It was Bryra who saved him, and by doing so, saved Gusselan and me as well. For that, I am grateful to her."

The four apostles appeared from the kitchen, and seeing Osmud and I hurried over.

"Tressya, may I say, we're a little concerned he's spending so much time on his feet," Tortilus said. "Perhaps it's a testament to our skill that he's able to do so, but we feel—"

"I was on my way to speak to him," I interrupted and pushed past the five of them for the front door.

The gloom of approaching dusk cast the garden bed in a dull gray hue. Further on, shadows shrouded the maze of hedges. Given his head start, I wasn't confident in finding him.

"Tamas," I called as I moved farther into the maze, pulling the collar of my shirt up high to protect against the creeping chill.

The towering hedges on either side exuded the smell of oily resin and fresh-scented mallee pine. When I reached the end of the first path, I couldn't recall which way Tamas had turned, my mind preoccupied with all Gusselan had told me.

"Tamas." I stilled, believing I heard scuffling boots from within the maze. "Don't you dare force me to go in after you."

I held my breath. Nothing. "Everyone in the manor thinks you've lost your head. And that includes me."

Still, I heard nothing, but Tamas always claimed he was the perfect predator.

"The apostles are worried you're exerting yourself. They've spent the last few hours congratulating themselves in the kitchen with Gusselan's ale, and if you stay in here any longer, they'll down the wine as well," I yelled.

"That wouldn't do," he said from behind me, looking too casual for all the worry everyone else was brewing over him. "No one need worry about the residual effects of the Salmun's magic. I can say that's long gone. So perhaps the apostles deserve a wine or two."

"So if you're no longer suffering the effects of Salmun magic, why are you acting like you've gone insane? Normal people don't march around in circles through a garden bed for hours, Tamas."

He released a huff of laughter, a sound that was comforting and familiar, easing the tight knot in my stomach.

"Razohan can't handle being confined to a sickbed."

I nodded. "Plausible excuse."

"Why don't you walk with me?" He offered the crook of his arm.

"Through a maze, in the dark?"

"Are you frightened we may get lost?"

"I was thinking we should deal with the more pressing issues."

"Which are?"

"I'd say being hunted by the Salmun is pressing. And the Mother won't sit idle while we disappear."

"Your Mother Divine is the least of our worries."

He believed this only because he was unaware of the actions she had taken to secure her position in the power struggle. Given the apostles had healed Tamas's sickness, maybe they had the power to save me from the curse the Mother placed upon me; there had to be a way to sever the link between the Mother's and my fates.

"The Salmun are a real threat."

He slowly prowled toward me. "I think you worry too much."

What was going on with him?

"And I think you truly have lost your mind. The Salmun's poison seems to have burned all sense in your brain."

He laughed, but I was dead serious. I glared at him, but perhaps the intensity of my glare was lost in the dim dusk light.

"Tressya. Tressya. Tressya. You always needed a little loosening." Every time he spoke my name, he took one step closer until he'd taken all my free space and air.

I would be lying if I said I didn't find his prowling distracting—more than that, I found it arousing—but there was something unsettling in his demeanor. Our situation had never felt more precarious, yet Tamas seemed indifferent to the dangers we faced.

"How many Salmun did you consume?"

Even that remark failed to alter his expression. His lazy, arrogant smile remained undiminished, and now he was twirling a loose strand of my hair around his finger, subtly brushing his knuckles against my chin to distract me from my question.

"Do you really want me to answer that?"

He released the strand, only to trace his finger along my jawline until he reached my chin. I was grateful the near darkness shielded his eyes, preventing me from seeing where his gaze lingered.

"Not really," I answered, sounding in a daze.

His enticing touch worked. Damn him. I should pull

away, but it had been too long since I'd felt Tamas' hands on me.

I succumbed to the magic of his fingers, let him cast his spell over me because I wasn't as strong as I wished to be. My body craved too much, and my heart craved even more. Neither the threat of the Salmun or the Mother, nor the possibility that Tamas had returned to the south for less honorable and sincere reasons, could make me easily dismiss him or what he was silently offering.

"Why did you come back?" The question escaped my lips before I could hold it back.

"You know why?" As he leaned down, the imminent threat of a kiss made every rational thought vanish, except for a lingering niggle in the back of my mind that implored me to maintain a semblance of sanity against his allure.

His response could mean one of two things, depending on the true nature of our relationship, and I was not convinced that his heart was aligned with mine.

That fateful night in the Ashenlands, after he'd risked his life by turning against the witch Romelda, I believed we were united in our hearts. Weeks had passed, and much had transpired since then. He had spent his time in the north, under Romelda's influence and surrounded by friends obviously opposed to keeping me alive.

I had encountered him in the throne room, even though he insisted he had come to me first, yet I had no way of determining the truth of his claim. Did he return to the south solely for the torn pages now in my pocket? There was no point in asking, as I could never be certain whether his answers were truthful.

I attempted to create some distance between us, but Tamas snapped out his arm and wrapped it around my waist, beguilingly, suffocatingly, anchoring me against him, holding me closer than we'd been before. Instead of focusing on the challenges we faced, as a stronger woman might have, the sensation of his warm body, pressing against mine, consumed all my attention. His scent, which had lingered so long in my memories, had become a craving I couldn't ignore, and I was a woman who'd been starved of affection for too much of my life.

Discipline. I needed the main tenet of the six pillars to help me float rather than sink in the ocean of my hunger. "What about the pages from the Senjel Oracles?"

"What about them?"

"No," I struggled to escape his embrace. "Stop it." He was being deceitful by omission. The hidden pages meant more to him than he let on. Twice he had stealthily entered Emberforge to search for them. I refused to delude myself into thinking he'd returned for me; his primary motivation for coming south was to hunt the Senjel Oracles.

"Easy, little queen." Tamas bound my wrists in a tight grip.

"Let go of me," I growled.

Using his lethal Razohan reflexes, he pinned my hands behind my back, anchored them in place with one hand. "Only if you ask me nicely," he crooned.

I lurched forward, intent on head-butting him in the nose to find air, as Tamas jerked his head away. He also caught my leg between his thighs to prevent my intended jab to his groin.

"This is the Tressya I know and love."

Love, as in a provocation he couldn't resist; love, as in a challenge he longed to conquer. This was all a game to him. I would do well to believe there were no other emotions attached to the word that his heart would acknowledge.

"This is the Tamas I've learned to hate," I sneered.

It was a lie, which made my heart bleed.

He suddenly released me, watching me stagger backward.

"If I had a dagger—"

"You would have attempted to stab it through my eye."

"Heart. It's more lethal that way."

He huffed a laugh. "I've missed your sharp wit."

"Because you're surrounded by dullards and grovelers."

"Because no one captures my full attention quite like you."

His captivating words ensnared any sharp retort I might have offered, yet I couldn't allow myself to succumb to his seductive allure and lose myself. Not until I was certain that my heart was unbreakable. "I can't share your sentiment. Neither do I want to. We should return to the manor."

He stepped toward me—was it a threat? I halted, wary of his motive. "You wanted to talk about these?" And he pulled from his pocket the folded pages I'd torn from the Senjel Oracles.

"How—?" In any manner of ways. He was a man as cunning as he was fast.

"I should've known there was a more sinister reason for manhandling me."

"My singular reason was pleasure. But this—" He waved them in front of me "—was a bonus."

Stealing them from me was hardly an act of trust, and I would make that clear except my curiosity won out. "And what do they say?" Would they easily reveal themselves to him?

"See for yourself."

He offered them to me.

I didn't want him to know I'd already tried. "In this light? I can barely make out your face, let alone read illegible scrawl."

"Then let us return to the light." He made to slip his hand to the small of my back, so I hurriedly retraced my steps through the maze and back toward the manor.

It didn't take us long to reach the sprawling portico. I mounted the steps and headed inside, conscious of Tamas' heavy footfalls close at my heels. I spared a glance into the grand reception room as I passed, seeing the apostles huddled around what appeared to be a book, before I took the stairs, two at a time.

I was halfway up when Osmud called out from behind us.

"Everything all right?"

I didn't stop my ascent, ignoring Tamas' reply, but he caught me up once I reached the landing, slipping his hand into mine and tugging me in one direction. I resisted withdrawing my hand, not knowing where I would go otherwise, until Tamas led me into his room and shut the door.

A candle remained lit, casting a buttery yellow glow across the walls. I glanced to the crumpled covers on the bed and thought of sex, then admonished myself for the thirst still lingering no matter my growing distrust and—I had to be honest with myself—dislike for this new Tamas.

"There's plenty of light now."

I turned from him and strolled toward the candle beside the bed. "What did it feel like when you were sick with the Salmun's magic?"

"That's a distraction."

"I'm honestly curious." I eased myself down on the side of the bed.

"Agony. And then I was saved. How about you look at the pages?"

I placed them in my lap, resting my hands on top. "Do you believe the apostles saved you? Are you truly free of the Salmun's influence?"

"That's what this is about. You think I'm possessed?"

"You're different."

"Better I hope."

I hitched a breath when he crouched in front of me, his muscular thighs outlined against his pants, his large body leaning toward me, caging me, as he placed his hands on my knees. How was it most movements he made had my mind so easily switching from thinking of safety and escape to thinking of me and him between the sheets? Hypnotized by how intoxicating his presence was to me, I simply stared at him like the dullard I accused him and his friends of being.

"Now, how about you take a look?"

And for him, this was nothing more than a way to find the Etherweave. Curse me for being the fool. I conceded, but

I doubted with him crouching at my feet before me, I could concentrate at all.

I lifted the blank pages up, hiding his face, and stared at them. Next I tried closing my eyes, calling on discipline to steady my mind, but the fact Tamas' hands still rested on my knees, warming my skin underneath, did nothing to gather my focus.

"What do you see?"

"Patience."

I sighed when his finger appeared at the top of the pages, then he gradually lowered them down until our eyes met.

"And?" He quirked a brow.

"How am I supposed to concentrate with you pestering me?"

"It shouldn't be this hard."

Feeling as though it was an accusation, I snapped. "You do it then." And I shoved the pages at him.

My disappointment surprised me. I'd never wanted to be queen, neither did I want to rule from the Bone Throne, but I had felt special in becoming an heir to something as significant as the Etherweave, only for me to discover everyone was wrong.

The Salmun had allowed the Tannard line to end, believing I was the rightful heir. Tamas had claimed the same, yet for the Senjel's pages to reject me.

Tamas slid in beside me on the bed, his attention on the blank pages.

"That's impossible," Tamas said, leaning in close. "How can that be?"

I handed them back to him. "It seems you were wrong

about me." I swallowed more of my disappointment, hating how much it leached into my voice. "So show me what they say."

Tamas took them, holding them up for me to see.

I gasped. "They're blank for you too."

He simply shook his head, tightening his grip on the edges of the pages.

"They don't respond to either of us. How can that be?" I uttered.

"The Salmun were wrong about how to bring the words to life."

"How are we going to make them work?" Then, I ripped the pages from Tamas's hand. "The apostles may know." And I hurried from the room before Tamas could protest.

Everyone glanced up from what they were doing when I stormed into the grand reception room.

"You lot." I glanced at the four apostles, still huddled around a book Tortilus had in his lap. "Come and look at this."

Everyone gathered around as I splayed the blank pages on the table.

"What are we looking at?" Osmud said, peering over Gusselan's shoulder.

Tortilus leaned closer as Plesy said. "They appear ancient. See these filaments." He pointed at the pigments of brown woven across the pages. "The process of making—"

"That's not what we're interested in," Tamas interrupted him.

I flattened the parchments with my hands. "Do you know any spells to reveal hidden words?"

"Well…" Tortilus glanced at his fellow apostles. "There are some, I would surmise. Selisimus?"

"If I could consult—"

"Either you know or you don't." Tamas slammed his hands down on the table.

"Well… Er…" Selisimus stuttered.

"Wait. Tamas, look," I said.

Thin black marks appeared where Tamas's and my hands touched the parchment in different places. They merged as one and spread outward like a snaking river, expanding across the parchment, and as they did so a sketch emerged in their wake.

I looked over at Tamas and found his gaze fixed on me.

"Twain is the bloodborn," he whispered.

I wasn't sure why he phrased it that way, but I understood his meaning; both heirs were necessary to unlock the secrets held within the Senjel's pages.

CHAPTER
TWENTY-ONE

TAMAS

'Do not do it,' Carthius said. Although his voice was calm, I sensed the warning. 'You bind your fates at her peril.'

"I'll do as I wish," I growled, ceasing my endless pacing and marching toward the bedside table where I'd placed the now blank pages.

His will is stronger than we anticipated, Fivia said.

This will make it harder. But with persistence, we will prevail. We are four. He is one. No human can match our might, Ineth replied.

He is not human, Ovia said. *I agree with Fivia. I can feel the strength of his will.*

That he is filled with the souls of many weakens our control, Carthius added

The connection with the woman is our greatest problem, Ineth said. *We will never truly own him while she is alive.*

"How about you all shut up and give me some peace," I said aloud.

They fell silent, leaving me to wonder if I was meant to hear any of that conversation. "You didn't expect me to join you in your secret communications, now did you?" I sneered.

In a collective effort, the Eone had exerted their influence over me, compelling me to snatch the pages from the table soon after Tressya's and my combined touch revealed what was hidden for all these years. But it wasn't the words I had expected to appear on the pages; instead, it was a map.

I swiped the now blank pages from the bedside table. The truth was, I didn't need the map to show me the location of the Etherweave. I was certain the Eone had already revealed its resting place, and now it was time to disclose it to Tressya, to share the truth and gain her trust.

Since waking from the Salmun's poison, nothing I'd done was rational, so I couldn't blame Tressya for questioning my sanity. My bonded partner, my mate, yet the connection between us was fragile, and that I couldn't tolerate. I would win her heart once again by revealing my secrets.

'Do not be foolish,' Carthius announced, already knowing my intention.

"I've realized one thing tonight," I told him as I marched toward the door. "Your control over me is tenuous at best."

'Tenuous, you say,' Carthius began.

'Never underestimate the Eone, my friend,' Ineth finished.

Nearing my bedroom door, my legs became increasingly heavy, each step feeling as though an anvil was strapped to both ankles.

'You let us in, young Razohan. You traded your life for your freedom,' Ovia helpfully reminded me.

"You tricked me," I gasped, fighting against their control. "You tricked me." In this moment, I realized the enormity of my mistake, the power I'd handed to them, for it wasn't just my mind they could influence. My body failed me too, succumbing to their commands. "I was willing to lose my life. But not Tressya's. Only it turns out Tressya wasn't even dying."

'If you care for her so much, then release her. You risk her life if you continue to keep her close. She plays no part in this journey,' Ineth said.

"You broke our bargain when you lied. I'll do everything in my power to sever our link."

'Link? Dear friend. There is no link. We are a part of you now.' I could hear the sneer in Ineth's voice.

'Tamas, listen to us,' Fivia said.

I attempted to block her out, redirecting all my focus toward reaching the door, determined to undermine their control over my body.

It wasn't entirely me in the maze last night. The Eone spun malicious lies in my head, trying to bind me to their will. Sometimes they won, influencing me in ways I loathed to witness, but I wasn't feebleminded, which infuriated and surprised them. And now they'd inadvertently exposed their vulnerability through their furtive communication, revealing the fear of their influence over me might be diminishing. In time I would explore what I'd learned, but for now I had to reach Tressya.

'You do not need the map,' Fivia continued.

"I'll put my dagger through my skull if you don't shut up."

'You have already seen the Etherweave, Tamas. You have been there already. You know where to go.'

I stopped fighting against them for control of my body. So I was right; the Eone had guided me to its location. "The castle? How can it be that simple? Why haven't the Salmun discovered it already?"

'Because the Etherweave and its tomb are visible only to those it calls to. That is you, Tamas,' Ovia said. 'The castle is our home.'

"Your home?"

'The defeat of King Ricaud released the Etherweave from its cage,' Ovia said.

"The rock is its cage. The Nazeen saw to that," I said.

'It was bound long before that. For centuries, the Bone Throne entombed the Etherweave, starting with King Agropea. When King Ricaud was defeated, the Etherweave tried to return to its masters, but we were no more. The closest it could come to finding us was our home, but the Nazeen intervened, entombing it inside a new prison; the rock it now resides within. But even the power of the witches could not prevent the Etherweave from coming home. There it awaits you.'

"You mean there it awaits you. My guess is the four of you will benefit the most when I take in the Etherweave. You'll have no use for me anymore."

'You are one of us now, young Tamas,' Carthius said.

"What a load of horseshit. But you needn't worry. I'll rid you from within me."

I sensed the weakening of their grip on my limbs; the argument distracting the Eone from their intent to prevent me from seeing Tressya. I lunged for the door, yanking it open with such force it flew back and slammed against the wall, sending a loud thud echoing through the manor, likely waking everyone within.

Before they attempted to exert any more control over my body, I rushed to Tressya's door, opening it to find her slipping on a shirt.

"What do you think you're doing here?" she snapped, pulling the fronts of her shirt over her chemise.

I closed the door behind me. "There was a time you never hid yourself from me."

"You thundered all the way down here to tell me that, making enough noise to wake everyone in the manor."

Soon, I would battle the Eone's influence once more. I pressed my hand to my forehead, already sensing their probing presence, like tiny spider bites prickling across my mind's surface as they searched for vulnerabilities, striving to assert total control. Time was running short for me to act freely before resisting their insidious attempts to dominate me consumed my focus.

I strode across to Tressya's window, snagged her hand as I went, and dragged her along beside me. She didn't resist me, which I was grateful for as I doubted I could convince her and resist the Eone's control at the same time. Once there, I pulled her down onto the window seat beside me.

She slumped down, releasing a plume of her scent.

"You smell good."

She'd taken to wearing a perfume unfamiliar to me, a

heady scent of depthless mystery, and I welcomed the pleasant distraction.

"Get to the point, Tamas. Why are you here?" The hardness in her voice forced a divide between us I was determined to scale.

I have so many plans for us. My heart pleaded.

'She will bring you down,' Carthius intervened, intruding upon a moment that should be private. Tressya's bedroom; there was only space for the two of us.

My jaw ached for how hard I clenched my teeth, wanting to force Carthius into the recesses of my mind. After a moment's breath, I lifted her hand, still caged in mine, and placed it on the pages of the Senjel Oracles.

"You're willing for me to see them now?"

I grimaced at the sarcasm in her voice while fighting the Eone's interference. Desperate to conceal the whereabouts of their castle, they were attempting to exert an immense amount of influence.

"I know where the—" I clasped at my throat, feeling the lump thickening, then rising. I shook my head, slumping forward, pressing my lips firm.

You bastards.

The force was too great. I had enough time to throw the pages away as I suddenly lurched forward, bent between my legs, and threw up over the rug.

Tressya gave a small squeak and curled her feet up onto the window seat. "Stars, are you all right?"

I grunted, wiped the last of the spittle from my mouth, then launched to my feet. Stepping over the mess, I stormed across the room, heading nowhere in particular.

"I'm going to shred you for that," I growled, then stopped, rubbing at my brow when I realized I was in Tressya's company.

Bathed in moonlight, she looked diminutive and vulnerable, curled up on the window seat, her eyes wide with shock as they met mine. Despite her appearance of helpless innocence, she was far from it, and right now, deep down, she knew she had been right all along: I was indeed insane.

"Tamas?" she said my name with uncertainty.

I held up my hand, warning her not to come closer. It was better I deal with the bloody Eone at a distance from her, for I could feel the restless urgings of my beast wanting out. This was the work of the Eone, and it distressed me to think they could control that part of me to hurt Tressya.

"I'm struggling at the moment," was all I said, feeling the edges of my claws spike through the tips of my fingers. The audacity of their attempt to control one of the core fundamentals of my nature ignited a fury within me, one that I was certain would be difficult to restrain if I allowed it to be unleashed.

'You dare do this, and I'll cut out my throat,' I spoke in my mind.

'Lies, young Razohan. We are privy to all your secrets. We feel the force of your life's blood flowing through your veins. It is strong. You do not want to die,' Ineth said.

'If you're privy to so much, you would know what I'm prepared to do to keep Tressya safe.'

I gleaned satisfaction in their silence.

"Come sit," Tressya said, patting the space beside her on the bed.

Bathed in moonlight, she looked like the queen she was; my beautiful queen. I paused for a moment, absorbing the sight of her, my mind overflowing with poetic words and my emotions saturated with the love I felt for her. Let the Eone sense that, let them understand Tressya was untouchable. And should they dare, I would ensure their eternal lives met a swift end.

The discarded pages flickered gently in the soft breeze wafting in from her partially opened window. As much as I wanted to sit beside her, I remained shaken by my emerging claws, and how swiftly the Eone had tapped into my beast form—I'd thought that part of me sacredly preserved, the very soul of my nature, under my command and no other. I couldn't risk it happening again, and even though I was sure they were suitably chastised for now, I needed a few more breaths to calm my rampaging heart. Rather than sit beside her, I swiped the pages up, avoiding glancing at the mess I'd made on the floor.

I straightened and stared out the window at the moon, before arching my head back and probing inward, searching for any evidence that the Eone remained close at hand.

Tressya stayed quiet, watching me intently, no doubt wondering what weird words would come from my mouth or bizarre actions I would make.

"It's buried in the Ashenlands." There, I'd said it, with no terrible consequences.

"Why am I not surprised? But how do you know?"

Those evil bastards; this time my tongue felt thick.

"Because I've—" My jaw felt locked in place.

Tressya slid off the bed and came toward me. Unable to

tell her to stay away, I held up my hand, preventing her from coming any closer. Of course, the little minx would ignore me. Instead, she took my hand, entwining her fingers with mine.

"You're afraid of what you might do." It wasn't a question. She sensed my struggle to control my beast. "At least the apostles' spells kept you alive. But they never quite cleared the Salmun's magic."

I nodded when I wanted to shake my head. With Tressya's hand in mine, I felt hairs bristle across the back of my neck, felt the tips of emerging claws once more, felt the snarl rush up my throat, contained by the lock on my jaw. Forcing my transformation was the worst invasion. Already I felt the surge of my beast from rioting to be set loose.

Ripping my hand from Tressya's hold, I managed a mumbled groan, then turned and fled her room, discarding the pages before I disappeared out the door. Stampeding down the dark corridor, driven by a madness seizing my mind, hairs sprouted on the backs of my hands and across my chest. Throughout my body, the bones expanded until they broke. What usually took a blink of the eye to complete unfurled in slow and torturous agony as I resisted the change, refusing to allow the Eone to take command of that one part of myself I needed safe.

With my feet partially transformed, my gait was clumsy on the stairwell. Without my usual graceful agility, I caught my left foot on the edge, tripped, losing my balance and tumbled all the way to the bottom, and that was enough for me to lose my grip on my human form. By the time I hit the ground at the base of the stairs, I was the beast.

For one horrible moment, I stayed on my side, staring up the stairwell, sniffing out my prey, seeking that lingering scent as saliva formed in my mouth, dribbling down my fangs and dripping to the wood floor.

I had naïvely believed my suffering was confined to the transformation alone. How mistaken I was, for the greatest anguish of my life was only just beginning. The Eone were turning Tressya into prey, overriding my control and inciting my beast's instincts to hunt

I breathed in her scent, savoring it with both my tongue and my nose, a tantalizing sample of the taste that awaited. My animalistic nature surged through my veins like a swollen river after a torrential storm, amplifying my hunger into an overwhelming force I was powerless to resist.

'Fuck you,' I cried, but the Eone remained quiet.

"Tamas," came Tressya's voice in the darkness.

My muscles twitched. The scrape of my claws along the wood floor echoed through the silent manor. In my mind's eye, I saw myself leap for the stairwell, mounting the stairs in two bounds. For one horrifying moment, I thought I would do it.

The Eone had unleashed their collective will, disrupting my concentration, muddling my thoughts, forcing me to my knees, forcing my beast to believe Tressya was a threat.

I unleashed a roar of despair, defiant in my conviction that they could never triumph in this manner. I was Razohan, imbued with the combined might of the Huungardred coursing through my veins. No essence could strip that away from me; no one should be able to control my beast but me.

Summoning every ounce of my strength, I ripped myself

from the ground, carving deep furrows in the floor as I surged toward the door. With a leap, I burst into the night air, punching through the barrier. I cleared the steps in a single bound and raced alongside the moon, disappearing into the hedge maze and out of sight.

The thrill of my escape consumed my mind and soul, until a rising fury seared through my heart, a united cry of rage for having been defeated. Even so, the Eone refused to release my mind from their vile clutches.

"Tamas," came the cry. The lonely echo of her voice halted me mid-flight.

A savage snarl tore from my lips as I lifted my head, inhaling the intoxicating scent of flesh and meat, along with something far deeper and more alluring. Even the beat of her heart and the rapid flow of her blood through her veins were laid bare for me to explore.

"Tamas." Her voice came closer.

The silly fool. What did she think she would achieve by hunting me down? A low growl rumbled through my throat as I turned from my flight and prowled toward her scent. I'd buried myself within the maze, but would have no trouble following her scent and hunting her down.

The part of my mind that remained free from the Eone's hold, screamed for release, struggled to assume control of my actions. By now that part of me had faded to an annoying hum, insignificant against my feral needs, cruelly drawn forth by the Eone.

"I know you're struggling," she yelled. "The part of you that makes you good, that makes you who you are, is still there. It's fighting. And I know it will survive."

How little she knew me. The foolish little thing, so weak her bones would snap with one bite. By following me into the maze, she'd trapped herself inside with me.

I retraced my steps, deadly silent in my stealth, while Tressya's approach echoed through my head with her noisy clomping tread. I rounded one corner of the maze and then another, sensing her scent growing stronger, while saliva pooled in my mouth.

Now, with only a hedge between us, my senses were attuned to the shallowness of her breathing, the rapid beat of her heart and the aroma of budding fear. It was too delicious to resist. Fine shudders of anticipation racked my body as I prowled around the last corner.

And there she was, her outline haloed in the moonlight. In her haste to dress, she'd missed button holes and left the lace of her breeches and boots loose. Her hair tumbled over her shoulders in a tangled mess as though she'd struggle through brambles for hours to reach me.

She froze on seeing me, her steely gaze never once releasing me.

"I always thought you were a magnificent beast," she said, as if that would save her life.

"Remember when I cursed growing fur myself? Well, I feel differently now. Especially when I see you as you are."

In my beast form, I could neither sneer nor ridicule her attempt to soothe my hunger with her placating words.

"Look," she said, pulling the pages from her pocket. "What was it you wanted to show me?"

What lay upon those pages was something she was never meant to see.

The roar surged up my throat the moment I sprang, launching myself across the distance between us. In that fated moment, something struck me in the middle of my chest, lancing a pain so sharp it strangled my roar. I lost my momentum and slumped to the ground at her feet, losing my hold on my beast form.

Biting back my wail of agony, I glanced down to see the hilt of a dagger protruding through my chest.

Tressya knelt beside me, placing her hand on my shoulder. "You know I could've easily put that through you heart, Razohan. As it is, I've embedded it a hand's span down and slightly to the left."

I collapsed my head forward, pressing my forehead into the dirt, and exhaled through my teeth.

"Come on." She attempted to heave me onto my back. "You'll lose too much blood wallowing in your misery."

I let out a laugh, a shard of agony piercing through my chest. The laugh was for Tressya, my cunning, courageous, resilient fighter, but also for my freedom; the Eone had receded, sulking in the dark corners of my mind, leaving me free of their influence.

"Laughing's not wise in your current predicament."

"I can't...believe...you stabbed me," I stuttered through the pain.

"I can't believe you were going to attack me." She announced with as much indignation as she could muster.

I rested my hand on hers and arched my head back so I could look into her eyes. She needed to see my conviction. "That wasn't me."

"I gathered," she said. "I'm going to withdraw the dagger."

"Can't you give a man a breath?"

"If I give you too many of those, you may lose your ability to take anymore."

"No thanks to you," I grumbled, overwhelmed with gratitude toward her for what she'd done. Engulfed in a seemingly endless stream of physical torment, my mind was clear, thanks to Tressya. And I would rather endure a hundred stab wounds than find her dead at my feet because of me.

She ignored my grousing and said. "I'm going to count to three."

"I know this trick. You'll pull it out in... Fuucckk," I shouted. "Stars above," I panted, as Tressya pressed both hands hard against the wound, having freed the dagger.

"That worked a treat," she said. "Now you have to change back into the beast so you can heal. But I warn you. I'll make sure it goes through your heart if you dare do that again."

I wanted to tell her *never*, but until I lunged at her moments ago, I had thought that would have been a given.

"I can't begin—"

"Stop. Heal yourself first, then you can grovel, because I can tell you now it's going to take a lot to crawl yourself back into my good graces."

I couldn't shift my gaze from her face, no matter how hard I tried. "Come here," I said.

"What?"

"You heard me."

For the first time, she looked unsure. Not when she faced

my huge, menacing beast form, not when she pulled the blade from my chest, but now, when I threatened to kiss her, did she hesitate.

"I willingly suffer this pain for what I almost did to you."

"Don't be stupid."

"Know had I succeed—"

She snorted a derisive sound. "As if you would've."

"I'm trying to speak from my heart, woman."

"Get it said, then heal yourself."

Instead of words, I snaked my arm around her neck and pulled her lips to mine. At first, simply resting my lips on hers, and swallowing her breaths. In doing so, I sent shards like broken glass into my chest. I inhaled the pain, taking it in deep, savoring it for what it did to my sanity.

Slowly, I ran my tongue across her lips, tasting the scent that had nearly driven me wild with hunger in my beast form. Now, as a man, her scent stirred emotions deeper than mere need, emotions so profound they overwhelmed me; my eyes prickled with tears. I fisted her hair and pulled her closer, refusing to let any of her breaths escape.

I cannot lose her. The power of my thought resonated through my soul, steeling my conviction. If I ever did anything to hurt her, I would gladly end my life with my hand.

"Tamas," she whispered, her lips tickling mine as she spoke.

"I'm weak, Tressya." I released my hold on her hair and buried my head in her nape.

"That's not true."

"I nearly killed you."

"Tamas. Come on. Heal yourself."

"I thought I was stronger than them. I thought I could defeat them."

"The Salmun?"

I shook my head. "The Eone."

She didn't reply.

I slung an arm around her waist, needing to keep her close. Feeling the warmth of her body reassured me she was here with me, alive, mine to love, mine to protect, mine to cherish.

"You can tell me everything when you're healed." She tried to peel my arm from her, but I resisted, draping it around her waist once again and pulling her close.

"The apostles didn't save me. It was the Eone."

Again, she tried to extract herself from my hold. "I really want to hear this story, but once you're healed."

"They created the Etherweave, Tressya."

She stilled.

"And now they possess my mind."

"Not entirely." She gently lifted my head from her nape and shifted to bring her eyes level with mine. "If the Eone possesses you so completely, you wouldn't..." She dusted a finger across my cheeks. "You wouldn't have come back to me."

Despite her kiss feeling as light as a feather brushing across my lips, lingering for several heartbeats, she poured into it the deepest conviction of her heart; she would fight before she ever let me go. I swallowed everything she gave, but grew ravenous for more, so I fisted her hair, tilting her head backward in the perfect position and smothered her lips with my own. I kissed her slow and deep, lingering until it hurt to keep my restraint in place, then let go and kissed her exactly the way a woman like her should always be kissed, untethered and raw, sucking in her soft moans, swallowing them down like they were the sweetest syrup. And when she struggled to pull her head away, I couldn't contain the growl that slipped from my lips.

"Tamas," she mumbled, my name slurring against my lips.

I grew cold the moment I released her.

"I swear I'll command your spirit to perform humiliating stunts if you dare die on me now."

"I surrender." And I relaxed in her arms, and she eased me back so I lay flat on the ground. "To you. Always."

CHAPTER
TWENTY-TWO

BRYRA

I WANTED to blame Romelda for my predicament, but I was equally at fault. Despite the plan going awry, the responsibility for the repercussions of my actions lay solely with me. I could have rejected Romelda's request, which would have been the honorable choice.

And now there was little reason for me to stay in the south. If I had any dignity, I would confess all to Tamas and Tressya, then face Romelda and admit my defeat, before explaining the reasons I believed she was wrong.

For two days, I'd patrolled what little wilderness surrounded the manor in beast form, ensuring neither the Salmun nor Tressya's Mother Divine surprised us, allowing nature to ease my conflicted heart. And for once, nature was not the answer. The only way to rid me of shame would be to return to the manor and reveal my soul. I had already left the forest and was on the trail that would lead me to the manor's door if I were to continue ahead.

Packed secure amongst the few things I'd brought was a large gem spelled with ethereal light to bear me through the Ashenlands. Once I had confessed, I would head north, using Romelda's gem, and return to my father's court. Few in the realm of the two-legged were honorable, and few deeds committed would I consider righteous. Nothing could entice me to venture south again.

About to transform back into my half-form, I detected a faint, unfamiliar odor—aromas that seemed out of place in the wilderness. I remained motionless, inhaling the fragrances carried by the wind: the rich, musty soil, the scent of decaying wood on damp, mossy ground, the resinous tree sap, and the delicate hints of various flowers.

The other aromas were distinct, hinting of human presence: the scent of clothes worn against warm skin, a tang of sweat, and the oiled leather of a horse's saddle.

For the last two days, I'd stayed out of sight from the few two-legged I'd heard passing on the few solitary paths through the wilderness that skirted close to the manor. I'd watched a shabbily dressed man walking beside his old horse and cart, a woman, bent and worn, carrying a load on her back while a young child skipped alongside her, and another youngling with long tangled hair, sitting upon a very large horse, so his feet barely straddled its girth. The horse, sensing my presence, had shied away from where I remained hidden, and the boy nearly tumbled from his seat.

As a beast, my size was difficult to conceal in this small patch of woodland, so I reverted to my half-form and concealed myself among the trees, anticipating the newcomer. I expected to encounter none other than local farm folk who worked the lands near the manor, so upon seeing the Mother astride a small black horse, my heart seemed to freeze in my chest. A sense of sickness spawned in my stomach, spreading like a blight infecting healthy leaves.

My only surprise was the time it had taken her to locate Tressya, as I was convinced she possessed some magical means of finding whatever she desired. The ways of the Nazeen had always been inscrutable to me, rendering the Mother an even darker mystery.

The poison Romelda expected me to use on Tressya remained magically smeared across the tip of the claw on my beast's side. I could afford her a few moments more to approach my hiding place, ensuring that my attack would come as a surprise. I'd pull her from the back of her horse before she could retaliate and swiftly slice my claw across her throat. She would be dead before she hit the ground—a merciful way to die.

It wasn't the Mother who caused Tamas to fall in love with Tressya; he did so of his own free will—a twist of fate not even Romelda foresaw. Therefore, it was unjust to blame the Mother for the wounds in my heart. I would blame her regardless. Because of the Mother, Tressya arrived in Tarragona. Because of the Mother, we failed in the Ashenlands, leaving half the northerners bereft of sons and daughters. Despite despising no one I had yet to know, I despised her.

My wounded heart felt she deserved no mercy. If I were utterly heartless, if I were fully human, the thought of her suffering a painful and slow demise would bring me pleasure. But it didn't, because that was not in my nature. Nevertheless, she had to die. The poisonous fate she'd created was already loose, but I would serve justice by ensuring she never lived to see the outcome.

Suddenly, her horse threw up its head, whining and sidestepping, likely sensing my presence. The Mother jerked on the reins, kicking its sides to encourage it forward, but the horse refused, prancing in place, a quiver of unease rippling down its flank.

The Mother cursed and stabbed her heels into its belly once more. Watching her cruelty toward the frightened animal, I ground my teeth and clenched my fists so tightly that my budding claws pierced my skin. Any minute, I was sure the horse would try to dislodge her from its back.

The urge to transform into my beast form sent prickling hairs spiking through the skin across my back, but now was not the time. As large as I was, I would expose myself too early, and the horse would likely attempt to flee. What I needed was for the animal to deliver her to where I wanted her, right in front of my path. At that precise moment, I would become my beast form and launch from the trees with blinding speed, catching her off guard.

My body twitched with the urge to transform, my muscles quivered with the desire to spring forth from my hiding place and onto the horse's back, but at the last moment, I heard humans approaching along the trail, but the conversation would be too faint for the Mother's ears.

I needed to act decisively, as my opportunity to deal with the Mother was quickly slipping away. Either I launched my attack now, cutting the Mother down and fleeing before the party arrived, or I waited until they had passed.

No, I couldn't wait. But I hesitated before releasing my half-form, realizing with growing horror that it was Tressya's voice I could hear approaching. I glanced toward the Mother, noting that she too had heard Tressya's approach.

This was Tressya's ninth pass on this trail. She was restless, eager to hunt the Etherweave, but stabbing Tamas had delayed their departure from the manor. Amusingly, the apostles had become her shadows, perhaps believing they could protect her from Tamas—no one would explain why Tressya had stabbed him, then fretted over him and insisted we give him time to heal properly before continuing our quest to track this power. I had returned to the small wilderness, determined I wouldn't get involved in whatever complications arose between Tressya and Tamas.

I cast another glance down the trail, spotting the party of five in the distance, and knew in that instant that I had lost my opportunity. As fast as I was, Tressya would still see me. Rather than assume the Mother fell victim to a wild animal, she would know it was my claw who severed her throat.

And what should I care if she knew what I'd done?

A slow rumble reverberated deep in my throat, my repressed frustration leaking through, because, for reasons I couldn't explain, I cared what Tressya thought; the woman I'd come to kill; the woman who stole Tamas from me, yet I wanted her respect, not her contempt.

Tressya had chosen Gusselan as a companion over her own Mother Divine when she fled. I'd heard the scorn in the words spoken between them, felt the tension, sensed the loathing, and questioned Tressya's loyalty to her order many times over. I understood one's loyalty to familial links. As an orphan, she would liken the Sistern to family. That I respected, but I have now come to realize she was looking for a way out, an escape.

And I could offer that to her as an apology for the wrongs I came here to commit.

Crouching low, hiding my large frame as best I could in the thicket, I waited while the Mother gazed along the path toward Tressya and her party. I observed her expression shift from the pinched ugliness of her frustration to the narrowed-eyed cunning of her black-hearted soul. The transformation in her features triggered a primal response within me, causing my claws to extend and my fangs to protrude through my gums.

The tension in my muscles turned to pain as I waited, judging my best time to strike, while listening to Tressya's approach. In her silence, I imagined the thoughts in her mind, wondered if her heart raced wild like an escaping deer in the presence of a wolf.

Strangely, in that moment, I felt the unbidden and sudden need to protect her. This went beyond merely correcting my mistakes; it was about ensuring her safety, for Tamas' sake, and for her own. I held Tamas in the highest regard, second only to my father, and so believed the woman he loved would embody his virtues, making her someone worthy of helping.

"Mother." Tressya's voice revealed none of her emotion.

"It seems I missed your message that you were traveling." The Mother stayed on her horse, giving her height over those present.

"I saw no need, as I knew you wouldn't have any problem finding me."

I caught the imperceptible tick on the Mother's jawline, the hard press of her lips. "Your traveling party is unknown to me."

At Emberfell, she'd struggled to portray herself as subservient to the queen. Out here, cracks emerged in the facade she had maintained, as her true nature gradually broke free.

"We are loyal apostles of Emberforge, servants to the Salmun." The one with the spikes of ginger hair spoke.

"Indeed." The Mother quirked a brow. "And what would the Salmun's loyal servants be doing so far from their temple?"

"We are the queen's guardians," said the stouter of the four. "And who may you be?"

If the change in her expression was a sign, she liked his audacity as much as his question. "It's curious their loyal servants seem privy to regarding the queen's whereabouts, when the Salmun has no clue."

The four exchanged a nervous glance.

"It's...a secret. Only few Salmun know...Orphus included," stammered the tallest apostle.

The Mother sneered, then sliced her gaze to Tressya. "You could at least have chosen a worthy guard to make your escape."

"We have our talents." The tall one stepped forward.

"Tortilus," Tressya warned.

"I'm sorry, My Queen, but she misjudges us because of our robes." The apostle was offended. As was typical with the offended, their outrage clouded their judgement. He turned back to the Mother. "We are not as we appear. Together, we possess a greater amount of magic than many assume. It would be unwise to underestimate us."

"The problem lies with underestimating me." A serpent's voice, smooth and slick, encircling your throat before you can utter a scream.

Then what came next surprised me. The Mother uttered an indescribable word, which made the one named Tortilus turn ridged. Soul voice. I'd heard the Sistern's weapon was their voice, but had never suspected it could be wielded with such efficiency and speed.

"You will bow—"

"No." Tressya stepped forward, blocking the Mother's direct path to Tortilus. "It's me you want. Release him."

Soon, very soon, I would wipe the triumphant smile from the Mother's face. And yes, I would take great pleasure in seeing her fear when she realized her life's breath was fading.

"Come now, Tressya. I don't want to humiliate you in front of your friends, but the poor boy needs a lesson in respect."

"No. I forbid you."

The Mother laughed. "You. Forbid. Me."

"She is the queen," said the last apostle to speak. His voice was a little above a whisper.

"Queen by my endeavors. Perhaps I could be lenient. After all, you have no idea who I am."

I could sense the rising fear in them. They exchanged nervous glances, shuffling uneasily on their feet.

"Shall I bend all four to my will? Or perhaps I shall just take you, Tressya dear, my most loyal disciple."

The air crackled with the sparks of power as they both shouted the same word. Tressya jerked backward, stumbling into the apostles standing behind her, while the Mother tumbled from her horse, kicking up a cloud of dust as she landed on her back. The horse's flight edged my urge to transform, forcing me to grit my teeth to maintain control over my half-form. I tasted the sweet tang of energy I often smelt when Romelda performed her magic enchantments. And for the first time, I realized the potential power words held, but lucky for me, the Mother's particular magic would hold no sway over my soul.

The Mother sprang to her feet with remarkable agility for someone her age—a trait I begrudgingly respected. Tressya remained undaunted. She positioned herself in front of the apostles as a protective barrier, her expression radiating open defiance.

"That is a surprise," the Mother said, though her disdain for Tressya seemed to falter. Behind the curl of her lip and the feigned confidence in her voice, I detected a hint of apprehension.

"I've kept many secrets. My loyalty toward the Sistern died long ago."

"You were never good at succeeding in anything. It takes years, child, to master your soul word as defense against another. Even if you have finally learned the truth of its power."

The Mother repeated the same word the two had shouted in unison, but this time the wash of power sent hairs piercing through my skin along my back. I had to stifle a growl as a fang jutted below my gum.

The impact on Tressya was more profound. I could see her struggling to maintain her grip. Her face contorted as though in pain, her arms tensed, fingers curling inward as she struggled against the Mother's control.

"Always a failure," the Mother crooned, reveling in her triumph.

"Your Majesty," said the ginger haired apostle.

"No," Tressya said through gritted teeth.

She scrunched her eyes shut, ducking her head to hide her face. Within moments, her arms loosened, her fingers uncurled, and she straightened once more. Her eyes were now clear of the fog of concentration, and her shoulders relaxed their tension. Had she won over the Mother's vile influence?

"Maybe not always," she said.

I was engaged in my own battle. The strains of energy tensing in the air made it difficult for me to maintain my half-form. The Mother's rage was a beast of its own, invisibly prowling the space between them. My own inner beast struggled against the confines of my half-form, yearning to break free and driven by a hunger to confront her tyranny.

The Mother's lips quivered, the only visible sign of her fury. "Then I shall have to make my words count," she said, then repeated Tressya's soul word again.

Tressya staggered backward, and she threatened to

topple from her feet. In her eyes I could see fury, but I also read fear. The Mother was winning.

The power in her voice reverberated through the trees, and I lost control of my beast. In less than a breath, I sprang from my hiding spot in the thicket and closed the distance to land upon the Mother. Mid-flight, I glimpsed Tressya falling to her knees, the terror on the apostles' faces, but I moved too swiftly for their cries to register. Best of all, I watched the shock on the Mother's face transform into utter horror. Not even she could muster a second's retaliation before my claw grazed her throat, opening it from one edge to the other.

Perhaps the slice of my claw would take her life before the poison did.

CHAPTER
TWENTY-THREE

TRESSYA

Is this how it felt as your life was fleeing? I had no command over my lungs, my legs or my heart, which felt held in the strongest vise.

The Mother's blood slowly spread across the path like a vine, its tendrils reaching for my boots. Her lifeless eyes stared up at the sky as an eerie silence enveloped us like a thick cloud. I tore my gaze from the Mother's body and glanced at each of the apostles. Instead of focusing on her, their eyes were fixed on Bryra, their mouths agape, eyes flared wide with a likely combination of fear and shock.

My attention also turned to Bryra, who'd already reverted to her half-beast form. A mix of gratitude and admiration surfaced from my shock at the unexpected turn of events. My body still tingled from the Mother's grasp, and my heart raced with the residual fear of knowing the Mother could have triumphed in our mental confrontation. In those seconds before Bryra had killed her, I was sure she had won.

It was foolish to think I could challenge the Mother's superior mastery of soul voice, even after my victory over the Salmun in their hidden cavern beneath Emberforge. However, mind manipulation is a distinct talent, and the Sistern are experts, with the Mother being a consummate artist in this skill.

"That's twice you've saved my life. Quite the feat for someone who came to end it."

I ignored the apostles' gasps.

She subtly dipped her head in acknowledgment of my thanks, showing no signs of the anxiousness one would normally feel at being discovered.

"We haven't seen you since this morning." It was a strange comment for me to make, given the Mother's body lay at our feet because of Bryra's ruthless speed and efficiency in killing her.

In truth, my mind was struggling to keep apace. And a dark seed inside my soul rejoiced for my freedom. Would I have taken the Mother's life? I stared down at her lifeless body, her mouth slightly parted as though she was about to utter another of her cruel retorts or issue another wicked command.

Yes, I would have done it, and undoubtedly felt the same as I do now if she had died by my hand. After a lifetime of hoping otherwise, I was grateful she had never shown a single spark of compassion toward me. Nor would I blame myself for enduring her cruelty all these years, considering I was brought into the Sistern as an infant and raised under the Mother's stern guidance, knowing no other life but that dictated by the Sistern.

"I had much to think about." Her gaze was solemn as she leveled it at me. "I prefer the serenity of the wilderness when I need to think."

"I understand."

"I failed my purpose, but now I've fulfilled another, I must return home. This is not my life."

"Not without seeing Tamas."

I watched the human side of her face as she held my gaze. I'd rarely a chance to scrutinize her half-beast form. Despite the wild and savage appearance of her beast side, her human side was beautiful. Though marred by a lengthy scar, I believed her skin would feel silken to touch.

She nodded, about to reply, but I beat her to it, turning my attention to the apostles. "Can you give us a moment?"

The four huddled together, with Wellard gripping Selisimus's hand for reassurance. Their continual shock kept them quiet; it was easy to forget their presence.

"'Er," Wellard uttered, dropping Selisimus' hand.

"Your Majesty, do you think that's wise?" Tortilus said. "I meant it when I said we were your guardians. It seems we have attracted many dangers." His gaze slid from Bryra to the Mother's body.

"We're in no danger now, especially with Bryra here." I glanced at Bryra, to see she'd yet to shift her gaze from me.

The four exchanged significant looks.

"We'll just be over here," Plesy said, eyeing Bryra suspiciously, as he dragged Tortilus, who seemed reluctant to leave, and Selisimus along. Wellard followed behind, casting worried glances at me from over his shoulder.

"No. I don't think—" Tortilus began.

"It's the queen's wishes," Plesy reminded him in a hushed tone.

"Yes, but I believe she doesn't understand the extent of the danger. And we, as masters of our craft—"

"Shut it, Tortilus. You and Plesy succeeded in one thing," Wellard intervened. "I'd hardly say we're masters of anything except getting ourselves into trouble."

"Besides, the old crone is dead. Anyone could see she was the real foe," Selisimus said.

Their voices faded as they continued down the path. I fought back a smile, watching them bicker among themselves. It wasn't wise to bring them along. I didn't have the heart to tell them their magical skills didn't save Tamas. Rather, the enigmatic Eone's possession saved him—and I had yet to ask Tamas to explain everything he knew about them. The Mother was just the beginning of the perilous fates ahead, and I doubted any of the four were equipped to handle what was to come. However, we needed all the help we could find, and traveling with magic wielders, regardless of how formative their craft would be helpful.

Once they'd moved out of hearing, Bryra spoke. "Tamas won't wish to see me after he hears my confession."

"I'm not so sure about that." I could only think of his attack on me last night. Perhaps he would welcome the idea of another's help in his quest to end my life.

I gave a small shake of my head. My sarcasm was ill placed. Tamas was gutted over what he'd attempted last night, and I feared his morose attitude would hang over him until he could free himself from the possession of these Eone. That was not the Tamas I needed right now.

And standing over the Mother's dead body was not the best place for a conversation, but it would be cowardly of me not to face the Mother's spirit.

"I don't understand you."

"Never mind." I glanced down at the Mother, knowing I had little time remaining until her spirit rose. "If I can forgive you, then he can too."

"But... I really don't understand you."

"Then you have a lot in common with almost everyone else who knows me."

The apostles shared fleeting glances in our direction.

"We still have plenty of enemies, and we need friends. If you can't believe my benevolence toward your actions, then believe I forgive you because I need you."

"How can you trust me?" She held up her right hand, the one that remained in beast form, to show me her claw. "Romelda spelled this claw before I left. It will remain lethal until my return to the north. Does that not concern you?"

"Far from it. I think that's very handy. I definitely think you should stay and help us."

Interestingly, the beast and human sides of her face moved independently. Surprise and confusion on her human side didn't easily transfer to her beast side. I was not adept at reading her beastly features, so I couldn't determine if she was contemplating finishing me or was merely deep in thought. But I would say the human side of her face was deeply confused.

"There were many chances for you to kill me, and yet I'm still alive. You also saved Gusselan and I when you could've turned you back and left us to our fate. It's Romelda who wants me dead. Not you."

"But I agreed to be a part of her plan."

"She was a coward to send you in her place. But that's not what I'm interested in right now. Romelda spelled your form too, didn't she? Can you become Ryia once more? While we're in Tarragona, it will be helpful for you to blend in by looking the same as everyone else."

"No. That was temporary."

"Then we'll make do."

"Your Majesty."

"What is it, Tortilus?" I tried to keep the frustration from my voice at his persistent use of the formal title. The apostles had edged their way closer while we talked, no doubt hoping to move themselves within hearing distance.

"We couldn't help hearing... It's only a suggestion, but if you need assistance, magically speaking, we aren't without talent. As we have showed."

I heaved a breath. "I have noticed your skill. Thank you, but for now I think it's best—" The Mother's rising spirit distracted me.

Her spirit form had taken longer to separate itself from its bodily tomb, but now she was free, I loathed to face her. Those eagle-sharp eyes fixed on me. But what truly wrenched dread from my throat, stealing my breath and ability to speak, was the maniacal glee in her expression. Anyone sane did not rise from death, looking immensely pleased.

"We know a few handy spells suitable for such an occasion." Tortilus turned to Plesy. "You've memorized a few, haven't you, friend?"

The Mother's spirit wielded command over my senses, intensified by a looming sense that a terrible fate would come to pass.

"What do you say, Your Majesty? It would take but a morning's work, I'm sure," Tortilus continued, his persistent pestering a faint hum easily ignored.

'Did you really think you would defeat me? Foolish child,' the Mother intoned.

My gaze flitted to Bryra, who was watching me intently, then to the apostles, seemingly oblivious to what was welling inside me. It felt as though my growing fear was saturating the surrounding air, leaving not enough for all of us to breathe.

'Discipline, the most formidable of all pillars, has enabled me to triumph. Generations of meticulous planning and perseverance, enduring hardship regardless of the cost, and here I stand, surpassing all the women who have preceded me, poised to fulfill what the Sistern has long strived to achieve.' Even in death, she maintained her formidable presence, her condescending glare, as if it was us, not her, who'd suffered an untimely demise.

"Tressya." The note of concern in Bryra's voice broke the Mother's hold on my attention.

"Leave," I said. "All of you. Go back to the manor."

"Your Majesty, we have yet to tell you—"

"Just go." My soul word rose within me, turning my shout into a command, which was useless against the living.

It was soul voice that commanded the living, soul word that commanded the dead.

"Apologies, Your Majesty," Tortilus persisted.

Selisimus tugged Tortilus by the arm. "Come on, you oaf."

This time Tortilus went readily with the rest of them, sensing the anger in my voice.

I ignored Bryra, who seemed determined to remain, and concentrated on the Mother's spirit while the apostles retraced our morning's path. Tamas would arrive as soon as they returned, relaying all the recent events. I preferred he wasn't present as I confronted the schemes the Sistern had devised over these last centuries. And since Bryra had fought in the Ashenlands war and was aware of my prowess as a spiritweaver, I saw no need to conceal the Mother's spirit from her.

"You're at my command now."

The Mother's sneer made my words rattle hollow in the air.

"Tressya?" Bryra said, following my gaze, though she would see nothing.

"The Mother's spirit has risen," I informed her.

'Very well,' the Mother intoned. 'She will be my first victim.'

"There is little you can do beyond the veil." Somehow, the words felt like a feeble lie. The Mother found them amusing, as evidenced by her persistent malevolent smile.

"She's stuck there, isn't she?" Bryra flicked her eyes from me to the space around the Mother's dead body.

'Yes.' I whispered when I should shout, because when it came to the Mother, I wasn't sure about anything.

The Mother ensured my knowledge of the death arts remained limited, as with the true power of soul voice. She was even more restrictive regarding Tarragona, and now I understood why. Had I not been so naïve about the destiny awaiting me, I would have known how to fight against her schemes, for I was sure, given her smug expression and contemptuous glare, everything had unfolded as she'd planned.

'You are my perfect instrument: meek when you should have fought, ignorant when you should have sought knowledge. Compliant to my cruelty, which I have enjoyed the most. I was not lying when I said your mother hated you even before you were born. But not even she could have imagined how perfectly you would play your part, the despised illegitimate child accomplishing more than I ever dreamed you would.'

"What poison is she saying?"

"Nothing," I mumbled.

'The Salmun posed my greatest challenge. That's why I opted for a less direct approach and placed you on the throne beside your husband, for the time being, moving you one step closer to the Bone Throne. However, I did not anticipate that you would dismantle the House of Tannard in just over a month. I never believed you would advance so swiftly to sit upon the throne as queen before I had achieved my goal. That you killed Radnisa is of little consequence to me. If not you, I would have been forced to perform the deed. I sent her across to keep you humble and never a part of my plan.'

I lost my composure and backed away—when facing the Mother it was an acceptable weakness, but few in the Sistern would not do the same.

I spent my life in reverence and fear of her, clinging to the foolish hope that she might one day regard me with a hint of warmth in her heart. Those were the guileless dreams of an orphan child, despised by all around her.

I should not feel so hopeless or fearful of her reach. Yet her confidence overshadowed mine. She had not spent her life planning this moment only to make a mistake. Not the Mother of the Sistern, who surpassed anyone in her meticulous scheming. Was dying a part of her schemes? Not by Bryra's hand, but given her triumphant expression, I would say yes. But how could she think she had won when she'd turned me into a spiritweaver, one capable of commanding the dead, meaning she was now under my command?

I inhaled deep, finding my calming breaths to still my savage heartbeat. Fear was my weapon, a mantra the Mother impressed upon me. I would use it now against her. She thought to control me with soul voice from across the veil, but I was the master.

Aetherius. My soul word surged swiftly, as if it had been lying in wait just beneath the surface, poised for this precise moment. I exhaled, feeling the power of my calming breath, feeling my soul word fashion my fear into armor.

"This is your resting place now, old woman."

Old woman. Those were sacrilegious words, words that no one within the Sistern would dare utter, but the Mother was no longer worthy of my reverence. Her death finally liberated me from that terrible, strangling noose. She no longer held my loyalty.

"What can I do, Tressya? How can I help?"

"This is not your fight, Bryra." I shouldn't let Bryra distract me like that. Not when I faced the Mother.

'You poor child. Innocent until the very end. That's what made you so perfect.'

She'd told me that day in the king's garden that she'd ensured our lives were linked. I couldn't fathom how her death would link our lives, but her perpetual sneer sent prickles of unease across my skin.

"You'll never know freedom, only the pain of your failure," I uttered, but I heard the wavering of my voice.

"This is my fault," Bryra continued. "It was I who sent her into the spirit realm, forcing you to face her alone."

"It was always going to be her and me." I whispered, knowing Bryra would still hear me.

This was exactly what the Mother desired: her formidable power pitted against her humble student, but I struggled to understand how she hoped to win. Her lineage was not connected to the House of Whelin, so she possessed no skill in the death arts.

She's simply a spirit. I reminded myself, as I felt my control over Aetherius wane.

Fear is my weapon. As discipline gave me the courage and strength to wield it.

"I was stupid to wish anything more from you than what you gave. I have you to thank for ensuring your cruelty was all I knew. It is a blessing I finally understand what I was lucky enough to escape."

She huffed a laugh.

"You could never comprehend the power of the spiritweaver," I continued, disturbed by her apparent indifference to my words, as if everything I said was insignificant to her overarching plan.

'Can you honestly tell me you know it better yourself?' she sneered.

"It's within my veins."

'But there are many aspects of the craft you don't yet understand.'

She was right. Radnisa had taunted me, saying I was naïve about my skill as a spiritweaver.

'I know your crimes.' She shook her head. 'Bringing the dead across the veil. What consequences have you unleashed?' She reveled in her malicious delight as she recounted my most terrible deed: forcing the dead into a war that wasn't theirs. Liberating Andriet from his deadly home was another accusation, one that, if Gusselan were to be believed, was equally heinous, though I struggled to view it as such a truly atrocious crime.

"Don't worry, you'll not share a similar fate. You're destined to remain on this wilderness path, troubling the peasant folk." No matter what I said, her smirked remained in place.

"I'm here for you, Tressya. Just tell me what you need. I may not possess magical abilities or the sight to see the dead, but I have my own talents, which are at your disposal if you need them," Bryra said.

'Tell the beast to stop prattling.'

"It's best if you left, Bryra."

She shook her head. "No. I won't leave you."

'I would call her brave if she wasn't so stupid.'

"Please, just go, Bryra. I think it's for the best. There's nothing you can do against a spirit. She's within my control now."

The Mother could only smirk, which ran anxiousness like fingers under my shirt, pebbling my skin.

Bryra frowned, hesitant to do as I asked. I nodded, encouraging her to listen. An uneasy feeling warned me she wasn't safe, but mostly, I didn't want a witness to my plans. The Mother wouldn't linger in limbo on this desolate trail; I believed she'd prefer solitude over spending eternity with ordinary folk, people she could no longer control with her soul voice. Therefore, I would banish her to the Ashenlands, the most morbid place to spend one's death.

"I'll return to the manor, let Tamas know what has happened here. No doubt he'll come quick."

I assumed her last comment was for the Mother's ears.

'Yes, run along like a good dog.' And the Mother launched toward Bryra.

"No," I shouted, my heart already blocking my throat as *Aetherius* surged forth with little encouragement from me.

I saw the surprise on the human side of Bryra's face as she half turned toward me again. But she was soon forgotten as the Mother, halted mid-flight from reaching Bryra, spun on me in fury. 'Soul word is it now?' Her voice was like nails. 'So that's the secret to commanding the dead. Let's see if you can stop me,' she cackled, diving straight for me.

The Mother uttered an unfamiliar word that bore no resemblance to soul voice.

"Stop," I shouted, my voiced laced with soul word, but the Mother was already upon me, and then she vanished, leaving behind a coldness so pervasive that my bones instantly turned to ice, my body wracked by violent shakes I couldn't control. I bent double, cradling my arms to my stomach, feeling as though I would snap in half if I went any further. This was the power the dead held over me, but it had never been this bad. I would never get warm again.

"Tressya." Bryra seized hold of my hands. "Stars, you feel like ice."

My jaw ached as I tried to prevent my teeth from chattering.

"Your skin is deathly pale, and your lips are blue, in so short a time."

I couldn't stop my teeth from clacking together to reply.

"Where's the Mother?"

I tried to shrug.

"Gone?"

I nodded, and she swept me close, pressing me into her warm body. "I don't know what happened. But this is strange. I've never seen the cold seize hold of someone so fast. If I change, I'll keep you warmer."

I nodded against her chest.

"Tamas will probably be here soon. The apostles would have alerted him to our encounter."

I nodded again, not wanting Tamas here at all, for I understood what had just transpired. Radnisa had teased me the night I killed her, taunting me with the notion that spiritweavers new to their skill were susceptible to possession. I had barely listened to her that night, preoccupied as we were with war, but now I finally understood why the Mother had kept me ignorant of the death arts and why she had turned me into a spiritweaver. It wasn't because she wanted me on the Tarragonan throne, wielding the Etherweave. She wanted to place herself there instead, forcing me to her command. The Mother knew I could learn to overcome soul voice. But as a spirit in possession of my body—was that something I could ever defeat?

CHAPTER
TWENTY-FOUR

TAMAS

I BARELY UNDERSTOOD THE APOSTLES' ranting, but two words stood out clearly: Tressya and danger. There was also mention of an old crone, now dead at the hands of the woman-beast who had appeared out of thin air, which could be none other than Bryra.

Osmud and I, in our beastly forms, raced side by side, reaching Tressya in no time. She lay huddled against Bryra's massive belly, appearing small, vulnerable, and strangely, freezing.

I shifted back to my human form, avoiding the Mother's lifeless body, and crouched beside Tressya. She was nestled in Bryra's plush fur, which failed to keep her warm. If not even Bryra's body warmth couldn't soothe her shivering, it must be some kind of curse at work.

"What happened?" I chided myself for the unmistakable fear that laced my voice.

My haste to reach Tressya, combined with my frequent shifting between forms, caused the skin around my nearly healed dagger wound to sting. However, I easily dismissed the discomfort as I knelt beside Tressya and gathered her in my arms, making room for Bryra to shift into her half-form.

"The Mother found her," was the first thing Bryra said.

"I understood little of the apostles' ramblings, but they said you killed her."

"I took her by surprise."

"So the bitch is dead," Osmud said. "That's a welcome relief. Now there's only the Salmun."

As Osmud spoke, I turned my gaze to Bryra, my mind swirling with questions. The most urgent one was why was she in the south. After regaining consciousness, I hadn't had the chance to press her for answers because she'd vanished. Truth be told, I assumed she'd headed back north. But for now, all questions would have to be put on hold until Tressya was safely and warmly back at the manor.

Avoiding Osmud's gaze—he was still skeptical about forming a partnership with Tressya—I quickly retraced our path, holding Tressya close to my body for warmth, as her own body seemed incapable of generating any heat. Despite her courage matching that of any warrior, she felt fragile and small in my arms. Anxiety became a heavy burden, draped over my shoulders like an oversized cloak of iron.

In beast form, I could reach the manor in half the time, but Tressya lacked the strength to hold on. I would have to return in human form, moving slower, yet still faster than any normal man could.

It was clear the Mother was behind Tressya's condition. However, I couldn't determine how, since, to my knowledge, soul voice was their only weapon. Yet, Thaindrus had mentioned the possibility of a Nazeen traitor. And this situation could very well be the evidence needed to confirm a Nazeen had assisted the Mother.

Jaw clenched, I mentally shook my concerns and increased my pace, desperate to return to the manor.

'This is not your responsibility, young Razohan.'

I growled at Ineth's interference.

'She is no longer the woman who has your heart,' Ovia added.

'Say one more word...' My thoughts were on Tressya, my desperation to reach the manor like claws seizing my heart, I had no threat to finish with.

'It is only a matter of time. We think only of your pain, my friend. Give her to your friends and leave. Make the break now. She will not last the night,' Carthius said. 'It is obvious she is cursed. A curse beyond reach.'

"Shut the fuck up," I snarled, realizing I'd said the words aloud too late.

Tressya tried to respond, but her teeth chattered so much, her words incomprehensible.

"If you need a break." Osmud suddenly appeared beside me, offering to take Tressya, thinking she was my burden because he didn't understand my real burden was buried deep within.

I felt the snarl rise in my throat, felt my lips peel back to reveal a fang at the thought of handing her off to someone else.

She's mine to care for. The thought was so sharp it felt like it sliced through my skull. I remained silent, knowing Osmud would understand my silence as a refusal.

It wasn't until I reached the steps of the manor that I slowed my pace. The apostles and Gusselan were waiting on the portico, but I waved them off and hurried inside, aware of Osmud and Bryra closely following. I ascended the stairs as if I had wings, and without conscious thought, headed towards my room, only realizing my direction when I arrived at my door.

Osmud appeared on the other side of the bed, pulling back the covers so I could lay her down. I caught his eye and nodded in gratitude for his thoughtfulness, despite his mixed feelings towards her.

"She needs more covers," I informed everyone who was now crowding into the room.

"Perhaps we can be of assistance," Tortilus dodged around Bryra and edged close to the bed.

"The first priority is warmth," I snapped.

"Of course. More covers," Tortilus barked, snapping his fingers at no one in particular, but already Osmud reappeared, carrying a high bundle in his arms.

"Oh good. Quickly now, let's tuck her in." Tortilus tried to help by reaching for an end of the blanket as Osmud draped it over Tressya's small form. However, a single growl from me made him jerk back and retreat.

"Apologies," he stuttered. "Come brethren," he waved

the other three apostles forward. "Plesy, remember that spell we were working—?"

"No," I intoned, snapping my arm out to wrap a clawed hand around Tortilus's upper arm. "Leave it for now." I tasted the subtle tang of blood on my tongue as the tips of my fangs descended.

Tortilus squeaked as the other three eased away.

"Perhaps it would be a better idea if we all left the room," Osmud said, giving me his best 'you're a crazy-ass-moron' glare.

"Except you." I glanced at Bryra.

Once everyone else had left us in peace, I planned to crawl in beside Tressya to warm her up and question Bryra about what had transpired on the path. I needed answers to save her. If this was a magical issue, the apostles were our best chance of saving Tressya, even though I doubted they had a lick of real magic between them. Romelda came to mind. If Osmud flew north, He could bring Romelda south within a few days. But what if Tressya didn't have a couple of days?

"Now's not the time," Osmud said, his voice heavy with concern. I was sure his thoughts were more with Bryra than with me, understandably so, given the harshness in my tone.

"I need to know—"

Feeling the cold brush of Tressya's hand against mine, everyone else faded into the background like mere furniture as I crouched beside her, taking her hand in mine and fighting the urge to roar with fury at the horrible chill of her touch.

She shook her head, which I took to mean she agreed

with Osmud. Bryra had attempted to save Tressya by killing the Mother, so perhaps I should go easy on her.

I clenched my teeth and Tressya's hand, forcing myself to remain calm, suppressing the evidence of my inner beast.

"Time to clear the room, folks," Osmud said.

"I'll bring warm broth," Gusselan said as she departed.

I rested my forehead on the side of the bed, softened by a well of gratitude for Osmud's presence. Both he and Tressya were right in preventing me from questioning Bryra at this time, not while I felt as though I was being edged into a walled enclosure. I didn't react well—understatement—to feeling caged; helpless.

As the door closed, I slipped beneath the mountain-high covers, gently lifting Tressya from the bed and nestling myself underneath. I sprawled her down the length of my body, her head resting on my chest. It was like layering myself in snow, and I bit back a persistent whimper of concern.

"It...it..."

"Shh." I stroked her back. "You don't need to talk."

"It...it...will...pass."

"Not soon enough," I grumbled, laying my head back on the pillow and wrapping my arms around her tight. "Rest knowing you're in my arms, Tressya. Nothing will harm you." I had to hope my will was strong enough to keep her with me, given I had no magical means of countering any curse.

I closed my eyes. *One day I will. When the Etherweave is mine, no harm will ever befall Tressya again.*

'This is true, young Tamas,' Carthius said. I inwardly

groaned at the reminder of my constant and infuriating companions.

'Once it is yours, there will be no stopping you. You will have the power to do what you desire,' Carthius continued. 'Always remember that. Keep that goal at the forefront of your mind.'

'I swear if I could rip you from my mind, I would.' But Carthius had a point. Once I imbued the Etherweave, I would be a magic wielder with no limits to the good I could do. *And the bad.* I had to always remember that.

***

By the time Tressya warmed, the sun lingered low on the horizon. She'd remained frozen for the rest of the night and the following day, only now, as the sun disappeared, had she finally warmed. Gusselan had come and gone with bowls of warm broth, which Tressya devoured as if she hadn't had a decent meal in a week, and then promptly fell asleep.

I had to snap at Tortilus three times when he poked his head inside the door, hoping I would be amenable to their magical attempts to dispel any curse Tressya might be under. The next time the apostle stuck his head through the door, I was ready with the blade I had freed from my belt. He would wear it through his skull if he dared to repeat his question even once more.

The room was now steeped in darkness, save for the bedside candle thoughtfully prepared by Gusselan before she departed. Were it not for the apostles' excited chatter in a distant part of the manor, I might have thought it deserted.

With the Mother's prompt arrival, the Salmun came to mind. They couldn't be far from tracking Tressya down, and I had no idea how many remained after the tunnel fight. Hopefully, Osmud and Bryra were vigilantly monitoring the paths near the manor.

Given the challenges we faced, I should have been pacing, striving to rein in my chaotic thoughts and seeking mental clarity, hoping to make wise decisions. However, in that moment, I found myself unable to muster any concerns or even move a limb, content to lie there with Tressya sprawled across me.

I gently traced lazy trails along her back, experiencing a newfound sense of contentment and tranquility. For the first time, my body didn't feel the urge to move. Instead, I felt as though I could grow old with her sprawled across me, her slow, steady heartbeats like the gentle flutter of a tiny bird's wings against my chest. The return of her warmth and the pressure of her petite frame against me spread a comforting heat through my chest and into my belly, kindling a slow-burning fire that, once ignited, would never extinguish.

If I could command the Etherweave, I would stop time, suspending us in this quiet cocoon for eternity, keeping the world from breeching our serene sanctuary, until I felt the twinges of the Eone's presence slowly merging within my mind.

Stay the fuck away. Silence ensured. Perhaps they sensed the savage snarl in my mental thoughts.

As if sensing my internal snarl, Tressya stirred. I held my

breath, not ready for her to awaken, knowing the moment she did, she would quickly climb off me while bombarding me with questions I had no desire to answer and insisting we plot our escape from the predicament we found ourselves in. Once more, I reflected on my state of tranquil lethargy and how little I cared about anything beyond the confines of this bedroom. There was time enough to worry about our fates once this night was over.

Too late, she was waking. She lifted her head off my chest, then made to rise.

"What do you think you're doing?" My voice was rough, a reflection of my suddenly darkened mood, as I preferred situations to unfold in my favor, and Tressya staying asleep, her warm little body pressing down on me, was my idea of bliss.

"It's nighttime."

"When all should be asleep." With a firm hand on her back, I eased her down onto my chest again.

"Tamas." She tried to resist me.

"No." I wrapped both arms around her, securing her in an embrace from which there was no escape. Ever.

"I'm overheating."

"Better than shivering."

"Please."

With effort, I kicked the mountain of covers down to our waists. "You'll feel cooler soon."

I closed my eyes, smiling to myself, as I felt her resistance ease. However, she disrupted my serenity by tracing the tip of her finger around my nearly healed wound, igniting a flame fiercer than the embers stemming from my heart.

"I'm sorry."

"You shouldn't be. It's no less than I deserved."

She lifted her head, resting her chin on my chest. "But you were...are...umm..."

"Possessed."

She rose, then laid her chin on her folded arms, splayed across my chest. "We haven't talked about that."

Not like this; not when the delightful sensation of her body stretched atop mine consumed my thoughts. There was no room in my head for anything else.

"Let the moment be as it is." I closed my eyes, avoiding her gaze as I battled a myriad of urges: some innocent, some dark, and some depraved.

"How did it happen?"

I released a low rumbling growl deep in my throat, which only made Tressya chuckle.

"Do I need to teach you another lesson, Razohan?"

I cracked an eye open. "Is that a bargain or a threat?"

"Both are equally effective."

"You do realize moments like these will be as rare as dogs with wings going forward? I think it best we savor it for the tranquility it affords us and let the chaos of our fates remain in the future for a little longer."

"The southerners had no word for these people, and so they called them the ancients. But you're saying they're the Eone."

I sighed, conceding defeat. Yet, I continued my gentle caresses across her back, holding onto the faint hope that it might eventually work to my advantage and coax her to lie back down across my chest.

"There are four of them."

"Four?! As in, four inside of you? Possessing you?"

"It's more than a little crowded."

"And they created the Etherweave?"

"According to them."

She rose until she straddled me, which was the next best thing to her stretched out atop my body, so I didn't complain.

"But they must be millennia old. How did they possess you?"

'Please, Tamas, now is not the time,' Ineth urged.

Curses that he'd reared so suddenly within my mind. My serenity broken, my jumbled thoughts were once more clouding my concentration, and the Eone slipped through without me noticing.

"It's a tedious story." My voice was perhaps a little too forceful. "There's only one part worth knowing. A fragment of their essence has survived to this day. That's how they found a way inside. And now they're a blight I long to burn from my mind."

The Eone remained surprisingly quiet.

"They want you to kill me?"

"They know what will happen if they dare try to influence me again."

I rested my hands on her thighs, hoping a gentle massage might divert her attention from her questions to more pleasant pursuits.

Tressya didn't respond immediately. When she finally spoke, her voice was quiet. "Do they?"

It was an uncomfortable question because I couldn't respond with a resounding yes.

"What happened with the Mother?"

"No way. You don't get to change the subject. This is serious, Tamas. If they can influence you—"

"Once. Only once. I'm Razohan, Tressya, a man filled with countless souls. No voices in my head will ever dictate my actions." I didn't mean for my tone to sound so harsh.

"As the second bloodborn, I'm a danger to their plans."

My grip tightened on her thighs. "No. Never. Not to me."

She rested her hands over mine, a subtle sign that my grip was too tight, and I didn't realize.

"Sorry," I mumbled.

"Now we really have a problem."

"There's no problem. They'll never risk endangering you because they know what I'll do."

How could I recapture the serenity of our moment? I was unable to take advantage of her ideal position sitting astride me, as I couldn't dismiss the truth in her words from my mind. Damn. It appeared as though she'd won, dragging me so thoroughly from our enchanted moment. My heart kicked up a fierce beat remembering last night. Any minute I would transform certain parts of my body, which were bound to send her to the other side of the room.

Calm the fuck down.

"They believe they'll gain access to the Etherweave by possessing you, Tamas. These Eone won't stop trying to dominate your mind. You're as much a danger to their plans as I am. You and I are the two people who stand in their way."

She is devious, Ovia said.

We must break her influence over him, Fivia added.

We shall. But we need to move carefully, Carthius said.

"They think you're devious."

The Eone vanished from my mind as emphatically as a slamming door.

Tressya's brows hitched.

"I told you it was crowded in here."

I firmly gripped her hips, signaling for her to stay put while I shuffled myself up to lean against the wall behind us. "Now you know my sordid secret. What happened out there today?"

"This is serious, Tamas. You can't change the subject. I want to know more about these Eone."

"You were a mess when I arrived. Not even Bryra's body warmth could restore yours. I think that's equally serious. So, what happened?"

She shook her head, scrunching up her nose. "You always do this. Returning my question with a question."

"And you always think you'll get the better in a conversation."

"Because my questions carry more weight."

I seized her wrists, pulling her arms forward, so they were either side of me, which drew her nearer, her face hovering dangerously close to mine. "I humor you most of the time."

"That's why you have a blade wound on your chest."

"Tressya, my queen, will there come a day when you surrender to me?"

Her eyes subtly widened, pupils noticeably dilating.

What she heard pleased her, igniting parts of me that should never be stirred unless she was ready for the consequences.

"Isn't the blade wound proof enough of my surrender?" She quirked a brow in question.

I stared into her eyes, then let my gaze drift down to her lips, making a deliberate show of it. "That it is. I wouldn't expect any less from my queen."

She fought unsuccessfully with a smile, slanting her gaze sideways to hide how delighted she was with the new title I'd given upon her.

"Bryra killed the Mother, which I'll be eternally grateful for."

This time, it was my turn to suppress a triumphant smile. She had succumbed, abandoning her own questions to respond to mine.

"You knew Bryra was here?"

"I did." She glanced over my head at the darkness outside.

"Do you know why she's here? I'm struggling to think how she made it through the Ashenlands without help."

Her gaze settled on me. "She saved your ass, you know. There's no way I could have gotten you out of the castle on my own."

"How did she get into the castle without drawing everyone's attention to her? And why does it sound like you're defending her?"

"Because you're bullheaded. Once you're angry, you won't hear the truth. You'll only hear the version of the story you want to hear."

"What version should I hear?"

"The one that says Bryra was your savior." Tressya tried to free herself from my grip, but I wouldn't release her until she gave me specifics.

There was no reason Bryra would venture south. She'd suffered during the Ashenlands war—Osmud filled me in, when normally Bryra would have told me herself—saying she was done with the world of the two-legged, and that her father needed her by his side.

"So why was she in Emberfell?" I barely suppressed the frustration in my voice. Tressya's secrecy compromised her safety, yet she expected me to turn a blind eye.

"You should know I'm possessed too."

I released her wrists. "What?"

Tressya sat back, and I followed. "What do you mean? Who? Since when? Why didn't you say something straight away?"

With a firm hand on my chest, she attempted to push me backward. I resisted, a spark of burning liquid pooled in my belly, molten fury, searing a hole through my gut.

"Stars, Tressya."

"You expect me to reveal all when you dance around my questions?"

"We've had this argument."

"Oh really, when?"

"I'm no stranger to bearing the weight of others' souls. Having voices other than my own in my head is not uncommon."

"That's because you're insane."

"Who is it, Tressya?" I flicked my gaze between her eyes, my stare sharp as a knife, hoping to carve out the answer from within. "Shit. It's the Mother? That's why you were like ice to touch. The Mother's spirit has possessed you?"

"Certainly not what I expected. I'm furious she outsmarted me."

"Tressya..." I struggled to find the words, as something beast-like surged from deep within, a wild and furious feeling slowly growing barbed wings.

She pressed a finger against my lips. "I can handle her."

Not even her finger on my lips would distract me as a primal savagery tore through my chest, leaving in its wake a shredded heart. I would use my claws as a pitchfork, and gouge that bitch from within if I knew it wouldn't harm Tressya. While I was at it, I would give Tressya a damn good shake. This situation was nothing short of perilous, yet she was treating it as a mere inconvenience.

I moved her finger aside. "I'm sure there's a way to bring the Mother back to life once I have the Etherweave, just so I can kill her again, in a bloody and violent way."

"Once *you* have the Etherweave?"

I barely heard her reply. "I can handle the Eone. But the Mother, I question you'll—"

"You're dealing with four. And they obviously still hold some of their power if they could save you from whatever foul Salmun poison made you suffer. The Mother's little more than an irritable spirit trapped within."

"The Eone is nothing without me. They know that. But the Mother nearly killed you." My voice rode along the wild fury within, coming out louder, harsher than I meant.

"Hardly." She folded her arms across her chest. "I was a

little cold. That's far from dying. You, on the other hand, tried to kill me."

"Never, Tressya." I vehemently shook my head.

She pressed her palm over my wound. "And what about this?"

I fell backward against the wall, groaning in frustration at how easily she flipped our argument. Sure, I had a momentary lapse of weakness, one that would never happen again. Never. I would grow stronger, fight harder, become smarter. The Eone would never have that much control over me again. My will was iron.

As if sensing the heat of my simmering anger, Tressya traced a finger around the wound, then let it glide along my chest, her eyes following the path she created. "The Mother has no surprises left. And at least I've gained one thing."

She had the audacity to think she could climb off of me while my anger was far from quelled. I tightened my grip on her waist, forcing her back onto my lap. She wasn't going anywhere until I decided otherwise.

She frowned at me.

"We haven't finished our conversation."

"I have soul voice," she stated, as if I were a fool for not anticipating her response. "Everything of hers is mine. It's not too dissimilar to what happens when you take souls, Razohan."

"Don't you think she would've planned for that?"

"The Mother knows nothing about spiritweaving. I mean…she knows nothing about what it's like. And how it's done. She's little more than a spirit now. And spirits are harmless."

Having spent countless enjoyable hours gazing at Tressya's face, I was familiar with the subtleties of her expressions. Thus, I could tell when she was lying or, at the very least, uncertain about the truth of her claims.

"Liar. You don't even believe what you're saying."

That finger of hers was having a hypnotic effect. I tried to resist dipping my gaze to watch the now gentle swirls she was making around my left nipple, almost absentmindedly, while she continued talking. "I know more about the Mother and spiritweaving than you know of the Eone. She'll prove an annoyance. Nothing more."

"An annoyance that wants to possess the Etherweave."

"Like the Eone. It seems we're a pair."

"I don't like this."

"You think I'm thrilled? Unlike the Eone, the Mother has no magic. She only has soul voice. And I have the power of my soul word. Besides, I'm not even sure soul voice would be effective when she's trapped inside of me."

"I'm not convinced—"

She jerked forward and kissed me, a firm kiss meant to silence me, not entice me. But, as sure as the stars come out every night, it didn't work as she hoped, because it was enticing.

When she went to pull away, I gripped her wrists. *No. No. No. My little viper.*

"I'm sorry, little queen," I whispered against her lips. "There's no backing out of what you started."

"Tamas, the Mother disapproves."

In shock, I let her go.

She smirked, then sat back, straddling me once more.

The little serpent. I flipped her over and nestled myself nicely between her legs, which was a bad move. My cock wanted to play. "What exactly does the Mother disapprove of?" I quirked a brow, bending forward to feather kisses along her throat, unable to stop my hips from rolling forward and gentling thrusting against her pants. The soft snarl I released was for the fabric that lay between us.

"Not that, for sure."

I couldn't help smiling at the purr in her voice.

"And if I did this?" I worked the tip of my tongue along her jawline, tasting the delicate sweetness of her flavor, very much like a blend of the finest meal, the most exquisite scent, and the most cherished memory all in one. I grew suddenly ravenous to taste more delectable flavors on her body. I dragged my nose across the delicate skin of her chest, inhaling as I did so. "There's not enough of you exposed for me to taste." My voice was harsh, as I felt my fangs descend.

"I'm sure she would find this outrageous," I whispered as I flicked open the first two buttons on her shirt with a fang and nuzzled my nose between the soft swell of her cleavage, partially hidden behind her chemise, longing to lick and nip all that luscious skin she kept hidden underneath her ill-fitting men's clothes.

Her soft sigh was the spark that ignited my hunger. "This all has to go," I growled.

"What about all your questions? I'm sure you have a dozen more." I heard the smile in her voice. More importantly, I felt the jump of her heartbeat under my tongue.

"I'm far more interested in scandalizing that old crone," I

mumbled. Anything that came before me getting my lips on her skin was long forgotten.

"And the Eone?"

"Who?" I flicked more buttons open with my fangs. "If you were further along in your transition from mere human to Razohan, we could have ourselves a lot of fun right now."

The edges of my restraint were slowly fraying. Give me another few seconds, and they would be torn asunder. The day Tressya traded her fragile human body for the strength of her beast would be the day I discovered how truly feral I could become.

"For now, I'll keep my claws and fangs tucked away and play nice."

"I thought you wanted to scandalize the Mother." Her voice slipped into the breathy whisper of anticipation, as I pulled her chemise from its hem up to her chin. Forcing my fangs away, I wasted no time tantalizing her nipples with my hot breaths and gentle sucks.

"Oh believe me, I will," I said between passing from one breast to the other. "I still have my fingers and tongue as perfect weapons in my arsenal."

"Is that all?" Her voice ended in a soft huff of a sigh.

"That's for starters."

"It's too late. She's already receded. I don't feel her anymore."

No longer caring about that stupid old crone, I used my tongue to crawl my way down her body, delicately swirling it around her belly button while I flipped the buttons on her pants. Tressya encouraged me with soft gasps and small grunts of anticipatory pleasure, sounds that headed to one place, spawning a need in me that would soon turn to pain if I was denied.

Damn, I need this woman. My desires were as primal as they were emotional. Being in her presence tantalized my senses as much as any unrestrained carnal pleasure. The last thing I ever expected or believed was that I'd find the other half of my soul while hunting for the Etherweave.

"You need to know my days will be spent in worship of you," I whispered against her skin as I slowly drew her pants down her thighs, following the fabric with delicate nips and kisses.

"Only days?" she mumbled, already sounding as though she was floating in bliss.

"Always. There will be no night and day, only us."

With garments discarded, I leaned back to behold what was in my heart, mine—perhaps not entirely, but I would continue to believe so until Tressya made her feelings about us unequivocally clear.

Every curve of her body was mine to explore, savor, and possess for as long as she allowed. I was ravenous, desperately eager to taste every inch of her skin and chart it with my hands, lips, and tongue until she craved a taste of my blood. And that's exactly what I did, sparing no inch of her body, pausing in places that made her giggle or utter soft little sounds of delight, relishing the way she soothed her fingers through my hair and drew her nails along my skin. The tantalizing curve of her nape, the extra soft flesh beneath her breasts, and the dip of her hips, particularly enthralled me—places that captured her scent and intensified it. In my clan, twenty-seven was considered young, yet it felt as though I'd wasted too much of my life without her. How was it the simple act of pleasuring this woman could make me feel so complete?

I could spend a lifetime enjoying the feel of her skin on my tongue, but the primal pulse of my blood yearned to taste that one part of her body reserved solely for me. I lowered, hitching one leg over my shoulder, then hummed my approval at the sight before me, before wetting my lips and nestling myself between her legs, eager to commit the fragrance of her most intimate part to memory. I wanted her, wanted this, wanted it more than my next breath, more than the Bone Throne.

I took my time toying with her, savoring her, learning the nuances of her desire, what secret places drew those gorgeous little sounds of pleasure, what use of my fingers and tongue caused the slight tremor in her thighs before it moved through to seize her entire body in the swell of her impending orgasm. This would be my place of worship. Here, I would stake my claim or perish in the attempt.

My arousal was a torturous bliss, a euphoric pain I willingly suffered when she fisted my hair, ground herself across my face, arched her back off the bed and cried my name like I was a god.

Over Tressya's cries of pleasure came the sound of heavy boots thumping down the corridor.

"Tamas," she gasped.

"They wouldn't dare," I growled, reaching over her to where I left my dagger on the bedside table before I slipped into bed to warm Tressya.

"What're you doing?" She pushed at my chest, and I snarled. Our moment was well and truly trashed.

"Whoever comes through that door wears it," I said, turning to look over my shoulder.

A blink after the door burst wide, I released the dagger. Osmud caught it before it impaled his eye. Behind him, Tortilus squeaked. Cramming in after them came the rest of the apostles. It seemed everyone thought my room was a thoroughfare.

"You'll want to hold on to this once you hear my news," he said.

Tressya was struggling to shift out from under me, but I stayed her with a hand, pulling her chemise down first before I growled. "Only one person need tell us the news," I barked, feeling the flames of anger lick the edges of my caged beast. The apostles scuttled from the room, tumbling over each other in their haste to be gone.

"Lucky I warned Tortilus to let me enter first," Osmud responded dryly, leading against the doorjamb, flipping the dagger as though bored.

"What is it?" Tressya said, seeming to forget she'd lost her pants with all the tension thickening the air.

"Turn around," I growled at Osmud.

He quirked a brow, then casually turned to look out the door as if this was no big deal, and normally it wouldn't be for us Razohan, but I didn't know how Tressya would feel about her lost privacy.

"The Salmun," Osmud replied.

CHAPTER
TWENTY-FIVE

TRESSYA

"Stars, where are they?" I said, buttoning my shirt, having already donned my pants.

"We'll talk downstairs," Osmud replied and pushed off the doorjamb, unexpectedly throwing the dagger as he half-turned to leave. Tamas deftly caught it mid-air before I uttered a cry and mumbled a word of thanks as he sheathed it at his hip.

I was at the door about to head out when Tamas caught my hand, spun me into him and kissed me, a furious kiss for the unspent passion. Our bodies pressed together, my heart pounded against its confines as if reaching to merge with his, my body still pulsed with my inflamed yearning. Being this close to him was infectious to my sanity. Pleasure was the last thing I should think of when we were far from safe, and the treacherous path ahead was more dangerous than the one we'd left behind.

"It won't end like this next time."

"Perhaps our heads will be on spikes next time."

"Have a little faith, my queen," he whispered against my lips, his voice a soft caress as he traced the side of my cheek with his now clawed fingertip. "This," he murmured, "is for the first Salmun I encounter."

"Well, Your Majesty, I'm—"

"Maybe I'll sharpen it on our little friend here first," Tamas growled, revealing his lethal looking claw to Tortilus, who appeared to have been lurking close by waiting for us to make an appearance, and sending him stumbling back into the wall.

"He's simply ensuring I'm recovered." I pulled Tamas hand down to his side. "Play nice," I admonished him under my breath.

Tamas paused beside Tortilus and leaned in, his clawed finger pressing ominously against Tortilus' neck. "Continue to encroach onto my territory, and this claw will embed itself somewhere fatal within your body."

Perhaps it was the intrusion into our private moment, my pulse still racing, my body still vibrating with my unmet needs, that contributed to my reaction, because Tamas' possessive warning sent a little anticipatory shiver through all the best places inside of me. I couldn't resist the addictive thrill of being desired, even if it carried a hint of possessiveness.

"We're all on edge," I said to Tortilus as a way of an excuse as I followed Tamas down the stairs.

"Of course, Your majesty, I under—"

I turned on him at the top of the stairs. "Let's drop the formalities, shall we? No offense, but I'll strangle you if you utter that title once more." Then I hurried down, chasing Tamas, who'd already disappeared into the grand reception room.

Tortilus did his best to keep pace with me. "You look well rested...er..."

"I am."

"With no lingering effects?"

"I haven't felt this good in a while."

He skipped two steps to come beside me. "If at any time you feel a reoccurrence of the bizarre happenings—coldness, fever, dizziness, an inability to think clearly—don't hesitate to let me know."

I tried not to smirk. "So you're a healer as well?"

"Not as such. But if it's magical healing you require—"

"I'll come straight to you, Tortilus."

"Yes, good, good."

By now we'd reached the bottom of the staircase and Tortilus hurried to slip in front of me, blocking my way. "Your Maj—Tressya, are you sure you can trust these people? Northerners in the south are only after one thing."

"Tamas and I are after the same thing. Besides, we'll get nowhere without their help."

"The woman... She's—"

"Of great value to us. Without her, I wouldn't be here."

"Oh, right. If you're sure. It's just...you have the four of us now. Between us—"

"I'll turn away none who want to help if their hearts are genuine."

"Absolutely, Your—" He caught himself. "We're prepared to serve you until the end. You are the rightful heir and most deserving to sit upon the throne."

I sighed, then mumbled under my breath. "I hope it never gets that far."

Everyone except Bryra was present when Tortilus and I entered the room. The other three apostles sat clustered together on a long seat, engrossed in the book open on Selisimus' lap. Tortilus excused himself and quickly joined them, leaving me to endure the scrutiny of the others. Meanwhile, Tamas, who'd had the foresight to bring the parchment pages, had spread them out on the round wooden table in the corner.

"Tressya," he motioned with a jerk of his head for me to join him.

Osmud's face remained a mask of composure, his gray eyes shimmering like moonlight on water, casting a captivating glow. Yet beneath that serene surface, one could easily find oneself drowning. They tracked my movements across the room without giving away any hint of his thoughts. I was certain Bryra had shared everything she knew about the incident on the path, so I wouldn't blame him for his suspicions.

Despite everything I'd said to Tamas upstairs only moments ago, I wasn't entirely confident about the Mother's possession. I heard no inner voice. My thoughts were clear, and my mind felt free. What did it even mean to be possessed? It was a question I would have to ask Tamas when we were alone.

As I neared her, Gusselan rose and took my hand. She said nothing; her question silent as she stared into my eyes. I gave her a weak smile, feeling as though her eyes had the power to penetrate deep inside my mind to where the Mother hid.

"You're warm at least," she finally said.

"The worst has passed."

She raised a brow, seemingly questioning my assertion. If by removing Andriet from his death place I risked destroying the divide, which diabolical consequence would spirit possession cost me? I didn't have the courage to ask.

"Place your hands on the parchment," Tamas instructed me once I was beside him.

I did as I was told. "Shouldn't we talk about our plans to escape the Salmun?"

"We already know the Salmun are on our trail, so it's imperative we find our way to the Etherweave. We must get there before the Salmun."

"Where's Bryra?" I said.

It was clear in the past the two had meant more to each other, as evidenced by Bryra's reaction upon seeing him ill. Tamas was a superb performer, or he'd genuinely let go of any intimate feelings toward her, and I would guess Bryra had yet to do the same. Perhaps it was Tamas she avoided—and any show of affection between us.

Osmud rose. "Keeping watch on the Salmun. I'm off to join her." Tamas glanced his way, gave one nod of acknowledgment, then returned his attention to the parchment.

At some point, Wellard and Plesy joined us at the table, leaving Selisimus and Tortilus engrossed in the book.

"Little of what is here makes sense." Wellard finally drew my attention to the map, preoccupied as I was with the more pressing matter of the Salmun's possible arrival.

"What if they come before we've even left the manor?" I said.

"They won't," Tamas murmured, appearing unconcerned by the threat of the Salmun. "That's what Bryra and Osmud are for. No one's surprising us tonight."

"In case it slipped your notice, the Salmun have magic. Osmud and Bryra don't."

With both our palms on the map, I leaned against Tamas. In the sudden lull between chatter, I realized I could hear his heartbeat, a heavy thudding rhythm in tune with my own. Looking up at him, I noticed the dark shadow of his early beard, and for one fleeting moment, I toyed with the idea of running the back of my hand across his jawline because it seemed not even a life and death moment would completely erase my desire for him.

As if sensing my thoughts, Tamas slowly turned his head, bringing us intimately close. "You don't need to worry about Bryra and Osmud."

"I can't be that confident."

"Because you want to protect everyone close to you."

"Is that a fault?"

"It's admirable until the point it gets you killed."

"Are you suggesting we should only think of ourselves?"

The hint of a twitch at the corners of his lips made me want to smack him. It seemed my beast-man loved provoking me.

"Nothing will happen to you. Trust me."

"I'm flattered that's your only thought, but I can't dismiss everyone else in this room."

Tamas flicked his eyes to Plesy and Wellard standing beside me. "The apostles have their magic. And Gusselan poses no threat to the Salmun. They are solely after you. If things turn bad, Osmud and Bryra will head north. That was my instruction. Leaving you, Tressya, as my only concern."

"I'm not the only one to wield the Etherweave in case you've forgotten."

He arched his head back and laughed. "You honestly think they're a threat to me?"

Hearing his heartfelt laughter was like the gentle embrace of a mother soothing her crying infant, yet not even the tranquility that such a feeling ensured quelled my frustration. It seemed he was determined to continue being an arrogantly heroic fool.

"It seems the Eon—You were always an arrogant fool."

"There's not much the Salmun can do against their rogue pet," he remarked, referring to the nightmare.

"They nearly killed you last time?"

Leaning in close, he brought our lips dangerously close. "That was before..." He hardened his dark eyes on mine, a predator ready to strike. Enticing, but right now a blaze was burning in my gut, steeling me against his enigmatic allure.

He was referring to the Eone. "Heroes still die."

"And make the best legends."

"If I put a stake through your heart, you won't be doing anything heroic."

"You already tried that, my queen. It didn't work."

I clenched my teeth, knowing I was getting nowhere.

"Perhaps you both can lay your argument to rest for now," Gusselan said, reminding the both of us we were not alone, something I readily forgot when around him.

I glanced around me, seeing Tortilus and Selisimus had lost interest in their book, while Wellard and Plesy had distanced themselves from the table.

"This is not over," I snapped at Tamas and slammed my hands down on the parchment, breathing furiously through my nose while I waited for him to do the same.

When he did, he'd positioned himself behind me, coming down over the top of me, caging me within his arms, between his body and the table. It was a definite show of dominance and possession—and I tried my damndest to ignore the tingling flutter between my legs, even if I wanted to jerk my head back and head-butt him in the nose for his obstinance.

The black ink, as if guided by an unseen hand, sketched itself with meticulous detail across the parchment. Each stroke breathed life into the map, the lines forming a twisted swirl of contours, tracing the high mountainous regions and the sinuous paths of rivers winding through deep valleys. This was not a mysterious adventure, so my tremor of anticipation seemed misplaced. Yet, I held my breath, awaiting the revelation of a momentous secret, while the map gradually came into view.

I scrutinized every corner, every contour, every fold and line, but there was nothing that appeared significant, nothing that was in any way marked to show our destination.

"What do you think we're looking for?" I said.

Peering over my shoulder, Tamas remained silent. I could feel his breath, and in the unsettling quiet, I could hear his heartbeat once more. It was in tune with mine, a phenomenon that only occurred during the rare instances when I delved into another's mind to seek their elusive soul word.

The sketch drew everyone present to the table, causing a crowd to form on the side opposite to us, and I suspected it was Tamas's snarling attitude that kept the others at bay.

"I've never left Tolum, so I can't say I know any of this forest," Plesy said.

"This map is depicting what once existed before the Levenian came," Tamas said. There was a hardness with a hint of a snarl in his voice. He was fighting the Eone. They didn't want him revealing any of this to us. "One thousand years ago, Tarragona was a vast forested land. Now, when you head north, all you see is a stretch of wasteland, as the Salmun has hidden what once existed behind a veil now known as the Ashenlands. Even these mountains are invisible."

"Like Plesy, I have never set foot outside Tolum. Though I know of the Ashenlands," Selisimus said.

"That's a lot of power magic," Wellard uttered.

"Dangerous lands," Tortilus mused. "We'll need our wits. And a few more of these." He waved the book he and the other three had been poring over.

"You're not coming," Tamas growled, swiping the parchment out from under my hands as he straightened. I saw the tip of a claw puncturing through the pages.

"With all respect..." Tortilus appeared lost for an appropriate title.

"Once we leave this manor, Tressya and I go alone." I was sure any minute he would grow fangs. It was a barely concealed struggled, but so far, he was winning.

"But we have magic," Tortilus countered. "You'll need magic to help you through the Ashenlands."

"Perhaps Tamas has a point," Wellard intervened.

But Tortilus seemed deaf to Wellard's plea. "Between the four of us—"

"You know nothing of what you'll face in the Ashenlands," Tamas barked, before closing his eyes and inhaling as he stuffed the parchment back inside his pocket.

"Excuse me, but can I make a suggestion?"

Everyone looked to Plesy.

"I was..." Plesy shrunk under Tamas' glare. "Going to ask which way you were planning on heading?"

"North, of course," Tamas all but yelled. "How else do you suppose we'll get there?" His mood was deteriorating. Perhaps we should cut this meeting short and get on our way before the Eone seized hold of his beast again.

"Yes, you see..." Plesy glanced at Tamas' pocket. "If you would just let me see the map again."

"What?" Tamas growled, slamming his hands down on the table.

Seeing Tamas hunched forward with his dark eyes blazing a glare capable of scorching anyone on the spot, I couldn't blame the apostles for taking a step back from the table. He looked every bit the beast-man struggling to stay human while his beast side prowled to break free.

When I noticed the protrusion of his claws along the tips of his fingers, I slipped my hand into his pocket and retrieved the parchment. I didn't need him to tell me he was struggling. They were unhappy about how many he'd exposed to the Etherweave's whereabouts.

"Stay with me," I whispered, as I gently ran my finger along his jaw.

His attention snapped to me, his eyes narrowed. Pressure creases formed at the corners of his mouth, and a muscle twitched in his jaw. I swear I saw a flicker of some untamed and vicious consciousness wavering in the depths of his dark eyes. It seemed the Eone didn't like me, which was hardly surprising given I was their direct rival for the Etherweave.

I leaned in and whispered in his ear. "You're in control, remember?"

Tamas let out a hard exhale, dragging his now fully extended claws down the table with a loud scrape before throwing up his hands, then folding them behind his head as if seeking a safe place to anchor them away from causing harm.

"It's not going to hurt, and we've got nothing to lose," I told him.

After I'd freed the parchment, he attempted to back away, but I grabbed his arm. "No, you don't. It takes both of us." I gave him little time to recover, knowing the Eone would rally and try again to win control over his beast, so pulled him toward the table and pressed his palm onto the pages once I had spread them out before us.

With one arm flat on the parchment, Tamas gave in, coming up behind me, sagging into me and resting his lips on the back of my neck. His heavy breaths were warm on my skin, and his heartbeat was no longer in rhythm with mine. It pounded against my back as if wanting to burst free from his chest. His other hand, he snaked around my waist, flushing me firm against him, and I knew this was his way of reminding himself what was important and fighting back control from the Eone. And I secretly loved that I was his anchor while he fought against their influence.

I placed my hand over his, as a silent acknowledgement for what he was going through, and waited, breath hitched, as the sketches reformed across the blank pages.

"What did you want to show us, Plesy?" I wasn't sure how long Tamas could keep up the fight.

"I think there's a better way than heading north."

"But the Ashenlands are north," I argued.

"And the Salmun will believe that's the way you've headed," Plesy continued.

"Because they'll suspect that's where the Etherweave is hidden," Wellard added.

"That's why they created the Ashenlands in the first place," Tortilus announced, as though discovering the final clue. "They long suspected it was there."

"So to prevent anyone from finding it—" Selisimus said.

"The northerners, in particular," Wellard interrupted.

"They cursed the land, preventing anyone but themselves from entering," finished Plesy.

"Good job, brethren," Tortilus said, looking extremely pleased.

"That sounds plausible. But which way do we go?" I said.

Tamas lifted his head and peered over my shoulder, seeming to find interest in what the apostles had said.

"I think you should head this way." Plesy pointed to Tolum, sketched in the bottom far left corner of the map. In particular, his finger rested on Emberforge.

"Ah, yes, I see what you mean," Tortilus said. "And we can retrieve a good deal more help." He patted the book still in his hands.

Feeling his inhale, as if he was about to speak, I squeezed Tamas' hand before he could grouch again that the apostles weren't welcome on our hunt for the Etherweave.

"Are you suggesting we return to the tunnel under the Bone Throne?" I said.

"Look," Plesy said, drawing a circle around Tolum. That's when I noticed what I'd missed before, too focused on the north and the Ashenlands. Tolum was poorly sketched, unlike every other place on the map. Emberforge was distinct, but beyond the temple, the rest of Tolum was nothing more than a dirty smudge, blending into the vast expanse of the Ashenlands. I realized then that not even the farming lands between Tolum and the Ashenlands were defined, nor were any of the counties labeled.

"By some magical means, the tunnel ends at the Ashenlands, and I'll bet my life it's not going to take us miles to get there," Tortilus murmured, unconsciously revealing his intent to join us once again.

Tamas rested his lips against the skin at the back of my neck once more, and I was certain that, unlike me, he had noticed these details himself. Perhaps his plan had always been to return to Emberforge, but he was reluctant to disclose it in front of our current companions, or perhaps the Eone had forced his silence.

I swiped the parchment from the table, folding it as I spoke. "We'll leave tonight."

"I'm packed," Tortilus chimed in.

I turned to Gusselan. "What's your choice?"

"You know my choice."

Before I could reply, Tamas took the parchment from my hand and held it close to the candle flame.

"What're you doing?" I cried as the apostles gasped in horror.

"We know our path."

"Not once we reach the Ashenlands."

"I do."

I stared at the parchment igniting into flames, then at his face, his uncompromising features, their harshness exaggerated in the candle flame and wasn't sure who was in charge right now; Tamas or the Eone.

CHAPTER
TWENTY-SIX

TRESSYA

Tamas had vanished into the night in search of Osmud and Bryra, intending to send them north. I argued we needed all the willing help we could get, and almost lost our argument because Tamas' stubbornness was reinforced by his irrational belief he was invincible, further bolstered by his possession of two potent weapons: the nightmare and the Eone—the latter not only a potent weapon, but a seriously dangerous and uncontrollable weapon I doubted even Tamas knew how to control—I could only hope he wasn't appeasing me by agreeing, only to do as he wished once he reached them.

I'd nothing to pack but the clothes I wore, so I was the first to the reception room with its lingering smell of burned parchment. The ashes lay on the table where Tamas had left them before he strode for the door, declaring he would track Osmud and Bryra down.

The sensation of being watched alerted me to someone's presence before I heard the door creak an aged welcome. I turned to see Gusselan closing the door behind her.

"I hate the idea of leaving you here."

"Not as much as I loathe the idea of racing across the Ashenlands. I can honesty say I'm happy to find my journey at an end."

As she walked toward the table where we had gathered early, her tense posture suggested she wanted to discuss something challenging or sensitive but was uncertain how to approach the topic, unlike the Mother, who never struggled to express her opinions, criticizing or belittling the listener in the process. I waited, giving her time to choose how best to say what was on her mind.

At the table she ran a finger through the parchment's ashes, leaving a dark smudge on the wood's surface. "Do you trust him?"

I paused for a beat, not expecting her to address Tamas and my relationship. Rather, I had thought she would query what had infected me with a chill so deep it was like I'd turned to ice. "Strangely, yes."

"He's as great a threat to your safety as the Salmun."

"He's a threat to many, but not to me." No one understood what Tamas and I had because no one saw the intimate moments we shared, no one could reach inside my heart to feel the strength he silently gave—Tamas was subtly rewriting all the laws laid down by the Mother, teaching me that love was power and not its opposite.

"Love doesn't always endure for eternity, especially when faced with the trials you must overcome."

"He's Razohan."

"He's a man. Their hearts are all the same."

"Then you don't know about or understand the mate bond between pairs."

She quirked a brow. "Is this an excuse he's used to subdue your doubt?"

I pulled up the sleeve of my shirt, revealing the scar from Tamas' bite. "The night he attacked the Sapphire Rose, I was at his mercy. He could've killed me. It's what he came to do. But rather than kill me, he gave me this."

"Then it's a malicious binding. A way for him to control you."

Gusselan, a disciple of her order, was likely raised to feel nothing but allegiance to her Reverend Mother. No doubt love was excised from her heart because it crippled one's purpose. Yet, as a mother herself, she understood the depths of that one emotion; she knew it was impossible to imprison the heart. Though, I doubted I could say much to make her understand, as just a few months ago, I would have thought the same as her.

"No."

He'd admitted biting me so he could track me, but only to keep me safe, and I would never voice those words aloud, hearing the naivety at their core.

"The mate bond is a bond of love for eternity."

"He told you that?" Gusselan made an exasperated sound. "A daughter of the Sistern should be smarter than that."

Feeling the slow climb of annoyance, I inhaled before I answered, needing my calming breaths to see the end of this argument. Naïve, ignorant and compliant were just three of the words the Mother had used to describe me. And now Gusselan thought to use the same. Recently, she was a mere stranger, so why should I care how she characterized me? Yet, I did—dammit.

"Perhaps I've misjudged you," she continued. "Since arriving in Tolum, you've committed many serious offenses, not least of which was freeing my son from his place of death. I fear your blind faith in this northerner and his companions may lead to your downfall—and potentially that of the seven realms."

"I wish I could make you understand. I know Tamas." *Do I?* "He's no more desirous of the Bone Throne than I am."

But he headed for the Bone Throne on his return to Tolum, did he not?

"If so." She lifted her hand from the ashes, rubbing the dark smudging between her fingertips. "Then why did he destroy the map?"

To ensure only he knew the way. "Because he already knows where to go." I mentally shook off Gusselan's concerns, telling myself to stay strong against her doubts. Tamas knew where to find the Etherweave because the Eone had told him, yet he was still intent on taking me. He had chosen me as his anchor, the one person to shield him from their relentless interference. There could be no greater demonstration of trust than that.

She faced me and took a step forward. I knew from the deep-set groove of her brows, I wouldn't like what she intended to say. "Don't make yourself a victim along the way. He needs no one's help to reach the Etherweave now."

"Perhaps he never did, but he brought me with him. If he wasn't intending on taking me, why rescue us from Emberfell? Far better for him if he left us to the Salmun."

"Maybe that's his fear. If the Salmun have you, they have access to the Etherweave. Perhaps that's why he keeps you close."

I turned away from her as the burgeoning beast of my fear struggled to rise within me, gnashing its blade-shape teeth. Gusselan was not present in our intimate moments to hear the words we shared; she was not privy to the rhythm of my heart as it beat in time with his. She didn't understand the trust, the vulnerability that felt like being warmly cradled in the arms of someone who would do anything to protect you. Or perhaps these were just my childish, fanciful dreams surfacing again?

Stop it. I clenched my fists, battling against the urge to succumb to the ugly, snarling beast within that wanted to tear my confidence and belief in Tamas apart.

"You need never worry about me." I kept my back to her. "I'll always survive."

"Will you this time?"

I tilted my head back, closing my eyes as if to shield myself from the possibility that Gusselan might be right. I shouldn't allow her to infect me like this, to let the worry seep in that I was remaining naïve by dismissing her concerns, by refusing to believe she could be right. I pressed my hand to the scar on my chest, knowing the Mother succeeded in possessing me because I allowed her to keep me ignorant. And what would happen if I repeated the same mistake with Tamas? The consequences were far worse.

I slowly turned to face her. "Thanks for your concern, but I have no chance of reaching the Etherweave without Tamas. Not if I hope to cross the Ashenlands." The nightmare was just the weapon against what lived within the Ashenlands.

She nodded. "Then don't let him play you for a fool."

The sound of the apostles noisily descending the stairs ended our conversation. We stared at each other for long moments before she stepped forward and took my hand. "Send Andriet to his rightful place. For all our sakes."

I hesitated, knowing the right reply, but unwilling to commit. Losing Carlin was the first time I felt my heart beat with the profound awareness that I was capable of feeling the depths of emotions the Mother was intent on destroying. Andriet's death was the next beat of my heart that made me truly understand that love holds the power to cripple as much as it strengthens the soul.

"I will." It was a promise I had to make.

He was still hurting, given he'd not sought me out at the manor, which he could have easily visited now he was no longer confined to his death place. As a spiritweaver, I had the power to summon him at any moment, yet out of shame, I hadn't done so, despite missing him terribly. However, I could no longer ignore what needed to be done. The Eone was real. Perhaps the legends of their war with the Divines were also true, which could mean the dire consequences might come to pass.

"Sorry we took so long," announced Tortilus on entering. "We were undecided which of our supplies we should pack."

"In the end, we took everything," Selisimus said. "We figured since we have no idea what we may face, it's best we depart with as much knowledge as we feel we need."

"I hope you don't mind if we take a little time in the sanctum of solaria. I can think of a few volumes I would like to add to our collection," Tortilus continued. "Healing spells and the like."

"You're forgetting Tamas said you weren't coming with us. He'll return you to Emberforge, I'm sure, but no further."

"True, but Tamas is a northerner and holds no authority in the south," Tortilus challenged.

I tilted my head back and took a deep breath, anticipating many arguments before Tortilus came to his senses. The other three seemed content to follow his lead. I couldn't decide which was the best option. Anyone wielding magic would be helpful and therefore welcome, but I had yet to determine how effective the apostle's magic truly was.

I was about to say something when I heard the scuff of heels on the steps outside as someone arrived. Hearing the heavy tread and powerful stride, I knew it was Tamas. I doubted the others heard anything yet, which had to be a sign of my Razohan heritage slowly making itself known—I couldn't help but smile at the thought. The pleasant tingle around the bite mark was also a giveaway, and despite the looming threat, flutters in my stomach took flight, narrowing my focus to the one person who was about to enter the manor.

"We can have this conversation with Tamas again if you like, since he's just returned."

Everyone's gaze shifted toward the door, then back to

me, before they exchanged looks. Moments later, the front door burst open, and heavy footfalls echoed toward the main room. As Tamas' heavy strides drew nearer, my heartbeat inched in anticipation just to lay eyes on him again—uncaring about the reason he'd left and whether he'd succeeded. The apostles edged closer to me, eventually positioning themselves behind me.

He charged through the door, wearing an expression darker than the night, his eyes settling on me first before flitting to Gusselan and the apostles.

"We leave now," he grouched.

"You caught up with Osmud and Bryra?" I said, a slight hitch to my voice, directly caused by the wild and somewhat ferocious glaze in his eyes; the predatory leader, the savage opponent, the man who opened my eyes and heart.

"They refuse to do as told by heading north."

At least I had a reason for his foul mood. I was worried it had something to do with the Eone.

He glared at me. "You're traveling with me."

"I guess that leaves us to travel with Osmud and Bryra," Tortilus announced.

Tamas snapped his gaze to the apostle. "To Emberforge, but no further," he grouched, then his gaze shifted to Gusselan.

"I'm not coming," Gusselan said

To which Tamas merely shrugged. "That's one less to concern ourselves with."

"How far away are the Salmun?" I said.

"Not far."

Wellard let out a shriek with the sudden and loud arrival

of Osmud and Bryra, both pounding down the hall as though the Salmun were already on their tails.

"That's our signal." Tamas launched for my hand, then dragged me across the room for the door.

"I want to say goodbye to—"

"You should've done that already," he grumbled, ignoring my struggle.

"Just go," Gusselan announced. "I would rather see you escape than hear you say a hundred goodbyes from your dungeon cell."

I surrendered to Tamas' urgency and allowed him to pull me across the room, knowing it was fruitless and foolish to fight him now with the Salmun so close to discovering us.

"What's your plan exactly?" I said once we were in the corridor, but rather than respond to me, he jerked his head toward the room. "Gusselan stays," he said to Bryra and Osmud and kept on his way.

"Shouldn't we wait for them?"

"No. Better if we travel separately. Separated targets make it hard to launch a coordinated attack."

"The Salmun are after the heirs to the throne, so we should travel separately. One of us has to survive," I said.

"No," he snapped, his restrained fury simmering like a brewing storm.

"We make it easier for the Salmun by sticking together."

"I'll not let you out of my sight, so don't waste your breath and our time on this argument."

Honestly, sometimes I could just punch him. I would loathe a man incapable of standing his ground, but Tamas' resistance at times was infuriating. "Is this raging mood partly because of the Eone?"

"It's because you're being a stubborn fool who won't do as you're told."

"And you're no different?" I announced, while skipping along beside him out the front doors. Now was not the time to get into an argument. "Fine, beast man, do your thing. But unlike Gusselan, I'm likely to pull hairs from your back."

"Just as long as you stay on." Those were the last words he spoke before he leaped from the portico and landed on the ground below as a beast.

My beast. Suddenly, a strange quiver erupted in my stomach, surging upward into my chest, transforming into an urgent call as it ascended. I felt an irresistible urge to run, to outpace the night, the moon, and the stars, leaving behind a wild song of freedom in my wake. Bizarrely, despite the looming danger, an irrepressible smile spread across my face, fired by the feral rhythm of my heart.

Tamas turned to face me, dipping his head low and pawing the ground as if impatient for me to climb aboard. For just a moment, I wanted to revel in the thrill of the promise; the promise of what awaited me as the Razohan within me emerged.

His growl forced me to move. I raced down the steps as he lowered one leg and leaped onto his back, slipping my legs either side of his large body, then leaned forward, grabbing a firm hold of a clump of his fur, my sole means of staying on.

He moved off as the others came out of the manor. When I glanced back at them, Tamas increased his speed, a silent urging for me to stay focused on the path ahead. I leaned over his forelegs, familiarizing myself with his gait. By keeping my thighs relaxed around his girth and allowing my body to flow in rhythm with his, I was prepared when he increased his strides, easily adjusting and moving in harmony with his pace.

I wasn't sure how far we needed to travel in this manner, and I wondered why he had chosen not to use the nightmare to return us to Tolum at twice the speed. Perhaps the memories of the last time he carried me in the nightmare's claws were still painfully fresh. Considering the Eone's persistent nuisance and their hatred for me, I shouldn't complain about the prospect of a sore ass. There was no telling what the Eone would decide once I was suspended miles above the ground.

While lost in my musing, Tamas suddenly veered left, catching me off guard, and I struggled to keep my seat. We moved swiftly; the forest bathed in the half-moon's glow blurring beside us. I leaned closer to his back, feeling his pace increase. What did he hear, smell, or sense to make him change his direction? With his increased pace, the wind ripped any sound from my ears.

My hair lashed against my face as I looked over my shoulder toward the motion I caught in the corner of my eye. Another beast advanced to our side; given the size, it was probably Bryra, who, even in her beast form, towered over Tamas. In the moonlight, I couldn't discern which of the apostles she bore. Shortly after, Osmud joined us on the opposite flank. Each of the northern beasts navigated the forest effortlessly, soaring over fallen logs as if they could fly, avoiding entanglement in the undergrowth.

I could only assume the presence of Osmud and Bryra beside us wasn't good news, considering Tamas had wanted us all to travel separately.

Bryra let out a low rumble in her throat, and the three northern beasts veered left in unison, as if reading each other's minds. They diverged at times to avoid thick-boughed trees but never strayed far from each other's sides. We moved so swiftly the chilling wind slipped under my clothes, yet I could easily endure the chill given I'd spent a harrowing flight gripped in the nightmare's claws.

A brilliant light pierced through the trees on my right, casting an intense flash that brightened the forest like a lightning strike. The muscles in my stomach clenched tight, and I had to tell myself to ease my fisted grip on Tamas' fur. The Salmun were the only ones capable of wielding such intense light. They'd come upon us so readily.

In the fading glow, I thought I saw something stirring among the trees. I bit back a shout, assuming the three northern beasts knew all too well that the Salmun's pets were on our trail. Unfortunately, they seemed able to keep pace with us.

Another flash of light revealed the extent of our plight. A swarm of the Salmun's creatures glided through the trees as effortlessly as fish through water. In the dying glow of Salmun's magic, I saw grotesque lizard-like creatures, their bodies covered in barbs. They used flaps of skin connecting their fore and hind limbs as sails and thick tails for balance. The shadows concealed the full extent of their natural defenses, but what I saw was enough to realize this battle would be formidable. There was no chance the three northern beasts could outrun them now.

With the Salmun's next assault, we veered abruptly left, forcing Tamas to leap over a boulder, which nearly unsettled me, before dodging around a tree. The next barrage of magic herded us right. At first, their tactics were perplexing, but it soon dawned on me they were not trying to confront us directly but to corral us, likely because of their uncertainty about our identities in the darkness.

Through the fading aura of the attack that flared above the trees like the morning sun, I saw the outline of giant galloping beasts with men on their backs. That's how the Salmun kept pace. Swift as horses, the animals moved on long, muscular legs. From this distance, they appeared comparable to Bryra in height and girth. For once, they seemed to be the only creatures the Salmun had created that didn't possess a terrifying array of intimidating defenses we couldn't hope to overpower single-handedly.

I wanted to warn Tamas, but again I was sure he'd already worked out their plan and noticed the Salmun astride their horse-like beasts. Besides, we were powerless to stop them. Our only hope was to outrun them, their magic and the lizard-like creatures, hunting us through the trees.

I leaned forward until I was practically laying across Tamas' back. The warmth of his beast form was a comforting caress along my legs, through my core, and now I could feel it on my face. Another time and I would close my eyes and wrap my arms around his massive form, nuzzling in to his woodland-scented fur. Beneath the scent of the woodlands, there was a deeper, animalistic aroma—primal, wild, and unmistakably masculine—that stirred the animal in me, the beast I'd yet to know, who was slowly shedding her shackles and making her presence felt, thanks to Tamas.

It had to be him. For twenty-three years, she had lived within me, subdued under the Mother's strict regime. A single bite from Tamas was all it took to unleash her, allowing her to stretch and extend her claws.

An eerie, mournful call rent the night, followed by a series of sharp yips. I glanced to my right, peering past the massive form of Osmud and into the trees, but the whipping wind brought tears to my eyes, and the darkness concealed the position of our enemies.

We burst from the forest; the moonlight casting a silvery glow onto a wide trail. None of the Salmun's creatures followed us into the open, but stayed within the darkness of the trees. The sound of snapping branches and excited yipping reminding us they continued to move alongside us.

A sudden shriek and in my periphery one apostle tumbled from Osmud's back, just as quick Osmud disappeared from beside us.

"Tamas," I shouted, but he kept his pace.

A cacophony of yowls and cries erupted from the forest ahead, signaling our enemy had moved forward, setting an ambush if we continued on the trail. It seemed we were surrounded. The Salmun had ceased using their magic, which had given away their position, and the forest descended into darkness.

"Tamas," I yelled. He had to stop. Osmud and the others

needed our help, but he seemed intent on making it to Tolum with or without his friends.

My decision was perilous, but I couldn't bear the thought of anything happening to the apostles or Osmud because Tamas was determined to get me to safety.

I shifted to the right, releasing my grip on Tamas' fur, and launched myself off his back, bracing for the blow. However, at the last moment, my instincts activated my reflexes, enhanced reflexes I'd first experienced while sparring with the two Tolum warriors. Instead of crashing heavily onto my side, I tucked tightly, spun mid-flight, and landed on my feet, bending my knees to soften the impact.

In an instant, Tamas was in human form by my side.

"What the fuck are you doing?" he snarled.

"The apostles need our help."

I was about to turn and rush back to where I suspected they would be, but Tamas snagged my arm. "Tressya," he snarled.

"You're willing to leave them behind?"

"For now, I don't have a choice."

"I'm not okay with that."

He yanked me toward him. "You silly little fool. The Salmun don't give a shit about anyone else but you. They would have left them behind if we kept going."

I had to swallow the truth. I was the silly little fool who'd let her fear for her friends get the better of her.

A chorus of excited yips erupted.

"Too late now," I breathed, as I pulled the daggers Bryra had stolen for me from my belt.

Tamas cursed.

"Now's the time to prove how loyal these Eone are to your command," I said.

"This won't go well."

Bryra came up behind me, two apostles by her side. "We're surrounded," she said without a hint of urgency or fear.

Close by, leaves rustled, boughs cracked and soft, throaty sounds revealed the lurking threat of the lizard-like creatures.

"We always were," I breathed, feeling a tickle creep up my spine, knowing how closely they watched us. At least on the trail we could see an attack coming.

The two apostles who'd ridden on Osmud's back rushed toward us, followed close behind by Osmud himself, and I resisted the urge to sweep all of them in for a relieved hug.

"I'm sure it's not that bad," Selisimus said.

"You can't say because you can't see," Tortilus snapped.

"Shut up," barked Tamas.

"Tortilus, now's a good time to work on some of your spells," I said.

"Yes, right...that's an excellent idea," Tortilus said. "Plesy, Wella—"

"Shut the fuck up," Tamas snarled, moving fast to cut off Tortilus' shout. "You're a bunch of fucking idiots."

That mood of his was growing worse. "There's no point staying quiet now," I breathed, gripping Tamas' hand now seized around Tortilus' throat.

"You should never have jumped," he shot to me.

"What's done is done."

He grunted. "We're fighting our way out of this one.

Beast form," he ordered the other two, and then he was gone, and in his place prowled his beast.

I gripped the hilts of my daggers tighter, letting my sharpening vision cut through the darkness. Curses my beast had yet to reveal herself, but blessed be my Razohan heritage for enhancing my combat skills. I would need every ounce of that strength to overcome the Salmun's creatures.

Tamas, Osmud and Bryra encircled us, forming a protective cocoon around me and the apostles at the center. I'd rather be part of the fight, but knew my presence beside him would distract Tamas too much.

The excited yipping escalated into a frenzy, then one male, Tamas or Osmud—identifiable by their size, though which male it was I couldn't tell in the dark—vanished toward the trees, only to reappear moments later, dropping one of the broken lizard-like creatures onto the ground.

That was the signal for chaos to reign. The forest erupted into pandemonium. Their screeching calls from the trees enveloped us in a haunting herald of our impending doom. I spun in circles, unsure where to face first, as the creatures hid in the trees on both sides of the trail, while the Salmun remained silent somewhere in the forest.

Discipline. I needed the strongest pillar now, more than ever.

Suddenly, the creatures abandoned the trees. Limbs spread wide, they glided toward us, blotting out the stars.

The northern beasts were spectacularly fast, a bewildering display of immense speed and agility I couldn't track in the night. The sudden wave of the Salmun's creatures fell before the speed of the northerners as they worked tirelessly to prevent any from breaking their protective circle and reaching us. But how long could they continue the fight?

"We need light," I shouted to the apostles, just as my instincts urged me to look skyward. I spotted a dark shape soaring just above the tree line—another of the Salmun's maligned creations had arrived to cause us strife.

I paused for a heartbeat—the darkness wasn't to my advantage—timing my strike perfectly. The winged creature turned in a wide arc and headed back overhead. I waited, studying its path and speed. When it suddenly swooped, my heart spasmed, my fingers twitching to release my dagger. *Not yet.* I took two calming breaths. *Almost.* I gauged the arc of its descent, then, with a swift upward jerk, threw my dagger. A sudden screech of fury confirmed my aim, then came the dull thud as it landed dead further along the trail.

Damn, now I'd lost a blade.

"Get on the ground," I barked at the four of them. "Work on that spell."

No sooner had I issued my command than more winged creatures descended from the night sky. They flew in swift, swooping down to settle on the trail, but Tamas and the other two had their hands full eradicating the lizard-like creatures.

I strove for calming breaths, centering myself for the fight, and focused inward, reaching for the she-beast lurking beneath my skin.

Help now, girl. Give me your speed and strength.

She complied with my request, channeling strength through my limbs. I inhaled deeply, absorbing the awe-inspiring beauty of her vitality, her might, her resolve.

I burst from the protective circle the northern beasts had tried to keep and unleashed my full force upon the deadly foe to the dying cry of my name from one apostle.

Moving swifter than the wind, I cut through the winged horde, taking heads before any could spear me with their beaks. Two tried to take to the skies, but I leaped up and staked them both through the chest before their talons were more than a foot off the ground. Soaked in the sprayed blood from their dismembered heads, I panted through the exhilaration of the power my beast gave me, then arched my head back and released a throaty snarl.

My lesson was not to bask too long, for the creatures were numerous and the night long. The winged were few compared to the lizard-like spawn, and before I knew it, I'd destroyed those that had come from the sky, and was left to face the oncoming tree dwellers who'd broken from the northern beasts' fight. Lucky for me, my vitality surged. I moved in rhythm with my heartbeat and my blade, learning to trust my enhanced senses to win this fight. I swiveled, turned, ducked and flexed, my hands moving swift, efficient and precise.

Tamas and his beasts delivered a deadly blow to the remaining horde, and at last, the onslaught waned. I swiped upward, felling a solitary creature that had leaped from the trees, when a sudden, blinding flash of light came from the forest on the right of the trail, accompanied by a deafening rumble, reverberating through the ground, knocking me off my feet and sending me sprawling backward.

"Mercy upon us," cried Plesy.

"It's the Salmun," Wellard shouted. "They've caught us."

I leaped to my feet, using the afterglow of the light to track Tamas, Osmud and Bryra, but only spied two of them. One of them was Bryra. *Damn you, Tamas.* I would bet my life he was the one missing, charging off with a hero's curse to save us, daring to take on the Salmun single-handedly.

"Stay down," I told the apostles. "Some handy spells would be good right now."

The four of them stayed huddled together on the trail, surrounded by dark blots of death—all the creatures we'd destroyed—as Osmud and Bryra positioned themselves to block the path from anything that should burst from the trees to the right of the trail.

"You heard her," Tortilus whispered. "Think brethren. What do we know?"

"My mind's blank," Plesy groaned.

I shut out their murmuring and shifted the hilt of my dagger in my palm. Magic would be a challenge to fight.

Despite Gusselan's warning, I would have to summon the dead.

'Do as I say if you want to survive.' The Mother. Her silence had made me think perhaps she'd failed to possess me.

'I can't say I'm overly joyful to hear your voice,' I thought.

'Shut up and listen to me.'

'Spiritweaver, remember, old crone? You've got no control over me from in there.'

A mighty roar echoed in the distance to our right, swiftly followed by a cry of surprise. Damn, Tamas. He was determined to become a heroic legend. As quickly as the voice was silenced, another streak of light transformed the night sky into a blinding white blaze. This time, I braced myself for the violent tremors beneath my feet, absorbing the shift and staying upright.

'You'll be dead if you don't cooperate.' The Mother's voice echoed through my head, sharp as an axe.

'With you?'

'Do you think I'm as eager to die as you?'

'You're already dead.'

'You know what I mean. Use your soul voice, Tressya. I've seen what you've done with it.'

'How dare you shift through my memories.'

'Stupid girl, that's what you're concerned about?'

'No, but when this is over, I'll burn you from my mind.'

Her silence was a reprieve from listening to her voice, but the Mother was powerful and cunning, so it was worth heeding her plan.

Bryra suddenly took flight, vanishing into the trees so fast she was gone in a blink. Gifted with such speed, perhaps the three northerners would survive the Salmun's magic after all. I'd killed so many of their filthy pets with my new found speed, agility and strength, and I was only just coming into my abilities as a Razohan.

"Go," I yelled to Osmud. "Help them."

He looked over his massive shoulder at me. I couldn't see his eyes, but I could imagine what they would tell me. Then he was gone, disappearing almost as fast as Bryra, smashing through the forest to join the other two and confront the Salmun head-on.

I breathed out, shedding the tension I'd felt discovering

Tamas, the crazy fool, had disappeared into the trees to the right of the trail alone.

'Glad you realize without me you're a spirit in limbo. So tell me,' I continued.

'Combined, we will be undefeatable against the Salmun. My power of soul voice added to your soul word, and we will scorch the minds of our enemies.'

Magic, turning the forest into a lethal display of Salmun might, distracted from the Mother's plan. The trees lit as though it was day. To my dismay, I saw not only the approaching Salmun on the backs of their beasts, but more of their distorted creations.

A single roar of fury split the air—Tamas—followed by excited yips and shrieks. I sucked in a breath, knowing Tamas, the bloody fool, was out there somewhere, thinking he could stand against the Salmun and their creatures on his own. At least Bryra and Osmud were now with him.

'We do this now.'

'Your lover is likely already dead. Heroism without cunning is death.'

Ignoring her and the words she spoke that raised a spear through my heart, I reached within for my soul word.

My soul word came to me like a wave to the shore, a deluge of Sistern power, eager to do my bidding. Whether the Mother was willing or ready, I didn't care, and with the next sound of a beastly roar, chorused by shrieks and screeches that ran like claws down my spine, I fisted *Aetherius* in my mind.

'Take my strength,' her voice echoed through my head.

Joined by the Mother's will, the power of *Aetherius*

expanded within, roiling like angry thunder, bursting to be free.

I shut out the chaos of the night and the magic of the Salmun, roaring my soul word into the darkness with the force of a tidal wave. It shot forth, an onrush that sucked the last of my breath and strength along with it. I fell to my hands and knees beside the apostles under the sudden and immense release, feeling hollowed out and empty. An eerie, oppressive silence filled the night air.

I knelt, scouring the darkness for signs the Mother and I had succeeded.

"What happened? Are we saved?" Plesy said.

My eyes soon adjusted to the moonlight, but I still couldn't see through the dense forest. The only sounds were the rustle of leaves from the gentle breeze. It seemed even the Salmun's creatures had vanished.

"Tamas," I shouted, leaving the apostles and racing for the trees.

"Wait," came Tortilus' cry.

I slowed when I spotted a black, disfigured form on the ground—one of the Salmun's pets. Dagger in hand, I nudged its body but got no response. Further on, I encountered another, and a little further still, I found three more. None of them appeared injured or dismembered. Presumably, the Salmun's will guided them. They were felled the moment I disabled the Salmun.

"Tamas," I cried.

Continuing on through the forest, I came upon the Salmun, scattered across the ground, some partially trapped beneath their motionless mounts.

"Tressya," Tamas yelled.

"I'm here." I hastened toward his voice. In the moonlight, I watched him bound toward me, trying to assess if he was injured by the way he walked.

We collided, forcing the wind from my lungs as we embraced.

"Are you hurt?" we said together.

"I'm fine," we replied together.

"You're a bullheaded madman," I admonished, with a punch to his arm, then buried my head in his chest, inhaling his sweat-filled scent. "Acting heroic without thought will get you killed. You were outnumbered, yet you faced the Salmun alone." It all came out in a rush. "It was unbelievably stupid. And you think to rule making decisions like that?"

He pressed a hand to the back of my head, holding me firm against his chest, so I could hear the ragged beat of his heart. "They weren't getting to you."

"Stop risking yourself to save me."

"You're asking me to do the impossible."

I pushed away from him, glaring up into his dark eyes, like hollow pits in the moonlight. "I saved all our asses just now. That's your lesson. Learn to trust in me."

Then, after feeding as much of my fury into my glare, I clawed myself back into his arms. I hadn't realized what I was holding in until the fight was over. It was only when I felt his hard body against mine, could I convince myself he was alive and unharmed. Finally, my bridled fear cascaded through me, a powerful current that swept all my courage and strength to my feet. I leaned into Tamas, forcing him to take more of my weight.

"I knew it was you. But how?" he said.

I shook my head, not wanting to involve the Mother just yet, not while I continued to feel battered and raw inside. I never allowed the thought that Tamas was dead manifest, but it had sprung unbidden all the same, lurking just below my awareness. In his arms, I was safe to let the thought free.

"How about we trust in each other, that what we decide to do is right?" he murmured, giving me the grace to keep my secret.

"I can't," I snapped. "You make so many terrible decisions."

He stroked my hair as I turned my head to rest my face on his chest, and I was rewarded with the rumble of his chuckle in his chest as it gently tremored against my cheek, the secure embrace of his arms holding me tight against him, and the warmth of his breath in my hair.

"My decisions are all about keeping you safe. I won't stop doing that."

"Stubborn beast," I mumbled against his chest.

"You sent Bryra and Osmud after me. They were supposed to stay with you," he growled. "But it seems they obeyed you over me."

'And you're the pathetic fool if you continue like this,' the Mother said.

"Stars, she's right." I struggled from Tamas' embrace.

"What are you talking about?"

"We can't stay here. The Salmun aren't dead. They'll rouse in time."

"What did you do to them?"

"It's just a little trick I've learned." I smirked, but Tamas likely missed it, or not, since he had the eyes of a Razohan. There was no point in being coy, neither did we have time. "It's not magic. I can't defeat them in that game. The Sistern's power deals with the mind. And it seems my soul word has quite the mental punch. Lucky for us, the Salmun's creatures are powerless without their masters."

"You remain an enigma to me."

If we weren't still in danger, I'd make sure Tamas knew what those simple words did to me.

The sound of the rest of our party approaching drew us apart.

"They're not dead," Tamas said, assuming a commanding voice, because he couldn't stop being a leader. "We have to reach Emberforge before any of them wake."

CHAPTER
TWENTY-SEVEN

TAMAS

"You've been at this long enough," I grumbled, pacing the star-marked floor, restless with the shadow of darkness creeping up my back—a formless presence that, if I lingered and gazed long enough, I might identify as guilt, intertwined with other turbulent emotions I'd prefer to keep undefined for now.

Selisimus and Wellard were making no progress, as far as I could see, which meant—curses—we needed all four to make this work.

"They'll take less time if you stop snapping at them," Tressya admonished, leaning against the throne's rock dais.

Tortilus and Plesy had abandoned us upon reaching Emberforge, claiming they needed only minutes to gather more supplies. By 'supplies', they meant volumes of spellbooks the Umbral Luminae had compiled over the last five hundred years. I humored them, thinking we'd shaken off two apostles, only to discover all four were needed to breach the Salmun's enchanted door at the back of the Bone Throne. At least, that's how it seemed, given how long we'd all been standing here waiting for something to happen. So far neither Selisimus nor Wellard were any closer to breaking through.

Our escape from the Salmun led us to the fringes of Tolum, where the three of us were compelled to shift forms. Bryra's half-form posed a challenge, and I seized upon that as a pretext to send her north, until Tressya interceded, insisting we needed all the assistance we could gather. Reluctantly, I conceded her point. Even with Tressya's emerging abilities and my weaponized form in the nightmare's shape, along with the Eone's pledged support, the two of us alone would find it difficult to overcome the formidable obstacles that lay in our path.

At Tolum, I'd commandeered a carriage to transport us to Emberforge, allowing us—especially Bryra—to travel incognito. Stained in the foul creatures' blood, none of us were fit to be seen. It was also the quickest way to travel, despite my inner beast bristling at the horses' sluggish pace. Thanks to the Salmun's absence from Emberforge, we reached the throne room with no complications.

"Osmud's taking too long." I forked my fingers through my hair, turning from the rest of them. I was sure to wear a groove in the stonework with all this pacing.

"He'll be back in time," Tressya reassured me.

Osmud, perhaps the only one with sense right now, had hastened away, also to collect supplies, but his collection would be more useful, namely food, water skins, weapons, and other such necessities.

"It's heating," Selisimus cried. "I can feel the heat from here."

"What does that mean?" Tressya said.

"Something's happening."

"Nothing we're needing to happen," I added. Tressya was right. I wasn't helping, but right now my mood was a foul beast, giving me nothing nice to say. The Eone were a constant annoyance, becoming more meddlesome now we had a team accompanying us on our hunt for the Etherweave.

In recent days, I'd noticed a troubling shift. Their voices were no longer the only affliction they gave upon me; their emotions infected me as well. As a soul-sucking shapeshifter, I was familiar with this kind of onslaught, yet this time, it felt different. Initially, it was easy to distinguish between their emotions and my own. However, as time passed, the boundary blurred and frayed, until I struggled to discern whose emotions were whose.

Despite the frustration this recent development brought, it offered some advantages. For instance, I realized their aversion to Tressya stemmed from fear—fear of her status as the other bloodborn and her potential to control the Etherweave, but primarily, fear of her formidable willpower.

'Peace, young Razohan. Do not weigh yourself with troubling thoughts," Carthius said.

'Peace you say. You've plagued me enough these last hours.' I'd didn't need this mental war at the moment.

'Your actions were irrational,' Fivia said. 'We were merely

trying to calm your thoughts, help you see a clear path forward—'

'Cut the shit. You want nothing more than to see Tressya suffer.'

'She does not deserve your devotion. She was never meant to be a part of this,' Ovia added.

They knew she was part of this. It had taken the two of us to reveal the map; they'd seen that. But Tressya was an obstacle in their plans because she wasn't under their influence; she wasn't their instrument to manipulate.

As the sound of hurrying feet approached, I momentarily forgot about the curse of the Eone and turned my attention toward the door. At last, Tortilus and Plesy had returned; I recognized their light, quick footsteps as opposed to Osmud's heavier tread. They burst through the door, accompanied by a handful more of their bloody friends.

"What do you think you're doing?" I snarled, striding toward them, causing them all to stutter to a halt.

It wasn't until I saw the eyes of the newcomers roam over my clothes, mouths agape, that I remembered my torn and blood-stained clothes. Seeing Bryra began a frenzy of whispers between them.

"These are members of Umbral Luminae."

"I don't give a shit what they're a part of. They aren't coming."

"Sir—" Tortilus began, but I cut him off with a swipe of my hand.

"No." My claws spiked through the tips of my fingers, but in the next breath I felt Tressya's hand take mine, as she ran her fingers across my claws.

"I'm sorry, Tortilus, all of you, but Tamas is right. We're not on an adventure."

"We know that...Tressya. Believe me, we do," Plesy replied. "We've seen so much these last days to understand what's at stake. The dangers we face."

"See, that's the problem," Tressya continued. "You don't know enough. What you've experienced is nothing to what lays ahead. I refuse to be responsible for so many lives."

"Hallelujah," Tamas breathed, to which Tressya rolled her eyes.

"United, we are strong," Tortilus said.

"Doesn't matter. None of you are bloody coming," Tamas said.

"But... That's not what was agreed," Tortilus protested.

I seized him by the collar, yanking him off his feet and dragging him, grunting and protesting, to where Selisimus and Wellard were attempting to breach the Salmun's magical lock.

"This is your job," I said, shoving him forward. "Place your hands on the rock and start chanting." I glanced over at Plesy. "You too. Get over here."

Tressya remained silent, not intervening in my rough handling of him. Although he was eager to assist, my patience and concern had worn thin. The Eone were taking their toll on me in numerous ways; providing endless distractions, sowing confusion, and intensifying my frustration. My inner beast was perpetually on the cusp of breaking free, yet it wasn't the sole threat; the nightmare was an even more formidable peril. Its impulses were beyond anything I felt familiar with or comfortable handling. I had only taken its form a few times, each instance a tremendous battle of wills when my mind was undistracted and unburdened by those seeking to control me. Given the current turmoil within me, I feared I might succumb and lose myself.

Plesy scuttled across and joined his brethren. I stepped around the rock, folding my arms across my chest and gave the rest of the group a stare as hard as my claws. None dared move, nor did they let out a peep of protest.

At the first sound of Osmud's return, I glanced over my shoulder. "You better be effective."

"I think it's working," Selisimus announced, distracting me from barring the advance of the other apostles.

I hurried around the dais as Osmud stomped inside. "This is quite a crowd."

"Onlookers only," I returned.

"Better be. There's too many mouths to feed." And he lugged the two weighted sacks higher on his back.

Once beside us, he dropped his cargo. "We'll share it amongst ourselves for ease of carrying. Any progress?"

"Plenty," Selisimus announced at the same time I said. "Not enough."

"I'll go with the optimist."

"At your peril. He's too happy," I snapped.

"And you're a mound of misery of late. I'd rather leave the clouds behind and take the sunshine with us."

"We're doing it," Selisimus uttered, sounding in awe of their success.

"All you need is faith," Tortilus said, fixing his gaze on me.

I flashed him a sneer, tipped with fangs, which wiped the

pompous cheer off his face, and watched—admittedly in awe tinged surprise—as a slice of rock vanished, revealing a steep stairwell that descended into the earth beneath the throne.

That shadow of darkness was once more pressing heavy against my back, so I turned away from our escape and addressed Osmud. "Let's sort the supplies."

"Oh, I brought these," Tortilus said, sounding way too proud and happy with himself for my liking.

"We'll manage," I grumbled, not even bothering to see what he meant. My patience with Tortilus had thinned to the point of transparency. I resolved to make him the target of my anger after his involvement in disturbing Tressya and I. In truth, it was Osmud who had interrupted us, but Tortilus was nearby, and so he would endure my frustration when I needed to vent. I couldn't give a damn if that was unfair.

"They're packs for carrying supplies. Very handy. And they have straps that slip over your shoulders like so," Tortilus said.

I rolled my eyes at Osmud, then spared one glance over my shoulder to watch him demonstrate how handy the straps were with his own pack. Covering the distance in two strides, I swiped his pack from his back, then tipped it upside down to empty the contents.

"What're you doing?" he said, as books tumbled to the floor.

"We can't eat those," I said, before stuffing supplies from one of Osmud's sacks.

"But I brought spares. There're enough packs for our

books and the supplies." Tortilus fell to his knees and, with reverent care, gathered the books from the floor, smoothing bent pages and ensuring to be careful with their spines. "Some are centuries old. They can't take such handling."

"Perhaps you should've left them on their shelves," Osmud replied, joining me in filling the spare packs the apostles had brought with them.

"Tamas," Tressya said.

Her tone wasn't admonishing, yet it carried an edge that made me inwardly sigh. She said nothing more, walking past me while eyeing me over her shoulder. I knew a fight was imminent, and I feared it would be one I was about to lose.

Once we were at a distance she deemed private, she turned, but I was determined to beat her to the first line.

"They're a burden we don't need. They'll slow us down and place us all at risk." I came in close, folding my arms across my chest and looking down on her as though I was a threat. It was a defensive stance because I already felt like I'd lost the argument.

"They might prove useful."

"Name one way, and I may consider it."

She would struggle to find even one. They were nothing but a burden.

"They're able to conjure light. I've witnessed it myself. That will be invaluable when facing the manifestations."

I placed my palm over her face, as I squeezed my eyes shut and silently cursed her astute mind.

She removed my hand. "I trust you're giving it serious consideration."

I circled it around her neck. "Osmud's likely brought plenty of flint and shavings. We'll create our own light."

"How did the northerners get through the Ashenlands?"

I leaned forward, pressing my forehead to hers. "Tressya," I whispered, her name coming out on a frustrated sigh. Romelda provided a magical light that pierced the darkest recesses of the impenetrable forest. Tressya was correct in her assertion that a flaming torch would be of no use to us.

"Good. That's settled. The four can come with us. The rest will stay to stall the Salmun."

I captured her chin, tilting her head up and forcing her to meet my eyes. "This is a bad idea. The four appear to be the smartest of their little troupe, let them stay and harass the Salmun, they'll likely do a better job. I'm sure Tortilus will drive them crazy with frustration."

Tressya looked around me. "Tortilus, find another pack for your books." Then she returned her attention to me. "You'll see that it's a good idea."

She went to leave, but I snared her wrist before she got too far. "Don't think it's going to be that easy next time."

She took a step closer, bringing her body, her scent, close enough to scramble my mind. *Keep your wits.* The little serpent was playing me with her feminine wiles. Unfortunately for her, I was a seasoned player in this game. Her stare wasn't combative, nor seductive, but a gentle mixture of both as she ran the back of her finger alone my jawline, and curses that I felt it as an arrow shooting straight for my cock. I couldn't stop my eyes from falling to her lips as she spoke.

"We'll make all our decisions as a team. As we did just now. And it worked well. Don't you think?"

She rose on her toes and feathered a kiss to my lips, before taking my bottom lip between her teeth and giving it a light nip.

It was no longer an arrow in my cock; it was a burning lance.

"Are all the packs full?" Tressya said, again thinking she could leave without my say. I snared her around the waist, hauling her close.

"The Salmun, remember?" And she smirked.

I grabbed her chin between my fingers, gently squeezing her cheeks. "I'm compiling a list of what you owe me." I pressed my finger to my temple. "It's growing long. You wouldn't believe what I've added." My traitorous eyes fell to her lips once again.

"Tressya," Tortilus called from behind me.

I grew fangs, but Tressya covered my mouth with her palm. Then, leaving me standing like I had my cock in my hands, she returned to Osmud and the apostles, who were busy transferring everything Osmud had brought into separate packs.

TRESSYA

THE APOSTLES LED THE WAY, guiding us with a bright light conjured in Tortilus' hand. It seemed that was one thing the apostles were adept at doing, and whenever they caught Tamas' eye, they countered his surly glare with a smug smile. Should I find a moment alone with them, I'd cautioned them to show some humility and grace. Inciting Tamas' ire could make this journey more arduous than necessary for all of us.

We'd ventured as far as the Salmun's ritual chamber when we came upon the false wall concealing the continuation of the tunnel.

"Gather around, brethren," Tortilus said. "Let us consult our approach on what must be done."

"I believe the Ebon Compendium contains some incantations that will be of use," Plesy said.

"Just get us through this bloody wall," Tamas growled from behind me.

"Patience, brother—" Tortilus managed before Tamas cornered Tortilus against the wall. "That's not a word you want to use with me, ever."

"Yes...yes, of course. Pardon me."

Osmud placed a hand on Tamas' shoulder. "How about we give the apostles room to perform whatever it is they need to perform?"

"The Salmun will be upon us before we get through this cursed wall," Tamas growl, his temper showing no signs of easing.

"And you're not making us go any quicker," Osmud countered.

Tamas begrudgingly took a step back but remained close,

fixing the apostles with a glare as if his intense scrutiny could hasten their decision.

The Eone were probably uncomfortable with so many accompanying Tamas to the Etherweave, but it was likely my presence was causing the most significant issues. I was sure Tamas was in a constant struggle with the Eone, striving to maintain control of his will and resist theirs. And I could only imagine what plans they hoped Tamas would enact—under their influence—to ensure I was kept far from the Etherweave.

"I never thought you'd have the impudence to show yourself here again."

I turned around to see Andriet's ethereal form casting a warm glow into the dark passage behind us. I covered my mouth with my hand, pressing my lips together to prevent myself from uttering his name. Tears threatened to spill, but I pushed them back and gazed at him, feeling my heart swell with genuine joy at the sight of him.

"Who's this band of heathens you've brought with you?" He floated around me, careful not to make contact, and that one gesture of courtesy threatened to reignite the tears still lurking within me.

"That one—" he declared, raising an eyebrow as he glanced at Bryra. "—is a Huungardred. A Huungardred within Emberforge. Oh, Tressya, my dear, you've fallen right off the seat of your throne."

I remained silent, offering no defense. The apostles were the only ones present unaware of my abilities as a spiritweaver, so there was no need to keep Andriet a secret, especially considering the challenges ahead. However, I wasn't yet prepared to reveal him.

"Yes, I'm familiar with this one," Andriet continued, drawing nearer to Tamas and sweeping his gaze up and down Tamas' body. Although he reached only as high as Tamas' nose, he sized him up as if he were a formidable adversary. "This is the one for whom you betrayed us, is it not?"

I shook my head because, indeed, through every decision and action, I had betrayed him, yet never in my heart. Still, I questioned whether that distinction held any significance for a man who'd lost his family and his life.

"And the other one looks just as wild," he remarked with a huff, eyeing off Osmud. "I doubt they're house-trained or even know how to use a knife and fork. At least you won't go hungry. These two are probably adept at catching prey with their bare hands and tearing it apart with their teeth. And don't even get me started on hygiene." Andriet leaned in, feigning a sniff at Tamas.

Tamas slowly turned his head, glaring in Andriet's direction, as if sensing the presence of something or someone nearby.

"I do believe this one knows I'm here. He's mostly a savage, so I'm not surprised. They say animals have keener senses than humans."

"Are we sharing this passage with someone else?" Tamas said, turning his head to face me.

"This is a fun game. Don't tell him, Tressya."

I buried my head in my hands, rubbing my fingertips across my forehead.

"Tressya?" Tamas warned, his voice deepening with a hint of menace that seemed to stalk through the passage like a restless beast.

"Possibly," I murmured from behind my hands, cautious not to further provoke Tamas, yet also not wanting to give Andriet the impression that I had forsaken our friendship.

"I should've known you'd choose his side. I can only imagine he's well-endowed and reasonably skilled in using it. Though as a savage, I'm sure he has a limited repertoire."

I had to smother my chuckle with my hand.

"Is this going to be a problem?" Tamas said.

"No."

"Bite your tongue, woman. A constant nuisance can become a greater problem than a major threat."

Tamas gave me a nod before refocusing on the apostles. Given he was burdened with enough issues on top of dealing with the Eone, I didn't want to cause him anymore distress.

"Wait. There's a spirit down here with us? Is that what you two are discussing?" Osmud interjected.

"Ah. The wildling's not thrilled about that notion. What an excellent discovery," Andriet added with a hint of delight.

"Emberforge is said to be—" Selisimus began, looking up from the book he'd been reading.

"You're meant to find us a way through this wall," Tamas interjected.

"Spirits are always around," I informed Osmud. "You're just fortunate enough not to notice them." I attempted to give Andriet a stern look, but he avoided my gaze.

"Come now, Tressya, don't spoil my fun. You owe me a

great deal, my girl. A thousand apologies and plenty of amusement," Andriet teased.

"Your Majesty can see spirits?" Plesy said, intrigued, forgetting the book to join in the conversation.

"Get us through that wall," Tamas demanded, pointing at the tome in Tortilus' hands, which three of the four apostles had abandoned, finding the revelation of my spiritweaving far more interesting.

"That's quite a lot of man to handle," Andriet remarked, giving Tamas another once-over. "He's got a temper, too. But I'm sure you know the trick to making him smile. I just hope he knows how to make you smile, considering all you've surrendered to be with him."

My heart ached at the truth; it mourned for losing Andriet but not for choosing Tamas.

"This should do. Look here." The three apostles returned their attention to Tortilus, who'd continued to hunt for the right spell to get us through this wall. They gathered closer, leaning in to follow Tortilus' finger across the page.

"It doesn't appear too tricky," Plesy said.

"Just do it," Tamas snapped.

"Steady, northerner," Tortilus said. "Magic takes time."

"Not if you're adept."

"We need a little time to study the words," Tortilus defended.

"Tamas, we should give the apostles some space to do what they need to do," I suggested, trying to sound as reasonable as possible.

"They need a little persuasion to keep up the pace,"

Tamas responded, his tone suggesting he was also attempting to stay reasonable.

I had no expertise in magic wielding, so I couldn't gauge the level of concentration required to perform it correctly. Nevertheless, I was convinced that Tamas' incessant hovering wasn't aiding the apostles in accomplishing their task.

"A tense standoff between lovers. My days shall not bore me."

"You're honestly not planning on coming with us," I grumbled, unfairly burdening Andriet with my frustration, and exposing everyone to our argument.

All eyes turned to me. Unable to juggle a spirit whispering in my ear amidst the escalating tension of the current crisis, I simply shrugged.

"No one else is joining us," Tamas snarled, not bothering to turn around. "Not even spirits. We've got too many hitching a ride as it is."

"Are we referring to the spirit here?" Osmud asked. "At least it won't consume any of our supplies."

"*It*," Andriet shrieked. "Deranged savage. Although he is speaking on my behalf."

"Is it going to be useful?" Osmud continued.

"Eat your tail, beast man," Andriet snapped. "I am what I am."

"Andriet will keep to himself and bother no one," I cautioned Andriet.

Again, I gained everyone's attention.

"Andriet!?" Tamas and Osmud replied together.

"The prince?" Tamas clarified.

"He's dumb, but he has big muscles, and likely an even bigger—"

"Yes," I interrupted him.

"I forgive you, Tressya. I've succumbed to a large cock myself. That was until Daelon, of course. Though his isn't tidy by any stretch—"

"He's going to be a major irritant to me, but harmless to the rest of you," I interjected.

Tamas finally abandoned the apostles and stomped toward me. "I thought he got killed in the Ashenlands." He barely kept the snarl from his tone.

"Don't make this into something, Tamas. Not now."

Andriet, close by, chimed in, "Listen to her, bullyboy. Though I must admit that predatory stalking stirred something in me."

I rolled my eyes. If this was the way it was going to be, I wouldn't survive. "What about Daelon?"

"That's not fair," Andriet reared backward.

"Are you talking to me or him?" Tamas said.

"You've got your own inner voices to contend with, so don't give me grief about mine." I jabbed my hands to my hips, glaring up at Tamas.

"That's it, Tressya darling. Let the beast man know your claws are just as sharp."

"How about you two—" Osmud said.

"Shut up," Tamas and I said in unison.

Andriet mimicked clapping his hands together. "Stars above, if only my Daelon were here to enjoy this spectacle."

"Ah… We've… Ah…encountered a slight problem." Tortilus stuttered.

It was as though the earth rumbled beneath our feet, interrupting Tamas' and my angry glares, only for Tamas to launch back toward the apostles as though a flaming arrow shot from a bow. "That better be a joke."

Tortilus shook his head, hugging the book to his chest.

"It seems…" Plesy tried to help Tortilus with an explanation.

"What?" Tamas loomed over the four of them, strangling them all to silence.

"You better slip the leash on your savage," Andriet helpfully informed me.

"Tamas," I started, but he raised his hand to silence me, and I noticed the slow emergence of his claws. The apostles saw it too, their eyes widening in alarm. Wellard let out a small whimper and pressed closer to Selisimus.

"Sort out whatever problem you've encountered," he said through gritted teeth, his inner beast sounding as if it was on the brink of being unleashed. "And get us through this wall before I decide you have no use and would look better impaled on my claw."

"What's the snag?" Osmud inquired, his question slicing through the tension.

"Well." Tortilus visibly relaxed, displaying the book in his palms once more, and pointing to a place halfway down the page. "At first appearance, it seemed straightforward. Only now, under further scrutiny, we've discovered we'll need certain…implements to perform such a spell."

Tamas raked his hands through his hair, bleeding his frustration over everyone present.

"What about the Salmun's chamber?" I said. "There's

bound to be—" We were standing just outside the cavernous room.

"This is really what we're going to do?" Tamas shouted.

"There's no alternative," I countered.

"The Salmun are close. I can feel it." He pounded a fist at his chest.

"Then stop wasting our time with these arguments."

"Why did we come this way?" He dragged his hands down his face.

"The map, Tamas," I replied.

"Because of that fuck over there." He jabbed a clawed finger toward Plesy, who was the first to notice what the map revealed of our path.

"He's really very feral, underneath all those muscles and masculine exterior."

Ignoring Andriet's quip, I replied with as much heat as Tamas. "You burned it, so we'll never know if there was an alternative path."

"The Ashenlands lie to the north. Instead, we're crawling around like moles."

"And your solution is to retrace our steps and head north?"

Tamas flung his hands skyward as he shouted, "Fuuuck," pouring all his pent-up fury into that single word.

And the wall replied by shimmering out of existence.

CHAPTER
TWENTY-EIGHT

TRESSYA

"Was that your doing, Tortilus?" Selisimus had asked, his concern seemingly more focused on the magic used to bring down the wall than on our final escape from the tunnels under Emberforge.

Tortilus at first had stammered, "I...um...it's possible, yes. I mean, I was focused on the spell at the time, considering all the alternatives in my mind that could complete it effectively." Then his explanation had gained momentum. "It's likely I inadvertently conjured up something entirely different that accomplished the task with far greater proficiency."

It was Bryra, ignoring Tortilus' excited explanation, who'd faced Tamas. "How did you do that?" Which got everyone's attention.

"It wasn't me," Tamas replied, but avoided meeting

anyone's eyes, including mine. He was lying. The Eone was responsible. Initially, Tamas seemed as shocked as the rest of us at what he'd done, so I could only imagine this was a new level of influence from the Eone, one Tamas never expected. The possibility that they could enact magic through him was something I didn't want to face right now.

For the rest of the journey down the mysterious tunnel, we stayed silent until we reached the end of the tunnel to find a door, which gave way under the might of Bryra's beast.

"Heading north would've been a terrible idea," Osmud said, the only one brave enough to step out of the passage and onto the loamy soil, covered in thick knotted roots clawing their way out of the strangling creeper. After the stagnant, oppressive air of the passage, the fresh breeze, albeit carrying the stench of fetid, animalistic filth, was a welcome relief. "So this is it," he breathed, arching his head back to the sky.

Tamas adjusted his pack, sweeping everyone into his glance. "We shouldn't linger here gawking."

He disappeared off into the Ashenlands, leaving all eyes on me.

"Tamas is right. If we linger here, we risk being caught by either the Salmun or the creatures of the Ashenlands."

"By creatures, you mean the abominations we faced while escaping the manor?" Plesy said.

"Those and worse," I replied, striding after Tamas until I noticed Andriet wasn't following.

I glanced back to see him standing at the entrance of the passage, which appeared as a wide fissure in the fabric of the Ashenlands, exactly as depicted on the map.

"Tressya?" Selisimus said. "We must be away."

I held up my hand. "Just a minute." And I crossed back to Andriet, who remained in the passage.

"I don't know what's come over me." He pressed a hand to his chest. "A spirit. What do I have to fear?"

This was his rightful home, and I was meant to return him. There was no doubt Gusselan's tale was true. Perhaps not in every detail, but certainly in the most crucial aspect: the part where I had created a perilous rift in the divide between the living and the dead by freeing Andriet from his place of death.

I stepped toward him. How did I say this without hurting the both of us? "Andriet, I made a dangerous mistake—"

"Nope." He shook his head. "I won't hear it."

I closed my eyes, gathering the strength I needed to admit the truth aloud. This was my fate: to rectify my mistakes and to endure the pain that would come with it.

"Freeing you—"

"Was your redemption for your multitude of lies and betrayals. I have seen the depths of your treason. My family lost their lives because you kept your secrets, and now I suffer. I was never meant to be here. You know that, Tressya. This was never to be my home. Cirro was my queen and Daelon my heart, but your actions took my family and stole my future." He reached for me in a silent plea, as if longing to touch me, but fearful of stepping into the Ashenlands lest he never return. The sorrow in his eyes pierced my heart. Hot tears burned at the back of my eyes.

"Andriet," I groaned, wishing I could succumb to cowardice and turn away, leaving him to continue his death in happiness. How could I find the strength to banish my one dear friend forever to the Ashenlands?

"But I returned to you, dearest friend, even though you ran from me. I returned to you because my heart bleeds when we're apart, and I want you to know I forgive you for your crimes because you have given life to my death."

Why did he have to say that? Because redemption was never meant to be painless. "It's likely my actions have ripped the divide between the living and the dead."

Andriet shook his head. "I'm sorry I can't feel anything but joy. I was once an honorable man, but death reduces us all to equals, so there's little point in trying to be anything other than selfish. I want the death you've granted me."

"At the expense of everything else."

"What else is there for me to worry about?"

He reached for me, stopping a breath's distance from touching me. "Look at this place, Tressya. You know its perversion, born of a malignancy, spreading like a disease, infecting the land to its very edges. You've experienced its malevolent embrace. Deep in your heart, you know I was never meant to spend my eternal days confined here."

Had it not been for me, Andriet might have died a natural death, his soul liberated from the agony of his limbo, hovering just beyond the veil of the living, tormented by witnessing life without ever being able to partake in it.

My guilt for what I'd done would be eternal, and for the sake of the seven realms, I should rectify the damage I'd caused. However, staring into Andriet's pleading eyes, I couldn't bring myself to make that choice, knowing it would be my ultimate betrayal to my best friend.

"Go back to Daelon, Andriet."

"Tressya," he gasped, verging on tears, which he would undoubtedly shed if he could. "My queen," he whispered, stretching one hand toward me, but never able to touch, forever trapped as he was within the curse of his maligned death.

Only the future would reveal the chaos I had unleashed upon the seven realms, but with Tamas possessed by the Eone and the Mother's spirit residing within me, the disruption to the balance of the natural cycle was inevitable. Therefore, I believed granting my best friend joy in death was my private path to absolution.

For all the times my heart was torn apart, his visible relief stitched it back together, his dry tears the thread.

"I'll return victorious." I wouldn't dwell on the Eone, their schemes, the future they envisioned, or that even as mere spirits, they could empower Tamas. Nor would I concern myself with the Mother's plans, because to win, I had to believe in myself and trust that I could handle any challenge ahead; to doubt was to fail.

"And when you do, you shall expunge the Ashenlands from the seven realms."

"I shall do one better and obliterate the Salmun."

"It's crazy how much I believe in you, despite the devastation you've brought upon my family. I've struggled with my feelings for my brother my entire life, and my father... I should've felt so much more upon their deaths, but I didn't." He shook his head, then gave me a wry smile. "I knew the moment I met you, you would be trouble of the most delectable kind. I knew everything was about to change; I just never anticipated the magnitude of what you were about to accomplish."

"Tressya," Tamas called.

Andriet crossed his hands and placed them on his heart. "Forever my heart. Now go, your beastly beast is calling you."

I gave him one final, lingering look, certain I had made the wrong choice in sparing him from his death place, yet oddly calm with my violation of the natural order. I should savor this moment, for it was unlikely I would find peace again soon.

"Let Daelon live his life without you. That's the kindest gesture you can make."

"Of course, my sweet. Whatever you say."

His wink would normally signify trouble, but Andriet loved Daelon too much to ever hurt him.

"Are you done?" Tamas said from beside me.

"Andriet has decided not to join us," I replied, forcing my attention on Andriet.

"I will haunt your days from now until eternity if you ever dare to harm her."

I smiled at his hollow threat, touched by the affection at its core.

"It seems night is drawing near," Tamas said, taking my hand.

I glanced up at the darkening clouds, obscuring the sun. "Or the Ashenlands is smothering the daylight."

"Either way, we should bury ourselves in the forest before we stop for the night. I'm sure the Salmun aren't far behind."

"I'll slow them down for you, Tressya, my dear. There are

plenty of my brethren wandering these stone walls, enough to form an army. Although we cannot physically touch them, we'll ensure they find it exceedingly unpleasant to pass through here."

I mouthed a thank you. "Andriet says he'll gather an army of the dead and bar the entrance to the Ashenlands. It won't be impenetrable, but it may slow them up, and give us a better head start." I glanced over my shoulder as Tamas led me away, to see Andriet still lingered in the passage's exit.

"How many dead are there in Emberforge?" With a gentle tug of his hand, Tamas slowed our pace, keeping us behind the rest of our party.

"I'm not entirely sure. They don't always make themselves known. Obviously King Ricaud and his—"

Tamas jerked me to a stop. "King Ricaud? You've seen King Ricaud? In Emberforge?"

"It's where the final battle was lost."

"You've spoken to him?"

"Briefly, the first day you sat on the throne."

His gaze looked beyond me, and I could tell his mind was turning inward, delving into the depths of his memories. "It was him."

"You felt him, didn't you?"

He blinked, then looked down at me, his dark eyes inscrutable for the thoughts locked inside. "It was the beginning." But Tamas had usually proved willing to keep the doors of his mind open for me. I couldn't fathom why he was honest most of the time, except for a sincere belief there was something special between us. And he wasn't alone. I'd betrayed everyone to be with him.

"I defied my fate for a long time. But feeling the spirit of King Ricaud pass through me altered my perspective. In that moment, I grasped the weight of my destiny."

"He rejoiced in knowing you. He believed his line was long dead."

Tamas wiped a strand of my limp hair from my cheek. "I made the right decision to fight for my place on the throne." Then he grazed his thumb across my bottom lip. "And my place beside you."

The Ashenlands and its perils vanished from my awareness, eclipsed by the gentle, feather-like caress of his thumb—mesmerizing, enticing, and powerful in its ability to bind me to him as firmly as the mark on my wrist. My mind turned to vapor, leaving me unable to think beyond wrapping my lips around his thumb.

The pulse of my heart flowed down to become the heavy throb between my legs, painful in waiting and wanting, until the mild stench of sewers, rotted meat and aged blood distracted me. I glanced down at my clothes, realizing for the first time how disgustingly filthy I was, stained by our desperate escape and fight: dried sweat, black blood, and a plethora of unidentifiable marks.

Sensing my thoughts, Tamas replied. "We wear our filth with honor." Why did he always make me feel as though we existed in a dream?

I smiled. Falling. As I always did whenever Tamas released the full potency of his power to make me want him. That was until his eyes seemed to devour my lips as a smug smile played on his own. Rather than wrap my lips around his thumb, I secured it firm between my teeth.

He sucked in a breath, baring the tip of sharp fangs. "You're always captivating when you're vicious."

"Never think I'm entirely entranced. I preserve enough of my sanity to remain wary."

"But you *are* entranced, and that's all that matters." And he flicked the tip of my nose with a finger, making me release his thumb.

He leaned down, closing the gap between us, bringing the promise of savage kisses, euphoric dreams, and the freedom from the chains that bound us to our future for one perfect moment. And this time I was totally and utterly enchanted, ready to die staked by our enemy just for one exquisite taste of him.

"You must know the truth about the mark. About what we are to each other." It was all he could say before he leaped away, doubling over as he clutched his stomach, before lifting his head and roaring in fury. His face flushed crimson, his eyes rolling into the back of his head.

Damn those bloody Eone. Why now? They must truly despise me to attack him like this, just as he was about to profess what lay in his heart.

"What did you do?" Osmud snarled, charging upon us.

I grabbed his arm and yanked him away from Tamas, refusing to backdown when he turned his venom-laced glare on me. "It's wiser to stay back."

Teeth bared, I watched as Osmud's fangs extended, dripping blood onto his lower lip before it ran in streams down his chin.

Behind him, Tamas sunk to his knees. "You bastards," he bellowed. "You fucks."

"You'll make it easier for him if you give him space." I tried to sound calm and reasonable amongst Tamas' hysteria.

"Is there nothing we can do?" Bryra said, coming alongside us. There was no accusation or judgement in her eyes, only concern. For that, I was grateful.

"They want to silence him. He has to learn how to fight them."

"Fight who?" Osmud growled, but Tortilus saved me from answering.

"I'm sure there's something we can do." Tortilus waved his hand to gather the other apostles around him. "Quickly, Selisimus," he urged as he spun, giving Selisimus his pack. "I need to retrieve the Chronicle of Ages."

"A lingering effect from the Salmun's curse, perhaps."

"It's very possible, Plesy. Let's consult."

My arms ached to cradle Tamas close to me, take his burden, fight his fight like I knew he would do for me, but his pain was because of me and the truth he was about to tell me. Touching him would likely exacerbate his anguish, because it was me the Eone wanted to destroy.

"What do you think about this one?" Plesy said.

"It's too lengthy, and the potential side-effects are too damaging," Tortilus replied.

"Forget it," I told them. "The worst is over."

I took a tentative step toward him as his breaths quietened, and his body visibly relaxed. He remained hunched over in the creeper, his eyes drifting closed as if channeling all his concentration.

"Tamas?" My voice was soft, cautious.

It was as if time itself held its breath.

Beside him, I bent, touching my hand to his back. The horror unfolded so suddenly, my mind lagged, but my instincts were fast enough to save me. His reflexes were blindingly fast, but my gradual transition into a Razohan gifted me the speed to spring backward, out of reach of his swiping claws. His snarl echoed through my ears, followed closely by another, and I realized it was me.

Tamas sprang to his feet, launching himself at me with ferocious speed, his face flushed red, a contortion of agony and fury. I barely dove away as the tips of his claws skimmed past my face with a whoosh of air from the power behind the swipe of his arm.

Someone yanked me away from behind with such force I stumbled to keep my footing and went down on my side. The enormity of Bryra's beast landed between us, bellowing a warning cry to Tamas.

Tamas responded with an equally threatening roar, only to sound strangled at the end. And that was the moment he won his fight against the Eone and crumbled to the ground.

With Bryra between us, I couldn't see his face, but I knew the devastation he would feel, the belief in his own weakness. He would be dying inside.

Slowly I rolled from my side to sitting, wincing at the pain from landing on a protruding root. I pressed a palm where it ached and felt the sticky damp. When I pulled my hand away, I saw blood. But the blood and pain became inconsequential compared to the significance of seeing claws where my fingernails should be.

"Tressya," Tamas rasped, as Bryra resumed her half-beast form.

He crawled across the ground toward me, his eyes haunted by his torment.

"Did I hurt you?" His gaze caught my blood, soaking the clothes around my hip. "I did," he wailed in anguish.

"You didn't. I fell. Forget it."

"I won't. You know I can't."

I battered his probing hands away. "You weren't quick enough to reach me, beast." And I shoved my claws in front of his face, close enough, one move, and he could've lost an eye.

He sat back, focusing on my claws. "Tressya," he gasped, his voice filled with awe. "This is…" He seemed at a loss for words. Instead, he took my hand and gently pulled it toward him, inspecting my claws. He ran his thumb across the sharp tips, and I marveled at the reverent care in his touch.

"She hasn't come to you fully yet, but this is still a significant moment. You're becoming who you really are. Strong and powerful." He raised my hand to his lips, closed his eyes, and placed a slow, deliberate kiss on my claws, warming my skin with his breath. I wanted to cradle this moment, shielded from our enemies' hatred and greed, but I had abandoned such fantasies long ago. Finally, Tamas lifted his lips and his eyes met mine. "My queen of both north and south, you're well and truly one of us."

It seemed Tamas wove a spell, entrancing everyone, for no one spoke. Our flight, the fight, the tension—all of it disappeared, leaving us suspended as if in a trance. I sensed that if I had been born in the north, celebrations would have followed this moment. Instead, we had to bury ourselves deeper into the Ashenlands, away from any pursuers, forgetting for a while that my beast and I were almost finally united.

"Your Maj—Tressya, what does this mean?" Tortilus finally broke the spell.

"It means, Tortilus, your queen has deceived you," Osmud added.

"Northerner blood runs through my veins." I informed the apostles, then narrowed my eyes on Tamas. "And it seems a sudden fright, or perhaps a fight, would speed my full transition." I arched a brow at Tamas. "My beast came forth to protect me just now."

His expression turned to winter. "Not on your life." He slowly rose to his feet as if not ready to release the small wonder of the moment, then offered me his hand. "Didn't you learn anything from what just happened?" He quirked a brow.

"Is someone going to tell us what *did* just happen?" Osmud said.

"You know, the only way you'll defeat them is to expose yourself to their influence. Repeatedly. It will weaken their whispers and strengthen your will."

"Who is *them*?" Osmud continued.

"You can't comprehend the struggle I'm facing, how pervasive they can be. They're in my head, Tressya." He jabbed a finger to his temple. "Sometimes their thoughts, their emotions—" he slapped his chest "—feel like my own."

I took his hand, and he pulled me to my feet, and I stepped toward him, placing my hand on his chest. "Then fight. Test the boundaries, dare to push beyond them, dare to destroy them and make your own. You're stronger than them. I know you are."

"Twice now I've nearly killed you. How is that strong?"

"Don't flatter yourself. You're alive because I aimed a little lower."

Tamas fixed me with his glare, his eyes darting between the two of mine. I could feel the violence of his stare, a desperate attempt to convince me he was right. But I truly believed he was wrong. "You may question yourself, but I don't."

Suddenly, he grabbed the back of my neck and pulled me toward him, kissing me with a fierce intensity that left me with no choice but to surrender. I fell into him, wrapped as much of myself around him and discovered with every sweep of his tongue the sheer pleasure of letting go, submitting to a craving so deadly, so unrelenting in its hold, I felt naked and hollow without it. He kissed me, and kissed me, using his tongue to bind us as deeply as his bite, stripping doubt and fear, descending us into a place where we couldn't hide from each other, where all secrets were bared. It was a bondage of raw honesty, frightening in its possibility, compelling in its promise.

In his kiss I felt his heartache for what he'd done, what he believed he could do, and his desperate need to avow it would never happen again. It was a sorry from the depths of his heart, and I responded by snaking my arms around his neck, tangling my fingers through his hair, dancing my tongue with his, pressing my body against his so that I felt him come alive; my secret language of forgiveness, acceptance, and strength.

He's here, he'll always be here, no matter the challenge, no matter the pain, no matter our fates; that was the answer his kisses gave my starving, yearning heart. And I unfurled.

"Okay, we get it," Osmud grumbled. "Before you two get naked, we have some serious distance to put between us and this passage."

CHAPTER
TWENTY-NINE

TAMAS

"Are you sure we can trust Tamas," whispered Wellard, revealing his ignorance about the capabilities of us Razohan. Not even a human, their hearing far inferior, would have missed his clumsy whispers.

"Tressya does. I guess that means we should as well," Tortilus said.

"What if she's blinded by... It seems they are... The northerner has a hold over her," Selisimus added.

"Our queen knows what she's doing," Tortilus retorted, raising his voice. "However, it would be wise for us to remain vigilant. When we break for the night, I suggest we consult our texts. There may be spells we can cast to protect Her Majesty from him...should he ever turn feral again."

"Perhaps we'll find a spell to bind the beast side of his nature," Plesy said.

My fangs involuntarily extended upon hearing him mention it, although I was skeptical about the existence of such a spell, and even more so about their ability to cast it.

"Excellent idea, Plesy. That should be the direction of our thoughts," Tortilus replied.

"Shall we inform Tressya of our plans?"

"Gracious, no, Wellard. I think it's quite evident after that display that she's incapable of thinking sensibly when it comes to the northerner. It's up to us to protect her from her soft heart," Tortilus continued.

"And what about the queen?" Selisimus' voice rose barely above a whisper.

He had to be referring to her admission that northerner blood ran through her veins.

"It seems the House of Tannard was following the wrong prophecy," Plesy replied.

"When we find a way to bind Tamas' beast side, perhaps we can do the same for her." Tortilus sounded assured they would succeed in finding such a spell, equally confident they had the capability of wielding such power.

I would put a claw to his throat for thinking such a thing if I could wipe the smirk from my face. Instead, I stopped, shucking my pack from my back. "This is far enough from the passage for now."

Since leaving the Manor in the middle of the night, a lot had transpired, and now, after almost a full cycle, we arrived at dusk without having stopped. The clouds above had thinned, unveiling a blanket of stars whose glittering light filtered through the canopy of trees.

"Praise Ovia, my feet are very sore," Wellard sighed, collapsing down on his ass and leaning back on his pack.

"You better be careful who you send your praise to, little apostle," I said, passing him as I headed back to Tressya.

Wellard leaned over to Selisimus. "What do you think he means by that?"

"He's a northerner. Their beliefs differ from our own," Tortilus whispered.

I shut out the rest of their conversation, as I spun Tressya around and eased the pack from her back.

"You think we're in far enough?" she said.

"This whole place is the Salmun's lair. No place is safe, but it's the best place for now. We can't go on all night. The apostles, at least, will need sleep if we don't want to be carrying them." I leaned in close. "And I smell water. I thought, maybe you'd like to…" I skimmed my eyes down the front of her clothes.

Given our haste, none of us thought to bring a change of clothes, but it didn't mean we couldn't take a dip to wash away some of the grime.

"I would love a wash."

"I'll prepare a fire," Osmud announced and moved off into the trees to collect wood.

Selisimus patted his grumbling stomach. "Pardon, but it's been a long time since I ate."

Beside him, Tortilus was already rummaging through his pack, and given he'd stuffed it with thick volumes taken from the solmira's shelves, I doubted he was thinking of food.

"Come with me." I curled my finger at Tressya, avoiding Bryra's gaze as I drew her away from our party.

"Tressya..." Tortilus called out, half climbing to his feet. "Do you... Perhaps it's not wise..." He glanced at the other apostles for support.

"Help Osmud prepare some food. We won't be long," Tressya replied.

I gave Tortilus a toothy smile, ensuring to bare my teeth, to which he quickly averted his gaze. Then, smiling to myself, I led Tressya into the trees.

We'd no time to discuss what happened at the entrance of the passage, and I desperately needed to apologize once more. Given my second attack, I knew my promises rang hollow, so my sincere apologies would have to suffice.

The silence between us as we strode through the forest ate at me. Thoughts swirled in my mind, but I needed time to sort them out, to express them accurately, to avoid saying things out of fear or in a misguided attempt to mend our relationship. Only the truth would suffice. I needed to find out if she could handle it. She needed the truth, so she could decide for herself if she will take the last leap. I was completely committed; she was my future, a decision I had made at the start with a premeditated plan while keeping my emotions at bay. But now, it was all about my heart, with no regrets. I needed to know if she was ready to join me, which demanded total surrender.

"Why do you suppose we have seen none of the Ashenlands' creatures?"

"Whatever the reason, it can't be good." There was no easy way to begin this conversation. "Tressya, I want to—"

"Forget it. You've already apologized enough. I think it's clear the Eone has a hold on you, so it's foolish, and possibly lethal, for us to pretend otherwise."

Her apparent lack of concern for the danger I posed to her amazed me. Yet, she'd proven more than capable of handling anything I threw her way. I couldn't stop thinking about her imminent transformation. It started with growing claws and fangs. Her full shift was closer than I'd expected, and here we were, far from safety. There would be no celebrations for the profound moment.

She might think this a random comment to make, but it needed to be said. "Your full transformation is close, and it pains me to think we won't be able to celebrate it the way it deserves to be celebrated."

She shrugged. "I've never done anything that deserves celebration, so it doesn't bother me."

I took hold of her elbow, turning her to face me. Although my Razohan eyesight allowed me to see her features in the starlit night, they weren't as distinct as I would've liked, given the importance of what I wanted to say. "I'll revere the moment." I touched my chest. "In my heart. And when we're free of this cursed place, the Etherweave coursing through our veins, I'll give you a celebration the likes of which the Razohan has never seen." Though inadequate to convey the depth of my meaning, the words came from my soul.

I was already hesitant to admit the truth of our bond, so her silence unnerved me. "Maybe I didn't say that right. You don't understand the profound meaning of a Razohan's first transition." I was making a mess here, so I changed course. "It's a lie."

She frowned.

"You, having never done anything that's worth celebrating. Since meeting you, you've constantly astounded me, outmaneuvered me, delighted me, captivated me, enraptured me—" Her kiss silenced the rest, a hard kiss because her words weren't adequate either. I felt her untapped pain bleed out, so coaxed her lips apart with my tongue and smiled at hearing her gentle moan.

I, for one, thought of nothing but us, but Tressya soon pulled us apart. "The Ashenlands, remember?"

"No." And I clawed her back into my arms.

"The Etherweave."

"Isn't going anywhere just yet." I nuzzled my lips into her nape, inhaling her scent.

"The Salmun."

I growled against her skin, then raised my head as she shifted away. I was about to protest when she cupped my cheeks between her palms. "You said it perfectly."

This time I was the one who frown.

"I understand how much the transition means."

"It's significant in Razohan culture, but to me, *your* transition means so much more."

She pressed her fingers against my lips. "I know."

"Because you're my bonded partner," I said around her fingers.

"I know."

"Your beast will make us equals. As bonded should be."

Now was the moment to reveal the true meaning behind those words, the true extent of what a bonded gained. But my throat suddenly thickened at the thought. Curse those damn Eone. I wanted nothing more than to surrender my blood to her, and the Eone knew it. Never would they allow her the same advantage I gained in taking her blood, and if I said anymore, the Eone would bring my beast forth once again.

"I killed my father." I blurted. If I couldn't admit the truth of our bond, I would reveal my ugly sins, bring myself low before her eyes, diminish any moral equivalency between us.

"That I didn't know." She drew her fingers away from my lips.

"Love can cause the deepest agony."

"I've never loved enough to know."

Hopefully, she was referring to her past, rather than her present.

"Father was willing to believe a lie to save himself from the torment of losing my mother. He believed by killing me, he'd become the heir to the Etherweave, which would give him the power to bring her back from the dead."

"I doubt that's even possible. Not so they are truly living again. Not even a spiritweaver can do that. However, I don't understand the extent of the Etherweave's power, so perhaps..." She took my hands.

"Ever since, I've questioned my right to inherit the Etherweave, what sort of ruler I would become filled with all that power, a man who murdered his own father."

"You actions sound justified. But knowing that doesn't

lesson your guilt." Her smile was sad. "I'm glad you told me. Now we know each other's deepest shame."

The silence that spread between us, her gaze locking with mine, told me the words she was about to speak held great importance to her. "Your father would have committed an unthinkable sin in killing you for power. The terrible guilt you feel for what you did, the fact you fear becoming a tyrant, proves the man you are. Tyrants never question or fear their actions."

"Yet I'm a slave to the Eone."

"You're not entirely. Even the most remarkable people fall. But such setbacks do not diminish their greatness. It's their ability to recover from adversity and persevere that truly defines their character, and you have never surrendered to them. Ancient people with ancient power, of course they're going to win. Being partially enslaved to them is no proof of a feeble mind. It's proof you're someone they need, someone of worth, and someone they fear."

"The depth of your forgiving heart, the loyalty you show me…nothing will ever humble me more." I stepped closer, dusting my fingers under her chin, gently tilting her head up to meet my gaze. "There's nothing I want more than what you've already given me."

About to kiss her, she moved her head away. "Really? I thought leading me away from the others to get clean was a ruse… I thought we were going to have sex."

I chuckled, wrapping my arms around her shoulders, hugging her to me. "Will there ever be a moment you stop delighting me?"

"Possibly never."

Never implied a long time. It implied a future. I rested my forehead on hers. "How is it that, in our darkest moment, I feel utterly content?"

"Because you believe in us. It makes no difference that our greatest rivals, two factions on opposing sides, now possess us. You have faith we'll succeed."

"I have faith in you. From the moment I met you on the Sapphire Rose, I knew it was going to be you who won."

Now was the time to tell her the truth. Before we said any more, she needed to know the advantages I gained from the bite mark, but how to tell her without the Eone's interference.

"There's something—"

She pressed a finger to my lips. "No. I don't like that tone. Don't you dare ruin this moment by reminding us of where we are."

"There are conversations we must have."

"Of course there are, but I refuse to be a part of them until after we've washed. At the very least."

I couldn't help but smile at her suggestion, yet she needed to decide to be with me only after fully understanding the truth about my mark. "What I have to tell you is best said before—"

"Would you shut up and stop being so serious?"

"I never want you to change your mind about me."

"For mercy's sake," she sighed. "What must I do to make you focus on us?"

She splayed her hands on my chest before slowly feathering her fingertips down my front.

As much as I wanted this, there would never just be the

two of us. After what happened after we left the passage, I feared the Eone's interference. "What about the Eone?"

"You want them to join in?"

I pressed her hands flat to my stomach. "I'll be at my weakest if we were to do anything. The Eone will distract me."

"What'll be your excuse next time? And the time after that? Unless you know a foolproof way to save yourself from them."

I inhaled, squeezing her hands as I closed my eyes. "Why do you always make me see reason?" Then, before another disabling thought could take hold, I tugged on her hand, leading her onward.

A faint musty odor, tainted by the decay of vegetation, grew stronger as I followed the sound of a gentle trickling stream. Through the wide girthed trees, I spied the glimmer of starlight reflecting off a black lake, the only light to penetrate the dark gloom of the forest. If not in the Ashenlands, I would think it beautiful.

"Do you think it's safe?" Tressya asked as I led her to its edge, obscured by the thick reeds and moss. Exposed roots that plunged into its depths, creating an eerie, natural ladder, bordered the lake's dark, foreboding waters.

"It appears tranquil," I replied.

"Nothing in the Ashenlands is to be trusted."

"I'll enter first. If I disappear, you'll know not to follow," I said, discarding my shirt.

Tressya stepped close, batting my hands away from the ties on my breeches.

"No blade?" I said, as she undid the laces.

Her slow, sly smile teased my cock hard. "I can oblige you with a blade if that's what you want."

Suddenly, I snared her nape, grabbing a thick knot of her hair and kissed her hard. "I'll take whatever you're willing to give," I spoke against her lips. I couldn't get enough of her taste, her smell. Of her. "My life was half-lived," I whispered, brushing her hair from her face, before cradling her cheeks between my palms.

"Your life will be half-lived if you don't stop talking." She pushed me backward, keeping one hand on the ties so they unraveled, opening the front wide, exposing my hardened cock to the cold air, which bounced out of its confines as though hunting her down.

"Now that's what I call a weapon," she breathed, her eyes flaring wide as she stared at my near-nakedness.

I slipped the rest of my clothes to my feet, and by the time I was done, Tressya had discarded her clothes, standing before me naked.

"You wasted no time."

"I was only half-satisfied back at the manor. I want the rest of what you owe me." She trailed her fingers up one of my thigh, angling inward, but I seized her around the waist and lifted her up. Understanding my intention, she wrapped her legs around me, and I groaned at the pressure of my cock nestled nicely between her legs.

Lost in her, it would make no difference to me if the whole of the north looked on, so I gave little thought to the Eone or the Mother.

In the Ashenlands, under the threat of vile creatures possibly lurking nearby, with the Etherweave looming and the Eone yearning for release, it made no sense for our kiss to be languid and exploratory, as though it were our first. It made even less sense for us to be like this, naked, consumed in each other and nothing else. Yet, when I was with her, the rest of the world faded into insignificance. And it seemed Tressya felt the same.

So when she ground herself against me, rubbing my shaft against the wet heat between her legs, releasing soft little moans as she deepened her kiss, all thoughts of potential danger went out of my head. This was it; the foundation of a joyous life. The pleasure of my woman was my sole priority.

"We need this, Tamas," she purred. "We need this because there's no guarantee."

"Whoa," I eased my head back, so I could look into her eyes. "Don't say that."

She gently shook her head. "Let this be what we remember when we need to be strong."

"Always."

"I mean it." She froze, staring deep into my eyes. "I'm sick of fantasies." Then she maneuvered herself to reach between us and grabbed my cock, while angling her hips to ease me inside.

I arched my head back, my eyes fluttering close on a groan at the sheer delight of feeling myself sheathed deep inside of her. Her warm walls hugging my cock tight.

She released a soft moan before she spoke again. "Everything can only get worse." She pressed her lips to mine, silencing me, then drew my bottom lip into her mouth, giving it a gentle nip before letting go. "But that doesn't mean we have to lose each other. I'll fight for you. You know that, right?"

"Curses, Tressya. Don't say that." Don't strip me down and humble me with your words. Not when the images in my head of any danger she might face were enough to drag my beast from slumber.

She gripped the back of my neck, her firm hold silencing me. "It needs to be said. We both need to hear it said."

I leaned in, pressing our noses together. "I've faced death, fought monsters, and defied fate itself, but nothing has ever scared me more than the thought of losing you. I'll scorch the seven realms to keep you safe, to ensure we'll always be together."

She nodded. "They'll do everything in their power to tear us apart."

She was referring to the Mother and the Eone.

"They'll never succeed. Not even the divide between the living and the dead can tear us apart. I'll never stop fighting for us."

She shook her head, as if refusing to listen to me. "Even once we possess the Etherweave, do you understand? They have the power to pit us against each other and turn us into each other's greatest enemy."

"No. You're wrong. That'll never happen."

She kissed me gently, then ground her hips, and I caught my breath at the exquisite feeling.

"But we'll always have this moment, and all the times before it. Those are our anchors, Tamas. We can find our way back to each other. We just have to remember."

Then she kissed me, silencing any reply I might have

given. For a moment, a strangling fist seized my heart at her seemingly prophetic words. She believed them deeply, but I couldn't. I wouldn't.

With one more gentle rock of her hips, the tight grip on my heart gradually loosened. Another rock of her hips, and her words transformed into moths, fluttering away into oblivion.

I lowered us slowly, hating the feeling of our lost contact as I settled her down on the discarded clothes. But Tressya rose. She signaled I should flip with a hand on my chest, then wasted no time in straddling me, impaling me deep inside of her.

This is how I would remember her: unrestrained and untamed, her eyes locked with mine as she rode me. Her stare was both a promise to me and a warning to our enemies—a severing gaze. Here was my queen, the Queen of the Bone Throne.

I came apart just watching her. Brimming close to climax, she threw her head back and snarled to the night, which drew me to the brink of my orgasm. As her walls closed tight around my cock in rhythmic pulses, her body suddenly spasmed. Seized in ecstasy, she jerked forward, dragging her clawed fingers from my chest to my stomach, and released another throaty snarl. The sharp pain from the slices she made with her claws was my undoing.

My release was like a savage storm. The immensity of the build of my ecstasy, the sudden release and I felt as though my body was splintering apart. I jetted my climax deep inside of her, joining her guttural snarls and gripping her waist tightly, as if it were the only thing preventing me from shattering into dozens of pieces.

With her collapsed on top of me, I felt her wild heartbeat raging in time with mine. I wrapped my arms around her, holding her close, savoring the smell of our sex, and the iron tang of my blood, savoring what we'd just shared. She'd branded me with her claws, and soon I hoped she would mark me with her bite.

"Tressya." I was loathed to break this spell, but I had to tell her the truth about my mark.

"Not that again," she moaned, pushing herself upright.

My blood covered her chest. I loved seeing her wearing it, knowing it resulted from her pleasure.

"Oh no. Tamas, I'm sorry." She looked at her hands to see them stained with my blood.

"Don't worry. It's more endearing than a love bite. Back home, bonded males will ensure the first wounds leave a scar and wear them with pride as to the pleasure they've given their bonded partners."

She huffed a laugh, and the sound caressed all the way down inside of me. Then, all too soon, she sobered. "We can't stay here like this."

"I know." My voice was heavy.

CHAPTER
THIRTY

TAMAS

I BIT BACK my protest when she climbed off me. Then I leapt to my feet at the thought of her reaching the lake before me. There was no telling what waited underneath. "I'll go first."

Using the fattest root as my way in, I gently eased my leg down its slimy surface until my foot slipped beneath the water, and the instant chill went straight to my head.

"This is going to be bracing." Then relinquishing my hold on the root, I dived shallow, feeling as though I'd plunged through ice.

My feet buried in silt as I punched to the surface, tasting the tannins in the water.

"That was reckless," Tressya said.

"The Eone wants me alive."

There was enough starlight without the moon to reveal her solemn face, even from here.

"Sorry, they're off-limits for discussion," I added.

"Actually, I'm curious about something."

"There'll be no answers until you're wet."

"Fine." She followed my lead, using the root as a ladder. "You never said it was like ice," she remarked, sticking her toes in first.

"You never asked."

As I spoke, her foot slipped on a slimy root, and she lost her grip, plunging into the lake. By the time I reached her, she was brushing her hair from her face and gasping from the cold. I pulled her against me, cradling her back to my chest.

"My Razohan heat will warm you." There was a distinct drop in my voice, which I couldn't help, neither could I refrain from tracing my lips across her exposed shoulder. There was no halting my desire for more, more of her and what we'd just experienced.

"I have questions," she said.

"And I might have the answers, but first I need my fill." Suddenly her presence, her body, pressed the length of mine, her skin, soft against my lips, became far more important. Even though I'd had an orgasm to blow my mind, I barely felt satiated.

"This is serious, Tamas, because I'm not sure how you'll respond to what I ask."

I continued to trail my lips to her nape while I spoke. "Dangerous territory to tread."

"You have magic now?" she blurted out, referring to my crumbling the wall under Emberforge, revealing the mysterious tunnel and our escape into the Ashenlands.

"Oh, that." I stilled. "I'm not sure what happened there. It had to be the Eone's interference."

"They still have a lot of their power if they can work magic through you?"

The Eone remained silent, but I felt a tightening in my stomach, as if my guts were being twisted with a pitchfork. They were tense, waiting for her questions and my response. It was surprising they hadn't resisted my wish to separate Tressya from the rest of our party, and our sex… Lucky for them, they'd stayed buried during that. For now, they seemed placated by Tressya's obvious astonishment at the extent of their talent, though I couldn't be sure, as they had withdrawn from me, taking their emotions with them.

"I'd say more, you know I would, but now's not a safe time to discuss them."

"So it's not safe to continue our conversation of earlier."

I tightened my hold on her, flushing her against me, hoping the iced water would save her from feeling anything sticking into her back—but who knows, my arousal felt pretty intense.

I was desperate to tell her. This was my moment. She needed to decide if she wanted to gain as much herself, which would involve taking my blood, marking me, binding us together for eternity. This was perhaps my only chance.

Sadly, something so profound and precious as the partner bond should never be shared with the Eone. It was nothing short of perverting the sacred, but what choice did I have? And I had to clear my thoughts before they gleaned the truth.

"About this?" I gripped her wrist, held close to her stomach, and rubbed my thumb over my mark, hoping the Eone would not discern my intent. I had strived to bury my memories of that moment on the Sapphire Rose, but there was no telling what the Eone could access now that I had opened myself to them

"Yes," she whispered.

I attempted to shield my thoughts from the truth and dulled my heart from the elation at the prospect of her accepting our union. This was something the Eone must never know. As I spoke, rather than focusing on what I was going to say, I occupied my thoughts with Garrat and the challenges he would now face in the north following my encounter with Kaldor. "I explained somethings already."

"So...the same would need to be done to make it complete," she said.

Cursed be my heart for betraying me as it sped up. "Yes. A blood exchange. A reciprocal arrangement in the full knowledge of what is given and what is taken." I wanted to be clear, so she would know exactly what I meant, but that was impossible.

Tressya was quiet for a moment, then hesitantly added. "I think I understand the giving side of it. What's the taking?"

"Everything," I breathed along her skin, feeling a tremor invade my body that had nothing to do with the cold. Even my heart seemed to suddenly stop beating.

"Everything?"

"Everything." I repeated the word, infusing it with a depth that could anchor it to the bottom of the lake.

"Everything!?" I could hear her thoughts churning, then

she made to escape my hold. "Even what is mine? My ability with spirit—"

"Shh," I whispered against her skin, tightening my grip on her—my pulse hammering through my veins—feeling as though she'd vanish if I let her go.

"So it never mattered if I was the first to reach the Ether—"

"Tressya," I whispered, as I covered her mouth with my hands. Perhaps it was already too late.

This was the deepest truth of my heart, the purest form of love I could give, yet I couldn't even voice its profound significance. "You needed to know," I murmured, closing my eyes as my tremors synchronized with the rhythm of my heart.

She pushed my hand from her mouth. "So it wasn't to track me?"

I shook my head, aware that she would feel the motion against her skin and possibly interpret it as a confirmation of her question.

"You wanted to take from me. Everything."

"It was to keep you alive," I whispered into her ear through gritted teeth. The worst part was the pain evident in her voice, adding weight to her accusation. I was powerless to explain it all, to make her understand while the Eone listened.

My thoughts betrayed me, slipping free of my noose, and the memory of our first meeting on the Sapphire Rose came unbidden into my mind, exposing the sacred moment to the Eone's scrutiny.

I pushed her away. "It's time to get out." My voice was rough, the warning a discordant note of ferocity.

She wasted no time wading to the edge and climbing her way out with the aid of the root. Twice she lost her footing on the slimy root surface, making me twitch to head over and help, but I didn't dare go near her, not now I'd revealed one secret to the Eone in that memory. If I was lucky, they wouldn't understand the full significance of what that memory meant.

Shivering from the cold, or possibly rage, Tressya fossicked around in the dark for her pants. "You've made it all so easy for yourself," she snapped.

"There are no barriers." My heart fell over a cliff, but I had to be honest.

"It all makes sense."

"No. You know my reason, but not the rest of the story. Not what came after." And because I couldn't express the raw makings of my heart, I added something else. "It could save us, Tressya." Once I wore her mark, it mattered little who controlled the Etherweave. Through our shared bond, neither the Eone nor the Mother could prevent us from accessing its power through each other.

"Or turn us..." she stopped before she'd begun dressing. "Do you really think either of our enemies will allow the other to survive?"

It was a topsy-turvy reply, but I grasped the gist of it. I tried to keep it as a scrambled jumble of words in my mind, refusing to pare it down to its intricate parts: the Mother and the Eone using Tressya and me as weapons against each other for control of the Etherweave. And what would happen to the two of us in the aftermath? Tressya's prophetic words haunted me.

"But kept a secret, it remains harmless," I said, wading to the edge and springing out. As long as our enemies were naïve to the significance of our bond.

"It can never be harmless."

Was she referring to the blight now dwelling within us both?

Suddenly, Tressya fell silent, sinking her head to her chest, dropping her arms beside her, as though she now bore a burden too great to face. Seeing her like this, motionless, I couldn't move. The darkness of the Ashenlands reached deep inside, pulling with it all the Salmun's perverted manifestations to gorge on my heart.

I had rehearsed this moment, dreamed of it, and in my dreams, Tressya smiled, kissed me, accepted me, loved me, and never once questioned our future. Of course, in my dreams, the Eone and the Mother were absent, and neither of us was forced to speak in riddles. But this was the worst possible way I could have told her.

"Unity brings strength." I clenched my fists, wishing for a more potent means to express my conviction than mere words, which can so easily ring hollow despite bearing the weight of my soul.

"Remember what you said." *Because I do*. I would never forget. Her promise was to fight for me, and mine was to destroy the seven realms to keep her safe.

None of what I said seemed to disturb her thoughts. She stayed motionless, as if her mind wasn't even here with me.

Look at me. Let me know what you're thinking. Her silence

strangled me. Her head remained sunk to her chest. Slowly I watched her hands fist beside her, a subtle sign of her emotional turmoil.

"It's our only hope."

Say something, Tressya. Don't shut me out. We needed each other. 'Twain is the bloodborn'. It was always meant to be the two of us.

I dressed quickly as she finally lifted her head. The depths of her blue eyes had pooled to darkness in the starlight, but there was no misreading her expression, cold like the lake, hard like stone, sharp like a blade. I'd never seen such an expression on her face before.

She shouted a word I couldn't decipher, sending a shimmering tingle through my body.

"What's going on?"

The power woven into the word was unmistakable. She shouted another, as incomprehensible as the first, but equally imbued with authority.

"Are you trying to control me, Tressya?" I ran my tongue across the tips of my fangs.

Another power-laced word was her reply, sending feathering tingles along my limbs. The Mother.

Damn that cunning bitch and her scheming mind. She understood every word we'd said, and now she would force Tressya to end me, ensuring there was only one wielder of the Etherweave.

"It appears I wasn't cryptic enough." I uttered.

'We gave you a reprieve, young Tamas,' Ineth said.

'Because you needed to know her lack of commitment to the feelings you so readily profess,' Carthius continued.

'We have known all along about the significance of the Razohan mark,' Ovia added. 'Your weak heart has kept her alive this long, for if we really wanted her dead, she would be, and you would have been powerless to stop us. And now, as you can see, she is owned by her Mother.'

'She has rejected you, Tamas, when you opened your heart to her,' Fivia said, as Tressya, driven by the Mother's greed to possess the Etherweave, shouted another incomprehensible word in her search to find the right word to cripple my soul.

'Hear it in her words, young Razohan. She seeks to control you, tame you, bring you to your knees before she destroys you.' Ineth's words were like fierce claws scraping across my mind.

I gritted my teeth against their harassment and the barrage of inscrutable words Tressya shouted as she attempted to penetrate my mind. A Razohan's mind was normally impenetrable because of the multitude of souls residing within us. It should be impossible for the Sistern to delve into the depths of our inner lives to find what they needed for control. However, the Mother was surprisingly powerful. By combining her strength with Tressya's, I sensed the first hint that they might actually succeed. And why wouldn't they, given how adeptly Tressya had disabled the Salmun?

"Fight her, Tressya. You're strong enough. I know you are."

"What if I don't want to be? She is my Mother Divine after all. What if I'm more than happy under the Mother's control?" Her voice was as serpentine as that of the wicked old crone—not soul voice though. She had yet to find that one word that would chain my soul to her command.

'It is time to release the burden of this woman that lays across your heart. She was always your disease. Now we give you the cure,' Carthius said.

I clutched at my temples, feeling the insidious creep of power worm its way into my head, as Tressya—the Mother — refused to relinquish her fight to control me.

"'We have to remember'. You told me that." I cried. "Don't let her win."

Another fiery lance of word-driven power crippled my body, sending me stumbling backward. How could the Sistern possibly win? How could the Mother find a way through the myriad of my souls to that one special place that dominated me?

Thaindrus was right. The Sistern had formed an alliance with one of the Nazeen, enhancing their ability to use soul voice. That was the only way Tressya was succeeding. It had to be.

"Bow before me, beast," Tressya yelled. The Mother's poisonous venom dripped from every word.

"You're my enemy," she spat. "That's the choice I've made."

In horror, I realized the sinister thread in her voice had woven through my mind, strangling my free will. I fell to my knees, driven by her command, and I stared up at her, silhouetted by the starlight, and saw the Mother's brutal fury etched upon her expression.

"Fight Tressya," I implored, loathing the feeling of mental chains. My mind was bound once before; the most harrowing experience of my life. My beast roared, desperate for release, but the binds of soul voice were as tight as Romelda's magic.

"It's on your knees I'll deliver your punishment," she crooned. Her words remained laced with soul voice power.

'Feel your powerlessness, young Razohan,' Ineth said. 'Let it permeate your mind with the truth. Those you love most will cripple you. At some point, everyone will fail you. Power is your only friend to seek. The Etherweave is your family, your lover, your savior.' His words echoed through my head.

I tilted my head back and roared to the stars, my helplessness funneling my rage.

"Tressya, please, hear me," I begged, unable to crawl my way forward to her feet.

"Stop sniveling, beast. It's embarrassing you," she growled, her hands clenched into fists. Then, with a voice dripping with scorn, she taunted, "The mighty Razohan, on his knees, begging, 'Please, oh please, save me.'" There was no trace of Tressya in anything she said. Was the idea of bonding with me so abhorrent that she'd allowed the Mother to take control? Or perhaps she was furious about my betrayal.

'Treachery, my friend, carves wounds that never mend. It can shatter you or forge you anew. The choice is yours. Vengeance is not a tunnel into darkness. It's a path to power. Embrace it, Tamas, and you will conquer,' Ovia said.

I sucked in a breath. "Tressya," I panted, feeling my throat thin. "You're stronger than her."

'Begging is not the way of the Razohan,' Fivia said. 'You

are a disgrace to your people.' It was as though she stood beside me, whispering in my ear. 'She is wicked, utterly wicked. A woman unworthy of your loyalty, and even less deserving of your heart. See how she revels in her triumph over you. Wicked, wicked woman.' Her last words flowed swiftly, as if she found great pleasure in saying them.

The Eone was as pernicious and deadly as the Mother. These were lies. They had to be. I shook my head, a savage cry tearing from my lips as I fought against their persuasion, against their emotional influence—against their hatred for Tressya, threatening to flood into my heart.

Arching my head skyward, I felt my fangs descend, claws break the skin behind my nail beds, hair prickle up my spine and along my shoulders.

The beast was not wanted now. I had to convince Tressya, help her break free from the Mother's hold as she'd done for me.

With Razohan blood pumping through her veins, Tressya dove for her discarded clothes. In the next moment, starlight glinted off the steel of her blade.

"I should've done this a long time ago." She rested her finger on the tip of the blade. "But it was too much fun, watching you play the fool." She slowly strode toward me before she lowered the blade in front of my face, laying the tip on my nose. "And you thought you were invincible to the power of the Mother's voice." She swiped the blade away, nicking my cheek as she did so.

A snarl escaped before I could swallow it down.

"Silly, silly, boy," she crooned.

'Choose us, Tamas, and you will transcend these petty

words and shift beyond anyone's reach. You will become power incarnate, breathing life into the word revenge,' Carthius said.

I closed my eyes, shaking my head, feeling torn between longing and insanity. Inside, my beast roared to break free from the Mother's binds.

"All silly little boys must learn their lesson," Tressya continued, soul voice strumming the cords on my heart. Only now her taunts were fading to the background as a violent tremor wracked my body.

'That is it, Tamas,' Carthius whispered. 'Open to your strength, my friend. Stop cowering in your fear. You are worthy. You are the one. The only one to wield the power of the Etherweave. You know it in your soul. There is nothing that can stand in your way. Not even these pathetic little word games. Break. Free.'

My beast punched through my restraints and severed the bind of the Mother's voice as I launched upward. Then, before my eyes, Tressya transformed into the most magnificent beast with a thick coat of dark auburn fur, shimmering like dried blood in the starlight.

She had found her beast. This moment should have been profoundly glorious, but The Eone had stolen all my emotions—draining joy from my mind and heart—except one. Fury. Which they played like a master with his lute.

We faced off, rising to our full height with lethal claws extended and fangs bared in a snarl. But then I looked into her eyes and saw the same intense blue that had captivated me the first day we had met. In that moment, I saw her confusion and fear, and realized the Mother had lost control over Tressya's mind once she was in beast form.

'Now, young Razohan. It is your time now. You have proved your strength. Come to us.'

I had believed my mark was a shield to protect us from our enemies, but there were too many lies, too much betrayal, and too many intent on severing what we had, determined to keep us apart.

The moment I lowered from my full height onto all fours, Tressya did too. I couldn't meet her eyes, couldn't even look at her face. Guilt permeated every pore, alongside a burning hatred; a hatred so pure it seared like a branding iron through my soul, directed entirely at Tressya.

In utter horror, I knew I'd succumbed to the Eone, to their strength of will. Hope, love, desire, none of it had been strong enough.

Aware she possessed the speed to keep pace with me, I leaped up, powering myself skyward with my beast's strength. Fleeing was all I could do to prevent a fight between us both. With the Eone's ability to wield their magic through me, Tressya didn't stand a chance.

Once clear of the canopy, I released the Razohan beast, transforming into the nightmare and ascending into the night sky.

CHAPTER
THIRTY-ONE

TRESSYA

"Tamas," I whispered, as the massive dark form of the nightmare spread its wings across the night sky, blotting out the stars.

The blade piercing my chest felt real, and the sense of desolation was just as deep. I sunk to my knees amongst the creeper and moss, burying my head in my hands, surrendering to an aching emptiness yawning inside of me. In the dark's silence, I felt utterly alone, totally defeated.

Tamas already triumphed by claiming me as his bonded, gaining access to any power I possessed. Regardless of the outcome, Tamas would be the wielder of the Etherweave, either through my abilities or by his own means. He didn't have to reveal that shocking revelation, yet he did so, at the risk of the Eone's and the Mother's wrath.

He knew everything, even from the moment he bit me,

yet continuously saved my life and protected me. In return, I silently accused him of betrayal at the precise moment when, in a show of devotion, he was offering his blood so I could take from him—even the Etherweave's power, if he reached it first.

With the Mother's baneful influence receding, I recognized what his offer truly meant; it was not about power, but the deep connection he longed to share with me, positioning us as equals, sharing our powers.

I wasn't born a Razohan and knew nothing of their traditions, yet I realized that by spurning him as I did, I likely wounded him in a deeply fundamental way. I gave him no chance to explain—cryptic as it might have been—and assumed he bit me so he could win. Then in my anger and hurt, I allowed myself to succumb to the Mother's influence. And now it felt like I'd ripped my heart out, all because I placed more faith in people's cruelty and betrayal than in their capacity for love.

He fled from me as the nightmare, knowing there was no hope of me chasing him, no hope of his friends hunting him down. That in itself was the greatest indication of the deep wounds I'd inflicted.

"You'll pay for this," I uttered, but the words felt empty. There was none of the fierce conviction within me revenge should evoke. I was empty.

'I saved you from your weak heart.'

Oh, how I wished I could gouge her out of my head.

"Then why do I feel caged?" There wasn't anywhere near enough fury in my voice while most of my heart rode on the back of the nightmare as it disappeared into the night sky.

'Your heart was always your prison, but you were blind to the truth. I've opened your eyes to the depths of his deceit. You finally realize the cage he's placed you in. I've liberated you, yet censure is all I receive in return.'

"Never dare influence me again."

'You're merely a child in this game. Children need guidance. They need to learn their place.'

"You exist because of me." I rose from my knees as though every limb ached, but really, it was my heart, spreading its sorrow throughout my entire body.

Slowly, I bent to retrieve my clothes and dressed as lethargically.

'And you survive, thanks to me. The Razohan is already dead, and you'll soon meet the same fate if you choose to ignore my guidance.'

I froze. "What do you mean?" I would have let out a scornful, humorless laugh at her notion of guidance had she not issued her ominous warning.

'Your naivety in relation to your talent was crucial, but now it's embarrassing. Yet it's important for you to remain ignorant until the end.'

"Cut the shit. Just answer me."

'Very well. The Razohan's usefulness is limited to those who wish to control him.'

"You know about the Eone?"

'There is no darkness once one crosses the veil. It's for this very reason I had to separate you from him.'

"Wait, I don't understand. What does that mean?"

'Spiritweaving has always been a rare and perilous talent, one that many feared once its true potential was revealed. Despite the risks, a few sought to harness it for their own gain. Eventually, those who possessed the talent were hunted and killed for their abilities, and gradually, the talent vanished from the realms, except within the lineage of a very few select individuals thanks to the Sistern. The lore surrounding its power also faded into obscurity, which worked to my advantage. This made it so effortless for me to keep you ill-informed.'

"What do you know?"

'Much, but what do I reveal?'

Calming breaths, I needed them more than ever when dealing with the mother. "Tell me, did you foresee Tamas? My guess is no. And I'm pretty damn sure you never expected him to mark me, claim me as his life's partner. And now this." I huffed a hard, humorless laugh. "He certainly stole my breath with that revelation. You never expected that level of interference, did you?"

'You underestimate me—'

"You're right. I did. But I stopped doing that a while ago. I'd say what he revealed alarmed you, otherwise why make such a bold, yet utterly futile attempt to defeat him? Did you really think you'd win against him?"

'You should praise me for what I've done for you. I bestowed this power upon you.'

"You say I'm a child in need of teaching, well just now you've demonstrated quite a bit. I'm understanding the extent of your influence over me, and I'm seeing your limits, because there was another thing you did not foresee. You lost control over me once I transformed into my beast."

After the initial shock subsided, the glory I felt upon

becoming the beast was indescribable. It was as if my entire life before had been meaningless, all my years spent waiting for a destiny I didn't know about. Now my beast had found me, I felt acutely aware of a connection to a race of people whose unique heritage isolated them from others, yet united them as one. For twenty-three years, I dismissed my dreams as the pathetic desires of someone doomed to be alone, misunderstood, and unloved. It wasn't until I encountered my beast that I realized I had been existing in a body that was only half complete, and living a life that was merely shadows when I could bask in the sun.

My beast empowered me to step out of the shadows, and it was Tamas who would become my sun.

"I may have begun naïve to this talent, and I might not yet comprehend its potential, but that's where you come in."

I took a long inhale, drawing air deep into my lungs, channeling my focus down to the core of my being, the seat of my power, where *Aetherius* resided.

"You're now my instrument."

'My life is in dedication to the Sistern. Everything I have done—'

"And everything you know is mine to exploit. If you won't give me the answers I seek, then I shall take them from you."

The sound of pounding footsteps pulled me from my mind. I lost my hold on *Aetherius* as the Mother's presence vanished. Suddenly I realized how cold I was, and the fact I still had to finish getting dressed. While shivering, it was an arduous task, but by the time Osmud and Bryra came into view, I was buttoning up my shirt.

"We heard noises," Bryra said, a polite way to say Tamas and I caused a raucous.

"Where is he?" Osmud said, glancing around before tilting his chin and sniffing the scents on the wind.

I pressed my lips together, thinking of a few lies I could say, but realized there was no point. "He's gone."

"Gone? What does that mean exactly?" Osmud demanded. I noticed small things as well as deeply transformative ones. For one, I could see Osmud's expression in the starlight more clearly, whereas before, his face would have been interesting shades of shadows. His expression was a blend of distrust and confusion.

"He took to the sky."

"He became the nightmare?" I failed to miss the accusatory tone in his voice.

I met his glare, anticipating the derogatory turn this conversation was bound to take from this point forward.

"He was our guide through this stinking shit hole." Osmud's voice rose dangerously close to yelling, his eyes radiating a fury I'm sure had been simmering beneath the surface since our first meeting, eager for any excuse to burst forth.

"Osmud," Bryra said, intentionally softening her voice to soothe his budding temper. "Why are you so quick to blame Tressya for all of this?"

"Because he's been an ass since he very first met her. And lately...well, lately I just want to knock his block off. If you want to understand the reason for his mood change, just ask her. She's the cause. I guarantee."

The apostles appeared, with Tortilus carrying his

conjured light in the palm of his hand. I should have felt pleasantly surprised to see he had some ability to manipulate magic, as I suspected, but it was inconsequential compared to losing Tamas and our way through the Ashenlands.

All four were wheezing and panting from their efforts to keep up with Osmud and Bryra. However, upon hearing Osmud's accusation, they glanced at me, and the guilt I'd carried for too long—both for my secrets and for hurting Tamas the way I did—made me feel as though I had every reason to apologize.

"You're right. He left because of me. But you know very little of the truth."

Osmud folded his arms across his chest. "Oh really. Why don't you enlighten us?"

My gaze lingered on each of them. This was Tamas' story to tell, but given our perilous situation, there was no point in withholding the truth.

"Tamas is possessed."

Wellard gasped.

"I'm not sure how or when it happened, but that's the reason for his deteriorating mood. He was constantly fighting to keep control of his mind."

Osmud shook his head, then forked his finger through his hair as he turned away to pace. Finally, he stopped and turned to face me. "That's your excuse. It's nothing but horseshit."

"Who possessed him?" Bryra said.

"Don't, Bryra. You're too intelligent to fall for this."

"An ancient people called the Eone. He claims they

created the Etherweave." I turned to the apostles, hoping to see some recognition of the name.

"The ancients?" Tortilus said.

"They call themselves the Eone. It's how he knew where to lead us," I explained. "Under the Eone's influence, he burned the map. He was never meant to bring any of us along on the final journey to the Etherweave—especially me."

"This makes no sense," Osmud growled.

"Begging your pardon, but it makes perfect sense. Tressya is a rival." Plesy said.

"Against a bunch of dead people," he spat, but the moment he said it, his eyes widened in understanding. "How very inconvenient of him to bring someone who commands the dead."

"I'm not sure how much influence I would have over them. Creating an ultimate power would require commanding significant power. And the fact they've existed in some form for a millennium—while retaining some of their ability—waiting for Tamas proves their mastery of magic."

Plesy continued. "I had thought perhaps the power was calling to him, guiding him to its location, but, yes, it makes sense, because if it was the Etherweave that was showing him the way, then it should do the same for you."

All six glanced at me.

"We must return to our books, brethren." Tortilus suddenly sprang to life, his enthusiasm for the challenging journey ahead undiminished by this new revelation. Belief was a powerful motivator, and that's why I wouldn't disclose to the apostles that it was actually the Eone, not their apostle skill, who saved Tamas from the Salmun's curse.

"I'm sure there's mention of this Eone in our collection somewhere. We're bound to find a reference, now we know what we're looking for. If we could learn more about them..."

His enthusiasm for magic and knowledge seemed endless. But by now I was musing over what Plesy had said. Would the Etherweave guide the true heir to its resting place?

'Is that true?' The Mother might know, but would she be honest with me?

'A question? Why don't you just exploit my knowledge?' Her clipped tone ran shrill across my mind.

'I will if I have to, but your cooperation will make things quicker.'

She stayed silent for immeasurable breaths. I was about to ask again when she answered. 'Your reliance on him weakened you. You were always subservient, allowing him to lead when you should never have followed. Not now, nor in the future.'

'I'll take that cryptic answer as a yes.'

'Let me war—'

'I've heard enough from you,' I mentally snapped at her.

I looked at Plesy. "Perhaps you're right."

"I am," he uttered in surprise. "Yes, I am."

"How's he right?" Osmud demanded, scratching his head.

"I'm not focusing on its call. I've shut it out because I was following Tamas."

Osmud huffed. "Alright then, point the way."

What if I was wrong about the Etherweave?

'You're not. It's time you had faith in what I created.' Her voice echoed inside my head.

"I need time." To listen for the Etherweave, and also to stop the Mother eavesdropping on my life.

"Time we don't have," Osmud growled.

"Patience, Osmud. I know it's not your strength, but unless you want us to be stuck here, Tressya is our only guide," Bryra said.

"Perhaps. But I'm sure there's plenty to be found in the texts, which will illuminate our problem," Tortilus suggested.

"Would you forget about your fucking books!" Osmud snapped. "And you..." He jabbed his finger at me. "...haven't told us nearly enough about these Eone."

"There's plenty of time for revelations once we return to camp," Bryra said. "If we hope to make any progress, we need rest and food." She turned to the apostles. "Feel free to study your texts for anything that may be helpful. We need as much knowledge about the path ahead as we can gather." She then glanced at me. "Take your time to listen, but not too long, if you know what I mean."

TAMAS

Above the forest, concealed beneath wisps of cloud and the deep gloom of night, there were no boundaries, only freedom. The temptation to unleash my constraints and merge with the wild, liberating chaos of the nightmare's primal urges—where I could escape the expectations of my position, break free from the chains of destiny, and indulge in the sheer magnitude of its physical power, poised for release—intensified into an almost overwhelming desire. Though its body was immense and its dominion over the Ashenlands absolute, its instincts were straightforward, its needs fundamental. The thought was calming to my soul.

My mental anguish and emotional suffering fractured under the assault of the icy wind, sweeping across my leathery wings with the sharpness of a blade, yet there was pleasure in that sensation.

Its feral mind and primal needs, however, became constant distractions that grew irritating. The creature was incapable of forming a coherent thought beyond following the scent of its next meal, of which there were many hiding in the forest far below us. It didn't help that I had my own needs, having had little to eat or drink since finding Tressya on the path, cold as ice.

As if sensing my struggle between retaining my sanity and succumbing to the freedom of the nightmare's insanity, a familiar beat pulsed through my chest, throbbing with need, beckoning me onward.

The Etherweave. I was not unaccustomed to its call, but in the Ashenlands, as I rushed toward my fate, the thrumming vibration of its call became an irresistible lure I couldn't dismiss. The power was coming to life, desiring its release.

Guided only by starlight, with the nightmare's exceptional sight, I spied the mountain from a distance, towering above the dark forest. My destination lay at its crest, encircled by a ring of winged protectors.

My stomach grumbled when the first taste of prey filled my nose. I opened my massive beaked mouth, savoring the taste of the scent as the wind moved across the fine filament of my tongue. There would be no harm in taking my fill before I entered the castle.

As I spiraled above the bone white castle, below, the smaller winged creatures, sensing my predatory approach, dispersed, skimming low across the forest canopy.

For a moment, a hazy thought clouded my concentration, and I lost focus on the chase. Shaking off the sudden confusion, consumed by the exhilaration of the hunt, I dived, tucking my wings, and then, at the last moment, snapped them wide, allowing the wind to slow my descent. The smaller creature dipped, hoping to find refuge in the trees, but with a single powerful flap of my massive wings, I was upon it. Stretching my neck to reach into a gap between the trees, I snapped it down in one gulp. It was barely a meal, leaving my stomach empty, so I rose, turning my head to seek the survivors, when the haze clouded my concentration once again.

'Do not lose yourself,' came the faint cry from within my mind.

I shook my massive head, beating my wings to soar once again high into the sky.

'Tamas, please.' It was a woman's voice, nothing more than a distant echo in my head.

The Eone. They were struggling to reach me while I had taken on the form of the nightmare. Free from the curse of the Eone's control; the thought was decidedly pleasant. However, their presence, though minor, reminded me of what was important. Losing myself in simplistic violence would not nourish my soul, nor would it relieve me of my responsibilities. The only thing it would do was tear me away from the woman I loved and my fate.

Surrendering to my fate, I spiraled down toward the castle, skimming into the gaping ruins so the tips of my barbs grazed the top stones, sending them crashing to the ground below. At the last moment, I snapped my wings closed and landed within the castle as a man. I cracked my neck and flexed my shoulders, feeling a sense of relief to be back in my skin.

'Welcome back, young Razohan,' Ineth said. 'Your mental control over such a savage beast is impressive.'

'We cannot linger,' Ovia said. 'We are so close. Can you not feel its call? The Etherweave longs for release, eager to unite with us once again.'

'A millennium we have waited. At last, our time has come,' Fivia said.

I attempted to fend off the surge of excitement overwhelming my emotions, determined to resist the sway they held over me. As a distraction, I glanced up at the night sky. "What about the prophecy that claimed the night would be lit as day?" Alone in this castle, I spoke aloud to them.

'You have us,' Carthius said. 'We are all you need to

succeed. Place your hands upon the Etherweave's cage and let us do the work. With our power flowing through you, the five of us will be strong enough to destroy the Nazeen's curse and bring the Etherweave forth.'

I hesitated, my thoughts drifting to Tressya. As soon as her image entered my mind, I tried to bury it, shielding her from the Eone's probing minds. My desire for her remained just as strong, the pain of her rejection doing nothing to dampen my feelings. Sharing the bond between us would have made us equals in every way. It was all I had ever desired. Only now I'd left her far behind.

I could leave, assume the nightmare once more, and return to her side.

'Stand firm and do not falter now, my friend,' urged Carthius.

A sudden tug in my chest drew me further into the castle's labyrinth, my legs moving under the Eone's guidance. I couldn't tell if my newfound curiosity and anticipation were my emotions alone or the influence of the Eone.

'You have become one of us, choosing to leave your burdens behind and join our cause. The task before you, young Razohan, is to fulfill your destiny and seize the Etherweave. By doing so, you will bring an end to the suffering that plagues the seven realms. You will be the harbinger of order amidst chaos, of benevolence amidst cruelty, for those who suffer under the tyranny of oppressors. The power is within your grasp to command,' Carthius continued.

'You are deserving of this, young Razohan,' Ovia reassured.

Curse her. She was turning my vulnerable thoughts into a weapon.

'Never let doubt cloud your mind. The Etherweave is yours. If not for the meddling of that vile order, which spawned such an abomination, your path would be clear and your fate unquestioned.'

Calling Tressya an abomination wouldn't earn my loyalty. It only reminded me whose side they were on: their own. "When I claim the Etherweave, what becomes of you? Will I be eternally bound by your interference, or will the Etherweave restore your lives?"

'Do not dwell on such matters now, not when we are so close to succeeding,' Ineth urged.

"The deeds you've compelled me to commit, the falsehoods you've spun—this is no alliance. You are neither my allies nor my friends. The rule of five will never prevail. Power will never allow the powerful to conform."

Regardless of my questions, they would only ever speak lies. I wasn't sure why I bothered with this conversation.

'You speak thus because you have yet to grasp the essence of our ways.'

"I want to be free of you—"

'You will be,' Fivia said.

"So you believe the Etherweave will grant you life again?"

'There is no cure for death. You know that, young friend,' Carthius said, using a soothing voice to calm my accusation. 'Even the woman who controls the dead cannot grant true life again.'

"Then what do you get out of this?"

'We are your guides of wisdom.'

I paced, scouring my face with my hands, feeling my agitation bloom. "Perhaps I should take my chances and give the others time to catch up."

They had access to my thoughts, control over my transition and body. They would never let me leave. Now I was here, they would ensure I stayed, and fulfilled their longing to control the Etherweave once more.

'You burned the map,' Ineth said. 'Now they are helpless, wandering the Ashenlands, vulnerable to the creatures that inhabit this forsaken place. If not the creatures, then the Salmun, impostors in this realm, will be their downfall.'

It was all thanks to the Eone that I had burned the map. They'd worked together to exert an immense amount of influence over me, and now they portrayed my actions as though I'd made a conscious choice to destroy it.

"I know my enemy," I said, mostly as a reminder to myself of what the Eone represented. I needed no response from them. "Tressya is too smart, too powerful against the Salmun. And Osmud and Bryra will have no trouble hunting me down."

'You forget you abandoned your followers to arrive here in the nightmare's form. I think you overestimate the power of your followers' abilities to hunt,' Ovia said.

She used subtle word games to twist my head. Their inimical mind tricks were the reason I was here... except... perhaps, I should accept some blame. The pain of Tressya's rejection had me tucking my tail like a young pup and running from the shame. But the hatred poisoning my mind had been the Eone's doing.

'How long do you suppose they will last in the Ashenlands? How many times will they have to fight before they have no fight left in them?' Carthius said.

"First you tell me to ignore the burden of my friends, now you're detailing the danger they're in. What do you expect me to do?" I shouted, wanting them out of my mind, or better yet, silenced. Permanently.

'The power of the Etherweave is your only choice, Tamas,' Ineth said. 'Accept its call. We know you feel its pull. Do not turn away from it. Embrace it, and you will become the arbiter of your friends' fates and the victor in this war.'

'Ignoring our guidance because of distrust puts your friends' lives at risk,' Fivia said.

By now, I was pressing my palms to either side of my head, wishing I could squeeze their voices into silence. But this was as much guilt as it was fury.

I strode to the gaping cavity in the center of the room and peered into its depths. This close, the Etherweave's call was as painful as it was exhilarating.

'That is right, Tamas. Feel its call. Feel its power,' Carthius crooned. 'Become the Etherweave's wielder, and you become master of your fate and the fates of the seven realms.'

The sweet smell of magic wafted up on a gentle breeze from deep within. The warming sensation that began in my chest and quickly spread along my limbs replaced the humming vibration of the Etherweave's call. Slowly, it turned into a searing heat reminiscent of the Ashenlands' pit. Far from uncomfortable, it was a temptation, an invitation to be renewed in the fire of the Etherweave's power.

Unable to resist the lure of the Etherweave's call or overcome the Eone's forceful control over my body, I leaped, calling upon my Huungardred strength to land safely far below. In the cavernous room deep beneath the castle, the flecks of white in the walls and floor shimmered blue, creating the illusion of standing underwater. Stalactites hung from the ceiling like frozen spears, and a faint, ethereal glow bathed the entire chamber. On the far side, a sizable rock sat—the Etherweave's cage—veined with intricate patterns of glowing energy, woven and intertwined like liquid sapphire, pulsed with a radiant blue light—the unmistakable power of the Etherweave. The raw power contained within cast an otherworldly luminescence that danced across the cavern walls.

'Answer its call, Tamas. It has longed for this moment. Longed for you,' Ovia said.

I approached, each step feeling the flames of rejuvenation, the promise of power. Standing within arm's reach, my whole body was tremoring with its song.

'Yes, Tamas, touch the rock,' Fivia said.

My deepest wish was for the both of us to claim this together, a dream I'd harbored since the moment I bit Tressya. I knew she was worthy of the power; I could only hope to be worthy of being her mate. But it seems I've deceived her in the former and failed her in the latter.

I should have told her the truth when I first saw her again, back when I was free from the Eone's venom. I could have explained my actions and the profound bond we now shared, without the Mother or the Eone shadowing our thoughts and controlling our actions, and Tressya would have had the grace to decide for herself what path she would take.

'Do not falter,' Ovia urged.

My choices vanished as destiny unfolded before me. The Eone would not allow me to turn away; even the call of the Etherweave bound me. I was transfixed, my body like stone.

Though she was bloodborn, perhaps wielding the Etherweave was never Tressya's fate. Maybe Romelda had been right all along.

If I took it now, I would fulfill the promises I'd made to myself. I would claim the southern throne for the north, gain the power to protect those I loved from any threat, and share it all with Tressya, my bonded, as my queen. Once I have the power, I would offer my blood to her, have her mark me as hers, so she would know the Etherweave's might.

I reached out and placed my hands on the rock.

'Yes,' Fivia gasped.

A sudden surge of pure elation from the Eone overwhelmed me as the heat from the rock, along with the contained power of the Etherweave, scorched the palms of my hands. I ignored the burgeoning pain, which intensified with every breath, grunting and clenching my teeth so tightly that my jaw ached.

'What is happening?' Fivia said, her voice edged with concern.

'It has been a millennium. It will take a little longer,' Ineth said. 'Open to us,' he demanded of me.

I grunted through the pain, baring my teeth, feeling my fangs piercing deep into my bottom lip. But the Etherweave didn't come to me.

'It is not responding,' Ovia cried.

'It will. He's resisting us.' The cruel cut of Carthius' voice only made me laugh.

'Stop this.' Ovia's shout resounded through my mind. 'Try harder.'

I released my hold on the rock and stumbled backward, revealing my blistered hands for all to see. All the while, I laughed, a cruel and taunting laugh.

'You cannot stop,' Fivia cried.

"It's pointless," I said, inhaling deep to ease the pain of my burns. "Can't you see?" I held my hands up, looking at my blisters. Then I laughed again. I spun in a circle, tilting my head backward, and laughed even more. "You were wrong," I declared. The laughter was my rejuvenation; it resonated through my soul.

He knows nothing, Ovia said.

He is mad, Ineth replied.

Perhaps he is right, Carthius said.

"Your minds are a millennium old, yet you still haven't figured it out?"

Because of the map, I should've guessed it myself.

Could we have been wrong? What if he is not the one, Fivia said.

"I am the heir. But you were wrong in believing Tressya played no part."

Just as the map would only reveal its secrets with Tressya's and my shared touch, it required the two of us to draw the Etherweave forth.

CHAPTER
THIRTY-TWO

TRESSYA

There was no escape from the overwhelming intensity of the bluish light, so bright it should have scorched my eyes, yet I felt nothing. I was numb to any sensations, as if separated from my body. It made no sense—unless this was a dream. Yet the vividness of the vision and the clarity in my mind made it feel like I was actually present.

People were speaking, but light and the sudden sensation of being abruptly thrown into a dreamscape—or whatever inexplicable experience had caught me inside—disorientated me. Where were they? Who was speaking? The apostles? Osmud and Bryra? No, the voices were unfamiliar, perhaps conjured from the depths of my unconscious mind.

I took calming breaths, determined to pull myself out of sleep, but I only seemed to fall deeper. The light lost none of its intensity, but my eyes gradually adjusted, and my disorientation eased. As with any dream, I felt powerless to control my body; my eyes remained fixed on what lay before me.

The object pulsed with a bluish light in rhythm with my heartbeat. Its intensity obscured its true form, but I noticed someone standing on the other side. The man was partially visible through a mysterious fog, his figure almost transparent against the intense rays of light.

The voices were speaking again, though I couldn't discern what they were saying. Now that my mind was clear, I realized the voices were coming from within my head, a sensation similar to speaking with the Mother.

A sudden hollow laugh reverberated through my head, throwing me out of my dream. I jolted upright to find myself beside the flickering remains of our campfire. Tortilus and Plesy were a short distance away, leaning against a tree trunk, engrossed in one of their texts, illuminated by a conjured light held in Tortilus' hand. With apparently only half the enthusiasm for knowledge, the other two apostles had fallen asleep beside them, Wellard's snores punctuating the night. Osmud remained with his back to me, gazing up at the night sky, and Bryra was nowhere in sight.

"Bad dreams?" Osmud remarked without looking back, his tone more accusatory than inquisitive.

I considered my response. "Weird is a better word. Where's Bryra?"

Tortilus and Plesy glanced across at me upon realizing I was awake.

"Patrolling. She gave me strict instructions not to eat you in your sleep."

I snorted a sound that had nothing to do with humor.

"Tamas wears a scar under his heart because at one point he thought the same thing."

"We've made no progress. There's no mention so far of these Eone. But we'll keep trying," Tortilus said as his conjured light faded. His focus appeared to be solely on acquiring knowledge and enhancing his magic, making him adept at overlooking signals and coming between escalating arguments.

Ignoring Tortilus, Osmud continued. "Glad to see he found some sense, however fleeting, between being led by his cock and the Eone's possession—if he's truly possessed."

"Before he disappeared, we fought, briefly, during which I found my beast."

Osmud fell silent, then slowly turned to meet my gaze. A moment of recognition passed between us, an almost tangible emotion that transcended any petty grievances—a bond as unifying as blood. We continued to lock eyes, and I felt a sensation akin to my ribcage being peeled open, my heart exposed for his scrutiny, as if he were evaluating its worth.

"That's significant," he said, still holding my eyes.

I didn't know if he expected a reply, so I continued to hold his gaze. Then he gave a small quirk of his lips, a concessionary smile, before turning back to stare at the stars. "Timing sucks, though. It can be a disorientating feeling in the beginning. And right now, we need everyone focused."

Tortilus slammed his book closed. "I'm sorry. Did you just say you transformed into...?"

Tortilus ceased to be heard by either of us. "It was..." Words could not capture the depth of what I had felt.

Tortilus and Plesy crawled toward the fire, leaving Wellard and Selisimus to their sleep.

"That's...good. Is it not, Plesy?" Tortilus continued, avoiding my eyes, his voice far from cheerful.

"Yes...yes, it was...going to happen, given...well."

"It doesn't matter." I saved Plesy from his misery. "I think I saw Tamas in my dream."

"You did?" the two apostles said in unison.

This time, Osmud swiveled to face me. "What made it weird?"

"The voices in my head."

"Told you the early stages of transforming will disorientate you. Or, perhaps, send you insane. If you weren't that already."

Immune to people's taunts, I ignored Osmud and shifted uneasily on my makeshift bed of clothes, uncertain how to articulate my dream.

Now that I was awake, I felt sure I had not been dreaming at all. What I witnessed was real. The reason I felt out of control of my body was because I had been in someone else's head, seeing through their eyes. It was unfathomable, but I believed I had actually possessed the dead. Was that yet another shocking tear in the veil?

Should I be honest and reveal the terrible mistakes I'd made in tearing the veil between life and death? The shame bled like an open wound. I expected Osmud's judgment, but what about Bryra and the apostles? Would they blame me for everything that had happened and was yet to happen because of my selfish choices?

'Did you know about this?' I felt sure the Mother would

be privy to everything that went on in my mind while I was asleep, but she remained stubbornly silent.

"I believe the voices were real. Only the people talking were dead."

Osmud huffed as if losing interest. "Anything can happen in a dream."

"I feel sure I watched Tamas through the eyes of someone else."

"Like I said, anything can happen in a dream."

Neither Osmud nor the apostles would grasp the significance of admitting I was certain I had breached the veil and assumed the body of someone on the other side—a feat that should be impossible while awake or asleep, except if you were a spiritweaver intent on destroying the veil with your continual mistakes—or deliberate actions.

"A disturbing dream indeed," Plesy agreed. "But why do you think the people talking in your head were dead?"

"They were on the other side of the veil," I said, springing to my feet, unable to stay still as my secrets clamored for release. "As a spiritweaver, I've done things I shouldn't have. Things that I believe may have weakened the veil separating the living from the dead."

"Like raising a dead army?" Osmud said.

"I didn't know. That's not true." I clawed my hands through my knotted hair. "I knew there were consequences, but I didn't realize how bad they were. And then releasing Andriet from his death place and being unable to return him."

"Yes, that was quite a shock?" Tortilus said.

Only to be drowned by Osmud. "How has that weakened the veil?"

"The Mother tricked me. And I'm sure her possession—" Oh shit, that was one share too far.

"Whoa, the Mother what?" Osmud demanded. He lurched to his feet.

"I'm sure Tamas is with the Etherweave," I blurted out, hoping to divert everyone from my bumbling revelation.

"Mercy upon us," Plesy cried. "He's released the Etherweave."

"No." I turned away, unconsciously pressing my hand against my heart. "I'm not sure. Something doesn't feel right. If he did, I'd know. I'm sure I would."

"Can we return to the part about the Mother and the possession?" Osmud interrupted.

"So you can feel its call?" Tortilus said. Both he and Plesy had joined us in standing. With all the noise, Wellard and Selisimus had also awoken.

"The possession is more important," Osmud barked. "How much of what you say comes from your Mother's influence?"

"None."

"Is Tamas truly possessed, or are you deflecting?" Osmud paced toward me.

"No. I mean, yes, he's possessed. And no, I'm not...what does it matter?"

"Because I want to know how much of what you say we can believe."

My eyes dipped to his hands, searching for evidence that he was sprouting claws, as I was—though I could easily disregard the mild discomfort. It was Osmud's stealthy and agile movements, combined with his piercing stare, scrutinizing every aspect of me, that triggered my recently acquired instinct and ability to grow claws.

I pulled up my sleeve, shoving Tamas' mark toward Osmud. "Tamas knows me." *I'm sure he does.* "He trusts me." *I think.*

"Then why did he disappear as the nightmare, ensuring you couldn't follow him?"

"Ensuring none of us could follow him. That was the Eone's doing." Possibly. I was putting a lot of faith in Tamas' ability to fight the Eone.

He deserted us to reach the Etherweave. But he had yet to release it. The scathing laugh I'd heard in my dream was his, directed at the Eone, no doubt.

Osmud suddenly tensed, turning his head to the side, momentarily ignoring me as he froze. I held my breath, tuning into my newly sharpened senses, and heard the rapid approach of pounding feet. For a moment, my heart raced with all the possibilities, but reading Osmud's expression, I felt confident it was Bryra.

Such was her speed that she burst into our campsite moments later. "We have company," she announced.

"Two legged or worse?" Osmud said.

"Much worse," Bryra replied.

"You lot get conjuring. We want the night to glow," Osmud demanded the apostles, who, for a moment, remained paralyzed by the fire.

"What did she mean?" Selisimus turned wide, anxious

eyes to his brethren. "What's worse?" Selisimus demanded. "Is the Salmun here?"

"You heard him, Selis. They need us," Tortilus said. "Gather close. Combined, we can conjure enough light to mask the night."

Osmud stabbed a finger at me. "Stay in human form. Now is not the time to lose your head."

Bryra's gaze shifted between Osmud and me. I gave a small shake of my head, then bent to retrieve my weapons, lacking the time and energy to repeat our conversation. I was sure Bryra suspected the Mother had done something to me, and I was grateful she remained silent, rather than confronting me with her suspicions.

A prolonged, resonant cry echoed through the trees, carried by the wind. Wellard let out a shriek, but Bryra's quick reflexes caught him before he could topple backward into the campfire.

I unsheathed my daggers. "Stay where you are," I told the apostles as Bryra, Osmud and I formed a protective circle around them.

"Give me your hands," Tortilus demanded, offering a hand to Wellard and Plesy. "You know the chant," he directed each of them.

"Come on, you fuckers," Osmud breathed.

'How far will my soul voice reach?' I reached inward toward the Mother. With our combined strength, I wondered if I could reduce the minds of the Ashenlands creatures to mush. The Mother remained silent, unwilling to share her knowledge in my desperate time of need.

So be it. I would claim the knowledge for myself. With a

calming breath and a focused thought, *Aetherius* flowed through my mind like a gentle breeze. I delved deep within my soul, scouring every shadowy crevice, until I found her hiding place in the deepest recesses of my mind. There was scant time to examine the insidious spread of her spiritual tendrils, and even less to scrutinize the toxic barbs of her grip, before I pierced the barrier she had erected to fend off my intrusion. It shattered under the force of my will, engulfing my vision in white.

I was suspended, formless, adrift in a white haze like billowing fog. All sensation faded to nothingness, leaving not even the beat of my heart to anchor me in my body.

'What is this? What is happening?' But the Mother gave me no answer.

Voices echoed in my mind, guiding my consciousness towards a singular point where the fog swirled, then slowly cleared. At that moment, I felt myself settle as if finally coming back to earth.

Curses on high, I had done it again—pierced the veil to end up back with Tamas, and I'd been powerless to stop it, and at such a terrible time to be lost in my head.

Tamas wasn't present, and now my vision was clear, enabling me to see the rock—the Etherweave's tomb for a millennium—beneath the pulsing bluish light. We stood in a cavernous chamber, its walls and floor reflecting the bluish luminescence from the Etherweave's beating heart. Overhead, a chute, tunneled up from the ground, lead to the vast expanse of the starlit sky.

I thought of my presence here in terms of we, because I sensed others beside me, sensed I was one of them, forming a deep connection that spanned millennia; I was within a soul that had persisted through the ages. Had I penetrated the veil and ended up in the mind of one of the Eone?

Suddenly, a figure descended through the open cavity from above, and my heart stopped at the sight of him. Tamas landed with a grace befitting his lineage, cast a measured glance at the rock, then arched his head back, as if to ease the tension in his shoulders.

Tamas. I tried to move toward him, but it was neither my body nor my mind that could bridge the gap. With mounting horror, I realized I was powerless to reach him in my current state. He belonged to the realm of the living, while I was trapped among the dead, caught in the mind of a woman whose ancient wisdom was not immune to the infliction of greed.

I sensed it consuming her mind as she observed Tamas moving slowly around the chamber, as if the emotion were my own. Surprisingly, she was impatient, odd for a woman who had lived through a thousand lifetimes. The restlessness in her veins sparked the newly united Razohan aspect of my nature; the beast within prowled, clawing at its cage, yearning for release.

Soon, Morwen. Soon, a male voice echoed in my mind, yet I could tell it didn't belong to the spirit I had invaded.

We have waited so long, replied Morwen, the woman whose mind I was inhabiting.

This had to be the mighty Eone.

She sighed. *I can almost smell the succulent aroma of life. I can almost savor its sublime beauty.*

The divide is weakening as we speak, came another male

voice, more melodious than the first. *Our time is almost upon us.*

He waits, he paces, came a second female voice, carrying a sinister edge with a lilt as sharp as a shard of glass. *A hostage, ignorant of the forces that have awakened. And now he is their prison.*

What did she mean by 'their prison?'

A fitting finale, came the first male voice.

Tamas was the prisoner of the Eone, his mind controlled by their will, so why would this woman believe Tamas was now their prison? And if she thought of the Eone as a separate entity, whose mind had I invaded?

I watched Tamas pace, my beast mirroring his restless movements with its own unease, sensing my confinement within this woman's mind.

Tamas was the least vulnerable person I knew. His courage and force of will were equal to his formidable presence. The restrained violence emanating from each step, and the tense readiness of his muscles, eager to be unleashed, were undeniable. But for now, the predator prowled as though caught within a cage, and I couldn't help perceive what Morwen and her cohort saw; his vulnerability to the forces that waited just behind the veil.

My arms ached to touch him; my body craved to unite us, to feel the security of his embrace, the reassuring warmth of his skin against mine, to remind myself that he was mine, and I was his, that our fates as bonded surpassed any destiny of power.

My longing for him eclipsed any hunger, any primal need for survival. I needed to confess that I was ready to surrender, that I yearned for him to be mine forever, because deep in my heart, I knew I was his. I wanted no barriers, no fragility of life to snatch him away, no obstacle that could prevent me from hunting him down and bringing him back to me.

Something large and heavy knocked me sideways with a *whoosh* of my breath, wrenching me from Morwen's mind. I landed on my hip with a guttural cry. Twenty-three years of discipline and training kept my dagger gripped firm in my hands, even as my claws punched through the tips of my fingers.

A crazed fury lay along the path of my beast. Osmud was right. That was not the answer to this fight. I resisted the longing to transform and instead swiped upward, slicing the creature in two, raining its blood down over me.

Having just been yanked from someone's mind, I felt momentarily disoriented as I sprang to my feet. I searched for Osmud and Bryra but found the apostles, who had formed a circle. Eerie screeches tore through the night, yet the apostles did not disrupt their chanting, busy conjuring a bright light swelling between them.

I dashed forward on seeing a shadowy creature flutter down from a nearby tree. A winged beast was a formidable target. And this one had a tail, forked with barbs that curled back on themselves like antlers. It swiveled its bat-like head back and forth, as if deciding its first target, then it spread its wings and took flight toward us. Intercepting its flight path, I severed its head, then dodged away to miss being felled by its body.

The night was alive with chaos. Death manifested in

countless forms. One apostle shrieked, but I disregarded his fear and lunged forward, confronting the sudden swarm of the Salmun's winged creations. In the budding blaze of the apostles' conjured light, I saw the striated veins wrapping like vines around their forelegs, the sharp angles of their protruding ribs, their elongated fangs, and the depths of their hollow eyes.

And I cut through them all until their body parts littered the ground at my feet. A snarl rumbled deep in my throat, and I wiped a drip of saliva on the back of my hand, realizing my fangs had punched through my gums.

"Tressya," Tortilus cried.

But I was already in motion, driven by my beast's primal instincts. My muscles tightened, primed for battle, prepared for the next approaching horde. They scuttled across the ground like spiders, with countless long legs, bulbous bodies, and small, venomous mouths.

My mind and body were in perfect harmony, feeling an added strength in the way I wielded my daggers and gracefully evaded attacks. My weapons extended beyond my daggers; they were in my reflexes, my speed, my skill, and even my enhanced senses that pierced the night, ensuring no enemy could remain concealed in the shadows. I decimated the horde, soaking my clothes in their blood, which leeched a stench of vomit and rotten fish.

A shadowy shape took flight from the trees and spiraled overhead. I watched, determining its height, its speed and the trajectory of its path. Then I threw one of my daggers, the steel blade glinting in the apostles' weak light.

The creature emitted a shrill screech when the blade

pierced its chest. Its flight became erratic, then faltered, before its wings folded and it plummeted from the sky.

Driven by an instinct I couldn't describe, I raced over to where it landed. It was a few body lengths longer than me, with leathery wings covered in thick black veins. Its snout was long, its mouth lined with nasty teeth to match its claws, protruding from scaled feet.

I crouched beside it, understanding the urge that drove me to do this. During the Ashenlands war, the Razohan had proven these foul creature's souls were for the taking, and as a Razohan, this soul was mine. I was positive at some point, assuming its form would be lifesaving, much as Tamas had saved my life by taking the form of the nightmare.

I placed my hand over its heart, instantly plunged into a labyrinth of darkness, flung along winding pathways with disorienting speed.

I was no stranger to invading another's body in the hunt for their soul word, and recently, their minds, but this was a dizzy array of confusing thought patterns that made no sense and were driven primarily by instincts alone.

Again, an inscrutable knowing told me to abandon its mind and to delve far deeper in search of its soul. It was like being flung into the ocean while still dressed in all my clothes. I was weightless and floundering, with no heartbeat to use as an anchor to keep me from spiraling into the unknown. The quest for its soul was a totally different experience to searching for soul voice, and I suddenly feared that I would fail with no way of knowing how to free myself.

Time became immeasurable. The landscape upon which I was flung was like an impenetrable forest. Visions churned through my head, then played out before my eyes in repetitive patterns. I wasn't sure if I should dismiss this invasion or if it led the way to the secret gem I was hunting for.

Suddenly, a light flared ahead, piercing through the darkened forest of the creature's inner life, the only marker I had found since daring this audacious feat. I focused all my energy on reaching it, but it was like battling the currents in the merciless sea.

The struggle was in my mind; none of my newfound physical strength could aid me here, only my strength of will.

"Tressya!" came Osmud's powerful cry.

My battle against the creature's inner forces wavered. Was he issuing a warning? Yet I needed to reach the light ahead. Before the voice, I had been gaining ground, but now the currents felt like arms around my body, pulling me away.

Claws punched through the tips of my fingers, fangs sliced through my gums. They alone were powerless against this mental struggle, but the sting steadied my concentration and reminded me of my purpose, of what was mine.

"Tressya!" Osmud sounded no closer, but there was a desperate edge to his voice. Definitely a warning.

I gritted my teeth and surged forward. In my mind's eye, I saw my hands reach out, claws poised to claim my prize, then I felt a drop of wetness on the back of my neck, followed by a trickle running down to my nape.

Osmud's cry had been a warning all right. Another of the Salmun's creatures reared behind me. No doubt ready to strike while I remained lost in the mind of my prey.

Come on! I mentally kicked at the barrier I felt, while

prickles sliced across my back, caused by the very much alive creature that had snuck up behind me, taking advantage of my distraction in chasing this soul.

This was all for nought if I lost my head. But dammit, I wanted this winged creature's soul.

Back me up, Osmud.

Brute force wasn't the answer. My success lay with *discipline*, the best of the six pillars, my calming breaths and *Aetherius*.

Aetherius burst forth, slamming through the barrier, plummeting me into the light as the hot breath of the creature behind me came warm across my nape.

Releasing my mental hold, I spun, striking out with my clawed hand, punching through the beast's chest and fisting my hand around its heart. At that exact moment, a dagger pierced its flesh, narrowly missing my hand.

"Fuck, Tressya," Osmud growled. "I nearly took your hand."

"Next time, have a little more faith."

Osmud kicked the creature off his dagger, and its heart came away in my fist. He glanced down at the still beating heart, oozing black blood from between my fingers, and grumbled. "Are you going to waste valuable time taking its soul as well?"

"One will do for now."

To my surprise, he flashed me a smirk. "I think I'm understanding what Tamas sees in you. But we're not done yet." Then he disappeared from my side and into the fray.

****

TAMAS

I crawled my way forward, using my claws as anchors to help me progress across the floor. Through sheer force of will, I managed a few more paces; still not enough, underscoring how little control I truly possessed.

"This is madness. You know I spoke the truth," I yelled, but my fury was futile. The Eone was unmoved by my threats, then pleas. "The Etherweave will never release without Tressya." Not for the first time I'd stated the truth, nor would it be the last.

Upon my failure to release the Etherweave, they expressed disbelief and horror before vanishing into silence. I naively thought they had retreated to sulk, but the moment I attempted to return to Tressya, they bound my body in an ironclad hold, resisting my attempts to transform.

I tried to take on the form of the nightmare, but the Eone had buried that aspect deep within my mind, compelling me to turn to my beastly nature. Yet, even that part of me remained confined behind a mental barrier, too formidable for me to shatter completely. I unleashed my claws, only to find the Eone exerting an overwhelming influence over my limbs. They even dared to attempt control over my thoughts and decisions once more, but my rage became a potent tool in shielding that part of my mind from their vile demands.

Despite my efforts, I remained powerless. Crossing even a short distance across the floor required immense effort. I felt as though I was trapped in rapidly setting clay, my mind seething against the formidable forces binding me—a Razohan's worst nightmare. Too often in recent months, I had found myself at the mercy of magic. Despite the promises I had made to myself, I couldn't prevent myself from falling victim to magic's grip.

Once I control the Etherweave. It was a poisonous thought I dared not voice, lest the Eone discover it. Yet, it simmered within me, mingling with my rage, which was scorching me like fire.

I collapsed forward onto my chest, exhaustion sinking into my limbs at having fought against my chains for as long as I had. I rolled onto my back, staring up at the night sky. "You'll lose your chance with your precious Etherweave if you let her die."

There must be another way. Finally Ovia spoke, consulting the other three, perhaps forgetting I was privy to their mental exchanges.

I lay silent and waited.

And if there is not? Ineth said.

She cannot be involved, Carthius said.

Most definitely. They have already claimed her as theirs in this war. How could this have happened? How did we fail?

Fear not, dearest Fivia, Carthius said. *We will prevail. They are not yet here.*

But it is so close. You must feel it, Fivia said. *I cannot be forever bound to this cage,* she lamented.

We are the Eone, Ineth declared, as though that alone guaranteed their triumph. *We cannot be stopped.*

But he is weak, Ovia said, which had to be regarding me.

Perhaps we chose the wrong one, Carthius said.

"Now that's interesting," I added. Instantly, they receded from my mind. "Don't go," I crooned. "I want to know more about who *they* are. And the fact you are referring to me as your cage. That is very interesting."

Silence.

I entwined my fingers and rested them on my chest. "Fine. I'll just lay on my back, staring up at the night sky, and wait for you to get chatty again."

They remained quiet.

"I may be weak and useless, but I sense the fear in you. Something is about to happen you didn't foresee and it frightens you. The mighty Eone. And now you have to face the very real possibility you may actually lose."

A millennium we have waited, Ovia said. *It is not possible.*

Ovia had retreated to mentally communicating with her companions, but I replied. "It's highly likely. In fact, you'll fail because your plan depends on me. If you want me off this floor, you'll have to grant me control over my body. And you know exactly what will happen once you do that."

'You are nothing more than our instrument,' Carthius said.

"True, but one that will hinder your manipulation. With every breath, I'll resist you, and Fivia there seems to believe you're in quite a hurry. I'm just not convinced you'll succeed."

'What if he is right?' I smiled on hearing the unease in Ovia's question.

'He is taunting us,' Ineth snapped.

"Am I? Then why do I sense this brewing anxiousness? It's not coming from me, I can tell you that."

'Do not let his provocations upset you,' Carthius said.

"Grant me one opportunity to aid my friends, and then

I'll attempt it once more." Twice the Eone and I tried to raise the Etherweave. Twice we'd failed.

'You yourself told us what you would do if we were to release you from our binds,' Fivia said.

I raised my arms, pleased to see I could easily place my hands behind my head. "I'll just make myself comfortable, shall I? Oh, and not to upset you, but Tressya will be here soon. I hate to say it, but you really did choose the wrong person between the two of us. She's far more capable. I'm sure she would find a way to raise the Etherweave all by herself."

My remark was met with silence.

CHAPTER
THIRTY-THREE

TRESSYA

Stinking filth, blood, guts and twitching bodies covered the ground, none of them human. How many creatures, I couldn't tell, but they littered our small campfire space like dark wells of tar.

"We need to move," Bryra said, her voice calm as ever, betraying no hint of the havoc she had just wreaked. "Being offspring of the Salmun, I'm sure our nemesis is somewhere close."

"If we had a little more time to—" Tortilus began.

"Get walking or we leave you behind," Osmud ordered.

I shook my head slightly when Tortilus looked to me for support, signaling I agreed with both Bryra and Osmud before stooping to retrieve my pack.

"I'll return this one to your pack," Plesy offered Tortilus, who snatched the book away from Plesy's hand as he clumsily slipped on his pack strap, then marched off after Osmud.

"Here." Selisimus offered me the last of the meat from the meal they'd prepared while Tamas and I were at the lake. "Apologies for how meager it is. You ate little when you returned to the fire, and I thought..."

"Thank you, Selisimus. Given our circumstances, this is a meal for a king."

I ripped off a piece of the cooked meat, which had now gone cold. However, within minutes of swallowing it, I surprised myself by spitting it out onto the ground, feeling as though the rest of the scant contents of my stomach would soon follow.

Selisimus and Wellard, who'd moved in beside him, jerked away. "Oh dear. Was something wrong with the meat?" Selisimus said.

"No, it was fine," I mumbled, pressing a hand to my stomach. The soul of the Ashenlands creature felt like a bellyful of unsettled food. "I have something else inside that's not sitting well with me." I resumed walking, ignoring both Bryra's frown and Osmud's smug expression. They both knew exactly what was happening, and I was sure Osmud was fighting the urge to say 'I told you so.'

I covered my nose with my hand, finding the acrid smell of day's old sweat like rancid meat.

"Excuse me," Wellard interjected. The last thing I was in the mood for was conversation. "This...er...This might be forward, but what were you doing when you crouched beside that creature?"

"Trying to prove something to myself."

"Did you succeed?"

I looked ahead at Osmud's back, then I dared turn my focus inward and felt the feral strain of the creature's soul, untethered and wild within. It clearly didn't like cooked meat.

'You have invited disaster by taking on this soul,' the Mother suddenly spoke.

'Now you want to be chatty.'

'And you expect me to share my space with such a creature?'

'My mind, my space. I decide what fills it.'

I turned my face to Wellard. "To answer your question. Yes, I succeeded."

'It will drive you insane,' the Mother continued.

'No more than you.'

'You can't control something that has no notion of logic. There's a reason spiritweaving is restricted to creatures capable of intelligent thought.'

'Tamas can. So too Osmud and the rest of the Razohan who joined the war in the Ashenlands.'

'People bred and raised with the knowledge of their heritage, taught from infancy on how to master their ability.'

"Don't you dare lecture me on—" I glanced across to Wellard, releasing I spoke aloud, then to everyone else, who were now staring at me. Oops. "Ignore me."

"Say hi to the old bitch from me," Osmud said over his shoulder.

"She's berating me for squeezing the creature's soul in alongside hers."

"You what?" Wellard said. "I'm sorry, but I'm struggling to keep up with everything that's going on."

"The severe old woman we met on the path now possesses Tressya," Tortilus said, forgetting his book for one moment. How he walked, conjure his dismal light and read the book was a feat in determination.

"Yes, yes, I understood that, but the rest is..." Wellard shrugged.

"If you were to ask me, which I know you're not, I'd say you were an idiot for what you did," Osmud remarked. Sarcasm, taunts, and advice I neither asked for nor cared to hear were the help Osmud offered me. "You can strip souls, but not the knowledge of how to care for them or use them. That takes practice under strict guidance. And something as untamed as an Ashenlands beast, I can tell you from experience they're no house pet. Savage things are hard to contain and even harder to control. Don't poke it. Let the soul simmer. It should quieten over time. And don't whatever you do dare think to assume its form. That will be your undoing. You're not strong enough to wrestle control."

'I'm loathed to admit I agree with the beast.'

"The Mother agrees with you. But she also thinks you're little better than the creature whose soul I've taken."

Osmud laughed. "Bring it on old crone."

The Mother's presence disappeared from my mind, leaving me alone with the restless prowling of an unshackled soul desirous to tear itself free from the bounds of its ethereal cage. Perhaps I was foolish in taking its soul when I was so new to taking on my Razohan heritage.

"As a Huungardred, I have no experience in such matters.

Our beasts are all we possess. There is no difference, even if our forms may say otherwise. But I've witnessed enough young Razohan learning their ability for the first time. And it can be a disorientating process. Please listen to Osmud. We don't need to lose the only other person who can guide us." Bryra hesitated a moment. "We also don't want to lose you."

While my enhanced vision didn't allow me to see everything as if it were daylight, I could at least make out her smile—a genuine offering of peace—in the darkness on the human side of her face. I was right in including Bryra on our quest; She was not only a valuable member but also, I believed, a friend, which was significant for me since I saw enemies more readily than friends. She'd chosen her own path, shifting her loyalty, something I understood all too well.

"I've some knowledge of such things, sadly not enough, but if I've understood correctly—" Wellard continued.

"I don't have a direction here," Osmud yelled from the head of our party.

Neither did I, just the agitated soul of a beast and the dull, faint throbs of a tune that somewhat resembled the beat of my heart. I could only imagine this was the Etherweave, though it offered me no real sense of direction.

Yet, everyone relied on me, just as I was relying on Tamas.

Okay, beast. Yes, Osmud had advised against provoking it. However, something as formidable as the nightmare couldn't roam the Ashenlands unnoticed by other winged creatures that inhabit the forest. Perhaps this new untamed soul would provide some clue where the nightmare had headed. And I was not as hopeless as everyone would believe in connecting with other souls.

The creature's soul seemed to be everywhere inside my thoughts, spreading like noxious creeper. As any wild animal locked in a cage, it felt as though the soul paced and prowled. It was impossible to get a sense of its thoughts or emotions, but an anxious need to take to the sky overwhelmed me. Osmud was perhaps right in saying it was best I didn't provoke the damn thing, but circumstances proved otherwise.

Given how readily it pervaded me, it didn't take me long to enter the creature's soul mind. Once again, I was thrust into a bewildering maze of twisting mental passages that lacked any apparent order or logic, driven by primal urges that nearly drove me to madness with their intensity, but through it all I caught glimpses into memories of the creature in flight and what lay before it.

"Tressya?" came Selisimus's questioning voice, and I realized I'd stopped and was pressing my palms to the side of my head as though trying to hold it together.

"What did I say?" Osmud snarled, yanking my hands from my head. I opened my eyes to meet Osmud's piercing glare. He was leaning down, his face so close that his eyes dominated my vision. His fury was unmistakable, even without Razohan sight.

"It's on the top of a mountain," I blurted out.

Osmud blinked, then straightened. "That's helpful." Spoken with sarcasm, as usual. "And you learned that from...?"

I tilted my chin, staring up at him. "It's not as hard as you make it out to be." And pressed my lips together to prevent myself from throwing up over him. Flight was disorienting, even when it was only a memory, and my feet remained firmly on the ground; perhaps that's what made it feel worse.

"Looks like I underestimated you."

"That's a common mistake."

He huffed a short laugh. "Did you get the direction of this mountain while you were poking around in its memories?"

"You wrenched me back before I could."

He gave an exaggerated bow. "Apologies, Your Majesty, I thought I was saving your life, or at the very least, your sanity."

"Did you get anything else helpful?" Bryra interrupted.

"It's a mountainous region. But the mountain we're after soars above the rest. There's a ruin at the top, perhaps a castle. I couldn't make it out. But I'm sure that's where Tamas headed." And I had a name for the Ashenlands creature. Pathfinder, for giving me the way to Tamas.

"I think I have something," Tortilus shouted, almost dropping his book. "Here, Plesy, look at this. I'm keen for a second opinion." He handed it across to Plesy, holding his conjured light over the page and jabbing his finger at the place he wanted Plesy to read.

"I wasn't sure what you were looking for, but I wasn't expecting this," Plesy said.

"You heard Tressya. This is important, perhaps the most important aspect of our current predicament."

"What have you found?" Wellard left me, moving across to join the other two, Selisimus doing likewise.

"A way to this mountain, I hope," Osmud grumbled.

"One of our predecessors has helpfully written a translation in the margins," Plesy replied. "Though it's difficult to read while on the move."

"I found it in The Opus of Verdantus," Tortilus said.

"What?" I crossed to the apostles, our current predicament forgotten because Verdantus was in the far realms, the Levenian's birth place. Avaloria, Gusselan's home, was a kingdom within Verdantus. "How is it you have something from Verdantus?"

"It's not an original. The Opus of Verdantus is a copy, meticulously transcribed. It contains some of Verdantus' lore and spell-craft. I know all this because it's written in the ancient tongue of Tarragona, not Verdantus. I found the book buried under dust. Quite a coincidence I picked it up, but I'm sure it's rarely been seen, certainly not in the last century or so, that's for sure. Translating it would be simple for me, given our extensive studies of the ancient tongue of Tarragona, if someone hadn't already scrawled the translation into the margin." Tortilus glanced at Wellard. "Though your studies are a bit lacking, aren't they?"

"What does it say?" I said.

"Telling me we need to find a mountain isn't helping," Osmud snapped. "So, focus on finding us a direct path to the Etherweave. And you lot, shut the fuck up about your bloody ancient books."

"But...I believe this is—" Tortilus continued.

"End of conversation," Osmud snapped.

"It's about the veil," Tortilus added.

Osmud fisted a palm, then looked at me. "Don't you fucking dare. Forget about it."

"I believe Tortilus is right in saying this is significant."

Osmud strode toward me. "The Salmun arriving any minute is significant. That Tamas is quite possibly about to release the Etherweave when he's not of sane mind and currently possessed by …whatever you called them. That is significant," he shouted. "I'm fighting for my brother. Who are you fighting for?"

"Everyone," I replied.

He pursed his lips, giving me a glare so sharp I was sure his claws and fangs would inflict only half as much damage. The ensuring silence hung over us like a leaden cloud while the air between us felt so brittle it would snap if anyone spoke.

Finally, he relented, ducking his head as he exhaled sharply.

"Can I speak?" Tortilus said.

"No," Osmud barked. "Yes," I said, our replies overlapping.

"It says here, the Aeternals and the Eone were never truly destroyed during the war for the Etherweave," Tortilus said, reading from the translation. "It's said their souls still linger while the Etherweave survives, but are imprisoned behind the veil that separates the living from the dead."

"The Divines," I whispered.

"Excuse me?" Plesy said.

I shook my head. "It's something Gusselan mentioned."

"It doesn't say much more, only that the veil must never falter."

Plesy leaned over the book, shifting Tortilus's hand away. "Otherwise the Aeternals and the Eone will walk the realms once more."

"I presume these two factions are a grave threat for such a warning," Wellard said.

"If they're not truly dead, how are they possessing Tamas?" Bryra said.

"Powerful magic," was my reply. "That's whose mind I'd entered."

"Begging your pardon, Tressya," Tortilus said. "We don't understand you."

"In my dream—only I guess it wasn't—I thought perhaps I'd entered the mind of one of the Eone."

"The dead whose eyes you believed you were looking through?" Plesy added, as if needing to clarify.

"Only it wasn't the Eone. It was the Aeternals. A woman called Morwen."

"How are you so sure?" Selisimus said.

"Because she said Tamas was now their prison. She had to be referring to the Eone. They're the ones who possessed Tamas, but this Morwen believes the Eone are imprisoned within Tamas, leaving the Aeternals free to take the Etherweave."

"I'm confused. Aren't you and Tamas the heirs to the Etherweave?" Wellard said.

"Tamas said the Eone created the Etherweave. But he learned that from the Eone, and they likely lied. Perhaps it was the Aeternals who were the real creators. Maybe that's why they believe they will succeed." I slapped my hands on my sides. "I don't know. I'm guessing here."

"Or maybe both the Eone and the Aeternals created it, and that's why neither died during this war the Opus of Verdantus mentions."

"Yes, Plesy, sound thinking," Tortilus said. "Both parties grew greedy, each wanting to control the Etherweave for themselves, and that is why the war began. And since both factions were equally powerful, none could defeat the other. Instead, they ended up caging themselves behind the veil."

"But now the Eone have mistakenly imprisoned themselves within Tamas when they possessed him, leaving the Aeternals the victors," Selisimus added.

"But the Etherweave is this side of the veil, and Aeternals are on the other side. How do they plan on winning?" Wellard said.

"The veil is weakening, and I'm certain they sense it. It may only be a matter of time before it falls." All eyes turned to me, but no one said a word, not even Osmud, who usually delighted in pointing out my failings. They had every right to accuse me, to shout and blame me, because it was my fault the veil might fall. But the Mother had also played me.

"So...you..." Plesy stammered. "Did you say that you entered the mind of one of the Aeternals? Like possessed them?"

I stared at him.

"Which means you crossed the veil." Tortilus caught hold of Plesy's meaning.

"Has that weakened the veil more so?" I heard the fear in Wellard's voice.

"That's also powerful magic." Tortilus's voice was full of awe.

I shook my head. "Not magic. I'm a spiritweaver…" A spiritweaver normally couldn't cross the veil. That's not what spiritweavers did. But how could I be sure, knowing so little about the craft?

'On your own, you don't have the strength to cross the veil,' the Mother added.

'And with our combined will, I do? Is that what you're going to tell me?'

"What happens to Tamas if the veil falls?" Osmud said.

I shook my head, unable to handle speaking with Osmud and the Mother simultaneously. "I have to reach him," I mumbled, half conscious of the words I spoke.

Osmud threw up his hands. "Finally, you're talking sense. If you would give us a definitive direction…"

'You possessed me to gain access not only to the Etherweave but also to the other side of the veil?'

'Stupid girl, why would I do that?'

"I can't," I murmured, focusing more on the cryptic words of the Mother, then giving Osmud a straightforward answer.

"Tressya? Are you all right?" Bryra said.

"Yes. The Mother is bothering me." I pressed my hands to my temples.

'Tell me the truth,' I insisted.

'The veil will fall. It is inevitable. That fate was prophesied even before King Ricaud died, over a millennium ago.' I could almost feel her rolling her eyes at my naivety. 'You needed to learn what you were up against. The Aeternals are right. You can forget the Razohan beast; he's at the mercy of the Eone. The Aeternals are your true nemesis. You had to learn as much, and that's why I forced your mind to reach across the veil while you were vulnerable in sleep, and again when you pathetically tried to force your way inside my head.'

'You did that?'

'Do not think I'm powerless as a mere spirit. But listen to me: you must reach the Etherweave before the Aeternals do. You know where to go and how to get there, faster than on foot. This means leaving this pitiable band of misfits behind.'

"Tressya, I'm sorry, but we should get moving." Bryra's voice came through in the echo of the Mother's words.

"Yes." I nodded.

There had to be another way to reach the Etherweave and Tamas without abandoning my friends, but how long did we have before the veil fell, releasing the Aeternals?

The Mother was referring to the untamed, stolen soul of the winged Ashenlands beast. She wanted me to assume its form and leave my friends. I would reach the mountain in no time, but that would mean leaving my friends vulnerable, and I couldn't take that risk. Still, I couldn't stop my attention from shifting inward, curious about the wild and savage soul tearing through my mind.

Someone seized my wrist in a cruel hold. "Not that way," came the fierce snarl.

I opened my eyes and stared into Osmud's barbarous glare. "Do that and you're no help to Tamas. It will consume you, Tressya." I wrenched my grip from him. "Trust me. I know. I've got plenty of souls inside of me, but that damn Ashenlands beast I took on during the war hasn't given me a moment's peace. And I've been doing this for a lot longer than you. Searching through memories is an ale house trick. You think you understand how to tame souls. Sorry, lassie, you don't know a thing."

I pressed my hand to my forehead, squeezing my eyes closed. "But there's nothing there," I spat in agitation, feeling no call from the Etherweave. "There's nothing."

The ground beneath me trembled as the night became illuminated with a display of brilliantly lit energy the likes of which I had never witnessed before.

"We're trapped," Wellard cried. "This is our end."

The Salmun had arrived.

This confrontation was unavoidable. No amount of haste could have forestalled it. "Let me deal with them. The rest of you stand behind me."

I faced the direction of their approach and waited. Enacting the Mother's ability in soul voice, combining it with my soul word, I should be able to deal with their advance easily enough. Though it was surprising how boldly and noisily they approached through the forest, sending out energy streaks to announce their arrival, given how decisively I had defeated them in our last encounter. Or perhaps there was a reason they didn't bother with stealth.

'Powerful adversaries are rarely fooled a second time,' the Mother said.

I glanced over my shoulder at the apostles, huddling together. Tortilus was rummaging through Selisimus' pack, allowing prized volumes to drop to the ground. "How about you guys come up with some magic of your own?"

"My thoughts entirely," Tortilus replied, his head half buried in Selisimus' pack.

"What's concerning you?" Bryra came up beside me.

"Twice I've tricked them. I doubt they'll be that easily fooled a third time. Your speed will be beneficial." I included Osmud in my glance. "Take to the trees now, before they arrive. Hunt them from behind. But don't take unnecessary risks."

Bryra nodded and then vanished, transforming into her magnificent beast form just before she disappeared from sight. Osmud lingered for a moment longer, giving me a wink, before he too disappeared.

I turned to the apostles, now gathered around a book. "You don't have long to come up with something useful," I warned.

"Are you sure?" Wellard addressed Tortilus, peering down at the pages of the book, while Plesy provided the meager light for them to read by.

"You heard Tressya. This is the best I can come up with."

"You're right. We have no time to scour every volume," Plesy said.

"Right," Tortilus announced. "Everyone sure of the words?"

The other three nodded.

"Mind the second stanza. At least one word gets caught on the tongue." He turned to me and elaborated. "It all must be said correctly for this to work."

"I believe you. Just do it," I said.

"Right, Brethren. We're needed. Time to prove our worth." And he held out his hands to Selisimus and Plesy, who distinguished his conjured light by a wave of his hand.

Whatever they intended to do was bound to fail. I felt

guilty for having so little faith in their abilities, but so far, all they had managed was to conjure light, which served only as an extra signal to the Salmun of our location.

I turned back to face our oncoming enemy and tried to shut out the apostles' chanting. Driven by my raging pulse, the untamed soul residing within lashed and swirled, interfering with my concentration to harness Aetherius.

'Contain the creature or control your mind,' the Mother snapped. 'I can't help you otherwise. It's like scooping sand with a loosely woven net.'

'I'm trying.'

The pathfinder's feral instincts were too addictive to ignore. I gritted my teeth, allowing my claws to pierce through the tips of my fingers and embed into the soft flesh of my fisted hands, hoping the pain would liberate me from the pathfinder's overwhelming desires.

A shimmering haze appeared before my eyes, and the sweet taste of magic danced on the back of my tongue, turning sour as I swallowed it.

"It's working," Wellard shouted.

"Concentrate," Tortilus admonished him.

I glanced behind me to see the shimmering haze encasing the five of us like a protective shield, reminiscent of the Salmun's magic on the night of the northerners' attack. The hue cast a soft glow around us. Hopefully, their shield wouldn't act like a candle flame, attracting all the creatures of the Ashenlands. The apostles were observing their handiwork with obvious amazement while keeping their rhythmic chanting.

I squinted through the darkness, but the Salmun kept

themselves out of sight, not making a sound. It would be foolish to think they were acting cautiously because of me. Had they fanned out to surround us?

A sudden cry of agony preceded a burst of light. I had a second to think of Osmud and Bryra when the Salmun's ferocious attack slammed into the shield. Wellard let out a cry and stumbled backward, losing contact with Selisimus and Plesy. A stark white light rippled over the shield like ants consuming a carcass, causing it to vibrate. In places, the shield flared a bright green upon contact with the Salmun's retaliatory magic before settling back to its dull glow.

"You fool," Tortilus hissed at Wellard. "Take his hand."

"Wellard," Plesy grumbled, leaning over to snatch Wellard's hand back.

Cracks, like spider's web, appeared in their shield.

"Hurry," Tortilus barked.

"We can't hold it," Wellard groaned, as if he had felt the Salmun's attack on a personal level.

"Don't be so feeble," Tortilus admonished him. "Tressya is relying on us."

No sooner had he uttered his determination, the Salmun hit with yet more force. This time causing the shield to bow and buckle. Wellard fell to his knees with a cry, while Selisimus growled through gritted teeth, resolved to hang on as best he could.

Somewhere off to our right, another piercing cry rent the air. Was that thanks to Bryra or Osmud?

Wellard was right. Two attacks and the apostles were already suffering. I inhaled deep and forced the breath out in a long, slow growl. Aetherius appeared ever so willing to do my bidding. And latched on to its power was the pathfinder, thinking it had found a way out. Its unhinged mind and predatory needs made it a heavy burden to drag forth and manipulate, and my soul word turned into an unmanageable force, infecting my mind with savage yearnings and monstrous ideas.

'Discipline,' the Mother shouted. 'You've lost control of your soul word. You'll lose control of the beast as well.'

I clutched my head and staggered backward, my claws digging through my scalp until blood trickled down into my eyes. I was only dimly aware of the third Salmun attack. Someone wailed, but it sounded too far away for me to care.

An agony unlike any I'd ever felt before wracked my body as I began shifting. This was the second time I had transformed, both times outside of my control.

'Fight for control,' the Mother commanded. Aetherius, my soul word responded, spurred by the power of the Mother's soul voice echoing in my head. But it was already too late. Her soul voice glanced off the armor that was the pathfinder's mental chaos, as it surged forth in my mind, diminishing my ability to wield my soul word. Quickly, the Mother's presence faded into the depths of my consciousness as the pathfinder's soul mind became my own.

Curses, I wasn't transforming into the Razohan beast, but something perhaps far more deadly.

My claws transformed into talons as sharp as blades, my arms extended into large wings covered in thick hide, and my torso twisted into a grotesque form with bowed hindquarters, an arched spine, and a protruding ribcage. I screamed through the torment as bones cracked and reshaped, my facial features elongated, and piercing teeth cut through my gums. Enduring such torture seemed impossible, yet I knew I would. This was the true gift of the Razohan, the power of shapeshifting, and I was determined to master it. All I needed was to maintain my sanity and resist being swept away by the pathfinder's savage whims once I became its form.

Briefly, I heard a shout and a name I recognized as my own before I succumbed to the urge to arch my head back and release a shrill screech. Overwhelmed by the desire to take flight, I spread my wings, but at the last moment, I resisted the impulse to soar into the sky, for I would surely be lost.

Suddenly, an uncanny noise rippled through the air, a deep resonant vibration that irritated my ears and reverberated down to my bones. I shook my large head, as if trying to dispel the sound, then noticed the clarity of my surroundings. At first, I attributed it to the pathfinder's enhanced vision, until I realized that the apostle's shield had vanished.

The Salmun had destroyed it.

CHAPTER
THIRTY-FOUR

TRESSYA

As fast as they diminished the apostles' conjured shield, shrill cries erupted from deeper within the forest. Cries of alarm swiftly silenced. Then a stark flash of gleaming white arced through the trees like lightning, illuminating the deep forest from within. It revealed the silhouette of the Salmun, spreading like a fan before us, and more of their vile creations. Some we had faced before, while others deformed creatures that likely once inhabited these lands before the Salmun created the Ashenlands.

I hoped I could thank Osmud and Bryra for the resultant cries of alarm, the fading gurgle of horror drenched in pain preceding the abrupt silence.

The pathfinder tilted its head to the side, watching impassively, seemingly indifferent to the Salmun, its master.

Though it was their creation, I felt no urge from the beast to join them in this fight. I could sense its feral nature, the wildness of its mind, which made me wonder if the Salmun would have to exert some force to bend it to their will, as they likely did for all the creatures that fought for them. Would Osmud and Bryra's attacks distract them from maintaining their mental control of their pets?

While wearing the pathfinder's skin, I couldn't instruct the apostles to disappear into the trees for shelter while we dealt with the Salmun, but perhaps there was nowhere safe now the horde could not follow.

The clamor of surprise and the howls of aggression stirred the pathfinder's craving for conflict. Sensing a straightforward conquest, it battled against my dwindling restraint, menacing to overtake my mental lucidity.

Assuming the pathfinder's body, I found myself beyond the Mother's assistance, with the battle to maintain sanity depleting my reserves. Gradually, fragments of my reasoning and portions of my memories faded, while the desire for freedom blossomed within me. Although, as a disciple, succumbing to forces greater than myself was unforgivable, the notion held a certain allure.

"Restrict your attack." Orphus rose his voice over the tumult. "We want her alive."

I struggled with the pathfinder, wanting to turn its head toward his voice, somewhere off to my left, but the creature wasn't interested in hunting down the prelate.

Hearing his voice and discerning his intention, I surrendered my last tenuous hold on my mental fortitude, permitting the pathfinder to rise and spread its vast wings. With two powerful beats, it soared above the tree line, trailed by a singular stream of brilliant white light marking its ascent. Concealed by the treetops, it narrowly avoided the initial Salmun attack. The magical energy passed close enough for me to feel its heat as it *whooshed* along its leathery body, scorching the treetops and casting a bright beam into the night sky, reminiscent of a solitary ray of sunlight.

Unwilling to leave a fight, the pathfinder continued to circle overhead, while moving further out of reach of any dangerous strikes. Cocking its head side-on, it peered through the canopy, using its supreme eyesight to watch for movement down below. Even the fragmentary glimpses through the dense canopy were enough for the creature to determine its prey's position. With no directive from the Salmun, the urge to hunt emerged from the pathfinder's primal instincts. And it seemed to see anything moving as prey.

Suddenly, a mental command pierced my focus, as incomprehensible as our soul word, but equally shattering to logic and free will. Orphus was trying to take command of the pathfinder. Without thought, *Aetherius* rose like armor, shielding both of us from the mental attack. The pathfinder shook its head and flared its wings, seeming to recover from Orphus' brief mental stab. I had little control over the pathfinder's mind, but at least *Aetherius* seemed powerful enough to keep Orphus out.

The Salmun had dispersed among the trees, their aggressive energy acting as a trail of blood to a predatory creature, and the pathfinder was primed for its feast.

THE RELUCTANT QUEEN

Once again, Orphus tried to assume control of my winged beast, but *Aetherius* stayed strong, and his commanding word and mental jab was nothing more than mere shouts and tickles.

Regrettably, the pathfinder was as drawn to the multitude of creatures accompanying the Salmun as it was to the taste of human flesh, even while I exerted my utmost effort to steer its appetite towards the Salmun.

Finally, it spied an opening between the canopy, a slim gap in which to strike. It plunged, folding its wings, shearing the branches away as it pitched downward, jaws agape and plucking one of the smaller creatures from a lower branch, biting the thing in half with one snap of its jaws. Not exactly the attack I'd hoped for, but in the chaos below it seemed none had noticed the pathfinder's approach, nor its vicious attack.

To navigate this situation, I tried to avoid contemplating the intricate connections between myself and the pathfinder, particularly whether, as a shapeshifter, it was truly I who tore the creature in half and consumed it. The only hint of emotion I felt for this action was a slight churning in my stomach; beyond that, there was hardly anything. This made me question how close I was to completely succumbing to the pathfinder's desires. That I could think independently must mean that my will was strong enough to resist being entirely consumed.

Orphus' voice rang out nearby, commanding his kin to set the trees ablaze. He seemed to have surrendered his fight to gain control of the pathfinder, instead deciding to either drive it out or eliminate the protective canopy, which meant the beast had to take to the sky, but the pathfinder dismissed my mental nudge. I became more forceful, calling on *Aetherius* to aid me, but soul voice had no power over animals, causing the pathfinder to simply shake its head as if ridding itself of an annoying insect buzzing around its ears.

A burst of white energy streaked through the trees on either side, miraculously skimming past the pathfinder's hiding spot. The leaves erupted in a blaze of fire, the heat uncomfortably intense against its leathery skin. I felt its instinct to screech in rage as if it were my own, but I attempted to suppress the sound, aware that it would reveal the beast's location.

Yet again, my quest for control proved futile as the pathfinder let out a high-pitched screech and launched itself from the branch, resolved to ascend through the flames toward freedom.

Suddenly, a cry from below heralded a forceful pull on its feet, as if bound by a magical tether as searing as a branding iron. The pathfinder issued another deafening screech while it frantically beat its wings in a bid for liberation. Despite its efforts, it was powerless to rise, only maintaining its current height.

The fury swelling within me was as much my own as it was the pathfinder's, but I was the one with the intelligence to devise a plan. This meant I had to impose my will on the creature, or we would both be doomed to the mercy of the Salmun.

Orphus would not win.

The Mother was correct in seeing me as a failure, because

of my blind adherence to her strict discipline, believing following the Sistern's training and her stringent guidance was my only way to success. If only I'd realized sooner the flaw in this belief. She was also accurate in saying I'd placed myself in Tamas' shadow, following his lead, despite being a bloodborn myself and an heir to the Bone Throne.

Now I am wiser. I must have faith in myself.

It's time you became my pet. I was new to my Razohan gift, but that didn't mean I was incapable of performing remarkable feats, which meant I had to embrace our unity and accept that, for now, I was indeed the pathfinder.

I could feel the burden of its wings as they strained to beat against the constraining magic, gradually drawing us toward the forest floor. I focused intently on the forceful rhythm of its heart and the arduous effort of its wings, determined to dissolve the mental barrier that separated us. Its soul was mine. Its body was mine. I was the pathfinder.

Regrettably, its exhaustion became mine to endure as well. Both my instincts and those of the pathfinder warned me that once on the ground, Orphus would ensnare us, restrain our wings, clamp our jaws with their blade-sharp teeth shut, and rip our talons from their beds, rendering us as helpless as an infant.

The pathfinder wanted to fight this trap. All it could see was the night sky, its home, and freedom. Yet I was smart enough to know struggling against the current of the Salmun's magic, which pulled us down like a rushing river, sapped our strength. We had only one opportunity. I had to act decisively, swiftly if we were to win.

Go with me, please.

It didn't work. I attempted to impose my will, urging it to turn and dive rather than attempt to escape. It resisted, but I clung to its instinct to flee, following it deep into the darkest corners of its mind, where all its primal instincts resided. I didn't coax. I unleashed a storm of rage, charging through its instinctual emotions, imprinting my own, the sheer force of my will, and the depth of my desire to prevail.

A brief flash of light flickered at the edge of my vision. I spared a moment to turn my large head toward the source of the light, catching another fleeting streak of dull, yellowish light arcing toward the Salmun below.

"Deal with them," Orphus hissed from directly beneath us. It was his magic that had ensnared us.

And it was the apostles, with their modest conjuring, who had dared to disrupt Orphus as he brought us down. The timing of their attack was perfect, even if their magic proved a pitiful attempt against the retaliatory attack of the remaining Salmun.

Seeing Orphus distracted, I wrenched the pathfinder's last resistance to my plan asunder, then tucked my wings and pitched us downward. We plummeted, aiming straight for our foe, while the apostles harried with more attacks from the cover of trees, stealing Orphus' attention for the precious seconds we needed. His magical binds remained tight, but the roaring of the fire as it set the forest ablaze obscured any sound of our rapid descent.

Perhaps it was some survival instinct on his behalf, but at the last, Orphus turned toward us. He threw out his arms, and I felt the terrible bind, once caught around our ankles, shift to ensnare our whole body.

He caught us, freezing us like ice mere seconds from taking his head. I thought to try and stretch our neck forward enough to snap at his face, but the bind felt impossible to break.

For a brief, crucial moment, I lost control of my emotions, and a fury like no other eclipsed my sanity, plunging me back into the dark morass of the pathfinder's instinctual desires. We struggled helplessly against our invisible prison, draining the last of our strength, while a desperate voice inside my mind insisted this was not the end.

For a few more seconds, we fought, gasping in heavy breaths, as Orphus slowly lowered us further to the forest floor. Finally, I regained control and settled us within the cradle of Orphus' magic. This was not a surrender but a recuperation before the final onslaught.

"I have misjudged you, Your Majesty," Orphus crooned. "In a great many ways. I feel it's only fair to warn you that your mental manipulations will no longer be effective. We have fortified our minds against such invasions."

The freeze on our body meant we couldn't even release a screech in opposition.

"I accept responsibility for allowing you to progress this far. I've been too lenient. The Salmun have grown arrogant and complacent, having dealt with weak and ineffective heirs and faced no significant challenges to our supremacy for centuries.

"Your bold persistence, strategic machinations, and

acuity have truly set you apart as a formidable adversary. Under different circumstances, I might have considered you a friend. However, our cause is too critical for such sentimentality. As the bearer of the Etherweave, you cannot remain untethered from the Salmun.

"The time of the Etherweave is upon us. The ritual must commence immediately. It is imperative we prevent the northern beast from assuming his role. And although it is regrettable that you have embraced your heritage, this issue is not insurmountable. Once you're bound to the Salmun, your shapeshifting abilities may prove to be of significant value to us, once we've stripped you of the Etherweave."

His long-winded speech revealed how little he had learned despite acknowledging the Salmun's complacency. He continued to harbor the belief in their inevitable victory, displaying a blatant disregard for his adversaries. He remained unaware of Tamas' whereabouts, indifferent to the chaos unleashed by Osmud and Bryra, and completely oblivious to the existence of the Aeternals and the Eone—a fact that worked to our advantage.

Gradually, he turned me over, forcing me to look up at the stars as he slowly lowered me to the ground. In this position, I would be lying on my wings, a potentially painful position that could hinder my escape. It was then I noticed the transparent shield cast by the remaining Salmun, enveloping us in a shimmering dome that offered protection from external threats. This explained his apparent indifference towards Osmud and Bryra, as well as the apostles.

"Come," he announced once I was lying on the forest floor. "We have no time to delay."

I noticed movement in my periphery, the Salmun drawing nearer, a scant number compared to what I'm sure had initially embarked on this pursuit through the Ashenlands. I owed thanks to Osmud and Bryra for thinning their numbers, but they'd played their part and were now confined outside the shield. It was time for me to save myself.

An eerie chill filled me with dread as a familiar low vibratory chant rang through my ears and the tingle of magic crept across my leathery skin.

Orphus leaned in close, so his breath tickled my cheek. "I'm going to need you a human for this to work, but I doubt you'll be obliging. I give you this moment to save yourself the pain you'll force us to inflict if you stay in this form."

As a Razohan, I had my improved speed, vicious claws and sharp fangs, but as the pathfinder I had many formidable weapons and a means of escape.

Orphus crouched beside us, subtly revealing the small dagger in his hands before locking eyes with us. The pathfinder perceived this as a direct threat and attempted to resume its struggles, to no avail. The magical binds remained unyielding. Thus, I focused on pacifying the creature's frantic urges and calming its struggles, a task that was far from easy. Eventually, I subdued its instincts, compelling it to lie passively in the grip of the Salmun's magic, staring up into Orphus' eyes.

The fierce burn of hatred ignited my determination to win.

"Perhaps you don't understand me. I discern no spark of intelligence in your gaze. What a pity. I had hoped to afford you some dignity, but it appears as though that won't be possible."

He stood. "Only her blood will do."

Their chants faltered.

"I must strip her of this form before we proceed."

Could he actually accomplish that, or was this simply another display of Salmun arrogance? I lacked sufficient knowledge about the Razohan shapeshifters' abilities to understand how deeply a new soul integrated into my body once consumed. I was certain Orphus was equally uninformed. My limited understanding of the Salmun's magic was also a problem, coupled with the unsettling certainty that Orphus would have little regard for the state of my sanity should he successfully extract the pathfinder's soul from within me.

Once again crouching beside me, he placed a cold hand over my chest. The bind of his magic was like being smothered in thick fur, oppressively hot, yet his hand felt like ice against my leathery skin. Within seconds of starting his low murmuring, it was as though spikes grew from the palm of his hand, piercing into my body.

Sensing the threat, the pathfinder's fierce longing for freedom resurfaced, and tethered to its instinct emerged an essence heavier than any primal urge, more potent than any emotion: the Mother's spirit. Bound, the pathfinder and the Mother were both ensnared by the mystical embrace created by Orphus' chant.

Having forced our connection, the Mother remained a perpetual outsider within my mind, yet the Razohan's ability to merge souls made losing the pathfinder a violation on my soul. The sensation was comparable to Orphus tearing my body apart and savagely attacking my heart.

My screams were sealed within my mind thanks to the Salmun's paralyzing magic as the pathfinder and the Mother were slowly ripped from my body. Along my back, the spike of sticks on the forest floor now digging into my soft human skin told me I was losing the pathfinder's form.

I couldn't let him do this; I couldn't let him prevail.

Aetherius was in my mind like a fast blowing wind. I lashed out with my soul word, searching for unity with the power of the Mother's soul voice. Such was the infinity with both, I found what I was looking for as though her soul voice had been searching for *Aetherius* for all this time.

Merging the two forces, I surged along the pathway he'd created by his magic and the touch of his hand on my body, following an ethereal tunnel, guiding me to my target. With all his concentration intent on removing the pathfinder's soul from my body, I found his mind vulnerable to the Mother's and my combined attack. So sudden was the force of our will, we sent him tumbling backward.

The link now severed, the Mother's spirit and the pathfinder's soul returned to reside within me. Without hesitation, I assumed the pathfinder's form once more and shifted sideways, freeing a wing.

Orphus was scrambling to sit. With a powerful beat of our liberated wing, we launched across the short distance to him in a blink before he could right himself, pinning him to the ground with our talons, ensuring they pierced his skin.

He shouted another incomprehensible word, some indescribable magic to bring us down, but he'd yet to finish the word when we tore his head from his shoulders.

Shouts erupted simultaneously with the collapse of the protective shield. Gazing at the brilliance of the stars twinkling above, I finally granted the pathfinder its freedom. We spat out the vile remnants of Orphus and soared into the sky.

Ascending higher, we soared above the blazing tree line, continuing our ascent, while the cries of the dying resumed behind us.

Below, the ravenous flames carved a path across the ground, while ahead, the stars illuminated a route into the distance. Rising above the dark canopy in the distance was a towering mountain peak. Our destination.

For a breath, I resisted the pathfinder's desire to disappear into the sky. If we continued, we would leave my friends behind in the Ashenlands with no guide.

One moment. That's all I needed to tell them which direction to head, but the pathfinder increased its wing beats, determined to leave the fire and the Salmun far behind.

Mentally I was too exhausted to fight the pathfinder's strong instinctual desire and in the end succumbed, trusting Osmud and Bryra would eliminate the remaining Salmun and ensure the apostles' safety. And if Osmud could see through his fury toward me for abandoning them, he might remember I mentioned a mountain and that he could possess a winged creature's soul if he so desired and guide the rest of them to us. We were already too high, the blazing forest growing distant, so I turned my thoughts to Tamas and the ominous prophecy in the Opus of Verdantus.

The pathfinder seemed as eager to reach the distant

mountain as I was, for we kept a straight path. Much smaller and lighter than the nightmare, our body was built for speed. One lazy sweep of our wings was all we needed to move swiftly through the night sky, diminishing the distance.

As we flew tiny sparkling lights flittered before our eyes like miniature stars falling from the sky. I'd never seen such a mystical sight, and unfortunately, while I remained the pathfinder, I was unable to ask the Mother what she thought of it all. Perhaps it was something common to the Ashenlands.

We continued to fly through the curtain of miniature stars, nearing our destination, when something heavy fell from above, sending us tumbling through the air and fast losing height.

The pathfinder released a shrill cry, spiraling downward toward the trees on the side of the mountain. *No!* I screamed to no avail. We had to reach the ruin, not descend into the forest far below. I tried to resist our downward spiral, but a much larger creature hit us from the right. Pain lanced our side as the brutal impact sent us tumbling once more, flailing our wings to no avail.

Just before we crashed through the canopy, the enormous jaws of our attacker clamped around one wing, sharp teeth tearing the leathery membrane. The wing tore and shredded in the fierce beast's grip, miraculously releasing us from its hold, but with one wing severely wounded, we couldn't continue flying.

Spiked branches peeled pack our skin as we broke through the canopy, snapping branches too small to arrest our fall. And by the time I hit the ground, the impact somewhat softened by the thick bed of creeper, I was crying in agony, having lost the pathfinder's form.

I curled into a ball, gritting my teeth and breathing through the intense pain that pulsed in rhythm with my heartbeat. Although it wasn't me who'd lost a wing, the agony felt just as profound. Each slight movement stretched the torn skin on my back taut, widening my wounds. I could only bite my inner cheek to stifle my cries and endure the relentless torment.

I took a deep, calming breath, embracing the pain, letting it surge through my body with the ferocity of a mallet driving a peg, using it to narrow my focus. Gradually, I shifted myself into a sitting position, matching each soothing breath with the sharp stabs of agony.

The forest's gloom enveloped me like a heavy shroud, close and suffocating. Far above, the stars glimmered through the dense canopy, their faint light like a candle flame in the dark, beckoning me to continue my ascent. I strained to recall how far the pathfinder had tumbled down the mountainside before crashing through the treetops as the attack had been swift, leaving only hazy memories.

Suddenly, the mysterious, miniature stars I had spotted high in the sky cascaded around me like a falling stars. Their soft glow chased away the shadows, providing just enough light for me to discern a path up the mountain. I'd spent one night in the Ashenlands during the trial, and I didn't remember seeing these tiny lights, though I was likely far from where the trials took place.

'Can you add some insight?' I prodded the Mother.

Silence ensued. It seemed likely the Salmun's attack had

left her reeling, or perhaps something even more dire had occurred. I was grateful for what her spirit presence had given me, knowing only too well it was our combined effort that won me my freedom from Orphus. However, in my current condition, I had neither the capacity to dwell on this nor time to waste pondering the Mother's silence.

Leaning on a fallen tree for support, I gradually rose to my feet and caught my breath. After a few moments of rest, I pushed away from the trunk of the tree and began my ascent, bathed in the glowing miniature starlight, which felt warm to the touch.

The relentless pain of my wounds made the climb excruciatingly slow, but as long as I focused on the path ahead and not the distance remaining, I knew I would make it. That was until I heard the noise of something crashing through the forest toward me from up high. I dreaded seeing whatever foul creature was stampeding toward me, but knew from the vibration under my feet and the sounds of snapping branches, it had to be large and heavy.

I quickened my pace, enduring the searing agony, and reached the base of a large tree, thinking to use it as shelter. Suddenly, a black shape rushed past at a speed too swift for me to see what it was and vanished down the mountain, leaving me stunned by how easily it moved through the seemingly impenetrable forest with such speed. But at least whatever it was no longer blocked my path to the mountaintop. However, I was likely to encounter more of its kind or worst beasts before I reached the top of the mountain.

The glittering falling starlight was becoming a nuisance, reminiscent of ashes from a fire, impaired my night vision and heated my skin where they landed. I brushed the shimmering flecks from my face, then glanced up to see I was standing under a dense canopy. Strangely, this offered no protection from the relentless fall of the tiny star-like specks.

I rested my shoulder against the tree, catching my breath once more, as I listened to the branches creak and the occasional eerie sounds drifting down the mountainside from creatures I preferred not to encounter. My beast was the only weapon I had for defense. Provoked by the Mother and misled into perceiving Tamas as a genuine threat, she'd come to me easily. But now, I didn't feel her at all; she was as silent as the Mother, yet Tamas had always relied on his beast to heal himself, and as a Razohan, I supposedly could do the same.

Whatever was falling from the sky was a distraction. I needed my beast's energy and healing to get me to the top of the mountain.

Aetherius awaited me, yet it was not my soul word I sought. The Mother's spirit remained elusive, which suited me fine since her presence was unnecessary. I kept my awareness hovering over the pathfinder's souls, hesitant to delve back in, but there was no sign of my beast.

A screech sounded alarmingly close. Opening my eyes, I saw the shadowy form of something large sweep across the canopy, obscuring the stars as it soared overhead after if sensing my presence. I had lingered in one spot for too long.

Wincing at the pain, I left the shelter of the canopy and hastened upwards, seeking refuge in the dense undergrowth and tightly packed trees while the continual presence of winged shapes passed overhead, driving me into deeper cover.

When something plunged into the branches above, I bit my bottom lip to suppress my cries and pushed onward, allowing no time to soothe the pain. Instead, I used it to sharpen my attention to my escape. Each step sent stabs of pain into my back, but after enduring enough of them, the throbbing became easier to ignore.

Another creature was rapidly making its way through the trees further down the mountainside, swiftly closing in on my position. I glimpsed its dark form as it leaped across a gap in the trees, breaking branches in its path, and yet another winged creature obscured the stars overhead, yet the glittering snowflakes remained every present.

I ran my thumb across the tips of my fingers, feeling nothing but fingernails. Next I searched for fangs along my gums, but they too remained hidden.

"I really need you now," I muttered before dashing upward to the next tree.

I vaulted over fallen debris, then doubled back, taking a moment to snap a decent length of branch free, sizing it up as a makeshift weapon. Although not as effective as a sword, it would suffice in its absence.

"Come on then," I breathed, feeling much better with some form of weapon in my hands.

By now I could smell their stench, decay and death, coming from everywhere I turned my head. Was I being herded?

"If that's the way you want to play." I inspected the branch and decided it wasn't sharp enough for my liking, so I spared myself precious moments fashioning the end into something resembling a spear. Once that was done, I continued ever upward.

My pace was smoother now I'd made friends with the pain, and I focused on moving with as much silence as I could muster, paying attention to the noises surrounding me. The creatures didn't bother to obscure their own movements, making it easier to track them. At least one was coming up behind me, and two were lumbering across the top of the canopy, rustling leaves and breaking branches under their weight.

Two choices lay before me. Either I continued up the mountainside on foot, wasting valuable time and risking attracting the attention of more deadly creatures, or I caught a ride. I took a second to decide, hoping my beast was on my side.

Upon reaching the next tree, I snapped off a branch similar in thickness to the one I already wielded and quickly fashioned it into a makeshift spear suitable for piercing leathery hide. Feeling more assured with weapons in hand, I continued on my way. Next, I made my way toward a pocket of clearing to my left, where starlight, unobstructed by the canopy, bathed the uneven terrain in a silvery glow.

I dashed across to the clearing, indifferent to the noise I made, intent on drawing my pursuers with me. Focus, timing, and precision were crucial, yet the damn tiny flecks of light proved to be an immense distraction. I was certain their numbers had multiplied since I first observed them cascading from above. By now, they were irritating my skin upon contact, leaving sensations akin to minor burns across my cheeks and the backs of my hands. Thanks to my Razohan sight, I navigated the clearing without succumbing to the debris and undergrowth and burst into the open space.

As I tried to look up, flecks of glittering light assaulted my eyes. For a brief instant, a fleeting vision captivated me, leaving me breathless with in its brilliance, though I questioned my perception. But when I blinked, it disappeared. I was left with the unshakable belief that I had seen faces gazing down at me.

Reeling from what I thought I saw, I almost missed the first attack. The creature burst from the canopy, similar in form to the creature who'd shredded our wings, swooping down with its impressively long beak as it sped across the clearing.

I was already off balance as I thrust my stake forward, staggering backward to keep my footing, my eyes irritated by the veil of tiny starlights.

Both of us failed to connect, the creature ascending into the night sky, while I fumbled to regain my balance amid the debris-strewn forest floor.

I spun around at the sound of a deafening screech and the beating of heavy wings, catching sight of a dark shadow diving from above.

You're mine. Another, looking the same as the first, or perhaps it was the first; it was all happening in rapid succession. The burning in my eyes was too distracting. I readied my branch, shielding my eyes with one arm as best I could while tracking its swift descent, timing the release of my makeshift spear.

A large, robust creature burst from the forest, unleashing

a raucous yowl as it charged toward me. On thick, muscular legs, it pounded across the ground, head lowered to expose its armored skull I would never succeed piercing with my stake.

The tiny starry lights had turned into a hazy blanket of white across my vision, so, instead, I tracked its raging approach through the vibrations beneath my feet, locating its exact direction. I dodged, thankful for the extra strength of my beast aiding my evasion, as I drove my makeshift stake down with a powerful blow, embedding it deep in the creature's massive side. Then, just as quickly, I ducked low as the sound of heavy wingbeats approached overhead. I felt the rush of air across my scalp as the winged creature struck, missing me by a hair's breadth.

The ground-dwelling creature was enormous, heavy, and cumbersome, making it an easy target for someone who could swiftly evade. However, I had only one makeshift spear remaining, which I'd hoped to use on the winged creature above.

I gave the bullock-like beast no opportunity to maneuver, as it became entangled in the underbrush and tore through the creepers. Seizing the moment, I struck again, targeting what I presumed to be its heart, and swiftly retrieved my other spear while the opportunity presented itself. Simultaneously, I kept a portion of my focus on the winged creature overhead, tracking its imminent return.

These Ashenlands creatures were incredibly resilient. My stabs seemed to do little more than enrage the beast before me, while I could sense the winged creature preparing to strike from behind.

I inhaled deep to steady myself, focusing mainly on the creature swooping down from behind, while waiting for the stomping, yowling beast to disentangle its legs.

The hairs on my neck prickled as the attacker from behind approached, and finally, the bull-like creature freed itself, then clumsily turned to charge at me. My muscles tensed, ready to dodge, but timing was crucial.

The ground dweller's advance was too sluggish for my plan. Perhaps this wouldn't work. I tightened my grip on both stakes, then, at the last, discarded one to improve my power and aim with the other.

I dove sideways at the last, half-turning as I did, and with Razohan strength, thrust upward, driving my stake through its heart as it extended its large, sharp beak to impale the bull-like creature through its eye.

The creature above thrashed its wings in a futile effort to break free, but my aim was accurate, and within moments, it plummeted to the ground. Using my Razohan speed, I avoided being trapped beneath its falling body.

I lunged forward as its massive body hit the ground, placing my hand near the wound I had inflicted. In less than a moment, darkness engulfed in me, leaving me disoriented, tumbling endlessly without a sense of direction. Having captured a soul once before, I was determined to do so again. All the while, I remained acutely aware of the sounds of my enemies drawing closer, even while trapped in a spinning, endless maze that scrambled my thoughts.

I felt as if I were suspended in time, adrift in an unfathomable abyss, gripped by the mounting fear that I might fail and be trapped within the creature's soul forever.

Discipline. I had to succeed. There was no alternative.

At last, I triumphed, seizing its soul in my hands and merging it with my own, allowing my form to dissolve and open myself to transformation. The agony of transformation was no less intense the second time, but it served as a salve, alleviating my fear of failure.

Once the transformation was complete, I unfurled my new wings and soared into the sky, allowing the creature to lead the way, for I knew precisely where it would head.

CHAPTER
THIRTY-FIVE

TRESSYA

It was a mental battle I was determined to win. I sensed its hesitation to enter the ruined castle, interpreting it as fear, yet that was precisely where I needed to go. This creature's mind was like a fortress. Unlike the pathfinder, I found no way to penetrate it. Even its basic instincts seemed locked away, as if in an iron cage.

Circling above, I surveyed the ruins of the castle, observing the desolate hall and passageways that spread like a labyrinth below. There was no visible movement, but I was certain Tamas was there, just as I was certain I would find the Etherweave buried deep within.

I had to get inside.

The creature's tough, leathery skin seemed impervious to the burning sensation of the tiny falling starlight, which appeared to have intensified, once again lighting the night. It was as if I were peering through a veil.

Sweet mercy. The realization set my heart pounding to be free of my chest. I had to enter the castle. I had to find Tamas. Yet, despite my persistent urging, the creature refused to yield and obey my commands. There was only one thing for me to do.

Don't abandon me, I pleaded with my beast. This was madness. It had to work. I refused to look down and gauge the distance I would fall as I released my grip on the winged creature. My transformation wasn't immediate. My mind slowly retracted, as if hesitant to let go, but soon I lost my wings and felt the wind rushing up my the legs of my pants as I free-fell toward the castle.

Help me. I plummeted toward the ground.

Damn. This would not end well. The fall was brief; I had little time to think of Tamas or regret all the things I hadn't done when I felt the excruciating pain of transformation and my beast burst forth in time for me to pass through into the interior of the castle. I gritted my teeth in anticipation of the impact, positioning myself to land on my feet and bracing for whatever pain would arise. When I hit on all four legs, I bit my bottom lip as the jar reverberated up my spine.

She came through for me in the end. Eventually, I would learn to summon her at will, but for now, at least she didn't seem intent on letting me perish.

I gazed up at the stars, observing the leisurely patrol of the creatures above the castle, before turning my attention to my surroundings. I found myself in a vast hall, half of its walls missing, as if some colossal hand had reached in and scooped out a portion of the interior.

Magic permeated the air, causing the fur along my back to bristle with a tingling sensation. It infused the atmosphere with a sweetness reminiscent of syrup, followed by a sharp aftertaste that singed the inside of my sensitive nose. The air was suffused with its flavor and a resonating tune that pulsed in harmony with my heartbeat. All I had to do was follow its call.

As I made my way down the hall, my transformation from beast back to human became complete. In my human form, I became acutely aware of the cold. The crisp night air, made even chillier by the gusting wind that seeped inside through the numerous rooms that had lost their outer walls, crept under my clothes. The castle walls offered scant protection against the fierce winds lashing the mountaintop.

The howling wind and my footsteps were the only sounds to accompany me as I ventured deeper into the castle, along with the constant presence of the glittering raindrops. By now, I had grown accustomed to the burning sensation they left on my skin in their wake.

Following an unseen path, guided through my kinship with the Razohan and my ancient link to the last king to sit on the Bone Throne, I ended up standing on the edge of a great cavity in the heart of the castle. I peered down into its depths, inhaling the thickening syrup of magic.

"Tamas," I called down into the cavity.

A burning ember landed on the back of my neck. I swiped at it to find nothing and turned to look up at the night sky while shielding my eyes from the glittering raindrops.

"Will you gut me if I touch you?" came Tamas' voice from behind me.

I slowly turned, allowing the deep resonance of his voice to guide me. For the longest breath, we stared at each other as if the two of us understood the fragility of this moment.

Although his absence was brief, it felt as though an eternity had passed since we last touched. Seeing him now, I couldn't contain my desire, my needs, or the raw power of my instincts. I leaped into his embrace, wrapping my arms around his waist and pressing my cheek to his chest, relishing the sound of his strong, forceful, and vital heartbeat, so reflective of his essence. In that moment, with the solidity of his body against mine, I felt as though we'd already triumphed. I knew I shouldn't disregard the consequences of my poor decisions over the last few months, but right now, it was all about us, about Tamas. I realized I didn't want to let him go, and that we were never rivals; we were always meant to be life mates.

"I take that as a no," he murmured against my lips.

"Neither of us are to blame," I added, before sinking into the familiarity of his kiss. After enduring the trials of the past few hours, this truly felt like coming home, even though the greatest threat still loomed ahead. I squeezed my eyes shut, pushing that thought away. Just for this moment, I allowed myself one more fantasy where the two of us were safe and nothing could come between us.

He pulled back, staring deeply into my eyes, drinking in my gaze, then my face, before returning to my eyes once more. He looked like a man who had finally discovered the wonder of life, humbled by its awe. "You found your beast." His words sounded laced with pride.

"She healed me." My body was pain free.

"Shit. You were hurt?" There was no mistaking the sudden alarm in his voice.

"It's nothing. And she wasn't the only thing I found."

He quirked an eyebrow.

"A lot has happened in your absence, even though the night has yet to pass."

As we stayed wrapped in each other's embrace, the castle and Etherweave receded from my thoughts. Not even the burning sparks of the glittering tiny stars falling around us like rain could distract me. Even though only a few hours had elapsed since Tamas took flight into the night, being together made time seem irrelevant. It felt as if we had always been by each other's side. The force of our destinies conspired to keep us apart, yet here we were, in each other's arms. Perhaps this was our true fate.

The Sistern meticulously orchestrated my existence through the manipulation of countless generations, all to set the stage for the Mother's ultimate plan to seize the Bone Throne. Her most significant accomplishment, unbeknownst to her and the generations of women who led the Sistern before her, was in uniting Tamas and me by ensuring my birth and arranging my marriage into the Tannard line.

The Mother underestimated the Razohan. She likely assumed King Henricus and the Salmun would kill him and could never have foreseen the bond that would form between us. Under her tutelage, she likely believed my heart to be as cold as hers and never imagined I would fall in love with my enemy.

"How are the others?" Tamas said.

"Orphus is dead."

He looked momentarily stunned. "You've been busy."

"I left Bryra and Osmud with the apostles and made my way here. I feel certain they will find this place."

"Sometimes it takes years for young Razohan to learn the ways of their beast."

"I didn't arrive on foot."

His brow furrowed.

"I had to learn fast. And it seems I'm a natural. I'll give thanks to the Mother for all her harsh discipline."

"What're you saying?"

"I took the soul of an Ashenlands beast. A winged one at that. Two, in fact. The pathfinder and I had problems getting here, so I had to take the soul of another to finish the journey."

Tamas set me back, holding my arms firm as he stared at me in open wonder.

"That you made it here is beyond words. To master the soul of another can take months. The fact you tamed the mind of a creature from the Ashenlands in…hours or less is beyond words. You truly are remarkable."

"Osmud mentioned all of that as well. Yet here I am."

He chuckled. "I'm genuinely in awe of you, Tressya. I vowed never to underestimate you again, yet here I am, once more humbled by the myriad of ways you've demonstrated your prowess. This is undeniably your destiny, far more than it is mine. From childhood, I was prepared for this fate, while you were kept ignorant, only to later battle fiercely to reach this point. There is no one more deserving of the Bone Throne than you."

"That's not true. I've made so many wrong decisions—"

Tamas silenced me with a gentle touch, pressing a finger to my lips, his eyes conveying a firm refusal.

I pulled his hand away, my voice earnest. "Don't idealize me. I'll only end up disappointing you."

"That's impossible," he countered softly.

"I'm just as flawed as anyone else. I've made countless mistakes."

He cupped my face tenderly in his hands, his gaze holding mine. "We all have. But what truly defines you is how you rise from those mistakes."

"I knew there were consequences to disturbing the dead, yet I didn't stop. Even once I understood the depth of those consequences, I still couldn't find the courage to send Andriet away."

"He was a very special friend, and something tells me you've had so few of those in your life." He traced a gentle line along my cheeks with his thumbs, his gaze as tender and compassionate as his words.

"Stop being so understanding."

"Why are you so intent on making me hate you?"

I lowered my head, pressing my face against his chest, reluctant to utter the inevitable. "I'm not. I want to feel like this forever."

He stroked my back gently. "Feel like what?"

"Like you'll always have faith in me."

He tilted my chin up with his finger, compelling me to

look into his eyes. "I wish I could make you understand that I always will."

"I've disturbed the balance between the living and the dead with everything I've done." Tamas knew what I'd done, but he had yet to understand the consequences. I'd been hesitant to reveal the true scope of my deeds, yet was determined to remove any obstacles between us, any hidden truths that might lead him to judge me, diminish his opinion of me, or erode his trust in me. If that was to be the consequence, I needed to face it now.

"From the way you said that, I assume it's not good news."

I relaxed my grip on him, creating a slight space between us. "I suppose you don't see the glittering rain."

He furrowed his brow in confusion.

"It's everywhere around us, and that you don't see it tells me it's all my fault. It's the consequence of everything I've done—raising the dead, freeing Andriet. The veil is thinning." I extended my hand, letting the shimmering specks of light gather in my palm until they flickered out, leaving behind a sensation akin to tiny burns from floating embers.

"The thinning veil is the least of our problems."

I shook my head. "If the veil diminishes all together, it will release things that are never meant to be released." I stepped away from him.

"The Eone?"

"No. Not them. On possessing you, I believe they've trapped themselves inside of you. Perhaps they didn't realize that at the start, or they were impatient to push you to the

Etherweave or..." I shrugged. "I can't imagine what they were thinking."

He forked his hands through his hair. "Let's slow this down for a moment. First, how do you know this?"

"The Eone has kept many secrets from you and made mistakes. I guess they must understand that by now and that's why they made you flee to the Etherweave."

"You haven't told me how you know this?"

"It's convoluted and connected to my skills as a spiritweaver, possibly influenced by the Mother's possession and her own deep connection with soul voice. I was able to..." I pressed my fingertips to my temple, searching for the right words. "I saw you here in this place. I saw your hand resting on the rock."

"You were in my head?"

"No, not yours. I was on the other side of the veil." I squeezed my eyes shut, giving my head a slight shake, as if to organize my thoughts. "That's how fragile the veil has become."

I glanced around us. The Aeternals were likely watching us at this moment, but the falling starlight was a now curtain I couldn't penetrate.

Tamas turned from me and paced away from the gaping hole in the floor and continued to pace, deep in thought. "That's why they're in such a hurry."

"The Eone?"

"Yes. They know the veil is falling, and they want to take the Etherweave before it does." Suddenly, he was upon me, seizing my arms in a fierce grip. "It takes the two of us to release the Etherweave."

"That's why you didn't release it."

He backed away and confused me by laughing. "It couldn't be anymore ironic."

"How?"

"The Eone possessed me after you raised the dead and freed Andriet from the Ashenlands, having anticipated the ensuing destruction of the veil." He rubbed his brow. "I've been fighting against their control for what seems an eternity now. They've only just relented. It's been punishing." He dropped his arm to his side. "They must have possessed me, hoping to use me to release the Etherweave prematurely, before..." He glanced at me. "Before whoever has chosen you as their own is released from the other side." His eyes widened as if he'd finally solved a puzzle.

"You're not making sense."

"It's something the Eone said. 'They have already claimed her as theirs in this war.' They were Carthius' exact words." He narrowed his eyes, staring directly into mine. "You're not possessed by anyone other than the Mother by chance?"

I straightened. "No." Then blinked. "It was the other way around...like I possessed her for a brief time when I looked through her eyes."

"Who's eyes?"

"Morwen's. I thought at first she was one of the Eone. But she's one of the Aeternals; the Eone's greatest enemy. They were the ones who claimed you were now the Eone's prison. I heard their conversation while in Morwen's mind. And I'm guessing Carthius is one of the Eone."

"Yes," he replied, chewing on a nail. "The Eone already

let it slip I'm their cage, a fact I think they hated revealing to me. But this means there are two powerful entities we have to worry about?"

"The Aeternals will return once the veil falls. As rivals to the Eone, they must be extremely powerful, which means we don't want their return."

"The Etherweave is our only hope," Tamas said.

I grabbed his arm. "Wait. As powerful and ancient as they are, surely the Eone wouldn't be foolish enough to trap themselves within you. Perhaps they believe once they possess the Etherweave, they'll have a means to free themselves from you. The Mother said you were lost to them, and I thought she meant the Eone had overpowered your free will. What if she actually meant they would destroy you once they freed themselves from their mental link with you?"

"We've no choice."

"There must be another way."

"This veil. How close is it to collapsing?"

"I don't know." I looked skyward. "It's getting worse." I held out my hands. "It's all around us. It's like we're standing under a waterfall of tiny stars. I can only imagine it's the very fabric of the veil disintegrating."

"Whatever we decide, we'll have to face powerful magic." Tamas' eyes blazed with a ruthless determination I had never witnessed before. He took a step toward me. "We seize the Etherweave and we fight. I've sworn too many times in recent months that I would never fall victim to another again. Time and again, that vow has been broken because the wrong people wield too much power. I refuse to let us and those we love suffer for the greed of others. With the Etherweave, we make it a fair fight."

"We might take on more than we can handle."

"We're left with no choice, Tressya. We either let fate consume us completely or we take control of it ourselves."

Tamas held out his hand. "Are you ready for this?"

I took his hand, staring up into his eyes. "For better or worse, this will change us forever."

"Our lives were irrevocably transformed from the moment we met. Countless forces have attempted to pit us against each other, but they never succeeded. They failed because they never grasped the truth about us."

"And what is that truth?"

"That our ultimate destiny has always been to be together."

"This will bind us," I said.

He gave me a slow smile, turning my hand over to expose my wrist. "I'm already bound."

I gazed at his lips, yearning to close my eyes and kiss him, allow the feeling of his lips pressed against mine to steal me away from the impending moment we hurtled toward.

"In the lake...before we..." Fought.

"Yes. It's exactly what I was going to do. I'd decided to offer my blood to you before I arrived back in Tolum. It was unfair that I had the advantage. You needed the same. But it's something you have to decide for yourself. There's nothing deeper, Tressya. It's something you need to be absolutely—"

"Just shut up and offer it."

"There's no escaping once you're—"

I pressed my palm over his mouth to silence him. "Didn't you just say our destinies were to always be together? Isn't that what this is?" I glanced at the mark he left on my wrist. "If you truly believed what you said—"

"It's not that, Tressya," he interrupted. "The partner bond is formed with full awareness of its implications, the depth of commitment it entails. I never wanted it for us merely to escape our current predicament."

"Yet you willingly tied yourself to me."

"The way it is, it's one-sided. It's too significant a commitment. I would never have forced you to reciprocate." He stepped into me. "I want this, Tressya, like nothing else I want this. But it must come from a place in your heart, a place of love and not fear."

"I know I've done some terrible things, made a lot of mistakes, but never doubt my commitment to us."

Tamas gently cradled my cheeks between his palms, tilting my head back to lock gazes with me. He opened his mouth, on the cusp of saying something, when a violent tremor rent the ground beneath our feet. He seized my hand to steady me as the tremoring grew more intense.

"What's happening?" he shouted over the deafening roar of the castle's stone walls collapsing around us.

I looked up, instinctively shielding my eyes from the blinding light that pierced through the night sky, its intensity akin to staring directly at the sun.

"I can't see," I mumbled half to myself. Tamas likely never heard.

Tamas pulled me close, using his body as a shield in case

any falling stone debris threatened us. "It's not safe to enter the chamber now. We need to get out of the castle before these walls fall on our heads."

He pulled me away from the gaping hole in the floor, the Etherweave's resting place. We stumbled across the trembling ground, as if we were walking on the back of a colossal beast awakening from its slumber. Above us, panicked screeches tore through the sky as the creatures circling overhead succumbed to the collapsing veil.

"No," I yelled, resisting his lead. "The veil." Then I almost lost my footing as the ground heaved like a giant sigh.

"It's not safe inside the castle, Tressya," Tamas shouted.

"It's so bright. I can't see."

"What did you say?" He turned, gripping me by the elbow, crushing me to him. "What did you say?"

"The veil's falling. It's lighting the night brighter than any day."

"Night lit as day," I heard him say amidst the dreadful din of the castle's gradual collapse and the cacophony from the multitude of Ashenlands creatures that had been circling overhead.

Tamas suddenly pulled me to the left, and in my periphery I caught the blur of something large plummet past us, down into the gaping abyss and the chamber below.

"Just as prophesied," he said. "The Etherweave is rising."

"We must reach it before it breaks from of its tomb."

"The castle's collapsing. It's too risky going down there. We could be buried alive."

I tried to shake myself loose from his grasp, half-closing my eyes to shield them against the intense brightness. "The

Aeternals will be freed any moment now. We can't risk them seizing the Etherweave."

"Maybe they can't."

We were both yelling at each other over the chaos, and I didn't have time to convince him, so I tried to wrench myself free. If I jumped into the cavity, he'd have no choice but to follow.

"Tressya," Tamas growled, refusing to release me. "The Nazeen spelled the Etherweave—"

"Are you really prepared to take that risk?" I shouted into his face, but my vision was destroyed by the brilliant light, obscuring his expression.

"Look around us. We have no choice but to escape." His grip on my arms was like a steel clamp, fingers digging into my flesh, leaving me with no alternative.

Help me now. She had to listen to me. Tamas attempted to pull me away from the entrance to the chamber below. It was challenging to resist his strength while trying to summon my inner beast. If not her, then I would harness the creature that brought me here.

I delved deep within myself, seeking the ferocious spirit of the Ashenlands beast. In a flash like lightning, its primal instincts answered my mental call, but just as quickly, I felt a sting across my nails and gums, accompanied by the metallic taste of blood as fangs erupted from my mouth.

My beast awakened. The euphoria of feeling as she engulfed my human form provided relief from the agony of transformation, as my bones shattered and reformed. Before she completely overtook me, I wrapped Tamas in a tight embrace, pressing him against my beastly chest, and lifted him off his feet. With a final lumbering stride, I leaped into the cavity.

As we fell, Tamas transformed, compelling me to loosen my tight embrace. By the time he reached the bottom, he had assumed his beast, but he quickly reverted to his human form. My transformation back took longer, and I endured the excruciating pain of my bones reshaping themselves until I was human again.

"Tressya," Tamas growled once I was myself again, seizing my arms and giving me a light shake. "We can't be down here."

"Look." I gave his anger scant attention.

He glanced over his shoulder toward the rock, consumed within a brilliant glowing orb of blue.

"We still have time." I grabbed his hand as I hurried over to the rock.

Tamas yanked me back, then pulled me against him, swiftly swinging me away as another large winged creature plummeted through the gaping cavity, landing dangerously close to where I'd been standing.

"This is too dangerous," he grumbled into my hair.

"Not once we—"

"The Eone," he breathed, his hot breath caressing my scalp. "They're waiting, eager. This is what they desire. By releasing it before the Aeternals arrive, we're playing right into their hands."

I turned within his embrace, tilting my head back to gaze into his eyes, marred by a pattern of torment. They'd brutalized him in countless ways.

"Then we take the advantage. Bend down," I demanded

as I reached on tip-toes to entwine my arms as best I could around his neck.

His brows furrowed in confusion.

"I want my mark to be more visible." I traced a finger along the side of his neck.

I saw understanding dawn on his face, sweeping away his confusion.

"We force the Eone to fight the both of us," I said.

Despite our limited time, he kissed me—a brief, intense, and fervent kiss that carried a lifetime's promise, a silent vow that overwhelmed my senses and stole my breath.

Then he suddenly tore himself away from me, stumbling backward, his expression morphing from horror to fury. The Eone. They would do anything in their power to keep us apart.

I hurled myself toward him, summoning the strength of my beast. Pain shot through my fingertips as my claws emerged. With one swift motion, I hooked his jacket, then, channeling the power of my beast into my legs, I sprang forward, wrapping my legs around his waist.

Tamas fought to dislodge me, his claws slicing across my back. The sharp pain pierced me like an arrow.

"I understand, Tamas," I shouted, knowing the self-loathing he would feel for inflicting this pain upon me, but the Eone weren't in full control of him, for if they were, Tamas would surely have torn me apart by now. Instead, his movements grew more clumsy, like those of a baby just learning to move.

The veins in his neck popped with the strain he was under, fighting against the Eone's bind as he tried to turn his head sideways, offering me his neck. My fangs descended, seeing the pulse of his blood through his artery. Not wanting him to suffer any longer, I struck like a snake, stabbing my fangs in deep.

I sensed the sacredness of the moment. It was meant to be taken slow, savored, shared. But if I did, the Eone may finally win and turn Tamas against me. Plus, I couldn't forget the castle's collapse, the Aeternals' arrival and the Etherweave's imminent ascension.

My fangs sank deep, and I savored the initial tang of his blood on my tongue. Suddenly, Tamas ceased his struggles, as if yielding to the sanctity of the moment—a force not even the Eone could suppress. He stood motionless, enveloping me in a tight embrace, cradling me against him as his clawless fingers pressed into my skin. I felt his groan as a deep rumble in his chest while I lapped at the wound I had inflicted, consuming as much of his blood as I could. Initially, my eagerness was driven by a desire to triumph over the Eone, but with each subsequent lick, I continued because it felt right, natural, and inevitable, an unseverable bond of utter trust I yearned to feel.

Consuming his blood didn't bring about any immediate changes in my feelings, nor did it trigger any sudden understanding or inner harmony. It seemed the change wasn't instantaneous, but instead would evolve and solidify over time, which was fine by me.

I pulled back and stared at Tamas, entwining my fingers around the back of his neck. His eyes drifted closed as he rested his forehead on mine.

"We will," I said in answer to what I knew was in his

heart, instinctively sensing that this moment deserved reverence for what we had just accomplished. We were bonded, united until death, and perhaps even beyond. But the cruelty of fate meant we couldn't allow ourselves time to explore our bond and how it changed us. Instead, we had to fight.

And just to prove my thought, the earth tremored, forming cracks at our feet. Above, chaos maintained its grip, sounding as though the entire mountaintop was disintegrating.

Tamas lowered me to the ground, then seized my chin and tilted my head up for a hard, lingering kiss. Right now, it was the only intimacy we could share.

"We do this," he whispered against my lips.

"Together," I returned.

The blue hue ascended like a colossal serpent, spiraling upward from its tomb. Yet, falling rock, raining down through the cavity above, hindered our quest to reach the Etherweave. We ducked and weaved around the most significant fallen stone blocks, but it appeared the castle itself was conspiring against us, repeatedly forcing us to divert our path or huddle together for protection.

"We have to make it," I yelled, feeling a genuine sense of dread that the Etherweave would escape into the Aeternals' clutches before we reached it in time.

"Tamas," I gasped. Sheltered by his body, I watched as the blue snake like energy continued to spiral upward toward the gaping hole overhead. The Etherweave was rising, and we were about to lose it.

"Use your beast," he yelled, his body already taking on partial beast form. Instead of waiting for me to do likewise,

Tamas swung me into his arms and leaped the final distance to the rock, then caught me between the rock and his body, using it as a shield from falling debris.

"Touch it," he yelled, reaching over me to place his hand atop the rock.

I turned in his embrace to face the rock, now scorching hot, almost unbearable to touch, and the pain intensified the longer I kept my hands on it. I gritted my teeth against the burn and looked up past Tamas to the sky, peering into the brightness to discern figures emerging through the white haze. There were four, two men and two women, magnificently elegant and regal.

"The Aeternals," I whispered.

The massive snake of blue light continued its ascent, almost piercing through the gaping hole and into the castle, toward the waiting Aeternals.

"It's not working," I murmured, shifting my gaze back to the rock, only to see Tamas' and my hands were now glowing blue. Even as the Etherweave spiraled into the sky, more of it snaked its way from the rock, up our arms, and further, until it reached my mouth and poured inside, both suffocating and enlivening me in its power.

"Tressya," Tamas' voice was strained. I felt his claws dig into my hip as a violent force threatened to wrench us apart. Following my instincts, I released my hand from the rock and spun within the cradle of his body, flinging myself into his embrace. I wrapped my arms and legs around him, anchoring myself close as a vicious wind whipped across my back. I arched my head back, looking up to see the long spiral of the Etherweave ascending through the floor cavity and into the waiting arms of the Aeternals above, who were still emerging from the amorphous white brilliance of the descending veil.

"They—" That was all I said before a white light so intense it seared my eyes engulfed us, accompanied by a deafening noise as if the entire mountain were collapsing.

We were thrown from the rock, hurtled through the air like debris caught in a ferocious gale. My inner beast surfaced, granting me the strength to cling tightly to Tamas' front. With equal force, he gripped a hold of me, keeping us together as the veil finally dissolved and everything around us disappeared.

AUTHOR'S NOTE

Thanks again for continuing with the series. Storytelling is my passion, and it's you, dear reader, who keeps that passion alive. I deeply appreciate that you've carved out some space in your life to explore Tressya and Tamas' chaotic world. Your support fills my heart and my creative well.

I have to jump back into my writing den for book 3, The Bone Queen, which will be the final in the series. I think. I planned it as a trilogy and unless something unforeseen occurs that's the way it will stay, but since I haven't finished it yet I can't be 100% sure.

Once again, a heartfelt thank you. May your life be endlessly filled with the things that ignite your passion.

Happy reading XX

About the Author

When I wasn't riding a camel through the Rajasthani desert, white water rafting the rapids on the Zambezi, bungee jumping off the Victoria Falls bridge or hiking the peeks in Pakistan, I was piloting a twin prop into remote first nation communities in northern Western Australia or staring down a microscope in a laboratory.

Now somewhat tamed, the microscope has morphed into a computer and I spend more time plotting dire situations for my protagonists than being in them myself.

I am the author of books that won't stay normal.

Also by Terina Adams

Ruinous Lies

Traitor in the Shadows

Labyrinth of Dreams

Thief of Hearts

Hells Gate series

Dark moon

Rising moon

White moon

Blue Moon

Dominus Trilogy

Dominus

Califax

Black Arcana

Sinner's Game

Deviant's Curse

Defiler's Soul